THE CAMBRIDGE EDITION
OF THE NOVELS OF

THOMAS LOVE PEACOCK

GENERAL EDITOR: Freya Johnston, *University of Oxford*

SENIOR EDITORIAL ADVISOR: Nicholas A. Joukovsky,
Pennsylvania State University

VOLUMES IN THIS SERIES

1. *Headlong Hall*

2. *Melincourt*

3. *Nightmare Abbey*

4. *Maid Marian*

5. *The Misfortunes of Elphin*

6. *Crotchet Castle*

7. *Gryll Grange*

THOMAS LOVE PEACOCK
CROTCHET CASTLE

Edited by
Freya Johnston and
Matthew Bevis

CAMBRIDGE
UNIVERSITY PRESS

CAMBRIDGE
UNIVERSITY PRESS

University Printing House, Cambridge CB2 8BS, United Kingdom

Cambridge University Press is part of the University of Cambridge.

It furthers the University's mission by disseminating knowledge in the pursuit of
education, learning and research at the highest international levels of excellence.

www.cambridge.org
Information on this title: www.cambridge.org/9781107030725

© Cambridge University Press 2016

First published 2016

Printed in the United Kingdom by Clays, St Ives plc

A catalogue record for this publication is available from the British Library

ISBN 978-1-107-03072-5 Hardback

CONTENTS

List of illustrations		*page* ix
General Editor's preface		xi
Acknowledgements		xxi
Chronology		xxiii
List of abbreviations		lv
Introduction		lix

CROTCHET CASTLE

I	The Villa	5
II	The March of Mind	13
III	The Roman Camp	23
IV	The Party	34
V	Characters	42
VI	Theories	52
VII	The Sleeping Venus	64
VIII	Science and Charity	75
IX	The Voyage	82
X	The Voyage, continued	89
XI	Correspondence	96
XII	The Mountain Inn	103
XIII	The Lake. The Ruin	107
XIV	The Dingle	111
XV	The Farm	116
XVI	The Newspaper	121
XVII	The Invitation	132
XVIII	Chainmail Hall	138

Contents

Appendix A: Peacock's Preface of 1837   152
Appendix B: Holograph fragment of Chapter 4 (c. 1830)   155
Appendix C: Holograph fragment of Chapter 5 (c. 1830)   156
Appendix D: Holograph manuscript of 'Touchandgo'
    (watermark 1827)   158
Appendix E: Holograph manuscript of 'Touchandgo'
    (watermark 1828)   164
Appendix F: Holograph fragment of Chapter 16 (c. 1830)   167
Appendix G: 'The Fate of a Broom: An Anticipation' (1831,
    1837)   170

Note on the text   172
Emendations and variants   177
Ambiguous line-end hyphenations   189
Explanatory notes   190
Select bibliography   316

viii

ILLUSTRATIONS

1 Title page of *Crotchet Castle* (1831) (Dunston B. 1428a, Title Page, the Bodleian Libraries, University of Oxford).   *page* 1

2 Holograph manuscript of 'Touchandgo' (TLP 55, Holograph poem (watermark 1828), Carl H. Pforzheimer Collection, The New York Public Library).   163

For kind permission to reproduce the images, and for supplying photographs, the editors would like to thank the Bodleian Libraries, University of Oxford, and the New York Public Library.

GENERAL EDITOR'S PREFACE

'That Peacock is a classic', declared the scholar and editor R. W. Chapman in 1924, 'now needs no proof; he has passed his century, and his reputation grows.' Such a judgement might have appeared sanguine even in the year in which *The Works of Thomas Love Peacock*, edited by H. F. B. Brett-Smith and C. E. Jones (1924–34), also known as the Halliford Edition, began to be published. During the early 1920s, Oxford University Press steadfastly resisted proposals for works by and about Peacock. But Chapman – learned, urbane Secretary to Delegates of the Press from 1920 to 1942 – was eager to see the novels back in print. He remarked in his Introduction to the World's Classics edition of *The Misfortunes of Elphin and Crotchet Castle* that the 'experiment' of publishing them, shortly after the initial five volumes of his ground-breaking edition of Jane Austen (1923) had appeared, might transform Peacock into a 'popular classic'.[1]

The present editors hope, in part, to realize that frustrated ambition. It seems fitting that the Cambridge Edition of the Novels of Thomas Love Peacock should appear not long after the Cambridge Edition of the Works of Jane Austen (2005–8). That the decades since the 1920s have been kinder to Austen than to

---

[1] Thomas Love Peacock, *The Misfortunes of Elphin and Crotchet Castle*, introd. R. W. Chapman, World's Classics, CCXLIV (1924), p. ix. On Oxford University Press and proposals for works relating to Peacock, see *Register of the Orders of the Delegates of the Clarendon Press* (Nov. 1913–June 1924), p. 308 (21 Oct. 1921), item 5227; p. 315 (4 Nov. 1921), item 5314. An edition of *Headlong Hall and Nightmare Abbey* was published as World's Classics, CCCXXXIV in 1929.

Peacock is no surprise; unlike Austen, Peacock is habitually, wilfully arcane. Nora Crook and Derek Guiton observe that 'His writings contain references as inaccessible to the common reader as medieval graffiti in cathedral towers'; the historical and architectural contexts are appropriate, as is the flavour of irreverence suggested by 'graffiti'.[2] Even if his comic fictions abound, like Austen's, with clever, good-looking women and with sparkling dialogue that culminates in marriage, Peacock's repartee can be hard to follow. On a first, unmediated encounter with him, many readers will feel, with Captain Fitzchrome (in Chapter 6 of *Crotchet Castle*), that 'the pleasantry and the obscurity go together'. Peacock does not aspire to the portrayal of interiority – perhaps the most cherished aspect of Austen's novels. Rather, his characters, both male and female, exist primarily in order to share, voice and test the limits of their ideas. His fictions, rebuffing intimacy, are inescapably political and intellectual. To approach the nineteenth-century novel via Peacock is therefore to see it as an outward-facing genre indebted to philosophical tracts, lectures, classical dialogues and the rhythms of parliamentary debate.

It would have amused Peacock, who tended to write contemptuously of academics and their institutions, that in 1921 Professor Herbert G. Wright's proposal for a new edition of *The Misfortunes of Elphin* was rejected by Oxford University Press, whereas the Snowdon Mountain Tramroad and Hotels Company, 'being desirous to provide holiday reading for visitors to the Principality', successfully lobbied for the same work's appearance in the World's Classics series, alongside *Crotchet Castle*, three years later.[3] Making the case for Peacock can be a tricky, unpredictable business. According to J. B. Priestley, he is 'a treacherous subject for

---

[2] Nora Crook and Derek Guiton, *Shelley's Venomed Melody* (Cambridge: Cambridge University Press, 1986), p. 13.·

[3] *Register of the Orders of the Delegates of the Clarendon Press* [Nov. 1913–June 1924], p. 308 (21 Oct. 1921), item 5227.

criticism'.[4] An erudite, eclectic and fastidious reader, possessed of an excellent memory, Peacock is a daunting prospect for editors, too; as Stephen Gill puts it, 'he was a bibliographer of sorts and a textual critic of some severity'.[5] One of the most striking things about his fastidious and omnivorous novels is just how many ancient and modern writers they lightly touch upon, in such a way as to reveal their author's delighted saturation in literature. To gloss his works therefore requires more than a few notes. 'Doing so much', thought Chapman, the Halliford editors 'might well have done a little more' in this regard: 'In the process of verification they must have traced many of Peacock's adespotic quotations; readers would have been grateful if they had given the references. It would be interesting, too, to know if Peacock often misquoted.'[6] 'Adespotic', in the hyper-abstruse sense in which Chapman uses it here (i.e. relating to classical, especially Greek, literature which is not attributed to any particular author), is so rare as not to appear in the *Oxford English Dictionary*, or indeed in Peacock's fiction, but there are plenty of other terms and allusions in his novels that will baffle the modern reader. Peacock's head, like Taliesin's (in Chapter 16 of *The Misfortunes of Elphin*), was 'brimfull of Pagan knowledge', sometimes misquoted. Volume editors have tried to keep in view the reader's need for information about and explanation of Peacock's myriad sources, and his relationship to them, while remaining conscious that annotations of his works are potentially limitless. Peacock wrote in a letter to Lord Broughton that he believed 'the author of an inscription always knows what he means, however difficult of apprehension his

[4] J. B. Priestley, *Thomas Love Peacock* [1927], reissued with introduction by J. I. M. Stewart (London, Melbourne, Toronto: Macmillan; New York: St Martin's Press, 1966), p. 195.

[5] Stephen Gill, review of Nicholas A. Joukovsky, ed., *The Letters of Thomas Love Peacock, Review of English Studies*, New Series, 53 (2002), 449–51 (p. 449).

[6] R. W. Chapman, review of the Halliford Edition of *The Works of Thomas Love Peacock*, vols. 2–5 (1924), *Review of English Studies*, 1 (1925), 239–42 (p. 241).

meaning may be to others'.[7] His comment suggests a puzzling quality to the epigraphs and other forms of quotation in the novels and elsewhere; but it also suggests that we might recover the author's meanings, if we will only persist in hunting for them. The Cambridge Edition aims to reveal his locally apposite, imaginative use of out-of-the-way sources and analogues. The appearance in 2001 of Nicholas A. Joukovsky's definitive edition of Peacock's *Letters*, incorporating details of the books Peacock read while composing his fiction, has paved the way for many new attributions. The seven novels he wrote between 1815 and 1861 have been enriched in the present edition by ampler cross-referencing to his other works, published and unpublished, and to their relevant literary, historical and cultural contexts, than has previously been attempted.

In his essay on 'French Comic Romances', Peacock remarked of Pigault le Brun that 'his successive works are impressed with the political changes of the day: they carry their eras in their incidents'.[8] The same might be said of Peacock's fiction, but he was equally interested in the capacity of his works to outlive their moment. Looking back on *Melincourt* some thirty-nine years after the novel first appeared in print, its author pointed out that 'Many of the questions, discussed in the dialogues, have more of a general than of a temporary application, and still have their advocates on both sides.' Some things might not be true, some decades later, but they had 'worthy successors' in the present. As Alexander Pope reflected with malicious complacency that his dunces would be perennially replaced with a fresh stock of dud writers, generation after generation, so Peacock envisaged his satires living beyond their original moment, as well as being marked by it (and needing some explanation accordingly).[9]

---

[7] Peacock to Lord Broughton (13 May 1861), *Letters*, 2.413.

[8] Halliford, 9.255.

[9] Peacock's reflections on the changes appeared in his Preface to the 1856 edition of *Melincourt*, while the reference to 'worthy successors' appeared in his Preface of 1837. In 'The Publisher to the Reader', Pope asserts of *The*

The numerous quotations from and allusions to other writers in Peacock's fiction suggest the company he chose to keep and in which he wished to be recorded. He would have agreed with Samuel Johnson that citing ancient writers, far from being mere pedantry, 'is a good thing; there is a community of mind in it. Classical quotation is the *parole* of literary men all over the world.'[10] That phrase, 'community of mind', sums up the sociable disputes to which Peacock's novels play host, and explains the gravitation within them towards the library as well as to the dining table. In *Crotchet Castle*, for instance, the library is a suite of interlinked apartments in which games, words and music are shown to be continuous with one another. The library is therefore structurally representative of the novel, revealing adjacency, sequence, continuity and difference between play, talk, literature and song.

There is a further sense in which Peacock's books might be viewed as miniature libraries: they share certain characteristics with commonplace books of quotation gathered around different subjects. It can be hard to differentiate a quotation from an allusion in Peacock; to tell why certain sources are named and flagged while others are left implicit or indeed almost entirely submerged. But one way of reading the novels might be as anthologies of classical material, as well as of the state of political life and reviewing culture at a given nineteenth-century moment (at one point in Chapter 16, *Melincourt* quotes an issue of the *Edinburgh Review* in place of a character's speech). A new edition of Peacock's fiction therefore requires attentiveness to old and contemporary orthodoxies, and to the bridges between them. He is a writer who manages to rehearse highly acrimonious debates without himself becoming either angry or jaded.

Dunciad that 'the *Poem was not made for these Authors, but these Authors for the Poem:* And I should judge that they were clapp'd in as they rose, fresh and fresh, and chang'd from day to day; in like manner as when the old boughs wither, we thrust new ones into a chimney.' Pope, *Poems*, vol. 5, pp. 205–6.

[10] James Boswell, *Boswell's Life of Johnson*, ed. George Birkbeck Hill, rev. L. F. Powell, 6 vols. (Oxford: Clarendon Press, 1934–50), vol. 4, p. 102.

Quotations serve, too, as forms of evidence, anchoring the claims made in the text, so that they contribute to the authority and probability that Peacock, following in Henry Fielding's wake, claimed was necessary in all kinds of fiction – however outrageous – and in the teeth of such historically incoherent works as Thomas Moore's *The Epicurean* (1827), which Peacock reviewed with majestic scorn.[11] In nineteenth-century reviews, lengthy quotations are often provided in order to ridicule and condemn a work, as well as to offer a representative selection from it. Perhaps the long footnotes quoting (for instance) Lord Monboddo in *Melincourt* combine these roles. They serve to establish a genuine basis for Sylvan Forester's arguments about his captured creature in Monboddo's own outlandish claims about orangutans, and in so doing they also poke fun at the nature of those arguments. In fact, the quotations are so substantial that, like the *Edinburgh Review*, they invade the text, forming part of Forester's speech in Chapter 6 – a chapter which amounts to a miniature encyclopaedia of arguments in favour of natural man. Such quotations are both seriously meant – they show attentive fidelity to source material – and satirically driven, since they also show how far from common sense such arguments may be taken. In other words, they resemble the notes to Pope's *Dunciad*.

Having said all this, and acknowledging Peacock's remarkable allusiveness, scholarly editing is not only about commentary and explanatory annotation. We have benefited handsomely from more than a century of sophisticated textual enquiry into Peacock, and from the formidable legacy of earlier bibliographical investigators. The Cambridge Edition is indebted to the diligence and skill of H. F. B. Brett-Smith and C. E. Jones, who set a very high standard in terms of the accuracy and completeness of their work. The first collected edition of Peacock, published in 1874 (dated 1875), was in three volumes; Brett-Smith and Jones oversaw the publication of ten. Their bibliographical retrievals and discoveries were legion; the

---

[11] See Peacock's review of Moore's *Epicurean*, Halliford, 9.3–4.

dearth of explanatory notes accompanying the texts was dictated by prevailing trends in editorial practice, rather than by their own preferences. Supplemented by David Garnett's two-volume edition of the novels (1948, 1963), and by Nicholas A. Joukovsky's numerous textual, critical and biographical gleanings, Halliford continues to offer the best and fullest selection of Peacock's writings as a whole.

Unlike Brett-Smith and Jones, who, in accordance with editorial thinking at the time, gave the preference to Peacock's revised lifetime texts, the Cambridge Edition of the Novels of Thomas Love Peacock employs as copytexts the first editions, in book-length form, of his fictions. This policy has been adopted partly because it seems to accord better with Peacock's authorial character; when given the opportunity to do so, he made few revisions to his novels. The first editions of those works also serve as the best witnesses of Peacock's satirical topicality, a vital source of his appeal and interest, and a distinctive aspect of his contribution to nineteenth-century fiction. In the case of *Nightmare Abbey*, for instance, now Peacock's best-known and most widely studied work, the text as first published in 1818 not only reflected but also directly participated in the literary and political debates of his time.

Our texts remain as close to the copytexts as possible. Spelling and punctuation have not been modernized and inconsistencies in presentation, titles (such as Dr. and Doctor) and grammatical forms have generally been left as they were found. Peacock's own footnotes are an essential part of his mock-explicatory, Scriblerian style; they are also a means, like his epigraphs, of displaying his literary allegiances and antagonisms. In this edition they remain at the bottom of the page – signalled by asterisks and daggers – as in the copytexts. The presence of editorial endnotes is contrastingly indicated by superscript numbers in the text.

The few corrections and emendations we have made to the texts, other than replacing dropped or missing letters, have been permitted only when an error is very plain, or where its retention might impede comprehension of the passage. For instance, missing quotation marks have been supplied, run-on words have been separated, repeated words have been excised and unclosed parentheses have been closed. Occasionally, where the copytext is corrupt and clearly does not reflect Peacock's intentions at the time of writing, it has been emended. For instance, at the beginning of Chapter 13 of *Nightmare Abbey*, the 1818 text reads 'or of a waggon, or of a weighing-bridge'. In this case, the 1837 correction 'or of a waggon on a weighing-bridge' appears to be a restoration of what he must have originally written or intended to write. All such changes to the texts have been noted in the final apparatus. Where relevant, in each volume surviving draft manuscript fragments have been transcribed, with explanatory headnotes indicating both their nature and their relationship to the printed text, in an appendix or series of appendices. All manuscript materials have been transcribed with their changes or erasures either reproduced or noted. Variant readings of such materials are not incorporated into the textual apparatus.

Peacock appears to have been sparing in the changes he made to the four novels (*Headlong Hall, Nightmare Abbey, Maid Marian* and *Crotchet Castle*) that were re-published by Richard Bentley in his Standard Novels series in 1837, but countless tiny alterations were introduced to this text. For many of those, Peacock is unlikely to have been responsible, although the concern he showed when correcting or altering orthography in the cases of characters' names, locations, dialect and pronunciation makes it generally unwise to attempt to determine which are his, and which are not. In the case of *Headlong Hall*, for instance, along with a number of misprints, there are some new substantive readings in 1837, one of which appears to be authorial. The Cambridge Edition accepts that many decisions about spelling, punctuation, capitalization, spacing, italicizing and paragraphing may not have been Peacock's, either in the copytexts or in subsequent lifetime texts, but we have no way of knowing for certain that they were not. All volume editors have therefore undertaken a complete collation of the copytext with other lifetime editions, but not all the accidental variants have been printed. Instead, we have reproduced all substantive variants between the copytext and other lifetime editions, and a number of variants in accidentals, including all those in the spelling of proper names.

Introductions to each volume are substantial and have a common basic structure. They incorporate original discussion of each work's genesis and composition, its publication history, reception and after-life. An extensive chronology of Peacock's life, revised by Nicholas A. Joukovsky from his edition of the *Letters*, is also provided in every volume.

Modern readers may ask what Peacock hoped to achieve through the elegant representation of opposing views in his imaginative, dialogic and dramatic prose. The answer is probably something akin to what he admired in French comic fiction: its capacity, by 'presenting or embodying opinion' through characters that are 'abstractions or embodied classifications', or representatives 'of actual life', to direct 'the stream of opinion against the mass of delusions and abuses' in the public arena.[12] Peacock commented of Paul de Kock that the author very rarely expressed a political opinion ('never', he says in 'French Comic Romances', modified to a 'very slight' indication of such opinion in 'The Épicier'); this elusive quality evidently puzzled and interested him.[13] What sort of a writer pursues opinion without committing himself? Does it make him tantamount to a mere reviewer? What kind of public is interested in opinions, and why? What is the status of literature in relation to public opinion? In a letter to Thomas L'Estrange (11 July 1861), Peacock wrote that 'In the questions which have come within my scope, I have endeavoured to be impartial, and to say what could be said on both sides.' Around the same time (20 June 1861), he suggested to Lord Broughton what talking heads might, at their best, have to offer:

The dialogues of Plato and Cicero are made up of discussions among persons who differed in opinion. Neither they nor their heroes would

---

[12] Halliford, 9.259.   [13] Halliford, 9.256.

have been content to pass eternity in the company of persons who merely thought as they did. They were enquirers. They did not profess to have found truth. They might have expected to find it in another life: but then they would no longer think, as they had thought, with those who agreed with them in this.[14]

Freya Johnston

[14] *Letters*, 2.425, 419.

ACKNOWLEDGEMENTS

We would like to thank the team at Cambridge University Press – Linda Bree, Anna Bond, Maartje Scheltens and Victoria Parrin – for their patience, encouragement and adaptability throughout our work on *Crotchet Castle*. In countless ways we have relied upon and benefited from the generosity and scholarship of our Senior Editorial Adviser, Nicholas Joukovsky. Kathryn Sutherland has been another source of expertise and of clear, sound advice. Keble College, St Anne's College, the Faculty of English at Oxford and the John Fell Fund provided very generous financial and administrative support.

We have gathered many other debts. Stephanie Dumke has worked meticulously and intelligently on the text and explanatory annotations; every aspect of this volume has benefited from her critical acuity. Henry Mason gave us a wealth of information about Peacock's classical allusions. Robert Stagg helped with the collation, and Rebecca Bullard with queries about Welsh. For their assistance with interpreting manuscript material and with various aspects of the volume's textual apparatus and annotations, we are grateful to Cathal Dowling, Peter Garside, Andrew Honey, James McLaverty, Anthony Mandal and Dale Thatcher. We would also like to thank Martin Maw, archivist at Oxford University Press.

The following booksellers and auctioneers were quick to respond to questions about their copies of the first edition of *Crotchet Castle*: James Burmester (Rare Books); Ed Lake (Jarndyce Booksellers); Ted Hofmann (Bernard Quaritch); Tom Linton-Mole (Antiquates). The Brett-Smith family of Princeton opened their parental home up to searches for a manuscript fragment of *Crotchet Castle*, which we sadly failed to recover; we appreciate their friendliness and generosity.

We have relied on the knowledge, efficiency and kindness of several librarians and specialists in rare books and manuscripts, especially Elizabeth Denlinger at the New York Public Library. Many thanks are also due to the staff of the English Faculty Library and of the Bodleian Library in Oxford; to Liam Sims at Cambridge University Library; to the staff of the Pierpont Morgan Library and the British Library; and to Sandra Stelts at the Pennsylvania State Special Collections Library.

Freya Johnston
Matthew Bevis

CHRONOLOGY
THOMAS LOVE PEACOCK, 1785–1866
NICHOLAS A. JOUKOVSKY

1785

18 Oct.

Born at Weymouth, or Melcombe Regis, Dorset, the only child of Samuel Peacock (born 1722/3), a London glass merchant whose father, Josiah Peacock, had been a linen draper and grocer at Taunton, Somerset, and Sarah Love (born 10 Nov. 1754), daughter of Thomas Love, a retired master in the Royal Navy from Topsham, Devon, who lost a leg as Master of HMS *Prothée* in the battle of the Saints, Rodney's great victory off Dominica, on 12 Apr. 1782. (His parents were married at St Luke's, Chelsea, on 29 Mar. 1780.)

?Dec.–Jan. 1786

Baptized by Henry Hunter, DD, minister of the Scots Presbyterian church, London Wall. (The Loves were Presbyterians, while the Peacocks were Independents.)

1786

Autumn–
Winter 1787

His father stops attending the Court of the Pewterers' Company (of which he is an Assistant) and apparently transfers his interest in his glass warehouse at 46 Holborn Bridge to his brother George (his brother Thomas having previously become a junior partner in the firm).

1791

before 31 Dec. His mother and her parents take separate houses at Chertsey. (His uncle William Love also settles his family at Chertsey in 1793.)

1792

Winter–Spring Sent to a private school kept by John Harris Wicks at Englefield Green, where he remains for six and a half years, spending his vacations at Chertsey and often visiting a schoolfellow named Charles at the Abbey House.

1793

early Feb. Death of his father (buried 5 Feb. at the Elim Baptist Chapel, Fetter Lane), after the purchase of two small annuities for his widow and one for his son.

1 Mar. Birth of his cousin Henry Ommanney Love (died 16 Sept. 1872) at Chertsey.

1794

Apr. His uncle William Love (born early Apr. 1764) promoted to the rank of lieutenant in the Royal Navy, having been a midshipman since 1778.

1 June His uncle Thomas Love (born 29 May 1752) serves as Master of HMS *Alfred* in Howe's great victory over the French.

Nov. Death of his uncle Richard Love (baptized 1 Mar. 1761) at Bombay, after having served in the Russian navy.

1795

4–14 Feb. Writes his first known poem, an epitaph for a schoolfellow named Hamlet Wade.

1797

before 24 Apr. Birth of his cousin Harriet Blagrave Deane Love (died 14 Feb. 1881) at Chertsey.

1798

June	Writes a poem on his 'Midsummer Holidays'.
before 18 Oct.	Removed from school, possibly due to failure of one of his mother's annuities. From this time he is entirely self-educated.

1800

before 11 Feb.–?1805 or 1806	Employed as a clerk for Ludlow, Fraser, & Company, merchants in the City of London, while residing with his mother on the firm's premises at 4 Angel Court, Throgmorton Street. During these years he has a circle of friends in the neighbourhood of Hackney, including William de St Croix of Homerton and, perhaps later, Thomas Forster of Lower Clapton.
Feb.	Receives an 'Extra Prize' from the *Monthly Preceptor, or Juvenile Library* for his first publication, a verse 'Answer to the Question: "Is History or Biography the More Improving Study?"'

1803

16 Nov.	Presents a (lost) manuscript volume of poems to Lucretia Oldham, 'the beauty of Shacklewell Green', with a dedicatory poem on the first leaf.

1804

Sept.	Writes 'The Monks of St. Mark' (later privately printed as a leaflet, probably in connection with the printing of the *Palmyra* volume in the autumn of 1805).
?Sept.–Oct.	Collects most of his juvenile verse, except the Lucretia Oldham poems, in a manuscript volume of 'Poems, by T. L. Peacock'.

?Autumn	Writes a verse drama entitled 'The Circle of Loda'.
1805	
Nov.–Dec.	*Palmyra, and Other Poems* published by W. J. & J. Richardson, with title page post-dated 1806.
10 Dec.	Death of his grandfather, Thomas Love, at Chertsey (buried 20 Dec. at the Presbyterian meeting-house).
1806	
Autumn	Solitary walking tour in Scotland.
18 Oct.	The annuity purchased for him by his father expires on his coming of age.
1807	
Feb.	His uncle William Love promoted to the rank of commander.
?Spring	Returns to live with his mother at Chertsey.
3 Aug.	Accepts a 'generous offer' of Edward Thomas Hookham and his brother Thomas Hookham, Junior, to supply him with books from their father's extensive circulating library at 15 Old Bond Street and to publish a projected poem, apparently in the same vein as *Palmyra*.
?Summer– Autumn	Brief engagement to Fanny Falkner broken off by the interference of one of her relations. She marries another man and dies the next year.
1808	
14 May– 2 Apr. 1809	Serves as Captain's Clerk to Sir Home Riggs Popham and, after 18 Dec., to Capt. Andrew King, aboard HMS *Venerable* in the Downs – 'this floating Inferno'. During this period he writes several prologues and epilogues for the officers' amateur theatricals as well as 'Stanzas

Written at Sea' (published with *The Genius of the Thames*).

1809

13 Mar.	Sends Edward Hookham a 'little poem of the Thames' and mentions 'a classical ballad or two now in embryo', perhaps 'Romance' and 'Remember Me'.
after 2 Apr.	Having left the *Venerable*, walks from Deal to Ramsgate and around the North Foreland to Margate, before proceeding to Canterbury and London, then eventually returning to live at Chertsey.
?Apr.–Dec.	Expands his 'little poem on the Thames' into *The Genius of the Thames*.
29 May	Begins a two-week expedition to trace the course of the Thames on foot from its source to Chertsey, with a stay of two or three days at Oxford.

1810

Jan.	Travels to North Wales, visiting Tremadoc before settling at Maentwrog, Merionethshire.
after 20 Jan.	Sends Edward Hookham the Prœmium to *The Genius of the Thames* while the poem is being printed.
Apr.–May	Attracted to the Maentwrog parson's daughter Jane Gryffydh, 'the Caernarvonshire nymph' – but by 12 June 'Richard is himself again'.
late May–early June	*The Genius of the Thames: A Lyrical Poem, in Two Parts* published by Thomas and Edward Hookham.
late June–?early Oct.	Affair with an unidentified 'Caernarvonshire charmer' ('not a parson's daughter'), ending in disillusionment.

27 Dec.	Death of his grandmother, Sarah Love, at Chertsey (buried 3 Jan. 1811 at the Presbyterian meeting-house).
1811	
7 Apr.	Leaves Maentwrog, after bidding farewell to Jane Gryffydh, 'the most innocent, the most amiable, the most beautiful girl in existence'. On his walk home by way of South Wales, he climbs Cadair Idris and calls on Edward Scott at Bodtalog, near Towyn, before proceeding to Aberystwyth and the Devil's Bridge, near Hafod.
?May–July	A 'long abode in Covent-Garden'.
Autumn	His mother's remaining annuity having expired at Michaelmas, she is forced by creditors to leave Chertsey. He and his mother are enabled by friends to occupy Morven Cottage, Wyrardisbury, near Staines.
?Autumn	Writes *The Philosophy of Melancholy* – 'in ten days', according to Edward Hookham.
before 14 Nov.	Revises *The Genius of the Thames, Palmyra* and 'Fiolfar, King of Norway' for a new edition, to which he adds 'Inscription for a Mountain Dell'. Consigns all his other poems 'to the tomb of the Capulets'.
18 Dec.	Grant of £21 from the Literary Fund.
1812	
Winter–Spring	Writes a (lost) farce entitled 'Mirth in the Mountains', which is read by James Grant Raymond, the actor-manager of the Drury Lane Company.
?Winter–Autumn	Translates passages from Greek tragedies, which he thinks of publishing under the title 'Fragments of Greek Tragedy'. Around this

	time he probably also writes and privately prints his Aristophanic Greek anapaests on Christ (no known copy).
late Feb.	*The Philosophy of Melancholy: A Poem in Four Parts, with a Mythological Ode* published by Thomas and Edward Hookham.
early Apr.	Second edition of *The Genius of the Thames, Palmyra, and Other Poems* published by Thomas and Edward Hookham.
before 20 May	Forced temporarily to leave Morven Cottage, Wyrardisbury, by his inability to pay local tradesmen's bills.
20 May	Grant of £30 from the Literary Fund. Edward Hookham, in his letter of application, expresses fears that 'the fate of Chatterton might be that of Peacock'.
20 May	Cosigns an East India Company bond for Peter Auber in the amount of £500.
?Summer– Spring 1813	Writes, with Raymond's encouragement, two more farces, 'The Dilettanti' and 'The Three Doctors', but neither is performed at Drury Lane. Other dramatic projects of this period include two Roman tragedies entitled 'Otho' and 'Virginia'.
July–Aug.	Thomas Forster visits him for a week at Wyrardisbury.
before 18 Aug.	Thomas Hookham sends Peacock's two recent volumes of poetry to Shelley at Lynmouth, Devon.
late Aug.– early Sept.	Visits Thomas Forster at Tunbridge Wells.
?Sept.–Dec.	In love with Clarinda Knowles at Englefield Green – 'this goddess of my idolatry'.

17–30 Sept.	Walking and sailing tour of the Isle of Wight with Joseph Gulston of Englefield Green, during which he visits his uncle William Love at Yarmouth and finds his cousin Harriet 'grown into a fine girl'.
4 Oct.–13 Nov.	Introduced to Shelley by Thomas Hookham in London.
late Nov.	Thomas Hookham sends Peacock's poem 'Farewell to Meirion' to Shelley at Tan-yr-allt, near Tremadoc.

1813

?Winter–Spring	Writes, and possibly prints, a prospectus outlining his educational theories and proposing 'to receive eight pupils, in a beautiful retirement in the county of Westmoreland'.
?Winter–Spring	Writes *Sir Hornbook*, which is illustrated by Henry Corbould before 1 June.
12 Mar.	Writes the poem 'Al mio primiero amore!' to an unidentified 'first love'.
?Apr.–June	Sees Shelley several times in London and meets Thomas Jefferson Hogg and William Godwin.
11 June	His epilogue to Lumley Skeffington's comedy *Lose No Time* is recited at Drury Lane, then printed in the *Morning Post* on 14 June.
16 June	Grant of £10 from the Literary Fund.
late June–late Aug.	Second visit to Wales, during which he wanders through Radnorshire, Cardiganshire and Merionethshire. Tentatively engages 'a very beautiful place in Radnorshire'. Returns by way of Bath.
Sept.	Visits Shelley at Bracknell, where he meets John Frank Newton, Harriet de Boinville and their circle.

4 Oct.–early Dec.	Accompanies Shelley and his family to the Lake District and Edinburgh.
Nov.–Dec.	*Sir Hornbook; or, Childe Launcelot's Expedition: A Grammatico-Allegorical Ballad* published by Sharpe & Hailes, with plates dated 1 June 1813 and title page post-dated 1814. (Second and third editions follow in 1815, fourth edition in 1817, fifth edition in 1818.)
1814	
Mar.	*Sir Proteus: A Satirical Ballad* published under the pseudonym of P. M. O'Donovan, Esq. by Thomas and Edward Hookham.
8 Apr.	Letter signed 'P.', pointing out a resemblance between *Hamlet* and Euripides' *Hippolytus*, published in the *Morning Chronicle*.
?Spring–Spring 1815	Begins and outlines two versions of 'Ahrimanes', an unfinished romantic epic in Spenserian stanzas.
12 July	Writes gloomy 'Lines to a Favorite Laurel in the Garden at Ankerwyke Cottage'.
28 July	After having consulted Peacock about his marital crisis, Shelley elopes to the Continent with Mary Godwin and Claire Clairmont. During his absence, he writes to ask Peacock 'to superintend money affairs'. Peacock does not meet the two girls until after their return on 13 Sept.
?Aug.	Proposes marriage to Cecilia Knowles at Englefield Green, having previously proposed to her sister Clarinda.
?Sept.	Watches the driving of the deer, by two regiments of cavalry, from Windsor Forest

	into the Park – 'the most beautiful sight I ever witnessed'.
25 Sept.–15 Nov.	Helps Shelley to raise money and to elude bailiffs, while residing with his mother in Southampton Buildings, Chancery Lane.
30 Sept.	Becomes involved in a plan to liberate Shelley's sisters from boarding school and run away to the west of Ireland, a scheme that would somehow enable him to marry Marianne de St Croix.
20 Oct.	Calls on Godwin in an unsuccessful attempt to effect a reconciliation between Godwin and Shelley.
?late Nov.–late Feb. 1815	Visits Zipporah Simpson, mother of John Arthur Roebuck, at Gumley, Leicestershire.
1815	
9–10 Jan.	Arrested for debt in Liverpool and lodged in a 'sponging house', after a mysterious affair with a supposed heiress named Charlotte.
Apr.	Considers emigrating to Canada and taking Marianne de St Croix.
13 May	Shelley reaches a financial settlement with his father, giving him an annuity of £1000 a year, from which he allows Peacock £120 a year.
?Summer	Settles with his mother at Marlow, near his uncle Thomas Love.
3 Aug.	Shelley takes a house at Bishopsgate, where Peacock is a frequent visitor throughout the autumn and winter months. Hogg later describes the winter at Bishopsgate as 'a mere Atticism'.
late Aug.–early Sept.	Excursion up the Thames from Old Windsor to beyond Lechlade with Shelley, Mary Godwin and Charles Clairmont.

early Dec.	*Headlong Hall* published by Thomas Hookham, with title page post-dated 1816.
?Dec.	Suggests the title for Shelley's *Alastor; or, The Spirit of Solitude.*
1816	
3 May	Shelley leaves England for Switzerland with Mary Godwin and Claire Clairmont. During his absence he asks Peacock to take custody of his books and furniture at Bishopsgate and to find another house for him and Mary.
late July	Second edition of *Headlong Hall* published by Thomas Hookham.
13/14–25 Sept.	Shelley visits him at Marlow.
5 Nov.	His prologue to John Tobin's comedy *The Faro Table; or, The Guardians* is recited at Drury Lane, then printed in both the *Morning Chronicle* and the *Morning Post* on 6 Nov.
5–9/10 Dec.	Shelley takes a house at Marlow and commissions him to supervise the fitting up of the house and the laying out of the grounds.
10 Dec.	Harriet Shelley's body discovered in the Serpentine.
30 Dec.	Shelley marries Mary Godwin.
1817	
27 Feb.–18 Mar.	The Shelleys stay with him while waiting to occupy their house at Marlow, where their spring visitors include Godwin and Leigh Hunt.
early Mar.	*Melincourt* published in three volumes by Thomas Hookham.
?Spring–Summer	Writes the unfinished tale known as 'Calidore'.
?Aug.–Nov.	*The Round Table; or, King Arthur's Feast* published by John Arliss.

before 28 Nov.	Completes *Rhododaphne*, which Mary Shelley copies on 4–10 Dec.
Dec.	Two of Shelley's letters from Switzerland 'To T.P., Esq.' published in revised form in *History of a Six Weeks' Tour*.
14–16 Dec.	Assists Shelley in revising *Laon and Cythna* for reissue as *The Revolt of Islam*.
1818	
?Jan.	Proposes marriage to Claire Clairmont, who has been living with the Shelleys at Marlow with her illegitimate daughter by Lord Byron.
29 Jan.	Goes to London, where he sees the Shelleys and Claire Clairmont almost daily until their departure for Italy.
early Feb.	*Rhododaphne* published anonymously by Thomas Hookham.
11 Feb.	Dines at Leigh Hunt's with the Shelleys and Claire, Hogg and Keats.
mid-Feb.	Shelley writes a review of *Rhododaphne*, which he gives to Leigh Hunt after Mary copies it on 20–3 Feb., but Hunt does not publish it in *The Examiner*.
11 Mar.	The Shelleys and Claire Clairmont leave London for Italy. During their absence Peacock sends them quarterly parcels and acts as Shelley's agent in business and literary matters.
20 Mar.	Back at Marlow, plans to write a novel set in London.
late Mar.–June	Writes *Nightmare Abbey*.
?17–24 June	Hogg visits him for a week at Marlow, during which they walk to Virginia Water and to Chequers.

7 July	Moves, with his mother, to a new house in West Street, Marlow.
7 July–26 Sept.	Keeps a journal.
16 July–23 Aug.	Writes, but does not finish, 'An Essay on Fashionable Literature'.
18–26 Sept.	Begins writing a political pamphlet.
early Oct.–early Nov.	On the recommendation of Peter Auber, goes to London as a candidate for a position in the Examiner's Office of the East India Company. Writes an examination paper on 'Ryotwar & Zemindarry Settlements', dated 2 Nov.
16 Oct.	Death of his uncle Thomas Love at Marlow.
mid-Nov.	*Nightmare Abbey* published by Thomas Hookham.
?Nov.–Dec.	Writes all but the last three chapters of *Maid Marian*.

1819

early Jan.	Begins regular attendance at the East India House, while living with his mother, and later his cousin Harriet Love, in lodgings at 5 York Street, Covent Garden.
Jan.	Begins reading proofs of Shelley's *Rosalind and Helen* volume.
18 May	Provisional appointment as Assistant to the Examiner of India Correspondence, with a salary of £600. His colleagues in the Examiner's Office include James Mill and Edward Strachey. Through Mill he subsequently meets Jeremy Bentham and other leading philosophical radicals.
1 July	Moves into his house at 17 Upper Stamford Street (later 18 Stamford Street), Blackfriars, where Harriet Love probably continues as a member of his household at least through Nov.

after 25 Sept.	Submits Shelley's tragedy *The Cenci* to Thomas Harris, manager and proprietor of Covent Garden Theatre, who finds the play objectionable on account of its subject.
20 Nov.	Writes a letter proposing marriage to Jane Gryffydh, with whom he has had no contact since Apr. 1811. According to Harriet Love, the letter was written under a 'feeling of bitter disappointment', at the suggestion of 'an old acquaintance' who called unexpectedly at the India House.

1820

22 Mar.	Marriage to Jane Gryffydh at Eglwysfach Chapel, Cardiganshire, while staying with his friends George and Justina Jeffreys at nearby Glandyfi Castle.
June–?July	Reads proofs of Shelley's *Prometheus Unbound* volume.
late June–early July	'The Four Ages of Poetry' published in *Olliers Literary Miscellany*, No. I.
?Sept.–Oct.	Holiday with his wife at Marlow.

1821

late Feb.–21 Mar.	In response to 'The Four Ages of Poetry', Shelley writes the first part of 'A Defence of Poetry' and sends it to Charles Ollier for publication in *Olliers Literary Miscellany*, but the essay remains unpublished because the Olliers fail to issue a second number.
10 Apr.	Appointment as Assistant to the Examiner confirmed, with a raise in salary to £800.
9 July	His poem 'Rich and Poor; or, Saint and Sinner' published in *The Traveller*, then reprinted in *The Examiner* on 22 July.

29 July	Birth of his daughter Mary Ellen in London (baptized 31 May 1822 at Christ Church, Southwark).
8 or 9 Sept.– ?1 Oct.	Holiday alone in Wales.

1822

late Mar.	*Maid Marian* published by Thomas Hookham.
late Mar.	Third edition of *Headlong Hall* published by Thomas Hookham.
8 July	Shelley drowns off Viareggio, leaving Byron and Peacock as joint executors of his will, dated 18 Feb. 1817. Peacock learns of his death on 6 Aug. in a letter from Leigh Hunt and writes to inform Sir Timothy Shelley.
?late Aug.– 16 Sept.	Holiday with his wife and daughter at Combe, near Wendover, in the Chiltern Hills.
3 Dec.	James Robinson Planché's opera *Maid Marian; or, The Huntress of Arlingford*, with music by Henry Rowley Bishop, first performed at Covent Garden, with Charles Kemble as Friar Tuck and Anna Maria Tree as Maid Marian.

1823

23 Mar.	Birth of his daughter Margaret Love in London (baptized 11 July 1823 at Christ Church, Southwark).
9 Apr.	Salary raised to £1000.
14 Apr.	Obtains a reader's ticket for the British Museum Library on the recommendation of a Mr Banks.
21 May	John Stuart Mill appointed as a junior clerk in the Examiner's Office.

28 June	After a quarrel with Mary Shelley, Byron declines to act as joint executor of Shelley's will, leaving Peacock as sole executor.
25 Aug.	Mary Shelley returns to London but does not see Peacock until after 18 Oct. because he is on holiday in the country.
before Nov.	Takes a cottage for his mother on the Thames at Lower Halliford.
6 Nov.	Begins protracted negotiations with Sir Timothy Shelley's solicitor, William Whitton, respecting financial provision for Mary Shelley and her son Percy Florence.

1824

5 June	Joins the Cymmrodorion, or Metropolitan Cambrian Institution.
24 June	Starts separate negotiations with William Whitton and others respecting the purchase of an annuity for Mary Shelley.
July–Aug.	Arranges for the suppression of Shelley's *Posthumous Poems* and an intended companion volume of prose works, at the insistence of Sir Timothy Shelley, who threatens to cut off Mary Shelley's allowance.

1825

30 July	Birth of his son Edward Gryffydh in London (baptized 14 Jan. 1832 at Shepperton).
before 26 Dec.	Intervenes to prevent the publication of Leigh Hunt's article on Shelley's *Posthumous Poems* in the *Westminster Review*.
?Dec.–Feb. 1826	Writes *Paper Money Lyrics*, but does not publish them, in order to avoid giving offence to James Mill.

1826

13 Jan.　　Death of his daughter Margaret Love in London (buried 21 Jan. at Shepperton). He later quarrels with William Russell, Rector of Shepperton, over the wording of his verse epitaph on her tombstone. His wife's grief gradually leads to mental illness.

Mar.　　Takes the cottage adjoining his mother's and moves his family to Lower Halliford.

15 Apr.　　Lets his house at 18 Stamford Street to Capt. Henry Robert Cole, retaining the use of two rooms and taking a friendly interest in Cole's son Henry.

?Spring–Summer　　Informally adopts Mary Ann ('May') Rosewell (baptized 20 July 1823, died 1 June 1883) because of her resemblance to his dead daughter.

June　　His poem 'Llyn-y-dreiddiad-vrawd; or, The Pool of the Diving Friar' published in the *New Monthly Magazine*.

1827

May–June　　Completes negotiations with William Whitton and Sir Timothy Shelley for a financial settlement for Mary Shelley and her son Percy Florence.

19 Sept.　　Birth of his daughter Rosa Jane at Lower Halliford (baptized 14 Jan. 1832 at Shepperton).

Oct.　　Article on 'Moore's Epicurean' published in the *Westminster Review*.

1828

?Feb.　　Begins an article on Leigh Hunt's *Lord Byron and Some of His Contemporaries* for the *Westminster Review*.

1829

?Jan.	The East India Company's Chairman asks him 'to look into the whole question' of steam navigation.
24 Jan.	His poem 'Touchandgo' published in the *Globe and Traveller*.
early Mar.	*The Misfortunes of Elphin* published by Thomas Hookham.
Sept.	Completes a long 'Memorandum respecting the Application of Steam Navigation to the Internal and External Communication of India' (printed in 1834).
21 Dec.	Lord Ellenborough, as President of the Board of Control, sends Peacock's memorandum on steam navigation to the Duke of Wellington, the Prime Minister.

1830

?Feb.–Aug.	Serves as opera critic for the *Globe and Traveller*.
Apr.	Article on the first volume of 'Moore's Letters and Journals of Lord Byron' published in the *Westminster Review*. Moore's protests apparently induce the editor, John Bowring, to change his mind about publishing Peacock's intended review of the second volume.
May	Capt. Francis Rawdon Chesney begins his reconnaissance of overland routes to India, stimulated by Peacock's questionnaires, sent the previous year through the Foreign Office to the British embassy at Constantinople and the British consulate at Alexandria.
Oct.	Articles on 'Randolph's Memoirs, &c. of Thomas Jefferson' and 'London Bridge' published in the *Westminster Review*.

12 Oct.	Birth of his natural daughter Susan Mary Abbott (died 4 Mar. 1921), probably to Alice Bunce Abbott. Susan is baptized on 1 Nov. at St Pancras Old Church as the daughter of Alice's brother John Abbott and Emmeline Spencer, but there is no other record of Emmeline's existence. Susan is raised by John and Alice as John's daughter.
8 Dec.	Appointed Senior Assistant to the Examiner, with a salary of £1,200. James Mill succeeds William McCulloch as Examiner.
1831	
Feb.–Aug. 1834	Serves as opera critic for *The Examiner*.
mid-Feb.	*Crotchet Castle* published by Thomas Hookham.
28 Feb.	Completes a long memorandum on 'Steam Navigation of the Ganges'.
Apr.–Mar. 1833	With Capt. James Henry Johnston, the Bengal Government's Controller of Steam Vessels, supervises the design and construction of iron steamers for the Ganges.
14 Aug.	His poem 'The Fate of a Broom: An Anticipation', a satire on Lord Brougham dated Mar. 1831, published in *The Examiner*.
Oct.	Holiday in Wales with his daughter Mary Ellen.
1832	
9 Feb. and 17 Mar.	Gives evidence before the House of Commons Select Committee on the Affairs of the East India Company.
early Oct.	Death of his mother (buried 11 Oct. at Shepperton).

1833

Jan. — Meets Chesney and induces him to print his *Reports on the Navigation of the Euphrates.*

10 Apr. — Signs an agreement by which his landlord, Thomas Nettleship, undertakes to pay for extensive reconstruction to connect his two cottages at Lower Halliford and convert them into a comfortable residence, while he undertakes to sign a twenty-one-year lease.

2 Dec. — Completes a long memorandum on 'Steam Navigation in India, and between Europe and India' (printed in 1834).

1834

16 Apr. — Submits a 'Corrected Estimate of the Probable Expense of Placing Two Iron Steam Vessels on the River Euphrates at Bussora, and Navigating the Same from Bussora to Bir and Back' to Charles Grant, President of the Board of Control.

9 and 20 June — Gives evidence as the leading witness before the House of Commons Select Committee on Steam Navigation to India, which accepts his estimate in recommending a Parliamentary grant of £20,000 for the Euphrates Expedition. The Appendix to the Committee's *Report* includes his memoranda of Sept. 1829 and 2 Dec. 1833, his estimate of 16 Apr. 1834 and other papers submitted by him.

11, 15, 17 and 31 July — Gives evidence for the East India Company before the House of Commons Select Committee on the Suppression of the *Calcutta Journal.*

Sept.–June 1837 — Supervises the design, construction, fitting and outward voyages of the *Atalanta* and the

Berenice, the first vessels to steam the entire distance to India.

1835

Jan.   Article 'On Steam Navigation to India' published in the *Edinburgh Review*.

Jan.–Mar.   Seriously ill with inflammation of the lungs.

10 Feb.   The Euphrates Expedition sails from Liverpool under Chesney's command.

Apr.   Article on 'Lord Mount Edgcumbes's Musical Reminiscences' published in the *London Review*.

Oct.   Article on 'French Comic Romances' published in the *London Review*.

1836

Jan.   Articles on 'The Épicier' and 'Bellini' published in the *London Review*.

17 Feb.   Appointed Assistant Examiner, with a salary of £1,500.

4–7 and 21 July   Gives evidence for the East India Company before the House of Commons Select Committee on Salt, British India.

27 July   Appointed to succeed James Mill as Examiner, with a salary of £2,000.

1837

Jan.   'The Legend of Manor Hall' published in *Bentley's Miscellany*.

Feb.   'Recollections of Childhood: The Abbey House' published in *Bentley's Miscellany*.

24 Mar.   *Headlong Hall, Nightmare Abbey, Maid Marian* and *Crotchet Castle* reprinted as No. LVII in Richard Bentley's series of Standard Novels, with a Preface dated 4 Mar.

22 Apr.–18 June   Seven of his *Paper Money Lyrics*, as well as 'Promotion BY Purchase and by NO

	'Purchase' and 'Rich and Poor; or, Saint and Sinner', published by Henry Cole in *The Guide, a new weekly newspaper.*
26 June	Gives evidence before the House of Commons Select Committee on Steam Communication with India.
July–Sept.	*Paper Money Lyrics, and Other Poems* privately printed by Henry Cole, with a Preface dated 20 July.
July–Apr. 1838	Supervises the purchase, refitting and outward voyage of the *Semiramis* (originally the *Waterford*).

1838

Jan.	'The New Year: Lines on George Cruikshank's Illustration of January, in the Comic Almanack for 1838' published in *Bentley's Miscellany*.
Aug.–Sept.	Two of his *Paper Money Lyrics* published in *Bentley's Miscellany*.
Sept.–Oct. 1841	As Clerk to the Secret Committee, supervises the procurement and shipment of iron steamers for the Euphrates, the Tigris and the Indus. Also supervises the design, construction, fitting and trials of a new class of iron steamers with sliding keels for sea or river service, four of which are finished in England and sent around the Cape (*Nemesis, Phlegethon, Pluto* and *Proserpine*), while two others are shipped in pieces to India (*Ariadne* and *Medusa*). Five of his 'iron chickens' see service in the later phases of the Opium War of 1839–42, the *Nemesis* winning great renown under Capt. William Hutcheon Hall.

3 and 7 Nov.	Two letters signed 'Philatmos', on the failure of the *Semiramis* to make the passage from Bombay to the Red Sea against the South-West Monsoon in July, published in *The Times*.

1839

Jan.	James Spedding's article on 'Tales by the Author of Headlong Hall' published anonymously in the *Edinburgh Review*.
21 Jan.	Recommends that the Board of Control employ Arthur Conolly for a mission to Khiva and Bokhara, with a view to placing British steamers on the Aral Sea and the Oxus and Jaxartes rivers.
17 Apr.	Death of his uncle William Love at Yarmouth, Isle of Wight.
mid-Dec.	Thirteen of Shelley's letters from Italy 'To T.L.P., Esq.' published in Mary Shelley's edition of his *Essays, Letters from Abroad, Translations, and Fragments* (post-dated 1840), which also contains an edited version of 'A Defence of Poetry', without Shelley's references to 'The Four Ages of Poetry'.

1840

?Summer	Takes his two daughters and his cousin Harriet Love on a trial voyage of the *Proserpine*, whose Second Officer is Edward Nicolls.
24 Oct.–4 Nov.	Pays the first of many visits to Sir John Cam Hobhouse at Erle Stoke Park, near Westbury, Wilts. (Hobhouse was Byron's friend and executor, but Peacock knew him officially as President of the Board of Control, 1835–41 and 1846–52.)

1841

19 May	His son Edward Gryffydh appointed as a midshipman in the Indian Navy. He arrives in India on 2 Oct., but returns on a medical furlough granted on 22 Apr. 1842.
11–16 Sept.	Keeps a log of a trial voyage of the *Pluto*, during which he lands briefly at Cherbourg, the only time he is known to have stepped on foreign soil.

1842

14 May	Letter signed 'Philatmos', on steamboat explosions and railway accidents, published in *The Times*.
late June	Makes 'proposals' of an unknown nature to Miss Jane Fotheringhame, perhaps for her to serve as Susan Abbott's governess and/or piano teacher.
Aug.	Writes 'Newark Abbey' (published in 1860).

1843

?Spring	*Sir Hornbook* reprinted by Henry Cole in the Home Treasury series.
?Autumn–Autumn 1844	Gives up his house in Stamford Street and takes chambers at 22 John Street, Adelphi.

1844

8 Jan.	Marriage of his daughter Mary Ellen to Lt Edward Nicolls of the Royal Navy (baptized 13 July 1817) at Shepperton.
11 Mar.	Edward Nicolls drowns in the Shannon estuary, while in command of HMS *Dwarf*.
24 Apr.	Death of Sir Timothy Shelley, allowing Shelley's will to be proved and executed.
21 Aug.	His son Edward Gryffydh becomes a clerk in the Examiner's Office.

27 Oct.	Birth of his granddaughter Edith Nicolls (died 20 Aug. 1926) at Shooters Hill.
1 Nov.	Proves Shelley's will at Doctors' Commons.
12 Dec.	Accepts legacies of £2,000 and £500 under Shelley's will.
1845	
June	Visits the Isle of Wight, possibly for reasons of health.
6 Oct.	Death of his aunt Jane Love, probably the widow of his uncle Thomas, at Chertsey.
1846	
?Mar.	His Greek anapaests on Christ (probably written and privately printed in 1812–13) published anonymously at Bruges in the Prolegomena (dated 27 Feb. 1846) to Thomas Forster's *Philosophia Musarum* (title page dated 1845).
9 Oct.	Sends Hobhouse a manuscript satire on Sir Robert Peel entitled 'Ancient Examples of Modern Political Virtue, I.'
1847	
8 Oct.	His daughter Mary Ellen Nicolls writes to inform Hobhouse that Peacock is severely depressed by 'a heavy pressure of debt' under which he has been labouring 'for some years'.
1848	
22 Dec.	Meets Disraeli at Erle Stoke.
1849	
?Winter–Summer	Projects a series of 'Tales for Three Sisters', inspired by Hobhouse's daughters.
9 Aug.	Marriage of his daughter Mary Ellen Nicolls to George Meredith (born 12 Feb. 1828, died 18 May 1909) at St George's, Hanover Square.

5 Sept.	Death of Hobhouse's daughter Julia, whom he commemorates in lines sent to Hobhouse on 18 Sept.
20 Sept.	Marriage of his daughter Rosa Jane to Henry Collinson (born 16 Nov. 1811, died 13 Jan. 1877) at St Martin's in the Fields.
17 Nov.	Marriage of his son Edward Gryffydh to Mary Hall (born 19 Aug. 1830) at St Marylebone.
1850	
16 Oct.	Birth of his granddaughter Rosa Collinson (died 31 Aug. 1899) at Hurcott, near Kidderminster. (Three younger Collinson children die in infancy or early childhood.)
?Autumn–Spring 1851	Takes a house at 1 Torrington Street, Russell Square.
24 Dec.	Meets Thackeray at Erle Stoke.
1851	
?Winter–Spring	Begins working on an edition of Aeschylus' *Supplices*.
1 Feb.	Death of Mary Wollstonecraft Shelley.
Feb.	Writes 'A Goodlye Ballade of Little John', satirizing Lord John Russell's attacks on 'Papal Aggression' (circulated in manuscript with illustrations by P. A. Daniel).
26 Feb.	Hobhouse created Baron Broughton of Broughton-de-Gyfford.
1 May–15 Oct.	After initially disliking the idea of the Great Exhibition and staying away for the first few weeks, he eventually 'became fascinated with it, and after his first visit haunted Paxton's glass Palace daily', according to Henry Cole.
late May–early June	Meredith's first volume of *Poems* published by John W. Parker & Son, with a dedication to Peacock, dated May.

?before 6 June	Writes 'A New Order of Chivalry' (circulated in manuscript and later published in *Gryll Grange*).
23 July–19 Nov.	Writes and privately prints his Greek lines on 'A White-Bait Dinner, at Lovegrove's, at Blackwall. July, 1851'. Also writes and lithographs a literal Latin translation. Lord Broughton translates the poem into English verse.
31 July	Marriage of Lord Broughton's daughter Sophia Hobhouse to John Strange Jocelyn (afterwards fifth Earl of Roden).
Autumn	The Merediths move into his house at Lower Halliford.
?Autumn	Begins collaborating with his daughter Mary Ellen Meredith on a projected revision of William Kitchiner's *Apicius Redivivus; or, The Cook's Oracle*, to be published by John W. Parker & Son.
Dec.	Article on 'Gastronomy and Civilization', written in collaboration with his daughter Mary Ellen Meredith and signed with the initials M.M., published in *Fraser's Magazine*.
23 Dec.	Death of his wife at Southend, Essex (buried 30 Dec. at St Mary's, Prittlewell, Southend). He learns of her death on Christmas morning at Erle Stoke but does not leave to attend her funeral.
1852	
?early Mar.	*Letters of Percy Bysshe Shelley* published by Edward Moxon with an Introductory Essay by Robert Browning. After examining the manuscripts and declaring them to be clever forgeries, Peacock gives Moxon permission to

	publish his own unedited letters from Shelley in their place, but nothing comes of the scheme.
Mar.	'Horæ Dramaticæ [No. I]: Querolus; or, The Buried Treasure' published in *Fraser's Magazine*.
Apr.	'Horæ Dramaticæ [No. II]: The Phaëthon of Euripides' published in *Fraser's Magazine*.
? May–October	After the deaths of John and Alice Abbott (27 Mar. and 16 Apr.), his natural daughter Susan Mary Abbott comes to live with the Merediths in his house at Lower Halliford.
?Summer–Autumn	Proposes marriage to Claire Clairmont's twenty-seven-year-old niece, Pauline Clairmont, who 'looked daggers at the dear old man'.

1853

13 June	Birth of his grandson Arthur Gryffydh Meredith (died 3 Sept. 1890) at Lower Halliford.
11 July	Gives evidence for the East India Company before the House of Commons Select Committee on Indian Territories.
?Autumn	Takes Vine Cottage for the Merediths, across the green from his house at Lower Halliford. Susan Abbott also leaves his house around this time.
?Autumn–Autumn 1854	Gives up his London quarters at 1 Torrington Street, Russell Square.

1854

27 July	Marriage of Lord Broughton's daughter Charlotte Hobhouse to Dudley Wilmot Carleton (afterwards fourth Baron Dorchester).

before 25 Sept.	His 'little book' of scatological Latin inscriptions *In Statuam Roberti Peel, Baronetti . . . Epigrammata Anathematica ad Singula Baseos Latera* privately printed on a friend's press.
1856	
Mar.	Writes a Preface for a yellowback edition of *Melincourt* published by Chapman & Hall.
12 Mar.	Tenders his resignation of the Examinership.
28 Mar.	Granted a superannuation allowance of £1,333.6.8. John Stuart Mill appointed to succeed him as Examiner.
1857	
12 Mar.	Sends Lord Broughton a Latin squib on the parliamentary coalition against Lord Palmerston's government. Broughton translates it into English verse.
before 29 Sept.	His daughter Mary Ellen, pregnant by Henry Wallis, asks Meredith for a separation.
Oct.	'Horæ Dramaticæ, No. III: The "Flask" of Cratinus' published in *Fraser's Magazine*.
5 Oct.	Death of his daughter Rosa Jane Collinson at 13 Cambridge Terrace, Paddington (buried 10 Oct. at Shepperton).
1858	
24 Jan.	Has his portrait painted by Henry Wallis.
late Jan.	Two of Shelley's letters to Peacock from Switzerland published in revised form in Charles S. Middleton's *Shelley and his Writings*.
Apr.	The first two volumes of Thomas Jefferson Hogg's *The Life of Percy Bysshe Shelley* published. Hogg caricatures Peacock in 1813 as the poor poet 'Otho' – a 'professor of

suicide' who made a strong impression on Harriet Shelley.

Apr. Article on 'Chapelle and Bachaumont' published in *Fraser's Magazine*.

18 Apr. Birth of his grandson Harold ('Felix') Wallis (died 4 Feb. 1933) to Mary Ellen Meredith and Henry Wallis (born 21 Feb. 1830, died 20 Dec. 1916) at Elm Cottage, Redland, near Bristol.

June 'Memoirs of Percy Bysshe Shelley' [Part I] published in *Fraser's Magazine*.

Autumn–Winter 1859 His daughter Mary Ellen Meredith goes to Capri with Henry Wallis for the sake of her health.

Nov. Article on 'Demetrius Galanus: Greek Translations from Sanskrit' published in *Fraser's Magazine*.

22 Nov. Marriage of his natural daughter Susan Mary Abbott to William Mayne Neill at All Souls, St Marylebone.

25 Dec. His son Edward Gryffydh receives a pension on the demise of the East India Company. He subsequently studies law.

1859

Mar. Article on 'Müller and Donaldson's History of Greek Literature' published in *Fraser's Magazine*.

2–20 Aug. Visits Lord Broughton at Corsham Court, near Chippenham, Wilts.

1860

Jan. 'Memoirs of Percy Bysshe Shelley', Part II, published in *Fraser's Magazine*.

Mar. 'Unpublished Letters of Percy Bysshe Shelley: From Italy – 1818 to 1822' published in

	Fraser's Magazine (followed by a 'Postscript to the Shelley Letters' in the May issue).
Apr.–Dec.	*Gryll Grange* serialized in *Fraser's Magazine*.
?Spring–Summer 1861	Writes 'A Dialogue on Idealities' and gives the manuscript to Charlotte Carleton.
June	Richard Garnett's article 'Shelley in Pall Mall', contradicting Peacock's account of the separation of Shelley and Harriet, published in *Macmillan's Magazine*.
21 Aug.–10 Sept.	Visits Lord Broughton at Tedworth House, near Andover, Hants. This proves to be the last of many visits.
Nov.	'Newark Abbey, August 1842, with a Reminiscence of August 1807' published in *Fraser's Magazine*.

1861

late Feb.	*Gryll Grange* published in book form by Parker, Son, & Bourn.
early Aug.	Onset of his daughter Mary Ellen Meredith's fatal illness, during which he visits her daily at Grotto Cottage, Oatlands Park, Weybridge.
22 Oct.	Death of his daughter Mary Ellen Meredith (buried 26 Oct. at Weybridge). He does not attend her funeral.
?Nov.–Dec.	Clari Leigh Hunt comes to live as a member of his family at Lower Halliford. She remains at least until Dec. 1863.

1862

| ?Winter–Spring | Writes 'The Last Day of Windsor Forest' (published in the *National Review*, Sept. 1887). |
| Mar. | 'Percy Bysshe Shelley: Supplementary Notice' published in *Fraser's Magazine*. |

June	Richard Garnett's 'Shelley, Harriet Shelley, and Mr. T. L. Peacock', dated 6 Mar., published in his *Relics of Shelley*.
?Summer	Robert Buchanan is a frequent visitor at Lower Halliford.
mid-Aug.	*Gl'Ingannati, The Deceived: A Comedy Performed at Siena in 1531: and Aelia Laelia Crispis* published by Chapman & Hall.
27 Aug.	Death of Thomas Jefferson Hogg.
1863	
?Winter–Spring	Suffers a decline in health and spirits, from which he never fully recovers.
1864	
22 Oct.	Makes a simple will, leaving his entire estate to his adopted daughter, Mary Rosewell.
1865	
Oct.–Dec.	His son Edward Gryffydh qualifies as a solicitor during Michaelmas Term. (He died 4 Jan. 1867 at 45 Hunter Street, Bloomsbury.)
?Dec.	Refuses to leave his library when his house is threatened by fire, saying, 'By the immortal gods, I will not move!'
1866	
23 Jan.	Dies while sleeping. Cause of death is certified as 'Climacteric'.
29 Jan.	Buried in the New Cemetery at Shepperton. His grave is later marked by a horizonal slab placed there by his cousins Henry and Harriet Love.
7 Mar.	His will is proved in London by Mary Rosewell, his sole executrix. The value of his effects is sworn under £1,500.
11–12 June	His library is sold at Sotheby's.

ABBREVIATIONS

References to Greek and Latin texts, unless otherwise stated, are to the editions in the Loeb Classical Library.

Quotations from the Bible come from the King James Version.

References to Shakespeare are to *The Riverside Shakespeare: The Complete Works*, ed. G. Blakemore Evans et al., 2nd edn (Boston: Houghton Mifflin, 1997).

References to Peacock's novels are given by chapter number and, unless otherwise stated, are to the texts as they appear in the Cambridge Edition of the Novels of Thomas Love Peacock, gen. ed. Freya Johnston, 7 vols. (Cambridge: Cambridge University Press, 2016–).

In *The Works of Thomas Love Peacock* (Halliford Edition), ed. H. F. B. Brett-Smith and C. E. Jones, 10 vols. (Constable, 1924–34), two novels are contained in volume 3 and a further two in volume 4. References to these are given in the following form: Halliford, 3/2.179; 4/2.213. The first number refers to the volume in the Halliford Edition; the second number, immediately after the /, refers to the first or second novel within that volume.

Quotations from Peacock's correspondence are accompanied by the date of the relevant letter and by the volume and page number in Nicholas A. Joukovsky's edition in the form 1.234.

Throughout the text and notes, place of publication, unless otherwise stated, is London.

Austen, *Works*   The Cambridge Edition of the Works of Jane Austen, ed. Janet Todd et al., 9 vols. (Cambridge: Cambridge University Press, 2005–8)

Butler, *Hudibras* Samuel Butler, *Hudibras*, ed. John Wilders
(Oxford: Clarendon Press, 1967)

Butler, *Peacock* Marilyn Butler, *Peacock Displayed: A Satirist in his
Context* (Routledge and Kegan Paul, 1979)

Byron, *Works* George Gordon, Lord Byron, *The Complete
Poetical Works*, ed. Jerome McGann, 7 vols.
(Oxford: Clarendon Press, 1980–93)

CC *Crotchet Castle*

Coleridge, *The Collected Works of Samuel Taylor Coleridge*,
Collected Works gen. ed. Kathleen Coburn, 34 vols. (Routledge
and Kegan Paul; Princeton: Princeton University
Press, 1969–2002)

Dictionary Samuel Johnson, *A Dictionary of the English
Language*, 2 vols. (J. and P. Knapton, T. and T.
Longman, C. Hitch, L. Hawes, et al.,
1755)

Dodson, *Crotchet* Charles Dodson, '*Crotchet Castle*, by Thomas
Castle Love Peacock: A Critical Edition', ed. Charles B.
Dodson (unpublished PhD thesis, University of
Nebraska, 1966)

Garnett, *Novels* David Garnett, ed., *The Novels of Thomas Love
Peacock* (Hart-Davis, 1948; 2nd impression
corrected in 2 vols., 1963)

GG *Gryll Grange*

Halliford *The Works of Thomas Love Peacock* (Halliford
Edition), ed. H. F. B. Brett-Smith and C. E.
Jones, 10 vols. (Constable, 1924–34)

HH *Headlong Hall*

Letters Thomas Love Peacock, *The Letters of Thomas
Love Peacock*, ed. Nicholas A. Joukovsky, 2 vols.
(Oxford: Clarendon Press, 2001)

McCulloch, *Principles*	J. R. McCulloch, *The Principles of Political Economy With a Sketch of the Rise and Progress of the Science* (Edinburgh: William and Charles Tait, 1825)
ME	*The Misfortunes of Elphin*
Mel	*Melincourt*
Mill, *Elements*	James Mill, *Elements of Political Economy* (Baldwin, Cradock and Joy, 1821)
MM	*Maid Marian*
NA	*Nightmare Abbey*
ODNB	*The Oxford Dictionary of National Biography*, ed. H. C. G. Matthew, 60 vols. (Oxford: Oxford University Press, 2004), along with revisions in the online edition up to 2014
OED	*The Oxford English Dictionary*, 2nd edn, 20 vols. (Oxford: Oxford University Press, 1989), along with revisions for the 3rd edn in the online edition up to 2014
Ozell	John Ozell, ed., *The Works of Francis Rabelais, M.D. . . . Now Carefully Revis'd* [revision of Urquhart-Motteux translation], 5 vols. (J. Brindley and C. Corbett, 1737)
Pope, *Poems*	The Twickenham Edition of the Poems of Alexander Pope, ed. John Butt et al., 11 vols. (London: Methuen; New Haven, CT: Yale University Press, 1939–69)
Rabelais, *Œuvres*	François Rabelais, *Œuvres complètes*, ed. Mireille Huchon, with François Moreau, Bibliothèque de la Pléiade, new edn (Paris: Gallimard, 1994)
Sale Catalogue	*Catalogue of the Library of the Late Thos. Love Peacock, Esq . . . which will be Sold by Auction, by*

	Messrs. Sotheby, Wilkinson & Hodge... on Monday, the 11th of June, 1866, and Following Day, reprinted in *Sale Catalogues of Libraries of Eminent Persons*, ed. A N. L. Munby, vol. 1 (Mansell, with Sotheby Parke-Bernet, 1971)
Scott, *Novels*	Walter Scott, the Edinburgh Edition of the Waverley Novels, ed. David Hewitt et al., 30 vols. (Edinburgh: Edinburgh University Press, 1993–)
TLP	Thomas Love Peacock
Van Doren, *Life*	Carl Van Doren, *The Life of Thomas Love Peacock* (Dent, 1911)

INTRODUCTION

GENESIS AND COMPOSITION

On 24 January 1829, 'Touchandgo', Peacock's boisterous satirical poem on rogue bankers, appeared in the *Globe and Traveller*.[1] At around the same time, he was asked 'to look into the whole question' of steam navigation;[2] that request yielded a 'Memorandum respecting the Application of Steam Navigation to the internal and external Communications of India', dated September 1829.[3] By the end of 1830, these divergent strains of topical commentary had united to produce *Crotchet Castle*. Navigation, steam, bureaucracy, paper money and 'all the recognised modes of accumulation on the windy side of the law' (Chapter 1) shaped Peacock's sixth novel. They began, perhaps, to combine after dinner, as various ideas are said to mingle in the Reverend Doctor Folliott's mind at the beginning of Chapter 8: 'fish and wine, Greek and political economy, the Sleeping Venus he had left behind, and poor dear Mrs. Folliott . . . passed, as in a *camera obscura*, over the tablets of his imagination'.

---

[1] *Globe and Traveller*, no. 8194 (24 Jan. 1829), p. [3], col. [2]. The verses were first reprinted in Halliford, 7.242–4.

[2] See Chronology, p. xl, and *Letters*, 1.lxxv–lxxvi, cxxviii; 2.226 n. 8; *Report from the Select Committee on Steam Navigation to India; with the Minutes of Evidence, Appendix and Index* (House of Commons, 1834), p. 5. Cf. TLP's holograph essay and notes on steam navigation, dating from the 1830s and 1840s, in the Carl H. Pforzheimer Collection, New York Public Library (TLP 134, 135, 136). See also John Tyree Fain, 'Peacock's Essay on Steam Navigation', *South Atlantic Bulletin*, vol. 35 (1970), 11–15.

[3] *Report from the Select Committee on Steam Navigation*, Appendix, No. 1, pp. 2–10.

'Touchandgo' was sparked by the flight on 27 December 1828 of Rowland Stephenson (1782–1856) – politician, art collector and defaulting Lombard Street banker – and his assistant, John Henry Lloyd. Thanks to a number of unsecured advances, authorized by Lloyd, the bank of Remington, Stephenson and Coleman, and Stephenson himself, were ruined.[4] A reward was offered, in vain, for his capture. With Lloyd, he fled to Savannah, Georgia, reportedly cashing the securities he had stolen and acquiring a brace of loaded pistols from a pawnbroker. The episode was so scandalous (the escape of 'the nefarious banker' and his clerk, via the Devonshire fishing village of Clovelly, was included in a book of illustrations published four years later)[5] that one contemporary reviewer, glossing *Crotchet Castle*, felt it wholly unnecessary to elaborate: 'We need not tell the reader what period or event of the last seven years is pointed to in the following extract.'[6] James Fenimore Cooper recalled people asking him in Italy and Switzerland why Stephenson had been permitted to remain in America, after landing in Georgia and being removed by bounty hunters to New York: 'I understood pretty distinctly', wrote Cooper, 'that there were reports current that the Americans were so desirous of obtaining rich emigrants, that they had rescued a criminal in order to reap the benefit of his gold!'[7] Stephenson was formally bankrupted under the twelve-month rule on 19 January 1830, thereby forfeiting his parliamentary seat. He never returned to England to stand trial. In a curious later twist, of the kind savoured by Folliott, his eldest son – another banker called Rowland (1808–95) – became, like Peacock, an eminent figure in

---

[4] See *ODNB* entry on Rowland Stephenson.

[5] John Britton and Edward Wedlake Brayley, *Devonshire and Cornwall Illustrated, from Original Drawings* (H. Fisher, R. Fisher and P. Jackson, 1832), pp. 58–9.

[6] Anon., *Mirror of Literature, Amusement, and Instruction* (2 Apr. 1831), p. 234.

[7] James Fenimore Cooper, *A Residence in France, with an Excursion up the Rhine, and a Second Visit to Switzerland*, 2 vols. (Richard Bentley, 1836), vol. 2, pp. 147–8.

the history of steam communication with India. He was knighted in 1856 (the year of his father's death) for services as a civil engineer and as managing director of the East India Railway Company.[8] It is not only in the protean realm of Peacock's fiction that the target and the vehicle of satire can suddenly appear to change places.

Of Peacock's sixth novel it may be said, as he wrote of Cratinus' *Flask*, that 'The fragments of this comedy are few and brief; but they throw some light on its scope and progress' – 'progress' being an especially charged term in Peacock's fiction.[9] No complete manuscript of *Crotchet Castle* exists, but the Carl H. Pforzheimer Collection of Shelley and His Circle (New York Public Library) contains some illuminating draft materials. Peacock began writing the novel soon after he completed *The Misfortunes of Elphin* (published in March 1829). According to H. F. B. Brett-Smith, the new tale was already well advanced by the beginning of 1829, but there is no real cause to doubt Peacock's statement, in his Preface to the Standard Novels edition (1837) of *Headlong Hall*, *Nightmare Abbey*, *Maid Marian* and *Crotchet Castle*, that the last novel had been written in its entirety in 1830.[10] The Halliford editors were led to think otherwise by their recovery of Peacock's unsigned verses of 1829, 'Touchandgo', from the *Globe and Traveller* newspaper, and by two newly discovered holograph manuscripts of the poem. One of those 'Touchandgo' manuscripts is a revised draft whose final readings correspond to those of the *Globe* text; the other is a shorter, untitled piece that is included in two surviving leaves of an early draft of *Crotchet Castle* (see Appendix D and Appendix E).

The comparatively brief version of 'Touchandgo', heavily corrected, is introduced by a snippet of Susannah Touchandgo's letter

---

[8] See *ODNB* entry on Rowland Stephenson (senior); there is no entry for his son.

[9] *Horæ Dramaticæ*, 'The "Flask" of Cratinus' (1857), Halliford, 10.72.

[10] See Halliford, 1.cxlv, 1–2; Nicholas A. Joukovsky, 'The Revision of Peacock's "Touchandgo" and the Composition of *Crotchet Castle*', *Notes and Queries*, 257/New Series, 59, no. 3 (2012), 386–7.

to her fugitive parent, in which she says 'My feelings have been very much hurt by reading some wicked verses about you in a newspaper', but that she 'could not help copying them, because they were about you'. We seem to be in contact with the genesis of the novel when we encounter Susannah's gentle, vulnerable perspective on crime and public gossip, matched (at this point somewhat awkwardly) by the knowing, robustly critical perspective of satire. Both these attitudes are evident in Peacock's journalism and reviews; the vulnerability typically surfaces in his responses to biography.[11] If we accept his claim to have written *Crotchet Castle* in 1830, and bearing in mind the recent discovery that his natural daughter Susan Mary Abbott was born on 12 October that year, it is tempting to read into the nascent character of Susannah (or Susan) a wish on the author's part to protect his illegitimate offspring, as yet perhaps unborn – as well as a need, at some level, to swipe at absconding fathers and to imagine the effects of such absence on their children.[12] After all, the name 'Touchandgo' need not refer solely to illicit financial activities.

The possible connection between Susannah Touchandgo and Susan Abbott is only one reason to query the Halliford editors' account of the likely dates of the novel's composition. Brett-Smith concluded from the manuscript incorporating the shorter version of 'Touchandgo' that Peacock must have started writing *Crotchet Castle* more than two years before it was published in February 1831. In other words, he thought that the newspaper text, printed in 1829, must postdate the manuscript, ascribing to Peacock the original intention of attacking Stephenson and Lloyd within the context of the novel, rather than in a freestanding satirical poem. This conclusion may have been reached partly because of the dates in watermark on the blue-grey Whatman paper on which both drafts of the 'Touchandgo' are written: 1828 (for the shorter poem and

---

[11] See e.g. *Memoirs of Percy Bysshe Shelley* (1858–60), Halliford, 8.39–40.
[12] See Nicholas A. Joukovsky and Jim Powell, 'A Peacock in the Attic', *Times Literary Supplement* (22 July 2011), 13–15.

extract from Susannah's letter) and 1827. But there was nothing to stop Peacock writing on that paper two or three years later, and the fact that Susannah refers to 'copying' the verses that follow out of a 'newspaper' and into her letter is a mischievous hint (entirely out of character for this loving, innocent daughter, and therefore absent from the published novel) that the *Globe and Traveller* text most likely predates the version of the poem that was included in the first edition of *Crotchet Castle*. Such is the view of Nicholas A. Joukovsky: 'The shorter, untitled version of "Touchandgo" in the draft of *Crotchet Castle* was not an early draft of the poem that would appear in the *Globe and Traveller*, but a later draft revision of the published poem, compressed for inclusion in the novel.'[13] Joukovsky's simpler explanation of how the 1831 text came into being gains in plausibility from the knowledge that, although most of the verse in Peacock's novels was original, *Crotchet Castle* also included 'The Pool of the Diving Friar' – a poem which had already been printed anonymously in the *New Monthly Magazine* for June 1826.[14] Peacock, it seems, was quarrying his back catalogue. This may or may not offer a hint as to why, following *Crotchet Castle*, it took him nearly thirty years to publish another, final novel. Given the demands of his official duties and the complexities of his private life, he may have found the process of composing sufficient new material, and of writing at length, more arduous than he had in the previous fifteen years.

The Pforzheimer Collection also includes one page torn from a notebook, containing (in pencil) ten lines of an early draft of Chapter 4 and concerning an 'expectant company' awaiting its dinner (Appendix B). The last, very brief section of this short manuscript, set off from the draft portion of Chapter 4, shows Peacock apparently beginning to sketch out the matter of an ensuing dialogue, planning his chief targets and allocating topics to speakers, perhaps with

[13] Joukovsky, 'The Revision of Peacock's "Touchandgo"', p. 387.
[14] See Nicholas A. Joukovsky, 'The First Printing of Peacock's "The Pool of the Diving Friar"', *Notes and Queries*, 219/New Series, 21 (1974), 334–5.

reference to a different chapter. Another page of an early draft of Chapter 5 survives in the Pierpont Morgan Library (Appendix C). Here, Sir Simon Steeltrap appears as Steeltrap FitzTreadmill Esquire. This draft, as far as it is possible to tell, serves only indirectly as a basis for the dialogue between Lady Clarinda and Captain Fitzchrome that appears in the published 1831 chapter, although some of its phrasing comes close to parts of that text, and it must represent a fairly early version of the relevant portion of the novel. It seems that Chapter 5, which in 1831 is entirely in the form of a conversation between two speakers, was at some earlier stage drafted as a third-person roundtable survey of all the main characters, given from the perspective of the narrator. In the 1831 text, each description originates with Lady Clarinda as she privately introduces and summarizes the company to Captain Fitzchrome; this lends the chapter a romantic and flirtatious as well as an ironic charge.

In the 1831 version of Chapter 5, Fitzchrome and Lady Clarinda refer to themselves occasionally in the third person; she addresses her suitor as 'the creature' (a word she uses more than anyone else in the novel) and as 'one Captain Fitzchrome, who is very much in love with a certain person that does not mean to have any thing to say to him, because she can better her fortune by taking somebody else'; he responds by calling her 'the beautiful, the accomplished, the witty, the fascinating, the tormenting, Lady Clarinda, who traduces herself to the said Captain by assertions which it would drive him crazy to believe'. The detached, self-descriptive tic implies that the couple are somehow aware that they are characters in a novel (in Chapter 13 of *Gryll Grange*, Lord Curryfin remarks to Miss Gryll, 'I flatter myself, I am a character', to which she replies: 'Indeed you are, or rather many characters in one'). That intimation contributes a flickering irony to their speech, a form of free indirect style which may reflect the origins of this entirely dialogic chapter in a third-person original. Another suggestion of such origins arises when Lady Clarinda says to Captain Fitzchrome 'You must know I had been reading several fashionable novels'; in 1837, 'had' becomes the less awkward 'have'.

However, if the point were being made by a narrator and in the third person, rather than in the form of a dialogue, it would be natural to say 'She had been reading several fashionable novels'. The characters' language appears to carry with it a residue of their author's earlier conceptions of how they might be handled and of what they might become. This can make the sparkle of Lady Clarinda's conversation − she is repeatedly described as a wit − come across as uncanny. There is a pathos and tragi-farcical charm in her combination of beauty, poise, intelligence and fatedness, a combination not unusual in heroines of nineteenth-century fiction, but one that is not usually played out through the primary medium of that heroine's dialogue.

The surviving manuscript fragments of *Crotchet Castle*, read alongside the text of the first edition, suggest that the novel's lovesick characters possess a sense of themselves as mechanisms or puppets, to be directed by their author and perhaps of necessity − sadly − conforming to certain fictional and social types. They exist in order to be bought and sold, as Lady Clarinda, a would-be novelist and a woman on the marriage market, repeatedly acknowledges. She is brilliantly self-aware, to the extent that she seems to know she is performing in a story of someone else's contrivance: not only because she features in a comic novel predestined to a particular conclusion, but also because she is a young woman whose character, accomplishments and inclinations are unlikely to count as much as will the rank and wealth of her future husband. The curious atmosphere resulting from her perfectly executed, often savage, conversational pirouettes, especially when they remind us of her own entrapment, is comparable not only to the 'rather too light & bright & sparkling' repartee of Elizabeth Bennet with Darcy in *Pride and Prejudice* (1813).[15] It also conjures up E. T. A. Hoffmann's satirical horror story *Der Sandmann*

---

[15] Jane Austen to Cassandra Austen, 4 Feb. 1813, in *Jane Austen's Letters*, ed. Deirdre Le Faye, 3rd edn (Oxford and New York: Oxford University Press, 1995), p. 203.

(1816), in which Nathanael falls in love with Olimpia, a peerlessly beautiful automaton (the tale went on to feature in Jacques Offenbach's *opéra fantastique*, *Les contes D'Hoffmann* (1881)) and Hans Christian Andersen's 'Den standhaftige tinsoldat' (1838), in which the titular hero falls in love with a paper ballerina. The two latter tales end in death and disaster – Nathanael throws himself to his death; Andersen's ballerina perishes in flames; the tin soldier melts into the shape of a heart – but it is far from clear how we are meant to respond to them. The crucial difference between the accomplished dolls and Lady Clarinda is that she is able to speak for herself, but at times it seems as if this distinction is unlikely to save her.

The evolution of Chapter 5 from manuscript to print supports the idea that its eventual form, that of the fictional dialogue, was the result of translating third-person narrative into speech. Peacock seems to have arrived at this characteristic feature of his novels of talk by moving away from third-person alternatives of framing a scene in order to refine them into dialogic and dramatic prose. One view of Peacock's career would encourage us to think that his fiction gradually departs from the schematic characterization and detached, satiric, philosophical manner of *Headlong Hall* in order to develop a more earnest, personal tone, as well as a commitment to psychological realism and to fuller, richer forms of characterization. But it is in the spirit of our contrarian author that we should counter that view with another, at least in relation to Chapter 5 of *Crotchet Castle*.

In 1972, Peter S. Hoff distinguished three voices at work in Peacock's sixth novel: that of an undramatized narrator, that of a clear-sighted character and that of a chorus of crotcheteers talking to (or at) one another. He described the clear-sighted character, Lady Clarinda, as exercising satirical methods quite different in kind from those of the undramatized narrator: 'Where the narrator's detached and gentlemanly tones depended upon the reader's own prejudices and ear for irony to carry the message, Clarinda's blunt and absolute language often forces a *reductio ad absurdum* upon its target.'[16] Hoff found the distinction between these two voices especially striking when each described the stock figure of the English country squire, arguing that, in the following passage from Chapter 5, 'Clarinda presents the squire just as she sees him, letting the picture speak for itself':

'By administering the laws which he assists in making, he disposes, at his pleasure, of the land and its live stock, including all the two-legged varieties, with and without feathers, in a circumference of several miles round Steeltrap Lodge. He has enclosed commons and woodlands; abolished cottage-gardens; taken the village cricket-ground into his own park, out of pure regard to the sanctity of Sunday; shut up footpaths and alehouses, (all but those which belong to his electioneering friend, Mr. Quassia, the brewer;) put down fairs and fiddlers; committed many poachers; shot a few; convicted one third of the peasantry; suspected the rest; and passed nearly the whole of them through a wholesome course of prison discipline, which has finished their education at the expense of the county.'   (Chapter 5)

Hoff comments of this baldly phrased inventory that 'Clarinda employs irony only once, when paraphrasing the hypocritical self-justification of Mr. Steeltrap ("out of pure regard to the sanctity of Sunday"). Otherwise no trace of narrative approval, real or feigned, appears in the description.'[17] By contrast, the voice of the undrama-tized narrator in Chapter 1 – who offers what is, in effect, an equally damning portrait of the same character – is ostensibly addressing Crotchet's inability to adopt the habits of a typical squire:

he could not become, like a true-born English squire, part and parcel of the barley-giving earth; he could not find in game-bagging, poacher-shooting, trespasser-pounding, footpath-stopping, common-enclosing, rack-renting, and all the other liberal pursuits and pastimes which make

---

[16] Peter S. Hoff, 'The Voices of *Crotchet Castle*', *The Journal of Narrative Technique*, 2 (1972), 186–98 (p. 191).

[17] Hoff, 'The Voices of *Crotchet Castle*', p. 191.

a country gentleman an ornament to the world, and a blessing to the poor; he could not find in these valuable and amiable occupations, and in a corresponding range of ideas, nearly commensurate with that of the great King Nebuchadnezzar, when he was turned out to grass; he could not find in this great variety of useful action, and vast field of comprehensive thought, modes of filling up his time that accorded with his Caledonian instinct. (Chapter 1)

Where Clarinda is harsh, plain and outspoken, Hoff argues, the undramatized narrator operates more subtly and indirectly. The effect on us of their distinctive approaches is to produce a composite, albeit wholly negative character of the true-born English squire. Clarinda, speaking harshly, exposes the absurd gap between what such a character is and what he ought to be; the undramatized narrator describes what he is as if it were indeed what he ought to be: 'an ornament to the world, and a blessing to the poor . . . valuable and amiable . . . great . . . useful', and so on.

As it happens, the manuscript fragment that survives of Chapter 5 also concerns the English squire; it therefore gives us some scope to pursue Hoff's distinction between the voices of *Crotchet Castle*:

The next neighbour of Mr Crotchet was ~~Squire Steeltrap~~ Steeltrap Fitz-Treadmill Esquire a great game-preserver and justice of peace. This worthy . . . contrived to be the terror of the peasantry whom he had stripped of their common rights & stopped out of their old ~~footpaths~~ paths, not even leaving them a strip of green for cricket: in return for which kindness they never lost an opportunity of pulling down his fences cutting off the heads of his young plantations & treading on the eggs of his birds . . . Somebody was always punished for these outrages: generally somebody who was not guilty: which added to the number of the aggrieved and emboldened the former perpetrators to a repetition of their exploits. (Appendix C)

Here, the third-person voice employs ironic terms of praise ('great', 'kindness'), but such irony combines with the overtly condemnatory language of Lady Clarinda: 'the terror of the peasantry whom he had stripped of their common rights & stopped out of their old ~~footpaths~~

paths, not even leaving them a strip of green for cricket'; 'Somebody was always punished for these outrages: generally somebody who was not guilty'. The 'outrages' of the squirearchy are more explicitly outrageous here, less obviously matter for comedy because the narratorial overlay of wry, disinterested urbanity is absent. What seems to have occurred between the earlier and later drafts of *Crotchet Castle*, then, is not only the transition (at times) from third-person narrative to dialogue, but the disaggregation of historical and satirical perspectives into Lady Clarinda's earnestness on the one hand and the narrator's detachment on the other. Lady Clarinda's opinions on social injustice possess a spoken urgency arising from her sense of things as they are right now; the narrator's knowing tone bespeaks a sense of the absurdity of human nature throughout the ages, and hence a different vantage point.

A single leaf of a more advanced draft of Chapter 16 was sold in 1998 by Jarndyce Antiquarian Booksellers in Bloomsbury, and eventually to Mr John Brett-Smith of Princeton, son of H. F. B. Brett-Smith, whose archive of Peacock material remains in his family's possession.[18] We have endeavoured, with the help of Mr Brett-Smith's descendants, to locate this item; searches of his private collection of books and manuscripts have not yet led to its rediscovery. Fortunately, there is a photocopy of the missing leaf in the British Library, which is the source of the text reproduced in Appendix F. This draft fragment of Chapter 16, in which Mr Chainmail unwittingly reduces Susannah to tears by revealing to her, via a newspaper, the announcement of Crotchet's imminent marriage, is very close to the text as published in 1831. There is a hint of a possible plot twist in Susannah's deleted words, 'It is not yet too', which suggest that it is not too late for something – but what?

PUBLICATION

Crotchet Castle cannot have been finished before the end of 1830, since its final chapters allude to political events that occurred in

[18] Jarndyce Catalogue 124 (Spring 1998), item 828.

November and December that year: Henry Brougham's acceptance of the Lord Chancellorship in Lord Grey's new government, and the 'Captain Swing' riots. *Crotchet Castle, by the author of Headlong Hall* was first published by Thomas Hookham, Jr., of Old Bond Street, in mid-February 1831. It was printed by J. and C. Adlard, of Bartholomew Close. The volume, a foolscap octavo in boards, cost seven shillings and sixpence. It included one page of publisher's advertisements, which announced that *Headlong Hall* was now in a third edition (priced six shillings) and that *The Misfortunes of Elphin* was available for seven shillings. It also noted that 'The other novels of the same author are MELINCOURT, NIGHTMARE ABBEY, and MAID MARIAN, which are at present out of print'. As was the case for *The Misfortunes of Elphin*, the printer's charges for *Crotchet Castle* were recorded in the Adlard Ledger, which indicates that 750 copies of both titles were printed.[19]

The Halliford editors propose that the 'correct' order of the preliminary leaves of *Crotchet Castle* is (1) advertisement, (2) fly-title, (3) title, (4) contents.[20] They note that this sequence required each pair of leaves to be sewn separately, and that consequently the leaves are rarely found in the right order. Evidence contained in the Adlard Ledger's entries for Thomas Hookham's account (5 February 1831), however, gives cause to question this explanation, and to suspect that the bifolium containing the motto from Samuel Butler's *Miscellaneous Thoughts —in Verse* ('Should the world resolve to abolish / All that's ridiculous and foolish / It would have nothing left to do, / to apply in jest or earnest to') and the advertisement was an afterthought. Since the final U gathering contains only six leaves, it is likely that one of the two pairs of preliminary leaves was printed as part of that gathering. Moreover, the location of the printer's imprint

---

[19] 'Ledger of the Printing Firm of Adlard' (c. 1825–32), Bodleian Library, Oxford (MS. Don. C. 84), p. 122. The entry for *ME* is on p. 121.

[20] Halliford, 4.213–14.

on the verso of the title page indicates that this was originally planned to be the first leaf of the book. The first line of the relevant entry in the Adlard Ledger confirms that each copy of the original printing was composed of '19 sheets' (not 19 and a quarter). The final line refers to '750 d[itt]o after[war]ds made up ¼ Sheet 12/- Alter[in]g Title 2/-' (this might have been a reasonable charge for printing two extra leaves and inserting them after the quires had been made up). So it is probable that the original prelims consisted solely of the title and contents leaves. In copies of the first edition that survive in the United Kingdom and North America and have been consulted by the present editors, the preliminary materials appear in various configurations:

(1) advertisement, (2) fly-title, (3) title, (4) contents;
(1) title, (2) contents, (3) advertisement, (4) fly-title;
(1) title, (2) contents, (3) fly-title, (4) advertisement;
(1) advertisement, (2) title, (3) contents, (4) fly-title;
(1) title, (2) contents, (3) no fly-title, (4) no advertisement;
(1) title, (2) contents, (3) fly title, (4) no advertisement;
(1) title, (2) advertisement, (3) contents, (4) fly-title.

In our copytext, the preliminary leaves appear as follows: (1) title, (2) advertisement, (3) contents, (4) fly-title.[21]

What may have occurred was that, after printing had begun, or perhaps even when it was completed, Peacock chose to add the motto from Butler on a separate leaf, and Thomas Hookham took the opportunity to include a conjugate advertisement leaf. In such a case, the leaf with the motto could have been intended either as a half-title or as a fly-title preceding the text. The advertisement leaf might have been folded to appear either before or after the half-title

---

[21] English Faculty Library Rare Book Room, Oxford, XM60.1[Cro]27029. For further details on the order of the prelims and copies of the first edition consulted by the editors, see 'Note on the text'.

or fly-title, but the two leaves could also have been separated, to allow the advertisement leaf to be pasted in at the end of the text, and the half-title or fly-title to be pasted in either before or after the bifolium containing the title and contents. With all of these possibilities to bear in mind, it is no wonder that binders were often confused, or that they occasionally discarded the advertisement leaf.

In 1837, the publisher Richard Bentley bought the copyright of *Headlong Hall*, *Nightmare Abbey*, *Maid Marian* and *Crotchet Castle* and reissued all four novels in a single volume, 'with Corrections, and a Preface, by the Author', as No. 57 in his series of Standard Novels. Bentley had originally agreed to include three novels for his 1837 edition, and *Crotchet Castle* was a late addition, 'presumably as a makeweight to bring the number of pages up to the average for volumes in the Standard Novels series'.[22] Peacock wrote a new preface for this edition and lightly revised and corrected all four texts. Many slight differences can be found between the 1831 and 1837 versions of *Crotchet Castle*. While there are only three substantial changes to the main body of the text, differences in spelling and punctuation crop up on nearly every page (for further details, see 'Note on the text').

Bentley seems to have paid only ten additional pounds for the copyright and stock of *Crotchet Castle*.[23] Since Peacock's new preface, dated 4 March 1837, could not have been written until after the decision was taken to include *Crotchet Castle*, it may have replaced an earlier preface to the other three novels. The Standard Novels edition appeared on 24 March at the usual price of six shillings. It was printed by Andrew Spottiswoode of New Street Square (in the early 1830s, the firm was also responsible for printing Bentley's

---

[22] *Letters*, 2.239 n. 3. For a full account of Bentley's series in relation to TLP, see the Introduction to *Nightmare Abbey*. This section of our Introduction is indebted to Nicholas A. Joukovsky's research.

[23] Bentley Archives, British Library Add. MS 46676A, fol. 30: 'Apl 37 Copyrt & Stock of Peacock's Tales purchased for inclusion in the Standard Novels £70'.

Standard Novels edition of Jane Austen). The author's name did not appear on the title pages, but it featured prominently in Bentley's advertisements. The original impression consisted of 3000 copies,[24] which proved enough to satisfy public demand until the series came to an end. By the 1840s, Bentley was in financial difficulties; the situation worsened in the ensuing decade. To help clear his firm's debts, he sold the remaining stock and copyrights of the whole Standard Novels series, along with the stereotype and steel plates, in an auction on 26 February 1856.[25] Peacock's four prose fictions were among the titles thus acquired by Ward & Lock, who used the stereotype plates for two 'yellowback' editions published later that year, one containing *Headlong Hall* and *Nightmare Abbey*, the other *Maid Marian* and *Crotchet Castle*. Peacock's preface was omitted. These cheap reprints, priced at one shilling each, appeared without his authority.

In 1858, Ward & Lock reissued all four of the tales from the Standard Novels edition in a single volume titled *Headlong Hall, Maid Marian, and Other Tales by T. L. Peacock*, priced at one shilling and sixpence in boards. Peacock mentioned this undated edition in a letter of 4 July 1861 to George Huntly Gordon.[26] While he had apparently seen a copy for himself, he did not realize that Bentley had sold the copyright of the four novels. The next British printing of *Crotchet Castle* would be after the author's death, in the collected edition of *The Works of Thomas Love Peacock, Including his Novels, Poems, Fugitive Pieces, Criticisms, etc., with a Preface by the Right Hon. Lord Houghton, a Biographical Notice by his Granddaughter, Edith Nicholls, and a Portrait*, ed. Henry Cole, 3 vols. (Richard Bentley and Son, 1875).

---

[24] William St Clair, *The Reading Nation in the Romantic Period* (Cambridge: Cambridge University Press, 2004), 629.

[25] See Elizabeth James, 'Sale of the Standard Novels: An Unobserved Episode in the History of the House of Bentley', *The Library*, 5th series, 33 (1978), 58–62.

[26] *Letters*, 2.423–4.

CRITICAL RECEPTION

Evoking the first three novels in its sociable, country-house back-drop, its opposition of ancients to moderns, and its incisive treatment of contemporary events and individuals, *Crotchet Castle* also borrows from the two historical romances which precede it a lyrical and pas-toral atmosphere and an easy affection for the past. Peacock might have coined for this book his term *romantesque*.[27] At the same time, *Crotchet Castle*'s effervescent farce is more ambitious than that of the earlier novels in its range of cultural and intellectual targets; it homes in on (among other things) progressivism, dogmatism, liber-alism, sexism, mass education and the follies of the learned – in short, on the absurdity of all human schemes and opinions. *Crotchet Castle* may be heterogeneous and complex, but it also embodies Peacock's characteristic elegance, lightness and concision, gesturing towards a vast range of literature. Folliott often quotes classical writers and thinkers; there are many footnotes; chapters are headed and liberally sprinkled with citations from a wide variety of texts, cultures and nations. The work constitutes an artistic, political and philosophical miscellany of sorts, thematically unified in its satirical emphasis on folly and dispute, and on the folly of dispute itself.

Given its range and tonal ambiguity, it is perhaps unsurprising that *Crotchet Castle* received mixed reviews when it was published in mid-February 1831. The first to appear, in the *Literary Gazette*, called Peacock 'the wittiest writer in England';[28] the next, in the *Athenaeum*, was also enthusiastic: 'This little volume is everything it ought to be – light, playful, sarcastic, amusing.'[29] Others were not amused. The *Monthly Review* felt that, although the style was polished, 'the wit is not at all remarkable for pointedness or elegance'.[30] *Fraser's* was adamant that the novel's author was 'an ignorant, stupid, poor devil,

---

[27] TLP to Edward Thomas Hookham (10 Feb. 1809), *Letters*, 1.27.
[28] Anon., *Literary Gazette* (19 Feb. 1831), 115–17 (p. 115).
[29] Anon., *Athenaeum* (5 Mar. 1831), 145–7 (p. 145).
[30] Anon., *Monthly Review* (1831), 117–34 (p. 134).

who has no fun, little learning, no facility, no *easiness*... the philosophy is rubbish, the wit trash'.[31] *Crotchet Castle* was witty and it was not witty. Some praised it for being Rabelaisian; some denounced it for not being Rabelaisian.[32] It was a 'satire'[33] with a point, containing 'matter whence a good moral or two may be extracted touching the times',[34] and it contained other stuff besides: 'so fine is the point, and subtle the humour, that the reader is at a loss to find them out'.[35] This last comment, from *The Examiner*, echoes Shelley's pronouncement on Peacock in his 'Letter to Maria Gisborne': 'His fine wit / Makes such a wound, the knife is lost in it.'[36] Yet what *The Examiner* formulated as a criticism, Shelley offered as a compliment. His metaphor raises a larger set of questions about Peacock's double-edged style, and about *Crotchet Castle* in particular. Is the knife lost because the wound it opens is so deep, thereby allowing the knife-wielder to get to the core of the issues he satirizes? Or is it lost because the wit is so fine that it becomes something more ambiguous than a single-minded attempt at point-scoring? From this perspective, the knife might be 'lost' because the object of its attack is forgotten, or forgiven.

Crotchet Castle's initial reception was 'mixed' not only because different journals had varying reactions; single reviewers had mixed feelings about it, too. When the *New Monthly Magazine* claimed that 'Mr Peacock has the most quaint, original, out-of-the-way species of wit of any writer of our time',[37] it was not clear whether the quaint

---

[31] Anon., *Fraser's Magazine*, 4 (Aug. 1831), 8–25 (pp. 17, 19).
[32] Anon., *Cambrian Quarterly Magazine* (1 Apr. 1831), 225–37 (p. 226); *Fraser's*, 4, p. 17.
[33] Anon., *Mirror of Literature* (2 Apr. 1831), 234–6 (p. 234); *Monthly Review*, 2.1, p. 134.
[34] Anon., *Metropolitan* (May 1831), p. 6.
[35] Anon., *The Examiner* (3 Apr. 1831), 211–12 (p. 212).
[36] P. B. Shelley, 'Letter to Maria Gisborne' (wr. 1820), lines 240–1, in *The Poems of Shelley, 1819–1820*, vol. 3, ed. Jack Donovan, Cian Duffy, Kelvin Everest and Michael Rossington (Harlow: Longman/Pearson, 2011), p. 455.
[37] Anon., *New Monthly Magazine* (Oct. 1831), 363.

out-of-the-wayness should be taken as a straightforwardly positive quality. The reviewer for the *Literary Beacon* was both 'gratified' and 'disgusted' by the novel: 'our feelings during its perusal may be likened to those of a person eating delicious oysters, interspersed occasionally with others of a contrary nature'.[38] Of the eleven reviews the novel received in 1831, the longest – and the most probing – was from Albany Fonblanque in the *Westminster Review*. Fonblanque was another who couldn't resolve his feelings about the oysters; having acknowledged the 'exquisite humour' of the novel, he added that 'it is pleasant to laugh without, at the same time feeling the twitchings of reason and conscience, sensations which we do not hesitate to say, have presented very considerable drawbacks on the amusement which we cannot help taking in all the writings of our author'.[39] He suggested that, although Peacock 'is liberal in all his political opinions . . . he attacks liberals only':

> We believe, sincerely, that it is not the warriors, but the followers of the camp, against which Mr. Peacock levels his shafts; he would probably be himself the first to regret his prowess if he thought he had put the whole army to the rout, and we are quite certain that he would much grieve, did he know, that by his very able sharpshooting upon the stragglers he was mistaken for the advance corps of the enemies of all improvement, whether in science or politics.
>
> It is a pity, that men are most inclined to satirise that of which they know the most . . . it is thus with Mr. Peacock.[40]

The movement from conjecture ('We believe') to likelihood ('he would probably') to assurance ('we are quite certain') does not manage to hide the feeling that Fonblanque is unsure what Peacock is up to in *Crotchet Castle*. Is the author a follower of the Utilitarians, or a satirizer of such followers? Or both? A year later, Leigh Hunt

---

[38] Anon., *Literary Beacon* (25 June 1831), 22–6 (p. 22).

[39] Anon. [Albany Fonblanque], *Westminster Review*, 15 (July 1831), 208–18 (p. 218).

[40] Fonblanque, *Westminster Review*, 208.

noted that 'the Utilitarians themselves are poetical!...if you want a proper Bacchanalian uproar in a song, you must go to the author of "*Headlong* Hall", who will not advance utility itself, unless it be jovial'.[41]

Given that Peacock's fictions are typically concerned to satirize not this or that opinion, but the very need to have an opinion (or to stick to it), it is curious that so many critics of *Crotchet Castle* should have felt the urge to deduce the author's opinions from his work. Debate has often focused on whether Folliott is Peacock's mouthpiece, or on the author's private feelings towards Brougham, or on whether he supports Chainmail's position, and so on. J. B. Priestley, who thought *Crotchet Castle* the best of Peacock's novels, suggested that 'What we should ask about him is not what purpose he had in mind but why his pleasure should take this form', 'form' suggesting (among other things) the distinctive formal properties of Peacock's works.[42] Purposes and pleasures need not be mutually exclusive (as Hunt recognized, Peacock was fascinated by what the jovial might have in common with the useful), but Priestley's point is a good one. Perhaps the best single thing written on Peacock in the nineteenth century, James Spedding's review of Bentley's 1837 edition of the novels, steered clear of trying to work out whose side the author was on and instead took pleasure in the breadth of Peacock's form, noting 'a certain sympathy, companionable rather than brotherly, with all'.[43] That said, Spedding quickly re-described this sympathy as 'a scepticism truly impartial and

[41] Leigh Hunt, from 'Preface' to *Poetical Works* (1832), in *The Poetical Works of Leigh Hunt*, ed. H. S. Milford (Oxford: Oxford University Press, 1923), p. xxix.

[42] Priestley, *Thomas Love Peacock*, p. 200. For Priestley's view that *CC* was TLP's best novel, 'more human, diversified and subtle' than the others, see pp. 131, 138. Reviewing Priestley's book, Raymond Mortimer concurred; see *Nation & Athenaeum*, 41 (24 Sept. 1927), p. 808.

[43] James Spedding, review of Bentley's edition of *Headlong Hall, Nightmare Abbey, Maid Marian* and *Crotchet Castle, Edinburgh Review*, 68 (Jan. 1838–9), 432–59 (p. 439).

insatiable',[44] which leads to another set of questions often raised about the tone of *Crotchet Castle*. If Peacock is disinclined to nail his colours to the mast, is his novel broadly indulgent of its characters, or unconvinced by them all? Is the even-handedness genial or cynical? Does the work's tone signal an achieved poise or a kind of slacking off?

Crotchet Castle was the first of Peacock's novels to be granted the dubious honour of a critical introduction; in the Cassell edition of 1887, Henry Morley noted that the book contained 'good-humoured exaggeration'; 'this critical satire' he thought, 'gave nobody pain'.[45] A few years later, in his collected edition of the novels, Richard Garnett said that '*Crotchet Castle* displays Peacock at his zenith . . . it is equally free from the errors of immaturity and the infirmities of senescence'.[46] But Garnett's response, with its Johnsonian appositional genitives ('errors of immaturity', 'infirmities of senescence'), also displayed an uncertainty about whether the book was affectionate or aggressive. On the one hand, 'the paradoxes and whims of *Crotchet Castle* are merry imps, to be even encouraged in moderation'; on the other hand, the editor includes an appendix about the Charity Commissions that Peacock satirized, and argues that the author's 'point is wholly blunted by its injustice'.[47]

Appreciation of Peacock's 'zenith' seemed to entail a sense of the novel as both permissive and pointed, and to call for a sense of his timelessness as well as for knowledge of his immediate historical context. Reviews of the Garnett edition agreed with his estimation, while disagreeing about the reasons for it. For William Payne Morton, *Crotchet Castle* was the 'most nearly perfect of Peacock's tales' because it was the most genial.[48] For Reginald Brimley Johnson, it was

---

[44] Spedding, review, 439.
[45] *Crotchet Castle*, introd. Henry Morley (Cassell, 1887), n. p.
[46] *Crotchet Castle*, ed. Richard Garnett (Dent, 1891), p. 7.
[47] *Crotchet Castle*, ed. Garnett, pp. 9, 189.
[48] William Payne Morton, *Dial*, 13 (Aug. 1892), 104–5 (p. 105).

the best because it embodied the strength of Peacock as 'satirist'.[49] The Macmillan edition of the novels (1895–7; reprinted 1955), illustrated by F. H. Townsend and introduced by George Saintsbury, also rated the book very highly; Saintsbury wrote that '*Crotchet Castle* is very frequently, and perhaps not erroneously, taken to be, all things considered, Peacock's most perfect work in his special vocation of modern satirist'.[50] However, the sentence is hedging its bets ('perhaps not erroneously'? 'all things considered'?), and it turns out that the modern satirist is chiefly to be praised for achieving a kind of balance that resists – without renouncing – the satirical impulse: 'It is, in fact, in this meeting of the ways, in the discarding of a personality which went near to bad taste, and the acquisition of an equity which is never merely insipid, that the charm of the work consists.'[51]

Twentieth-century responses to *Crotchet Castle* continued to explore the peculiar nature of this charm – and continued to be interested in determining the book's critical edge, or lack of it. Carl Van Doren noted that the novel 'has generally enjoyed the reputation of being Peacock's maturest and most characteristic work'.[52] The 'characteristic', though, turns out to have two characteristics (there is a tendency in the best critics of Peacock to multiply and hence often to contradict their own terms). The first is that of the social commentator: 'Nothing gives so good an idea of Peacock's actual position as to call him the Court Jester of Utilitarianism. Like a jester, he belonged to the Court'; the second is that of the withdrawn observer: '[the novel contains] evidences of a dignified retirement from commotion. The characters never take themselves so seriously as to imperil the quiet of the scene.'[53] Sociability and

---

[49] Reginald Brimley Johnson, 'Thomas Love Peacock, Satirist', *Novel Review*, 1.5 (Aug. 1892), 406–15 (p. 409).

[50] *Maid Marian* and *Crotchet Castle*, introd. George Saintsbury (Macmillan, 1955), p. xxii.

[51] *Maid Marian* and *Crotchet Castle*, introd. Saintsbury, p. xxv.

[52] Van Doren, *Life*, p. 191.   [53] Van Doren, *Life*, pp. 196, 199.

isolation remain in harmonious counterpoint throughout *Crotchet Castle*, a novel that is distinguished by its scenes of solitary communion with nature as well as by its scenes of witty dispute over a communal meal. Priestley echoed Van Doren's divided position in his estimation of the book, seeing it as the place where Peacock 'becomes a satirist of politics, which is not quite the same thing as being a political satirist', even if 'not one of the crotchets that are produced at the table in Crotchet Castle suggests any possible abstinence from the hock and champagne'.[54] Like Van Doren, Priestley implies that Peacock's attitudes inform those of both his narrator and his crotcheteers, but while the narrator's affable tone may include a satirical undertone, the crotcheteers' apparent commitment to their causes is not about to spoil their dinner. The novel lives a double life – sometimes posing as an anatomist of follies and vices, sometimes as an indulgent host to them.

This double life has continued to inspire mixed responses. David Garnett introduced his 1948 edition of *Crotchet Castle* by noting that 'I personally prefer both *Nightmare Abbey* and *Gryll Grange*'.[55] And yet, Garnett does concede that, in *Crotchet Castle*, Peacock's dialogue 'has indeed reached perfection'.[56] A debatable aspect of this 'perfection', it seems, is the way in which the structure of the dialogue itself – even though it is fuelled by speakers arguing for victory – never quite allows anybody to come away victorious. Reviewing the edition in *The Listener*, Humphry House turned to the argument about Walter Scott in Chapter 9 of the book: 'There is a whole view of Scott, presented, left poised for consideration.'[57] This poise sounds like an achievement, an inconclusiveness that is worked for and gained, but House also sensed that it might be felt as a lack or as a missed

---

[54] Priestley, *Thomas Love Peacock*, pp. 196, 142.
[55] Garnett, *Novels*, 2.645.   [56] Garnett, *Novels*, 2.648.
[57] Humphry House, 'The Novels of Thomas Love Peacock', *The Listener*, 42 (8 Dec. 1949), 997–8 (p. 998).

opportunity; although he thought Peacock was aiming for a 'critique of romanticism', he pointed out that 'he never quite becomes a satirist; he hasn't the anger'.[58] J. I. M. Stewart echoed these terms when he praised *Crotchet Castle* as 'the perfecting of Peacock's art . . . the chief work of his full maturity': 'His life's work . . . can be viewed as the critique of romanticism – yet in regard to the romantic idea he never quite finally knew where his heart lay.'[59]

Not knowing your precise relation to 'the romantic idea' – or indeed to ideas more generally – might be conceived as a strength or a weakness. Mario Praz plumped for the latter, arguing that *Crotchet Castle* was 'nerveless work' from a 'dried-up' author.[60] A. E. Dyson also felt that the book was 'the least pleasing of the novels', that Peacock had lost his nerve, and that he had then hidden behind 'a two-sides-to-every-question geniality'. Quoting Lady Clarinda's comment on Folliott – 'He . . . says rude things in a pleasant, half-earnest manner, that nobody can take offence with' (Chapter 5) – Dyson added: 'This "manner" is one which Peacock clearly admired; yet how much complacency, how much insensitivity, how much intransigent reaction, must it have sanctioned in its time?' To which it might be answered that the manner has the potential to sanction other things too (tact, say, or good humour, or imaginative sympathy, or a broad social concern). Dyson goes on to imply that Peacock is in league with 'cosy reactionaries'; whether or not one is convinced by this categorization of the author's politics, Dyson's premise is clear: Tory politics makes for bad novels.[61] George Meredith, hardly the

---

[58] House, 'The Novels of Thomas Love Peacock', p. 998.

[59] J. I. M. Stewart, *Thomas Love Peacock* (Longmans, 1963), pp. 26, 24, 29. See also Lionel Madden, *Thomas Love Peacock* (Evans, 1967): '*Crotchet Castle* exhibits more fully than any other work Peacock's merits as a writer' (p. 116).

[60] Mario Praz, *The Hero in Eclipse in Victorian Fiction* (1956; repr. Oxford: Oxford University Press, 1969), pp. 98–9.

[61] A. E. Dyson, *The Crazy Fabric: Essays in Irony* (Macmillan, 1965), pp. 61–71.

most sympathetic of Peacock's readers, offered a more discriminating summary of Folliott in relation to his author and the politics of *Crotchet Castle* in 1907, suggesting that 'Dr Folliott has [Peacock's] ideas as a scholar, & his diction. A Tory of Tories [Peacock] would readily welcome a festive Radical to his table.'[62]

Even as the politicized evaluations were being made by Praz, Dyson and others, some commentators were criticizing the novel for *not* escaping from politics, or – to confuse matters further – praising it for doing just that: while Ian Jack complained that 'the perplexities of the time hang heavily over this book . . . *Crotchet Castle* lacks the freedom from the pressures of everyday reality',[63] Kenneth Hopkins celebrated the book for the opposite quality: 'we are inescapably in the Peacockian world, from which in truth, we have no wish "to escape"'.[64] By the 1960s, then, *Crotchet Castle* had become Peacock's zenith and his nadir; witty and nerveless; liberal and conservative; engaged and escapist. The novel not only staged and explored disagreement; perhaps inevitably, it seemed to encourage it.

The next decade produced ground-breaking work on *Crotchet Castle*, starting with Charles Dodson's edition (published in 1971, along with *Nightmare Abbey* and *The Misfortunes of Elphin*). Dodson's book was based on his PhD dissertation, '*Crotchet Castle*, by Thomas Love Peacock: A Critical Edition', a study that began to hint at the sheer range of Peacock's sources, models and allegiances (Dodson noted Priestley's mischievous yet instructive claim that the novelist was 'an aristocratic individualistic republican radical with a strong Tory bias, whose good pleasure it was to be always against his government').[65] Some commentators were inclined to enjoy these vertiginous combinations, and to see *Crotchet Castle* as a pleasurably

---

[62] See Sylvère Monod, 'Meredith on Peacock: An Unpublished Letter', *Modern Language Review*, 77 (1982), 278–81 (p. 279).

[63] Ian Jack, *English Literature 1815–1832* (Oxford: Clarendon Press, 1963), pp. 220–1.

[64] *Crotchet Castle*, introd. Kenneth Hopkins (Folio Society, 1964), p. 15.

[65] Dodson, *Crotchet Castle*, p. xxvii.

tricky sort of book. Carl Dawson noted that 'Folliott is another of Peacock's characters who are more nearly right than wrong but who are never entirely either', adding that the fictions were like 'mock Socratic dialogues without a guiding Socrates'.[66] One of the most thoughtful articles yet written on *Crotchet Castle* was published in the same year as that of Dawson's study; Douglas Hewitt read the book as a 'novel of ideas' and weighed up the values and dangers of removing the guiding Socrates. On the one hand, Douglas noted, 'We do not so much investigate the ideas in such books as imagine what it would be like to hold them. We may be said to entertain them . . . Our vicarious enjoyment, indeed, is often the enjoyment of entertaining somewhat outrageous ideas or a succession of incompatible ones.'[67] On the other hand, Douglas worries about the way the book 'implicitly disparages all ideas':

We need to feel that there is intellectual rigour and integrity in reserve; otherwise the frivolity asserts itself as a judgement on the writer rather than on the ideas . . . In *Crotchet Castle* we recognize some ideas which are potentially serious and we are disappointed when they are transformed into abbreviated parodies of themselves and hustled quickly away, with the verdict going to complacent prejudice masquerading as sensible moderation.[68]

In some ways this echoes the concerns of Dyson and Praz; it also revisits Spedding's uncertainty about how readers might distinguish a companionable sympathy from an insatiable scepticism – or from a cynical complacency.[69] But it is not always clear where 'the

---

[66] Carl Dawson, *His Fine Wit: A Study of Thomas Love Peacock* (Berkeley: University of California Press, 1970), p. 266.

[67] Douglas Hewitt, 'Entertaining Ideas: A Critique of Peacock's *Crotchet Castle*', *Essays in Criticism*, 20 (1970), 200–12 (p. 201).

[68] Hewitt, 'Entertaining Ideas', p. 210.

[69] This has been a recurring feature of TLP criticism. See e.g. Roger B. Henkle, *Comedy and Culture: England 1820–1900* (Princeton, NJ: Princeton University Press, 1980), on 'Peacock's balanced perspective – or maybe it was his cantankerous skepticism', p. 67.

verdict' is 'going' in *Crotchet Castle*, and the most thorough analysis of the novel's influences to date offers a very different sense of the terrain.

For Marilyn Butler, the novel was Peacock's 'quintessential book, with something in it of all the others'. It displays not so much prejudice masquerading as moderation, but research masquerading as frivolity: 'the impression of social chaos is a calculated effect in *Crotchet Castle*, the fruit of serious analysis'.[70] As 'the most topical and densely-packed of the satires', the book delineates, for Butler, a coherent socio-political outlook:

It is not a satire on the March of Mind from a Tory point of view; it is a satire on the rich governing classes, landed and commercial, and their new philosophy of wealth – the practice and theory of materialism, seen from the viewpoint of a humanist . . . Peacock is trying to sift what is genuine in liberal ideals from the large accretion of hypocrisy, self-interest and pseudo-science . . . An unthinking and shallow liberalism may be a more insidious orthodoxy than the Toryism he battled against in his earlier writing life.[71]

This vision of Peacock as battler, not bottler, has much to recommend it, and Butler's defence was impressively detailed (she devoted more space to *Crotchet Castle* than to any other novel – around fifty pages). In true Peacockian fashion, Butler's erudition did not settle the debate, but rather encouraged others to restage it. Bryan Burns responded that the novel 'has no fight in it . . . Peacock seems to be fiddling while England burns . . . *Crotchet Castle* offers us a cooler world in which less is at risk, and this means that the novel itself is domesticated and rather diminished.'[72] A year later, introducing his Penguin edition of the novel, Raymond Wright felt that coolness was a vital aspect of the novel's critical edge, and in some ways he

[70] Butler, *Peacock*, pp. 183, 185.   [71] Butler, *Peacock*, pp. 188, 223, 229.
[72] Bryan Burns, *The Novels of Thomas Love Peacock* (Croom Helm, 1985), pp. 167, 168, 175.

reiterated Butler's argument: 'Peacock was ingenious in arranging encounters' in which people 'exposed their own follies in exposing each others'. In response to the claim that the author now seemed to be attacking the progressive party, Wright answered: 'We need not conclude from this, as some of his critics have done, that he was turning conservative, but merely that . . . he distrusted logicians and new orthodoxies as well as old ones.'[73]

The fact that no critical orthodoxy has emerged about *Crotchet Castle* would perhaps have pleased its author. Of the discussions that have appeared in the last twenty years or so, two in particular have opened up new avenues of enquiry. Gary Kelly claims that the novel is 'as successful as anything Peacock ever wrote . . . shapely, but not predictable; complete, but not closed'.[74] He goes on to suggest that the romance plots running alongside the dialogues gesture towards a resolution of sorts. The suitors of the women are singled out from the talkers, set slightly apart from them:

their betrothal to the scintillating heroines indicates that they have potential beyond the hobby-horses on which they discourse with other talkers . . . [the heroines] are figures for the full humanity which the heroes are striving and fighting toward in their dialogues with the other men in the novels . . . one could argue that the real match for heroines such as Lady Clarinda is not the hero such as Captain Fitzchrome, but the novels' implicit, gentrified, intellectual (male) reader.[75]

One could argue this, although one also wonders what Lady Clarinda might have to say in response to such a sanguine assessment of marriage. Still, Kelly's approach is an instructive attempt to think about how the dialogues in *Crotchet Castle* might be related to the other modes and genres that compete for space within the novel.

[73] Raymond Wright, ed., *Nightmare Abbey/Crotchet Castle* (Harmondsworth: Penguin, 1986), pp. 33–4.

[74] Gary Kelly, *English Fiction of the Romantic Period 1789–1830* (Longman, 1989), pp. 235, 247.

[75] Kelly, *English Fiction*, p. 246.

Gary Dyer's work on Peacock's fiction also tries to look beyond the dialogues by seeing them in relation to other sources – in particular, to what Mikhail Bakhtin refers to as 'the dialogic culture of Voltaire and Diderot, which had its roots in the Socratic dialogue, the ancient menippea, and somewhat in the diatribe and the soliloquy':

> Yet rather than simply mirroring the ideal of a public sphere where putative equals engage in rational debate, Peacock's satires critique it . . . showing that there is no entirely open or free conversation, that power shapes consensus as surely as reason does . . . The discursive form essential to the bourgeois public sphere was the periodical, and the era on which we are focusing was of course the golden age of the quarterlies. Peacock expresses skepticism about these journalistic forums in which the major issues of the day are debated by property-owning citizens, or, rather, their experts in legitimation.[76]

Crotchet Castle has a particularly close eye on such experts. In Chapter 4, Folliott notes that 'There is a set of persons in your city, Mr. Mac Quedy, who concoct every three or four months, a thing, which they call a review: a sort of sugar-plum manufacturers to the Whig aristocracy.' Mac Quedy retorts: 'Not in our city, exactly; neither are they a set. There is an editor, who forages for articles in all quarters, from John O'Groat's house to the Land's End. It is not a board, or a society: it is a mere intellectual bazaar, where A. B. and C. bring their wares to market.' This emphasis on the disparity within the apparent homogeneity of a 'set' is a salutary warning to anybody who might seek to tell the story of Peacock's reception either as a Whig version of history or as a journey towards consensus. In 1933, Jean-Jacques Mayoux observed that 'le premier aspect du style de Peacock sera celui-là: ses phrases sont volontiers des récipients'.[77]

---

[76] Gary Dyer, *British Satire and the Politics of Style, 1789–1832* (Cambridge: Cambridge University Press, 2006), p. 121.

[77] 'Peacock's style is notable in this respect: his sentences are open to everything' (editors' translation). Jean-Jacques Mayoux, *Un épicurien anglais: Thomas Love Peacock* (Paris: Nizet and Bastard, 1933), p. 530.

The divided critical reception of *Crotchet Castle* supports the wisdom of this claim.

INFLUENCES, ANALOGUES AND CONTEXTS

One of the tutelary geniuses of *Crotchet Castle* is the satirist Samuel Butler, from whom Peacock took the epigraph for his title page and for Chapters 2, 6 and 7 of the novel. Butler had already provided the titular epigraph to *Nightmare Abbey*, as Peacock announced to Shelley in a letter; he would do so again in Peacock's last novel, *Gryll Grange*.[78] Butler's *Hudibras* (1662–78), to judge from Peacock's surviving correspondence, was always a favourite work: a mock-heroic poem consisting largely of character sketches and debates, loosely associated with one another through passages of narrative and shot through with material composed at various stages in Butler's career (perhaps the example of *Hudibras* encouraged Peacock to recycle two of his own poems, originally published in newspapers, in *Crotchet Castle*). The incisive yet meandering *Hudibras* – a serpentine model for the opening sentence of *Crotchet Castle* – and the sceptical, uncommitted, yet troubled stance of the author, make the poem a lineal ancestor of Peacock's fiction.

The first sentence of *Crotchet Castle*, encompassing ancient and modern cities and rivers, breathes the spirit of the work:

In one of those beautiful vallies, through which the Thames (not yet polluted by the tide, the scouring of cities, or even the minor defilement of the sandy streams of Surrey,) rolls a clear flood through flowery meadows, under the shade of old beech woods, and the smooth mossy greensward of the chalk hills, (which pour into it their tributary rivulets, as pure and pellucid as the fountain of Bandusium, or the wells of Scamander, by which the wives and daughters of the Trojans washed their splendid garments in the days of peace, before the coming of the Greeks;) in one of those beautiful vallies, on a bold round-surfaced lawn, spotted with juniper, that opened itself in the bosom of an old wood,

---

[78] TLP to P. B. Shelley (15 Sept. 1818), *Letters*, 1.152.

which rose with a steep, but not precipitous ascent, from the river to the summit of the hill, stood the castellated villa of a retired citizen.

When Virginia Woolf paid tribute to Peacock's art, she focused on this sentence:

it would be difficult to describe the relief it gives us, except metaphorically. First there is the shape which recalls something visually delightful, like a flowing wave or the lash of a whip vigorously flung; then as phrase joins phrase and one parenthesis after another pours in its tributary, we have a sense of the whole swimming stream gliding beneath old walls . . . we are in a world so manageable in scale that we can take its measure, tease it and ridicule it.[79]

One reason for the relief, perhaps, is Peacock's flirtation with danger: 'defilement', it turns out, is only 'minor'; the ascent is 'steep, but not precipitous'. Accidents in his fiction tend not to issue in disaster, and the various falls in his novels offer as many lessons to pessimists as they do to optimists.[80] Another cause for relief is that – although the scene is awash with detail and digression – the periodic syntax finally works its way home to dry land, giving the reader, as it gives the retired citizen, a place to rest. Yet Woolf's indecision about the most appropriate metaphor ('like a flowing wave or the lash of a whip') brings into view other aspects of Peacock's style and outlook, for the whip is brandished by a writer who is not always keen to move with the current of the times.

The lash of a whip belongs to a satirist possessed of forensically 'fine wit', and wit itself is said, like a river, to flow.[81] Then

---

[79] Virginia Woolf, from 'Phases of Fiction', in *The Bookman*, 69 (1929); repr. in *Granite and Rainbow: Essays*, ed. Leonard Woolf (Hogarth Press, 1958), pp. 93–145 (p. 131).

[80] For mishaps that fail to end in disaster in TLP, see e.g. Cranium's fall in ch. 8 of *Headlong Hall*; Scythrop and Toobad's collision and fall downstairs in ch. 3 of *Nightmare Abbey*; the assault on Folliott in ch. 8 of *Crotchet Castle*; and the thunderstorm in ch. 10 of *Gryll Grange*.

[81] On TLP's 'fine wit', see 'Letter to Maria Gisborne', line 240, in *The Poems of Shelley, 1819–1820*, vol. 3, p. 455; on flowing wit, see e.g. Austen, *Works: Pride and Prejudice*, p. 30: 'her wit flowed long'.

again, the flowing wave also recalls William Hogarth's line of beauty, an S-shaped curve or serpentine figure graphically and stylistically recreated on the digressive pages of Laurence Sterne's *The Life and Opinions of Tristram Shandy, Gentleman* (1759–67).[82] In Hogarth's *Analysis of Beauty* (1753), S-shaped lines indicate liveliness and activity; they excite the viewer's attention by contrast with the straight, parallel or right-angled intersecting lines which represent death, ugliness or stasis. Straight rivers may be easier to navigate, but they are somehow duller work, too. Hogarth's praise of the serpentine assumes the principle of variety on which *Crotchet Castle*'s satirical picturesque is founded; he stresses that any artistic composition must unite different sorts of line and that it must please by striking, agreeable contrasts.[83] On the second page of the manuscript draft of 'Touchandgo' that includes a portion of Susannah's letter to her father, Peacock sketched a squiggly, river-like line downwards from the word 'tradition' through 'spot', 'stream', 'neighbourhood' and 'every' (Appendix E). The line of beauty identified by Woolf and celebrated by Hogarth and Sterne may well have been in the author's mind as he wrote, as his eye was drawn to the river that performs syntactically like the Sternian graphic wiggle in *Tristram Shandy*, bisecting the intellectual landscape it describes and teasing readers eager for the completion of the sense. Indeed, the parentheses described by Woolf gesture towards a world that, despite its scale, is not wholly manageable: 'not yet polluted' bespeaks a pressing concern (no significant legislation to address pollution of the Thames by refuse and sewage was passed until 1857); the recollection of 'the days of peace, before the coming of the Greeks'

[82] Laurence Sterne, the Florida Edition of the Works of Laurence Sterne, gen. ed. Melvyn New, 9 vols. (Gainesville: University Press of Florida, 1978–2014), vols. 1–3: *The Life and Opinions of Tristram Shandy, Gentleman*, text ed. Melvyn New and Joan New, notes by Melvyn New with Richard A. Davies and W. G. Day (1978–84), vol. 2, pp. 570–1 (vol. 6, ch. 40).

[83] William Hogarth, *The Analysis of Beauty*, ed. Ronald Paulson (New Haven, CT: Yale University Press, 1997), pp. 48–59.

glances at the precarious nature of idyllic moments and at warring factions to come (the phrase is a close translation from a moment in Book 22 of the *Iliad*, a wistful aside as Achilles pursues Hector round the walls of Troy). The narrator, like the old man of whom he speaks, may be 'retired', but he remains a 'citizen' – on the periphery, yet still engaged. The whole sentence is at once languid and lucid; it is not yet clear what sort of journey readers are undertaking.

One destination of the journey is Wales, for that is where the Thames leads some of the characters of *Crotchet Castle*: 'I am fitting up a flotilla of pleasure-boats', Crotchet Jr. explains in Chapter 2, 'to carry a choice philosophical party up the Thames and Severn, into the Ellesmere canal, where we shall be among the mountains of North Wales'. This is also where Susannah Touchandgo retires when her engagement is broken off, seeking solace in 'the land of all that is beautiful in nature, and all that is lovely in woman' (Chapter 12). In his previous novel, *The Misfortunes of Elphin* (1829), Peacock had drawn on his travels in the country, and on his extensive reading of *The Cambro-Briton* (1819–22), the *Myryrian Archaiology* (1801–7), Edward Davies's *The Mythology and Rites of the English Druids* (1809), and Richard Colt Hoare's *The Itinerary of Archbishop Baldwin Through Wales* (1806). A review of *The Misfortunes of Elphin* in the *Cambrian Quarterly Review* had praised it as 'the most entertaining book, if not the best, that has yet been published on the ancient customs and traditions of Wales'.[84] By the time *Crotchet Castle* was published Peacock had been married to Jane Gryffydh for eleven years and had become even better versed in Welsh history and literature.[85] Some critics have claimed that *Crotchet Castle*

---

[84] Anon., *Cambrian Quarterly Review*, 1 (1829), 231–40 (p. 240).

[85] On TLP's references to Welsh myths and traditions, and his 'positive contribution to the Welsh cultural revival', see Shawna Lichtenwalner, *Claiming Cambria: Invoking the Welsh in the Romantic Era* (Newark, DE: University of Delaware Press, 2008), pp. 164–73 (p. 173). See also Damian Walford Davies's Introduction to *ME* in this edition.

satirizes 'Romantic Wales', yet there is much in the novel to suggest that Peacock also values the place as his close friend Shelley came to value it – both as a site of personal rejuvenation and as one that opposed the corrupting, modernizing influence of the English metropolis.[86] In *Crotchet Castle*, to travel up the Thames and away from England is partly to retreat into the past, and partly to wonder what the present might learn from it.

The Thames often gave Peacock mixed feelings. In 1809 he wrote to Edward Thomas Hookham:

The Thames is almost as good a subject for a satire as a panegyric. – A satirist might exclaim: The rapacity of Commerce, not content with the immense advantages derived from this river in a course of nearly 300 miles, erects a ponderous engine over the very place of it's nativity, to suck up it's unborn waters . . . A panegyrist . . . might say . . . this noble river, this beautiful emblem, and powerful instrument, of the commercial greatness of Britain.[87]

Crotchet Castle is preoccupied with commerce; the development of rivers – and of progress narratives more generally – is never far from view. In his Preface to the 1837 Bentley edition, Peacock admits that some things have changed in the six years since he first published the book: '"Crotchet Castle" ends with a rotten borough . . . the rotten boroughs of 1830 have ceased to exist, though there are some very pretty pocket boroughs, which are their worthy successors.' So the more things change, the more they stay the same. The Preface ends by turning to the political orator who hovers in the background of the novel:

---

[86] On *CC* as a satire on Celtic antiquarianism, see Jane Moore, '"Parallelograms and Circles": Robert Owen and the Satirists'; on Shelley and Wales, see Cian Duffy, '"One Draught from Snowdon's Ever-Sacred Spring": Shelley's Welsh Sublime'; both in Damian Walford Davies and Lynda Pratt, eds., *Wales and the Romantic Imagination* (Cardiff: University of Wales Press, 2007), pp. 243–67 and pp. 180–98.

[87] *Letters*, 1.35.

political mountebanks continue, and will continue, to puff nostrums and practise legerdemain under the eyes of the multitude; following, like the 'learned friend' of Crotchet Castle, a course as tortuous as that of a river, but in a reverse process; beginning by being dark and deep, and ending by being transparent.

People may behave like rivers, and rivers may resemble people: Father Thames is a common personification in eighteenth-century poetry. If the satirical voice of *Crotchet Castle* helped to make Brougham's stratagems transparent, the voice which now speaks to us is under no illusions about the limits of its power to combat such sophistry. There are more where the 'learned friend' came from, and they will keep coming regardless. Trying to stop the flow of words would be like trying to stop the flow of a river.

Crotchet Castle is the most aqueous of Peacock's novels, and the book's liquidities make it enjoyably – and sometimes infuriatingly – tricky to plumb. Besides the more obvious structuring devices (the setting by the Thames, and the river expeditions at the novel's centre), it seems that people are likely to get wet in this book: some characters long for water; others are terrified of it; many of them richly deserve to get soaked. Early chapters speak of 'the sacred thirst of paper-money' and 'blowing of bubbles, the bursting of which sent many a poor devil to . . . the bottom of the river'; Mr Firedamp is concerned about 'the question of water against human life . . . I feel the malignant influence of the river in every part of my system'; Mac Quedy sees 'romance and sentiment' as mere hot air to be condensed into 'a drop of cold water in a moment'; Folliott envisages political economy as a dodgy 'system of state seamanship'; Mr Crotchet praises 'a great reservoir of learning' while Lord Bossnowl wonders whether the whole party makes up 'the ship of fools'; Susannah sings 'My heart is gone beyond the sea' and Mr Chainmail offers a rendition of 'The Pool of the Diving Friar'. Meanwhile, everyone spouts a torrent of words: 'In this manner they glided over the face of the waters, discussing every thing and settling nothing' (Chapters 1, 2, 5, 18, 9, 2, 11, 16, 10).

Peacock was alert to such figures of speech; reviewing Moore's *Letters and Journals of Lord Byron* whilst he was writing *Crotchet Castle*, he quoted Moore's commentary on the poems to Thyrza – 'a confluence of sad thoughts from many sources of sorrow, refined and warmed in their passage through his fancy, and forming thus one deep reservoir of mournful feeling' – and retorted: 'though streams may fill a reservoir, they cannot form one'.[88] *Crotchet Castle* has water on the brain, and for Peacock water seems to bring with it the not-always-welcome feeling of being saturated in debate. In 'An Essay on Fashionable Literature', writing on the influence of newspapers, magazines and quarterlies, he noted: 'The spring tide of metropolitan favor floats these intellectual deliciæ into every minor town and village in the kingdom where they circle through their little day in the eddies of reading societies'. *Crotchet Castle* has plenty to say about 'all this petty splashing in the pool of public favor'.[89]

One of the novel's most prominent courters of public favour is the absent yet ever-present 'learned friend', the tireless Brougham. One reason Peacock thought of water when he thought to allude to him in the 1837 Preface was because he saw Brougham as a convenient figurehead for what Folliott calls the Steam Intellect Society (the Society for the Diffusion of Useful Knowledge, SDUK, set up by Brougham in 1826 to publish cheap and accessible works on scientific and artistic subjects). The Preface to the first annual volume of the *Penny Magazine*, published by the SDUK and reaching sales of 200,000 in 1832, gives a sense of what Folliott is getting upset about:

The steam-boat upon the seas – the canal – the railway – the quick van – these as well as the stage-coach and the mail – place the 'Penny Magazine' within everyone's reach in the farthest part of the kingdom as if he lived in London, and without any additional cost. This is a striking

---

[88] Halliford, 9.124–5.
[89] 'An Essay on Fashionable Literature', (*NA*, Appendix B). The passage containing the words 'all this petty splashing in the pool of public favor' is marked for deletion in the MS.

illustration of the civilization of our country; and when unthinking people therefore ask, what is the benefit of steam-engines, and canals, and fine roads to the poor man, they may be answered by this example alone.[90]

Peacock had begun to cast aspersions on this wholly positive progress report in *The Misfortunes of Elphin* (1829), in which readers were told that their ancestors

had no steam-engines, with fires as eternal as those of the nether world, wherein the squalid many, from infancy to age, might be turned into component portions of machinery for the benefit of the purple-faced few. They could neither poison the air with gas, nor the waters with its dregs: in short, they...drank pure water, like unscientific barbarians.   (Chapter 6)

Despite the commitment of the SDUK and other groups to what they termed 'civilization', Peacock's comparisons between past and present were never simply to the detriment of either side. As his narrator put it in *The Misfortunes of Elphin*: 'The Druids had their view of these matters, and we have ours; and it does not comport with the steam-engine speed of our march of mind to look at more than one side of a question' (Chapter 6).

Peacock's inclination to look at more than one side of a question leads in unexpected directions in *Crotchet Castle*. Readers are treated to predictable complaints about 'those whose brains are high-pressure steam engines for spinning prose by the furlong, to be trumpeted in paid-for paragraphs in the quack's corner of newspapers' (Chapter 15), but they are treated to something less straightforward, too: the geographer Mr Philpot, for example, who 'thinks of nothing but the heads and tails of rivers, and lays down the streams of Terra Incognita as accurately as if he had been there'. When Philpot edifies 'the company with speculations on the great changes that would be

---

[90] *Penny Magazine*, 1 (1832), preface; quoted in Rosemary Ashton, *Victorian Bloomsbury* (New Haven: Yale University Press, 2012), p. 71. See also her chapter on 'Steam Intellect: Diffusing Useful Knowledge', pp. 58–81.

effected in the world by the steam-navigation of rivers' (Chapter 10), he is not just another crackpot, but also a portrait of the artist as a middle-aged man. Peacock's high position in the East India Company (he became a senior assistant to the Examiner, James Mill, in 1830) led to his growing expertise in steam navigation. His Memorandum on the subject in 1829 was sent to the Prime Minister, the Duke of Wellington, and he was later called before parliamentary Select Committees to advise on the matter. Peacock had also thought about the heads and tails of rivers for some years, writing in his Memorandum that 'high-pressure engines seem essential to the very great success in the upward navigation of powerful rivers' and quoting Captain Ross, with no irony, in Philpotian mode: 'Steam navigation... sets at defiance the monsoons, the currents, and the calms.'[91] Peacock supervised the design and construction of the first vessels to steam the whole distance to India, and he would later champion the use of iron steamers (according to family tradition, he was 'the first man to say that iron could float'). He proudly asserted to Sir John Cam Hobhouse in 1839 that 'this vessel, the first of her class, opens a new æra in steam-navigation, and gives to any government, having large rivers and an extensive sea-coast, a new arm of great and irresistible power'.[92] The author's earlier Memorandum, written as he began to turn his attentions to *Crotchet Castle*, ended with the following proclamations:

The steam navigation of rivers has made the fortune of the North-Western Territory of America, and given to population and industry throughout that immense tract of country an impetus to which there seems no limit for many generations. The protecting arm of a civilized government is all that is required to do as much for the now thinly-peopled and devastated regions that border the great rivers of Asia. The country on the banks of the Oxus appears to have many points

---

[91] TLP, *Report from the Select Committee on Steam Navigation*, pp. 3, 5.
[92] *Letters*, 2.264. 'I am in high spirits about my iron chickens', he wrote to Harriet Deane Love a year later (*Letters*, 2.269).

of resemblance to the Prairies of Louisiana. The vicinity of the Sea of Aral abounds with coal. The Russians have unlimited resources in coal, wood, iron, cattle and corn. They have now steam-boats on the Volga and Caspian Sea. They will have them before long on the Sea of Aral and the Oxus, and in all probability on the Euphrates and the Tigris. It is not our navigating the Euphrates that will set them the example. They will do every thing in Asia that is worth the doing, and that we leave undone.[93]

When, in Chapter 10 of *Crotchet Castle* ('The Voyage'), Philpot names many of the same rivers (the Euphrates, the Oxus, the Tigris, along with the Missouri, which is alluded to above), he is not merely a surrogate for his author; he is also forging his own alliances with the Steam Intellect Society. *Crotchet Castle* is not only a satire on the hot air of modernity. Peacock's allegiances (too often read simply as Folliott's allegiances) are not easily fathomable, and the cross-currents of his sympathies make the book hard to navigate.

Although *Crotchet Castle* enjoys mocking the political economists, the philosophical radicals, the utilitarians, the praisers of steam and other progressive figures, it is worth recalling some of Peacock's more impassioned letters to Shelley; he enthusiastically wrote, for example, that 'Bentham has laid a mighty axe to the root of superstition', and that 'Cobbett is indefatigable . . . it is impossible that his clear exposures of all the forms of political fraud should fail of prod<u>cing a most powerful effect.'[94] All of Peacock's journalistic writing appeared in liberal or radical publications. Thomas Jefferson – who himself, like Peacock, had Welsh connections – was one of his heroes, and his article on Jefferson's memoirs, written whilst he was composing *Crotchet Castle* and published in the utilitarian *Westminster Review* in 1830, was perhaps his most sustained defence of pioneering, experimental impulses.[95] *Crotchet Castle*, like Philpot and like Peacock in

[93] TLP, *Report from the Select Committee on Steam Navigation*, p. 10.
[94] *Letters*, 1.153, 123.
[95] Dumas Malone claimed that Jefferson was of Welsh descent in *Jefferson and his Time*, 5 vols. (Boston: Little and Brown, 1948–74), vol. 1, p. 5–6.

his Memorandum to the Select Committee, also looks to America. Touchandgo and Robthetill abscond there, and this gives Peacock the opportunity to cast side-glances at some aspects of the young country's institutions and inclinations. As Touchandgo informs his daughter, 'This is the land, in which all men flourish; but there are three classes of men who flourish especially, – methodist preachers, slave-drivers, and paper-money manufacturers . . . I am accordingly a capitalist of the first magnitude' (Chapter 11). However reprehensible such conduct may be, there is something in Peacock which imaginatively warms to escape-routes, new starts and voyages into unchartered territory, regardless of their motivating factors or consequences. In his Memorandum he had noted that 'The country on the banks of the Oxus appears to have many points of resemblance to the Prairies of Louisiana.'[96] Peacock was looking out for his employer's commercial interests, but an earlier letter to Shelley (another risk-taking émigré) hints at something more adventurous; commenting on Birkbeck's *Notes on America*, he wrote:

He has emigrated with his whole family . . . where he has purchased a *prairie* . . . Multitudes are following his example even from this neighbourhood . . . The temptation to agriculturists with a small capital must be irresistible: and the picture he presents of the march of population and cultivation . . . is one of the most wonderful spectacles ever yet presented to the mind's eye of philosophy.[97]

From the 'march of population and cultivation' in the 'mind's eye', it does not require a great leap of imagination to arrive at the 'march of mind' that is so often a target of ridicule in *Crotchet Castle*. And yet, the tone of Peacock's letter is admiring, enraptured even. One might argue that it expresses the views of an earlier version of the author, and that he had since grown older and wiser. But the feelings persisted, and they find complex expression in *Crotchet Castle*'s

---

[96] TLP, *Report from the Select Committee on Steam Navigation*, p. 10.
[97] *Letters*, 1.152.

fascination with intrepid voyagers of all kinds. David Bromwich has observed that 'Peacock's sympathies are so generous that one suspects him of having been a member of every group he satirized'.[98] Indeed, one suspects him of continuing to be a part-time member even after he has seemingly left the club.

Peacock's review of Jefferson's *Memoirs* defends liberal principles even as it remains cognisant of their attendant dangers. Jefferson, he writes, 'was less dismayed by the temporary excesses of the French Revolution, than fixed in his abhorrence of the inflictions of unrestrained power which had preceded and caused it', and Peacock approvingly quotes the statesman on the need to entertain other excesses: 'The only security for honest and unoppressive government is in a free press. The agitation it produces must be submitted to. It is necessary to keep the waters pure.'[99] The agitated waters of *Crotchet Castle* involve a submission to this kind of freedom. Take the moment when Peacock has Philpot answer Mr Crotchet's question, 'How shall we employ our fund?': 'Surely in no way so beneficially as in exploring rivers. Send a fleet of steam-boats down the Niger, and another up the Nile. So shall you civilize Africa, and establish stocking factories in Abyssinia and Bambo' (Chapter 6). Peacock is the kind of author you imagine must be smiling whenever he writes the word 'Surely'. The writing is at once indulgent and self-parodic (he is recalling his own rhetoric in the Memorandum, including his emphasis on 'civilized government'), but it is also glancing at his colleague James Mill, whose plans to reform India along utilitarian lines were first raised in his *History of British India*.[100] By the time the second edition of *Crotchet Castle* was published, Peacock had succeeded Mill in the East India Company; when asked by the Select

---

[98] David Bromwich, ed., *Romantic Critical Essays* (Cambridge: Cambridge University Press, 1987), p. 184.

[99] Halliford, 9.155–6, 167.

[100] See TLP's earlier letter to Thomas Jefferson Hogg (2 Oct. 1819): 'I have read through at home the first volume of Mill's India . . . Mill has accompanied me in many Sunday excursions' (*Letters*, 1.167).

Committee for his views on civilising the empire, he dryly replied: 'I am not sure that it would be any benefit to the people of India to send Europeans amongst them'.[101] His novel shares this scepticism, even as it entertains the pleasures – and the values – of sending people up real and imagined rivers without a paddle. When Lady Clarinda describes Philpot as somebody who 'lays down the streams of Terra Incognita as accurately as if he had been there. He is a person of pleasant fancy, and makes a sort of fairy land of every country he touches' (Chapter 5), she is also describing his creator, who enjoys fancying fairy lands into existence to see what might come of it.

Crotchet Castle's attitudes to various forms of 'progress', then, are complex. The word and its cognates were the rallying-cries of the utilitarian thinkers with whom Peacock associated, especially Mill ('That he is a *progressive* being is the grand distinction of Man. He is the only progressive being upon this globe').[102] Peacock often uses the word himself with no hint of irony; he thought Jefferson's journals should be read 'as confirming rational hopes of the progress of knowledge and liberty' and that much of America's 'progress' was 'indebted to him'.[103] Still, when the word appears in *Crotchet Castle*, it is hedged by quotation marks (Mr Crotchet has kept 'due pace with the "astounding progress" of intelligence'; Chapter 1), or it signals degeneration ('but the means, by the progress of time, having become inadequate to the end, the almshouse tumbled to pieces'; Chapter 8), or it leads to argument ('he agreed with Mr. Mac Quedy against Mr. Chainmail, that it was in progress to something much better than either, – to which "something much better" Mr. Toogood and Mr. Mac Quedy attached two very different meanings'; Chapter 10), or it is unexpectedly blocked ('till the base of a rock sinking abruptly

---

[101] TLP, *Report from the Select Committee on Steam Communication with India* (House of Commons, 15 July 1837), p. 55. On TLP's guarded response to Mill, see Van Doren, *Life*, p. 146.

[102] James Mill, 'Education', from *Essays* (1828), repr. in *Political Writings*, ed. Terence Ball (Cambridge: Cambridge University Press, 1992), p. 189.

[103] Halliford, 9.185–6.

in the water, effectually barred his progress'; Chapter 13). Perhaps Peacock's most delightfully double-edged use of the word appears with reference to Captain Fitzchrome: 'his inclination to proceed farther, diminished progressively' (Chapter 12). In *Crotchet Castle*, it seems, it may be progressive to avoid progress.

The antecedents and analogues for Peacock's own progressive fictional forms have been debated with as much fervour as have the debates in the books themselves. Richard Cronin has suggested that the closest counterparts to the novels of talk are the *Noctes Ambrosianae*, serialized in *Blackwood's* from 1822 to 1835. In addition, there is *The Pamphleteer* (1813–1828), which Peacock read, along with other contemporary examples of dialogue-writing (Walter Savage Landor's *Imaginary Conversations*, Robert Southey's *Colloquies*) and the magazine- and journal-form itself, which was, according to John Gibson Lockhart, 'not bound to maintain any one set of opinions, in regard to any one set of objects, through-out the whole of its pages'.[104] As a contributor to *The Examiner*, Peacock would also have taken note of William Hazlitt and Leigh Hunt's 'Round Table' series, in which Hunt explains: 'we are, lit-erally speaking, a small party of friends, who meet once a week at a Round Table to discuss the merits of a leg of mutton, and of the subjects on which we are to write'.[105] Humphry House suggested that 'Peacock was doing in his own medium the same sort of thing that Hazlitt was doing in the essays that were published in *The Spirit of The Age*; and Hazlitt is the best introduction to Peacock'.[106] Certainly, Hazlitt's introduction to Coleridge in that book – 'The present is an age of talkers' – is written in a Peacockian spirit (as is his portrait of Coleridge himself). But there are other analogues and

---

[104] See Richard Cronin, *Paper Pellets: British Literary Culture After Waterloo* (Oxford: Oxford University Press, 2010), pp. 163–6.

[105] William Hazlitt and Leigh Hunt, *The Round Table: A Collection of Essays*, 2 vols. (Edinburgh: Archibald Constable and Co.; Longman, Hurst, Rees Orme and Brown, 1817), vol. 1, p. 4.

[106] House, 'The Novels of Thomas Love Peacock', p. 998.

models that are of particular importance both to the overall design and to the finer details of *Crotchet Castle*. The first, in keeping with the aqueous nature of the novel, draws attention to how we might turn water into wine.

As many commentators have pointed out, *Crotchet Castle*, compared with the earlier novels, displays a marked increase in references to food and drink: crotcheteers stop mid-speech to say 'Sir, I will thank you for a leg of that capon' or 'I will thank you for an anchovy'; Mr Chainmail talks with 'his head swimming with two or three horns of ale' while 'The water-loving Mr. Philpot had diluted himself with so much wine' (Chapters 2, 15, 18). Peacock had long been attracted to the symposium-form ('symposium' means 'banquet'), especially to its engagement with both intellectual and bodily comedy.[107] Philostratus noted in *Imagines* that 'Dionysus himself is coming by sea to take part in a *komos*...He is bringing with him Laughter and Komos, the most exuberant of deities and the most fitting for a symposium.'[108] *Crotchet Castle*'s protagonists are swimming in these Dionysian waters. More specifically, Peacock's love of Petronius's *Satyricon* (he owned five editions of the work and frequently praised it)[109] leaves its mark on the novel. The *Satyricon* – notably the set-piece on Trimalchio's Feast – draws together satirical and symptotic impulses, and perhaps also draws on a disputed etymology for 'satire', from *lanx satura* 'lit. "full dish"...alleged to have been used for a dish containing various kinds of fruit, and for food composed of many different ingredients' (*OED*).[110]

---

[107] See Stephen Halliwell, *Greek Laughter: A Study of Cultural Psychology from Homer to Early Christianity* (Cambridge: Cambridge University Press, 2008), pp. 100–54.

[108] Philostratus, *Imagines*, 1.25.3.

[109] See *Sale Catalogue* 490–2 and 659–60. For TLP's references to the *Satyricon*, see e.g. *Letters*, 1.80, 2.311, 316, 329, 332, 334, 461. See also Halliford, 9.354–62.

[110] The mixed dish in the banquet-hall as a sign of liberality, and perhaps of a certain kind of liberalism, was cherished by TLP; see 'Recollections of Childhood: The Abbey House' (Halliford, 9.33).

Trimalchio is a model for Crotchet himself, a nouveau-riche social climber who made his money in ship-building ('I built five ships, got a cargo of wine... I built some more, bigger, better and also luckier'), and who invites his guests to debate all matter of things as he offers them plenty of food and drink.[111] This debauched symposium is a structuring device for *Crotchet Castle*, allowing its author to indulge in speculative flights of fancy while also laughing at the way in which talk may not tally with action, or theory with practice. When Mac Quedy says to Folliott at the end of Chapter 6 that 'We are all agreed on deliberative dinners', and the doctor replies 'Very true; we will dine and discuss', the table is laid for a sympotic denouement:

MR. TRILLO.

Well, gentlemen, I hope this chorus at least will please you:

> If I drink water while this doth last,
> May I never again drink wine:
> For how can a man, in his life of a span,
> Do any thing better than dine?
> We'll dine and drink, and say if we think
> That any thing better can be,
> And when we have dined, wish all mankind
> May dine as well as we.
>
> And though a good wish will fill no dish
> And brim no cup with sack,
> Yet thoughts will spring, as the glasses ring,
> To illume our studious track.
> On the brilliant dreams of our hopeful schemes

---

[111] Petronius, *Satyricon*, section 76, p. 177.

The light of the flask shall shine;
And we'll sit till day, but we'll find the way
To drench the world with wine.

The schemes for the world's regeneration evaporated in a tumult of voices. (Chapter 6)

That schemes for the world's regeneration should 'evaporate' here is Peacock's way of satirizing how apathy may sometimes disguise itself as engagement, but the sympotic ideal – the view that such 'deliberative dinners' may lead to enlightenment – is not necessarily abandoned. The serio-comic inflection of the Socratic dialogues in classical symposia bequeathed to Peacock a conviction that amusement could be a catalyst for reflective thought, and indeed that amusement could be a *form* of such thought. In his later essay 'Gastronomy and Civilization', he surveyed the classical terrain before noting: 'Our public and great city dinners, where political, scientific, and literary bonds are cemented by common enjoyment... are productive of great good. Hearts expand simultaneously with mouths... the mahogany of a goodly table frequently becomes the bond of reconciliation between ancient feuds.'[112] Trillo, Mac Quedy, Folliott, & co. are not simply being laughed at by their author; they embody an ideal as well as remind readers of the misuses to which that ideal may be put.

The symposium – along with the classical comedy that both echoed and parodied it – is one model for the philosophic and physical humour of *Crotchet Castle*.[113] Another influence, though, complicates the picture, and it can be approached by considering a

---

[112] Halliford, 9.396–7.

[113] See Halliwell, *Greek Laughter*: 'Old Comedy – itself in some way an offshoot of the *komos* – is a prime place where symposiac imagery/thematics can be seen at work' (p. 127 n). In 'The "Flask" of Cratinus', TLP focused on the continuation of this line in Menandrian comedies (Halliford, 10.83–4).

letter Peacock wrote to Thomas Jefferson Hogg while on holiday in September 1822:

I have lived in the open air from morning to night day after day in the woods and on the hills. I have read Γοργιας and Ιον [Plato's *Gorgias* and *Ion*], the Georgics, the greater part of Tacitus, and as usual Cobbett's Register: and every word of every evening's Statesman, which I took in during my absence from London.[114]

Like the many versions of pastoral to which we are treated in his fictions, Peacock's country idyll is within earshot of the city – just as his classical reading is complemented by an immersion in contemporary news. In *Crotchet Castle*, the chapter entitled 'The Farm' is immediately followed by one called 'The Newspaper'; Chainmail may be in retreat, but he is not in hiding: '[he] received newspapers by the post, which came in three times a week' (Chapter 16). In Peacock's last novel, *Gryll Grange*, Dr Opimian gives a sense of what Chainmail is waiting for the mail to bring: 'what is the epitome of a newspaper?', he asks, 'A great quantity of talk, called by courtesy legislative wisdom' (Chapter 7). That talk is parliamentary. Cobbett's *Political Register* contained the first elaborate and connected record of parliamentary discussion ever published in England; the 'Debates' section of the *Register* was sold to Hansard in 1812, a couple of years before Peacock began work on his first novel (he would come to own seventy-four volumes of the *Register*).[115] His garrulous fictions often took their bearings from parliament as well as from Plato.

Early in *Headlong Hall*, by mentioning 'immediate adjournment', 'seconded . . . motion' and 'a large majority', Peacock had given a hint about where his characters had learned to speak as they do (Chapter 5). Several pages of *Crotchet Castle* also read like tongue-in-cheek versions of Hansard; the honourable gentlemen do not quite talk to each other, but make speeches at one another (in Chapter 6,

114 *Letters*, 1.192.   115 *Sale Catalogue* 127.

Folliott refers to Mac Quedy's 'exordium'; in Chapter 10, the narrator refers to Folliott's 'perorations'). The public was accustomed to seeing talk of Peacock's fiction alongside parliamentary talk; when the 1837 edition of *Crotchet Castle* appeared, *The Examiner*'s praise of Peacock's writing as 'full of a genuinely liberal and ameliorating spirit' was followed on the next page by a transcript of debates in the House of Commons.[116] The first reviews of *Crotchet Castle* in 1831 appeared as the country was gripped by debates in parliament which preceded the Great Reform Act (the first bill was introduced on 1 March; the second reading passed by a single vote on 23 March). As rioting increased and as extra-parliamentary pressure groups demanded reform (between October 1830 and April 1831 over 3000 petitions were returned to parliament), Peacock had been writing the final chapters of a novel in which a hall filled with august gentlemen-talkers is surrounded by rioters: 'The scheme of Christmas gambols, which Mr. Chainmail had laid for the evening, was interrupted by a tremendous clamor without' (Chapter 18). The cause of the clamour is variously attributed to 'poverty in distress', to 'the march of mind', and to 'increase of information', but one thing is clear: if Peacock's speakers are orators of a kind, then Chainmail Hall functions as a House of Parliament that is threatened from within as well as from outside Peacock's fictional world. It is as though the author's commitment to such debates is now itself up for debate – or rather, as though the novel's debt to parliamentary forms and formalities must be balanced by finding a way to include voices that were otherwise refused entry to such arenas.

Spedding suggested that Peacock played the fool, before adding that the fool was precisely what early nineteenth-century England needed: 'The House of Commons, being at once the most powerful body on the earth, and the most intolerant of criticism, stands especially in need of an officer who may speak out at random without

[116] *The Examiner* (28 May 1837), 341.

fear of Newgate.'[117] This conception of the fool's office – and of his stance in relation to the language of political power – is in keeping with Peacock's ways of seeing and hearing. Discussing what he termed 'modern language politic' in his poem *Sir Proteus*, Peacock added a note: 'This language was not much known to our ancestors; but it is now pretty well understood by the majority of the H – – of C – –, by the daily, weekly, monthly, and quarterly venders of panegyric and defamation.'[118] *Crotchet Castle* is searching for a language that might resist this sell-out; despite Peacock's claim that 'our ancestors' were less often beleaguered by such sophistry, he knew better. The novel's classical antecedents and influences drew attention to how public speech needed to be watched; the *Satyricon* begins at a school of rhetoric, with one speaker, Encolpius, denouncing 'loud empty phrases . . . honey-balls of phrases, every word and act besprinkled with poppy-seed and sesame'.[119] Peacock's other vital model for comic dialogue with a socio-political edge was Aristophanes, a writer he often thought of when reading oratory in the newspapers ('The proceedings in Parliament confirm me in the maintenance of my "right to read Aristophanes"').[120] Indeed, Aristophanes' plays were seen by Quintilian as a tool for developing oratorical excellence, and by Peacock as 'a mighty instrument of moral and political censure', a 'poetical denunciation of rascals' that exercised 'a very salutary control over profligates and demagogues'.[121]

As *Crotchet Castle* nears its end, discussion turns to the demagogue once more:

MR. CROTCHET.

I suppose, Doctor, you do not like to see a great reformer in office; you are afraid for your vested interests.

---

[117] Spedding, *Edinburgh Review*, 68 (1838–9), p. 433.
[118] Halliford, 6.285.
[119] *Satyricon*, section 1, p. 3.   [120] *Letters*, 2.336; see also 2.407.
[121] Quintilian, *Institutio Oratoria*, 10.1.65–6; Halliford, 10.76–7.

THE REV. DR. FOLLIOTT.

Not I, indeed, sir; my vested interests are very safe from all such reformers as the learned friend. I vaticinate what will be the upshot of all his schemes of reform. He will make a speech of seven hours' duration, and this will be its quintessence: that, seeing the exceeding difficulty of putting salt on the bird's tail, it will be expedient to consider the best method of throwing dust in the bird's eyes. All the rest will be

> *Τ ιττιττιτιμπρό.*
> *Ποποποί, ποποποί.*
> *Τιοτιοτιοτιοτιοτιοτίγξ.*
> *Κικκαβαῦ, κικκαβαῦ.*
> *ΤοροτοροτοροτοροΛιΛιΛίγξ.*

as Aristophanes has it; and so I leave him, in Nephelococcygia.

(Chapter 18)

In other words: in Cloud-cuckoo-land. Folliott is riffing on the onomatopoeic coinages from Aristophanes' *Birds* in order to signal birdsong – and to signal the empty nature of Brougham's rhetorical posturing – but critics who have seen Folliott as no more than a mouthpiece for Peacock miss the complexity of the moment. Although both Peacock and Folliott see through the speaker, readers are not necessarily being invited to feel relieved that the latter's 'vested interests are very safe'. For the novel to draw attention to the disingenuous nature of Brougham's reformist credentials need not mean supporting reform itself, but it may goad the audience into pondering what else remains to be said – and done ('and so I leave him' is an invitation for readers to wonder where *they* have been left). Peacock's other mentor – Cicero – has an exchange in *De Oratore* which is instructive here, one in which Crassus takes Antonius to task for arguing with him: 'I rather suspect you are really of a different opinion, and are gratifying that singular liking of yours for contradiction, in which no one has ever outdone you; the exercise of this power belongs peculiarly to orators, though nowadays it is in regular use among philosophers'.[122] Peacock had a similar liking, and *Crotchet Castle* tries to find ways of translating the to-and-fro of political opinions back into a genuinely enquiring sympotic form by never allowing anybody's peroration to feel like the last word. A few months after *Crotchet Castle* was published, Henry Cole recalled Peacock saying that 'the predominant opinions of a community' were 'always a lie and a Tyranny'.[123] In this novel's community, no one opinion is predominant.

Crotchet Castle blends political and philosophical arenas to intriguing effect, but there is another forum that makes itself felt in the novel, one that foregrounds a different voice. Talk of symposia sometimes led Peacock to consider an exchange in which a 'crotchet' was not simply an opinion, but also a musical note: 'Shelley has left behind him some volumes of Plato but he has taken with him the 1st and 10th & the Symposium is in the latter... Have you seen Il Barbiere di Seviglia?... To me it was delightful. I never heard music speak so intelligibly and with so much of the *vis comica*.'[124] Peacock's enthusiasm for opera was put to use at around the time that *Crotchet Castle* was written and published (he began serving as opera critic for the *Globe and Traveller* in 1830, and for *The Examiner* in 1831); another affectionately self-parodic portrait of the author can be seen in Mr. Trillo, the 'dilettante composer' who 'maintains that the sole end of all enlightened society is to get up a good opera' (Chapter 5). But it is the ladies who are the vital figures here; Susannah's voice, for example, 'had that full soft volume of melody which gives to common speech the fascination of music', and her aspect 'had more of the *contadina* of the opera, than of the genuine mountaineer', while the incomparable Lady Clarinda thinks

---

[122] Cicero, *De Oratore*, 1.62.263. On TLP's admiration of Cicero (second only to Aristophanes), see Robert Buchanan, *A Poet's Sketch-Book* (Chatto and Windus, 1883), p. 104.

[123] Cited in the *ODNB* entry on Peacock; Cole, MS journal (8 Apr. 1831).

[124] TLP to Thomas Jefferson Hogg (?1–27 Apr. 1818), *Letters*, 1.121.

'an opera-box a very substantial comfort' and is later to be found 'singing' (Chapters 15, 13, 3, 7). V. S. Pritchett once remarked of Peacock's novels that 'in the mad brainy world the women alone . . . have sense and sensibility', adding later that 'Peacock really launched the cultivated heroine in the English novel'.[125] In parliament and in symposia, ladies' voices were not generally admitted, but in the opera they often stole the show. Peacock saw links between modern opera and Greek drama, which he associated with 'the progress of freedom and intelligence'.[126] His beloved Epicurus allowed women into his School, whereas at the Academy and Lyceum only males were admitted. When Lady Clarinda says of Mac Quedy and Mr Skionar that 'a little of them is amusing, and I like to hear them dispute. So you see I am in training for a philosopher myself', she is intimating that this particular gentlemen's club is missing something (Chapter 5).

The mingling of romance plots with intellectual debate is more ambitiously and dextrously handled in *Crotchet Castle* than it is in Peacock's earlier works. Douglas Hewitt suggests that the love story of Mr Chainmail and Susannah is 'a mild satire on artificial modes but it is sufficiently charming to remind us of those ranges of feeling which the rest of the book ignores'.[127] This rings true, although the novel does not exactly ignore these modes even when it ushers us into the drawing-room:

Mr. Trillo went on with the composition of his opera, and took the opinions of the young ladies on every step in its progress; occasionally regaling the company with specimens; and wondering at the blindness

---

[125] V. S. Pritchett, 'Mr Peacock', in *New Statesman & Nation*, 20 (13 July 1940), 42–4 (p. 43); *New Statesman & Nation*, 45 (16 May 1953), p. 586. See also Edmund Wilson, 'The Musical Glasses of Peacock', in *Classics and Commercials* (Allen, 1951), who saw TLP's form as essentially operatic: 'These girls of his – frank, independent, brave, intelligent and rather intellectual – stand somewhere between the heroines of Shelley and the heroines of Jane Austen', p. 409.

[126] Halliford, 9.226; see also Halliford, 9.437.

[127] Hewitt, 'Entertaining Ideas', p. 204.

of Mr. Mac Quedy, who could not, or would not, see that an opera in perfection, being the union of all the beautiful arts, – music, painting, dancing, poetry, – exhibiting female beauty in its most attractive aspects, and in its most becoming costume, – was, according to the well-known precept, Ingenuas didicisse, &c., the most efficient instrument of civilization, and ought to take precedence of all other pursuits in the minds of true philanthropists. The Reverend Doctor Folliott, on these occasions, never failed to say a word or two on Mr. Trillo's side, derived from the practice of the Athenians, and from the combination, in their theatre, of all the beautiful arts, in a degree of perfection unknown to the modern world.   (Chapter 10)

This is one of the very few moments in the novel when the word 'progress' is not set up for a fall. Mr Trillo's enthusiasm is smiled at but not laughed at, and the fact that debates about 'true' philanthropy and 'the opinions of the young ladies' are raised in relation to 'the blindness of Mr. Mac Quedy' is significant. Critics have tended to see Mac Quedy as modelled on the political economist John Ramsay McCulloch, and there is indeed much of McCulloch in him, but James Mill, Peacock's colleague at the India House and champion of both Utilitarianism and political economy, is a formative influence on the character too. Mill considered himself the figurehead of the 'true philanthropists', yet in his essay on 'Government' he felt it important to note:

One thing is pretty clear, that all those individuals whose interests are indisputably included in those of other individuals, may be struck off without inconvenience . . . In this light . . . women may be regarded, the interest of almost all of whom is involved either in that of their fathers or in that of their husbands.

This paragraph, John Stuart Mill would later remark, was the worst his father ever wrote; Thomas Babington Macaulay and several others zeroed in on it.[128] Peacock draws on the debate between

---

[128] Mill, 'Government', in *Political Writings*, p. xxi.

Mill and Macaulay at several moments in *Crotchet Castle*, but here it is instructive simply to note the latter's reading of Mill's paragraph: 'Without adducing one fact, without taking the trouble to perplex the question by one sophism, he placidly dogmatizes away the interest of one half of the human race.'[129] When, in *Crotchet Castle*, Lady Clarinda informs Captain Fitzchrome that Mr Mac Quedy 'has satisfied me that I am a commodity in the market' (Chapter 5), only then to tell him that *she* shall decide to whom she will sell herself, she is parroting the language of the political economists whilst also casting aspersions on some of their less enlightened assumptions. Clarinda is one of the best things in the novel – not least because she manages to send up the presuppositions of the crotcheteers' debates while refusing to be swallowed up by the romance plot. 'You always delighted in trying to provoke me; but I cannot believe that you have not a heart', Fitzchrome laments; to which she retorts: 'You do not like to believe that I have a heart, you mean. You wish to think I have lost it, and you know to whom; and when I tell you that it is still safe in my own keeping, and that I do not mean to give it away, the unreasonable creature grows angry' (Chapter 3). Kingsley Amis put it well when he asked, 'Who wouldn't consent to liquidating that whole tribe of after-dinner lecturers for the sake of a few more pages of the matchless Clarinda taking the stuffing out of Captain Fitzchrome?'[130] That said, other parts of the novel are in sympathy with her refusal to submit to Fitzchrome's terms. When Mr Trillo hears the gentlemen talk in Chapter 6, he thinks their language 'runs itself into a chorus, and sets itself to music', but much of the music of *Crotchet Castle* comes from Clarinda's mellifluous ironies.

---

[129] Thomas Babington Macaulay, 'Mill on Government', *Edinburgh Review*, 49 (1829), repr. in Mill, *Political Writings*, p. 291. Macaulay was also alluding to another well-known attack on Mill: William Thompson's *Appeal to One Half of the Human Race* (Longman, Hurst, Rees, et al., 1825).

[130] Kingsley Amis, 'Laugh when You Can', *Spectator*, 194 (1 Apr. 1955), 402–4 (p. 403).

Peacock wrote *Crotchet Castle* in the period Boyd Hilton summarizes as 'The Crisis of the Old Order'. That crisis took many forms: the Test and Corporation Act repeals; Catholic emancipation; the reform debates; workers' protests and rioting; and electoral instability – the 1830 election was the first since 1708 to be followed by the fall of a government. Many of these things can be felt in the novel alongside debates about political economy, the 'march of mind', financial corruption, and so on; it is one of those works, as Peacock says of Le Brun's writings, that 'carry their era in their incidents'.[131] Indeed, when trying to sum up the age's 'inclination to see the world in terms of opposites', Hilton quotes Mr Crotchet himself: 'The sentimental against the rational, the intuitive against the inductive, the ornamental against the useful, the intense against the tranquil, the romantic against the classical; these are great and interesting controversies, which I should like, before I die, to see satisfactorily settled.'[132] But what distinguishes *Crotchet Castle*'s approach to the oppositions it explores is Peacock's need to perceive congruence within apparent conflict, and to disrupt any sense of allegiance that borders on complacency – as though to imply that his culture's obsession with allegiance might itself be part of the problem.

In 1827, in the first piece he wrote for that bastion of utilitarian thinking, the *Westminster Review*, Peacock reviewed Moore's *The Epicurean*. He might have been expected to toe the line and to weigh Epicurean pleasures against a utilitarian calculus, but instead he criticized the need to see the parties as mutually exclusive. Having scorned Moore's complacent allergy to the word 'utility', and having demolished his shallow caricature of Epicurus' position as a debauched hedonism, Peacock noted:

Epicurus taught that happiness, or the greatest portion of permanent pleasure, is only to be attained by strict obedience to the dictates of

---

[131] 'French Comic Romances', Halliford, 9.255.
[132] See Boyd Hilton, *A Mad, Bad, and Dangerous People? England 1783–1846* (Oxford: Clarendon Press, 2006), p. 312.

right reason; that strict obedience to those dictates constitutes the virtue called prudence, and that all virtue is either prudence or a derivative from it ... Thus Epicurus first taught, that general utility, or as Bentham expresses it, 'the greatest happiness of the greatest number,' is the legitimate end of philosophy; and it is curious to see the same class of persons decrying the same doctrine as impracticably dry, when the word utility precedes the word pleasure, and as too practicably voluptuous when the word pleasure precedes the word utility. So much are small minds the slaves of words.[133]

Epicurus and Bentham might seem to be unlikely bed-fellows, but then Bentham – with whom Peacock, after all, 'had been extremely intimate – dining with him *tête à tête*, once a week for years together'[134] – described himself as 'something between epicurean and cynic'.[135] *Crotchet Castle* is neither 'impracticably dry' nor 'practicably voluptuous', and its equability of tone was, for Peacock, a form of prudence – prudence which was itself conceived as useful pleasure.

AFTERLIFE

Charles Dickens launched his career in fiction with an apparent nod to *Crotchet Castle*. In its first chapter, *The Pickwick Papers* (1836–7) alights on the same pedagogical and scientific targets as those which had been sent up in Peacock's sixth novel. The 'Transactions of the Pickwick Club' is a footnoted, pseudo-documentary record of how Samuel Pickwick's scientific paper, 'Speculations on the Source of the Hampstead Ponds, with Some Observations on the Theory of Tittlebats' has been received by a 'celebrated' body. Aping the language of Brougham's SDUK, the Club warmly endorses Pickwick's labours and urges him to travel far and wide, to publicize his discoveries and thereby to pursue 'the advancement of knowledge, and the

---

[133] TLP, 'Moore's Epicurean', Halliford, 9.47, 48–9.
[134] E. Grant Duff, *Notes from a Diary, 1851–1871* (John Murray, 1897), p. 60.
[135] Jeremy Bentham, cited in Kathleen Blake, *The Pleasures of Benthamism: Victorian Literature, Utility, Political Economy* (Oxford: Oxford University Press, 2009), p. 50.

diffusion of learning'. Pickwick's complacent protest, 'that if ever the fire of self-importance broke out in his bosom the desire to benefit the human race in preference, effectually quenched it', and his deliciously absurd pride in extending the fame of his Tittlebatian Theory 'to the farthest confines of the known world', restage the jokes made at Brougham's expense in *Crotchet Castle*.[136] Conjuring the superb prospect of Pickwick's scientific travels, Dickens seems to have in mind several of Brougham's catchphrases, especially 'The schoolmaster is abroad', originally invoked with reference to Brougham's efforts to educate the masses. As Brougham reportedly announced of this character, 'There was another person abroad, – a less important person, – in the eyes of some an insignificant person, – whose labours had tended to produce this state of things. The schoolmaster was abroad! (cheers and laughter)! and he trusted more to him, armed with his primer, than he did to the soldier in full military array, for upholding and extending the liberties of his country.'[137] Here, apparently, is one inspiration for the figure of trusty Mr Pickwick: armed with his treatise, disseminating scientific knowledge and philanthropy across the land, against a backdrop of social, political and agricultural unrest (Dickens has Pickwick allude, in this opening chapter, to the Swing Riots; the 'rabble-rout' scene in Chapter 18 of *Crotchet Castle* is inspired by the same events).[138]

Dickens appreciated Peacock's talents as a writer, publishing the latter's 'Recollections of Childhood' in *Bentley's Miscellany* (1836) while composing *Pickwick*.[139] Like Peacock, whose name may be faintly echoed in 'Pickwick', he was sensitive to developments in

---

[136] Charles Dickens, *The Pickwick Papers*, ed. James Kinsley (Oxford: Clarendon Press, 1986), pp. 1–6.
[137] Speech, Opening of Parliament (29 Jan. 1828), *The Times* (30 Jan. 1828), p. 3. See also *CC*, ch. 8.
[138] 'The praise of mankind was his Swing', *Pickwick Papers*, p. 6.
[139] 'Recollections of Childhood. By the Author of *Headlong Hall*', *Bentley's Miscellany*, vol. 1 (1837), 187–90.

education and popular science, as well as in the administration of charitable bodies; unlike Peacock, he was often enthusiastic about their potential. Dickens sought, in *Pickwick*, to attract the same readers of cheap literature who had been captured by Brougham's *Penny Magazine*. He won their favour partly by revisiting Peacock's jokes about jargon-friendly reforming societies and learned associations. Two 'Full Reports' of 'Meetings of The Mudfog Association' in that journal (1837–8), satirizing the relentless 'Advancement of Everything', are again openly indebted to *Crotchet Castle*.[140] Like Peacock, Dickens bracketed political economy alongside chemistry and geography as interdependent forms of enquiry; the social and natural sciences were, for both men, aspects of the same movement towards the professionalization of all forms of knowledge, and evidence of a mushrooming bureaucracy. For Dickens, as for Peacock, the delusive self-approbation, speechifying, jostling and petty disputes endemic in any gathering of specialists were fodder for comedy; like Peacock, Dickens also noticed how eager such crank debaters remained, crotchets notwithstanding, on a first-class meal.

Writing in the *Comic Almanack* for 1835, Dickens' future illustrator George Cruikshank gleefully continued Peacock's spoof of 'Henry Broom', citing a 'Society for the Confusion of Useful Knowledge' and 'their successful endeavours in be-*Knight*-ing the public intellect', as well as lampooning in his mock 'Proceedings of Learned Societies' the misuse of science by 'the state engine' and the methods of the New Poor Law Commissioners.[141] By 1842, Cruikshank was floating the idea of a yet more luminously redundant organization, 'for the Confusion of Useless Knowledge', whose foundation had apparently been proposed and supported at the annual meeting of the 'British Fill-us-off-ical and Feeding Association, at Ply-mouth'.

[140] See Jay Clayton, *Charles Dickens in Cyberspace: The Afterlife of the Nineteenth Century in Postmodern Culture* (Oxford: Oxford University Press, 2003), pp. 94–8.

[141] *The Comic Almanack, for 1835* (Charles Tilt, 1835), pp. 36–7.

The chief target here was the *Penny Magazine* and its bite-sized chunks of knowledge; portion control was bound up with progressive ideals:

It is intended, by the Company, to supply the present enormous mental appetite of the public, with a full feed of science and literature, in a series of sixpenny bits, or bites . . . The Company propose, in order to ensure the greatest possible degree of ultimate perfection, to commence some of the subjects in bits.[142]

But just as Dickens pitched his own serial works at the readers of the *Penny Magazine*, so Cruikshank's bitty and various *Almanack* embodied the same miscellaneous, quickly digestible forms of entertaining knowledge that it ridiculed. Throughout the 1840s, building castles in the air and eating a lot continued to be inseparable activities. Brougham was now the target of endless *Punch* cartoons; he figured as Mr Quicksilver in Samuel Warren's novel *Ten Thousand a-Year* (1841) – a best-selling account of interminable litigation which probably inspired *Bleak House* (1852–3) – having already spawned the character of Foaming Fudge, who briefly appears in Benjamin Disraeli's *Vivian Grey* (1826–7), and 'the learned friend' in *Crotchet Castle*.[143] In 1848, John Henry Newman's philosophical novel of conversion, *Loss and Gain*, combined reference to the latest Vice-Chancellor of Oxford University as 'a new broom' with a certain 'Dr. Crotchet . . . for years kept out of his destined bishopric'.[144]

---

[142] *The Comic Almanack, for 1842* (Tilt and Boyne, 1842), p. 32.

[143] 'Mr QUICKSILVER, a man of great but wild energy . . . The first and the last thing he thought of in a cause, was – himself' (Samuel Warren, *Ten Thousand a-Year*, 3 vols. (William Blackwood and Sons, 1841), vol. 1, p. 378–9). 'Foaming Fudge can do more than any man in Great Britain . . . he had one day to plead in the King's Bench, spout at a tavern, speak in the house, and fight a duel – and . . . he found time for everything but *the last*' (Benjamin Disraeli, *Vivian Grey*, 2 vols. (Henry Colburn, 1826–7), vol. 1, p. 187).

[144] John Henry Newman, *Loss and Gain* (James Burns, 1848), pp. 29–30.

'Nothing but innuendoes, figurative crotchets', complains the editor-narrator of his maddeningly oblique subject, Herr Teufelsdröckh, in Thomas Carlyle's *Sartor Resartus* (1833–4). These 'crotchets' – 'whimsical' turns, or fanciful intellectual devices – may well have been influenced by Peacock.[145] Carlyle's peculiar, brilliant novel first appeared in serial form in *Fraser's Magazine*. He began to write it in October 1831, and was perhaps stimulated to do so by the publication of *Crotchet Castle* earlier that year. Such a hypothesis is rendered more likely in view of the fact that Carlyle and Peacock had a common friend in Edward Strachey, who in 1820 was appointed an examiner at East India House in London, and who worked with Peacock (Strachey shared the utilitarian leanings of another colleague, John Stuart Mill).[146] Carlyle and Peacock were drawn to the same authorial models: Butler, Cervantes, Swift, Voltaire, Rabelais and Sterne (among many others).[147] *Sartor Resartus* is clearly influenced, as is *Crotchet Castle*, by Sterne's meandering whimsy and by Swift's mock-rhetoric of improvement, but the two works also offer satirical comment on philosophy, a sceptical view of biography, an experimental form and an atmosphere that is simultaneously factual and fictional, comic and serious, speculative and historical. Each work is in its own way theatrical, intellectual and densely allusive.

Although Peacock does not seem to have been indebted to Thomas Hurlstone's dramatic farce *Crotchet Lodge* (1795), or to its spin-off *The New Crotchet Lodge* (1799), his sixth work of fiction may have stimulated dramatic experiments in the same line. In 1852, Ernest Oswald Coe's three-act comedy *Crotchet Hall* appeared;

---

[145] Thomas Carlyle, *Sartor Resartus*, ed. Mark Engel and Rodger L. Tarr (Berkeley, Los Angeles and London: University of California Press, 2000), pp. 138–9.

[146] See *ODNB* entry on Edward Strachey.

[147] On possible allusions to TLP and Butler, see Carlyle, *Sartor Resartus*, pp. 321–2.

Mrs Alfred Phillips' *Uncle Crotchet. A Farce, in One Act* was performed a year later.[148] *Crotchet Hall* features the absent-minded Dr Crotchet, who hails steam as a 'great physical wonder: not equal, though, to my moral engine, my great transcendental'. It is a debating drama of sorts, centring on the marriage market and its discontents, in which one character expresses his fondness for hearing 'both sides of every question'. Dr Crotchet sounds alternately like Dr Folliott and Mr Mac Quedy, both intellectually abstruse and in favour of an 'extended scale of universal advantage'.[149] His concluding remark, however, following a series of escapes and confusions, is in the venerable literary and philosophical tradition of utter bafflement:

I can explain nothing – I know nothing: I don't even know where I am; and I have no clear notion of what happened; for it has never been clearly explained to me. I believe all this to be a delusion: we are in a world of delusions, of vague impressions, called knowledge, and of doubtful facts, termed history.[150]

In Mrs Alfred Phillips' *Uncle Crotchet*, which is no more than loosely connected with Peacock, an ageing Theophilus Crotchet plans to marry one of two foundling girls he has brought up as Roman virgins according to his own eccentric system at Crotchet Hall. Convinced that modern speech and behaviour have degenerated, the jokes at his and the other characters' expense focus on good and bad kinds of education, and on the clash of ancient with modern. As in *Crotchet Castle*, classical statuary is a means both of improving and corrupting young people.

While still an undergraduate at Oxford, W. H. Mallock began work on a satirical novel depicting the contemporary state of

---

[148] Ernest Oswald Coe, *Crotchet Hall. A Comedy in Three Acts* (Frederick Shoberl, 1852); Mrs Alfred Phillips, *Uncle Crotchet. A Farce, in One Act* (Thomas Hailes Long, 1853).
[149] Coe, *Crotchet Hall*, pp. 24, 38, 78.   [150] Coe, *Crotchet Hall*, p. 78.

intellectual and ethical life. After serialization in *Belgravia* (1876–7), this was published in book form as *The New Republic: Culture, Faith and Philosophy in an English Country House* in 1877. It won the author immediate acclaim. The novel, set over the course of a weekend at a country-house party in Devon, takes the form of a crotcheteers' symposium involving scientists, men of religion, writers and private citizens. Mallock claimed as his models Plato's *Republic*, Petronius' *Satyricon* and 'the so-called novels of Peacock'.[151] Very little happens in the book, other than conversation. *The New Republic* is designed as a serious critical appraisal of various *bien-pensants*, but its motivations are very different from Peacock's; Mallock was chiefly affronted by 'the reasoning of liberal Oxford'.[152] *The New Republic* is also, more overtly than any of Peacock's works, a *roman à clef*, skilfully parodying the views of Matthew Arnold, Walter Pater, Thomas Huxley, Benjamin Jowett, John Ruskin and John Tyndall – each of whom appears in transparent disguise and reveals a 'peculiar crotchet of his own mind'.[153] (Arnold himself, in 1861, had glanced in Peacock's direction when he referred to 'opinions which have no ground in reason, which are mere crotchets, or mere prejudices, or mere passions'.)[154] In duplicating his real-life models, Mallock thought he was behaving as a 'disciple of Peacock', yet Peacock had in fact tried not to write 'direct from life'.[155]

Like *Crotchet Castle*, *The New Republic* employs the device of one character introducing the rest of the cast to another.[156] And Mallock's heroine, Miss Merton, is, like Lady Clarinda, a beautiful, hard-headed truth-seeker who punctures the hypocrisy and

---

[151] W. H. Mallock, *Memoirs of Life and Literature* (Chapman and Hall, 1920), p. 65.

[152] Mallock, *Memoirs*, p. 63.

[153] W. H. Mallock, *The New Republic* (Leicester: Leicester University Press, 1975), p. 51.

[154] Matthew Arnold, *The Popular Education of France, with notices of that of Holland and Switzerland* (Longman, Green, etc., 1861), p. 165.

[155] Mallock, *Memoirs*, p. 65. [156] Mallock, *New Republic*, p. 14.

intellectual pretensions of the male crotcheteers. 'Under the innocent covers of this little book – half novel, half dialogue essay',
observed a reviewer in the *New York Times* of the 1878 edition of
The New Republic, 'much more is hidden than is meant to appear on
the surface'. Fearing that, for some readers, Mallock's anti-sceptical
'socio-political essay-novel' might prove hard to digest, the reviewer
was nevertheless keen to praise the 'clever points, sharp sayings' and
'amusing contrasts' to be found therein. The combined forces of
hospitality, satire and philosophy continued to deserve and reward
our attention – even if, when all is said and done, 'Each person goes
his or her way without regard to the arguments of the others, and
the symposium is at an end.'[157]

Mallock's account, written many years later, of his methods and
attitudes during the composition of his *New Republic* are suggestive
of Peacock's in *Crotchet Castle*, and perhaps in themselves attest to
another kind of authorial afterlife. While drafting and redrafting
the book, Mallock recalled discovering that his sense of human
absurdity had become sharper than ever. That sense of heightened
clarity influenced his final choice of epigraph for the beginning of
the novel, a choice that recalls Peacock's insertion of Butler at the
forefront of *Crotchet Castle*, as well as his habitual practice of writing
'a dialogue' in order 'to get a clearer view of my own notions':[158]

In my effort to give point to what were really my own underlying
convictions, I wrote *The New Republic* six or seven times over, and in
doing so it became clearer and clearer to me what my own convictions
were. They ended in an application of the method of a *reductio ad
absurdum* to everything; and this fact I finally indicated in the words of
a Greek epigram which I placed as a motto on the title-page – 'All is
laughter, all is dust, all is nothingness, for all the things that are arise
out of the unreasonable.'[159]

[157] 'Mallock's New Republic', *New York Times* (20 Apr. 1878), p. 3.
[158] TLP to Thomas Jefferson Hogg (?1–27 Apr. 1818), *Letters*, 1.121.
[159] Mallock, *Memoirs*, pp. 67–8.

Mallock felt keenly that 'such a conclusion' was unsatisfactory, even if 'the absurdities of current liberal philosophy' had driven him to it.[160] Knocking things down must be the first step towards building something new. Perhaps that first step is proposed by the sociably crotcheteering question that concludes *Sartor Resartus*: 'have we not existed together, though in a state of quarrel?'[161]

[160] Mallock, *Memoirs*, p. 68.   [161] Carlyle, *Sartor Resartus*, p. 218.

CROTCHET CASTLE.

BY THE

AUTHOR OF HEADLONG HALL.

Le monde est plein de fous, et qui n'en veut pas voir,
Doit se tenir tout seul, et casser son miroir.

LONDON:

PUBLISHED BY T. HOOKHAM,
OLD BOND STREET.

1831.

1 Title page of *Crotchet Castle* (1831)

Should once the world resolve to abolish
All that's ridiculous and foolish,
It would have nothing left to do,
To apply in jest or earnest to.

BUTLER.

CHAPTER I.

THE VILLA.[1]

Captain Jamy. I wad full fain hear some question
'tween you tway.   HENRY V.[2]

IN one of those beautiful vallies, through which the Thames[3]
(not yet polluted by the tide, the scouring of cities, or even the
minor defilement of the sandy streams of Surrey,[4]) rolls a clear
flood through flowery meadows, under the shade of old beech
woods, and the smooth mossy greensward[5] of the chalk hills,
(which pour into it their tributary rivulets, as pure and pellucid
as the fountain of Bandusium,[6] or the wells of Scamander, by
which the wives and daughters of the Trojans washed their
splendid garments in the days of peace, before the coming
of the Greeks;)[7] in one of those beautiful vallies, on a bold
round-surfaced lawn, spotted with juniper, that opened itself
in the bosom of an old wood, which rose with a steep, but not
precipitous ascent, from the river to the summit of the hill,
stood the castellated villa of a retired citizen.[8] Ebenezer Mac
Crotchet, Esquire, was the London-born offspring of a worthy
native of the "north countrie,"[9] who had walked up to London
on a commercial adventure, with all his surplus capital, not very
neatly tied up in a not very clean handkerchief, suspended over
his shoulder from the end of a hooked stick, extracted from the
first hedge on his pilgrimage;[10] and who, after having worked
himself a step or two up the ladder of life, had won the virgin
heart of the only daughter of a highly respectable merchant of
Duke's Place,[11] with whom he inherited the honest fruits of a
long series of ingenuous dealings.

Mr. Mac Crotchet had derived from his mother the instinct,
and from his father the rational principle, of enriching himself

at the expense of the rest of mankind, by all the recognised modes of accumulation on the windy side of the law.[12] After passing many years in the alley,[13] watching the turn of the market, and playing many games almost as desperate as that of the soldier of Lucullus,* the fear of losing what he had so righteously gained, predominated over the sacred thirst of paper-money;[14] his caution got the better of his instinct, or rather transferred it from the department of acquisition to that of conservation. His friend, Mr. Ramsbottom, the zodiacal mythologist,[15] told him that he had done well to withdraw from the region of Uranus or Brahma, the Maker, to that of Saturn or Veeshnu, the Preserver, before he fell under the eye of Jupiter or Seva, the Destroyer,[16] who might have struck him down at a blow.

It is said, that a Scotchman returning home, after some years' residence in England, being asked what he thought of the English, answered: "they hanna ower muckle sense, but they are an unco braw people to live amang;" which would be a very good story, if it were not rendered apocryphal, by the incredible circumstance of the Scotchman going back.[17]

Mr. Mac Crotchet's experience had given him a just title to make, in his own person, the last-quoted observation, but he would have known better than to go back, even if himself, and not his father, had been the first comer of his line from the north. He had married an English Christian, and, having none of the Scotch accent, was ungracious enough to be ashamed of his blood. He was desirous to obliterate alike the Hebrew and Caledonian vestiges in his name, and signed himself E. M. Crotchet, which by degrees induced the majority of his neighbours to think that his name was Edward Matthew.

---

* Luculli miles, &c. HOR. *Ep*. II. 2, 26. "In Anna's wars, a soldier poor and bold," &c. — POPE's *Imitation*.

The more effectually to sink the Mac, he christened his villa Crotchet Castle, and determined to hand down to posterity the honors of Crotchet of Crotchet. He found it essential to his dignity to furnish himself with a coat of arms,[18] which, after the proper ceremonies (payment being the principal), he obtained, videlicet:[19] Crest, a crotchet rampant, in A sharp: Arms, three empty bladders, turgescent, to show how opinions are formed; three bags of gold, pendent, to show why they are maintained; three naked swords, tranchant, to show how they are administered; and three barbers' blocks, gaspant, to show how they are swallowed.[20]

Mr. Crotchet was left a widower, with two children; and, after the death of his wife, so strong was his sense of the blessed comfort she had been to him, that he determined never to give any other woman an opportunity of obliterating the happy recollection.

He was not without a plausible pretence for styling his villa a Castle, for, in its immediate vicinity, and within his own enclosed domain, were the manifest traces, on the brow of the hill, of a Roman station, or *castellum*, which was still called the Castle by the country people.[21] The primitive mounds and trenches, merely overgrown with greensward, with a few patches of juniper and box on the vallum,[22] and a solitary ancient beech surmounting the place of the prætorium,[23] presented nearly the same depths, heights, slopes, and forms, which the Roman soldiers had originally given them. From this *castellum* Mr. Crotchet christened his villa. With his rustic neighbours he was of course immediately and necessarily a squire: Squire Crotchet of the Castle: and he seemed to himself to settle down as naturally into an English country gentleman, as if his parentage had been as innocent of both Scotland and Jerusalem, as his education was of Rome and Athens.

But as, though you expel nature with a pitchfork, she will yet always come back;* he could not become, like a true-born English squire, part and parcel of the barley-giving earth;[24] he could not find in game-bagging,[25] poacher-shooting, trespasser-pounding, footpath-stopping, common-enclosing,[26] rack-renting,[27] and all the other liberal pursuits and pastimes which make a country gentleman an ornament to the world, and a blessing to the poor; he could not find in these valuable and amiable occupations, and in a corresponding range of ideas, nearly commensurate with that of the great King Nebuchadnezzar, when he was turned out to grass;[28] he could not find in this great variety of useful action, and vast field of comprehensive thought, modes of filling up his time that accorded with his Caledonian instinct. The inborn love of disputation, which the excitements and engagements of a life of business had smothered, burst forth through the calmer surface of a rural life. He grew as fain as Captain Jamy, "to hear some airgument betwixt ony tway,"[29] and being very hospitable in his establishment, and liberal in his invitations, a numerous detachment from the advanced guard of the "march of intellect,"[30] often marched down to Crotchet Castle.

When the fashionable season filled London with exhibitors of all descriptions, lecturers[31] and else, Mr. Crotchet was in his glory; for, in addition to the perennial literati of the metropolis, he had the advantage of the visits of a number of hardy annuals, chiefly from the north, who, as the interval of their metropolitan flowering allowed, occasionally accompanied their London brethren in excursions to Crotchet Castle.

Amongst other things, he took very naturally to political economy,[32] read all the books on the subject which were put forth by his own countrymen, attended all lectures thereon,

---

* Naturam expellas furcâ, tamen usque recurret.

HOR. Ep. I. 10, 24.

and boxed[33] the technology of the sublime science as expertly as an able seaman boxes the compass.

With this agreeable mania he had the satisfaction of biting[34] his son, the hope of his name and race, who had borne off from Oxford the highest academical honors; and who, treading in his father's footsteps to honor and fortune, had, by means of a portion of the old gentleman's surplus capital, made himself a junior partner in the eminent loan-jobbing[35] firm of Catch-flat and Company.[36] Here, in the days of paper prosperity, he applied his science-illumined genius to the blowing of bubbles,[37] the bursting of which sent many a poor devil to the jail, the workhouse, or the bottom of the river, but left young Crotchet rolling in riches.

These riches he had been on the point of doubling, by a marriage with the daughter of Mr. Touchandgo, the great banker,[38] when, one foggy morning, Mr. Touchandgo and the contents of his till were suddenly reported absent; and as the fortune which the young gentleman had intended to marry was not forthcoming, this tender affair of the heart was nipped in the bud.

Miss Touchandgo did not meet the shock of separation quite so complacently as the young gentleman: for he lost only the lady, whereas, she lost a fortune as well as a lover. Some jewels, which had glittered on her beautiful person as brilliantly as the bubble of her father's wealth had done in the eyes of his gudgeons,[39] furnished her with a small portion of paper-currency; and this, added to the contents of a fairy purse of gold, which she found in her shoe on the eventful morning when Mr. Touchandgo melted into thin air, enabled her to retreat into North Wales, where she took up her lodging in a farm-house in Merionethshire, and boarded very comfortably for a trifling payment, and the additional consideration of teaching English, French, and music, to the little Ap-Llymry's.[40] In the course of this occupation, she acquired sufficient knowledge of Welsh to converse with the country people.

She climbed the mountains, and descended the dingles,[41] with a foot which daily habit made by degrees almost as steady as a native's. She became the nymph of the scene; and if she sometimes pined in thought for her faithless Strephon,[42] her melancholy was any thing but green and yellow: it was as genuine white and red[43] as occupation, mountain air, thyme-fed mutton, thick cream, and fat bacon, could make it: to say nothing of an occasional glass of double X,[44] which Ap-Llymry,* who yielded to no man west of the Wrekin[45] in brewage, never failed to press upon her at dinner and supper. He was also earnest, and sometimes successful, in the recommendation of his mead, and most pertinacious on winter nights in enforcing a trial of the virtues of his elder wine. The young lady's personal appearance, consequently, formed a very advantageous contrast to that of her quondam lover, whose physiognomy[46] the intense anxieties of his bubble-blowing days, notwithstanding their triumphant result, had left blighted, sallowed,[47] and crow's-footed, to a degree not far below that of the fallen spirit who, in the expressive language of German romance, is described as "scathed by the ineradicable traces of the thunderbolts of Heaven;"[48] so that, contemplating their relative geological positions, the poor deserted damsel was flourishing on slate, while her rich and false young knight was pining on chalk.

Squire Crotchet had also one daughter, whom he had christened Lemma,[49] and who, as likely to be endowed with a very ample fortune, was, of course, an object very tempting to many young soldiers of fortune, who were marching with the march of mind,[50] in a good condition for taking castles, as far as

---

* Llymry. Anglicè flummery.

not having a groat is a qualification for such exploits.* She was also a glittering bait to divers young squires expectant,[51] (whose fathers were too well acquainted with the occult signification of mortgage,) and even to one or two sprigs of nobility, who thought that the lining of a civic purse would superinduce a very passable factitious nap upon a thread-bare title. The young lady had received an expensive and complicated education; complete in all the elements of superficial display. She was thus eminently qualified to be the companion of any masculine luminary who had kept due pace with the "astounding progress" of intelligence.[52] It must be confessed, that a man who has not kept due pace with it, is not very easily found: this march being one of that "astounding" character in which it seems impossible that the rear can be behind the van.[53] The young lady was also tolerably good-looking: north of Tweed, or in Palestine, she would probably have been a beauty; but for the vallies of the Thames, she was perhaps a little too much to the taste of Solomon, and had a nose which rather too prominently suggested the idea of the tower of Lebanon, which looked towards Damascus.[54]

In a village in the vicinity of the Castle was the vicarage of the Reverend Doctor Folliott, a gentleman endowed with a tolerable stock of learning, an interminable swallow, and an indefatigable pair of lungs. His pre-eminence in the latter faculty gave occasion to some etymologists[55] to ring changes on his name, and to decide that it was derived from Follis Optimus,[56] softened through an Italian medium, into Follè Ottimo, contracted poetically into Folleotto, and elided Anglicé into Folliott, signifying a first-rate pair of bellows. He claimed to be descended lineally from the illustrious Gilbert Folliott,[57] the eminent theologian, who was

---

* "Let him take castles who has ne'er a groat."

POPE, *ubi suprà.*

a Bishop of London in the twelfth century, whose studies were interrupted in the dead of night by the Devil; when a couple of epigrams passed between them; and the Devil, of course, proved the smaller wit of the two.*

This reverend gentleman, being both learned and jolly, became by degrees an indispensable ornament to the new squire's table. Mr. Crotchet himself was eminently jolly, though by no means eminently learned. In the latter respect he took after the great majority of the sons of his father's land; had a smattering of many things, and a knowledge of none;[58] but possessed the true northern art of making the most of his intellectual harlequin's jacket, by keeping the best patches always bright and prominent.[59]

---

* The devil began: (he had caught the bishop musing on politics.)

> Oh Gilberte Folliot!
> Dum revolvis tot et tot,
> Deus tuus est Astarot.

> Oh Gilbert Folliott!
> While thus you muse and plot,
> Your god is Astarot.

The bishop answered:

> Tace, dæmon; qui est deus
> Sabbaot, est ille meus.

> Peace, fiend; the power I own
> Is Sabbaoth's Lord alone.

It must be confessed, the devil was easily posed in the twelfth century. He was a sturdier disputant in the sixteenth.

> Did not the devil appear to Martin
> Luther in Germany for certain?

when "the heroic student," as Mr. Coleridge calls him, was forced to proceed to "*voies de fait.*" The curious may see at this day, on the wall of Luther's study, the traces of the ink-bottle which he threw at the devil's head.

CHAPTER II.

THE MARCH OF MIND.

Quoth Ralpho: nothing but the abuse
Of human learning you produce.
                            BUTLER.[1]

"GOD bless my soul, sir!" exclaimed the Reverend Doctor Folliott, bursting, one fine May morning,[2] into the breakfast-room at Crotchet Castle, "I am out of all patience with this march of mind. Here has my house been nearly burned down, by my cook taking it into her head to study Hydrostatics, in a sixpenny tract, published by the Steam Intellect Society, and written by a learned friend[3] who is for doing all the world's business as well as his own, and is equally well qualified to handle every branch of human knowledge. I have a great abomination of this learned friend; as author, lawyer, and politician, he is *triformis*, like Hecate:[4] and in every one of his three forms he is *bifrons*, like Janus;[5] the true Mr. Facing-both-ways of Vanity Fair.[6] My cook must read his rubbish in bed; and as might naturally be expected, she dropped suddenly fast asleep, overturned the candle, and set the curtains in a blaze. Luckily, the footman went into the room at the moment, in time to tear down the curtains and throw them into the chimney, and a pitcher of water on her night-cap extinguished her wick: she is a greasy subject, and would have burned like a short mould."[7]

The reverend gentleman exhaled his grievance[8] without looking to the right or to the left; at length, turning on his pivot, he perceived that the room was full of company, consisting of young Crotchet and some visitors whom he had brought from London. The Reverend Doctor Folliott was introduced to Mr. Mac Quedy,* the economist;[9] Mr. Skionar,† the transcendental poet;[10] Mr. Firedamp, the meteorologist;[11] and Lord Bossnowl, son of the Earl of Foolincourt, and member for the borough of Rogueingrain.[12]

The divine took his seat at the breakfast-table, and began to compose his spirits by the gentle sedative of a large cup of tea, the demulcent[13] of a well-buttered muffin, and the tonic of a small lobster.

THE REV. DR. FOLLIOTT.

You are a man of taste, Mr. Crotchet. A man of taste is seen at once in the array of his breakfast-table.[14] It is the foot of Hercules,[15] the far-shining face of the great work, according to Pindar's doctrine: ἀρχομένου ἔργου πρόσωπον χρὴ θέμεν τηλαυγές.‡ The breakfast is the πρόσωπον of the great work of the day. Chocolate, coffee, tea, cream, eggs, ham, tongue, cold fowl, all these are good, and bespeak good knowledge in him who sets them forth: but the touch-stone is fish: anchovy is the first step, prawns and shrimps the second; and I laud him who reaches even to these: potted char and lampreys are the third, and a fine stretch of progression;[16] but lobster is, indeed, matter for a May morning,[17] and demands a rare combination of knowledge and virtue in him who sets it forth.

MR. MAC QUEDY.

Well, sir, and what say you to a fine fresh trout, hot and dry, in a napkin? or a herring out of the water into the frying pan, on the shore of Loch Fyne?

---

* Quasi Mac Q. E. D., son of a demonstration.
† ΣΚΙᾶς ΟΝΑΡ. *Umbræ somnium.*
‡ Far-shining be the face
  Of a great work begun.

PIND. Ol. vi.

THE REV. DR. FOLLIOTT.

Sir, I say every nation has some eximious[18] virtue; and your country is pre-eminent in the glory of fish for breakfast. We have much to learn from you in that line at any rate.

MR. MAC QUEDY.

And in many others, sir, I believe. Morals and metaphysics, politics and political economy, the way to make the most of all the modifications of smoke; steam, gas, and paper currency; you have all these to learn from us; in short, all the arts and sciences. We are the modern Athenians.

THE REV. DR. FOLLIOTT.

I, for one, sir, am content to learn nothing from you but the art and science of fish for breakfast. Be content, sir, to rival the Bœotians, whose redeeming virtue was in fish, touching which point you may consult Aristophanes and his scholiast in the passage of Lysistrata, ἀλλ' ἄφελε τὰς ἐγχέλεις,* [19] and leave the name of Athenians to those who have a sense of the beautiful, and a perception of metrical quantity.[20]

MR. MAC QUEDY.

Then, sir, I presume you set no value on the right principles of rent, profit, wages, and currency?

THE REV. DR. FOLLIOTT.

My principles, sir, in these things are, to take as much as I can get, and to pay no more than I can help. These are every man's principles, whether they be the right principles or no. There, sir, is political economy in a nutshell.[21]

MR. MAC QUEDY.

The principles, sir, which regulate production and consumption are independent of the will of any individual as to giving or taking, and do not lie in a nutshell by any means.

---

* Calonice wishes destruction to all Bœotians. Lysistrata answers, "*Except the eels.*" *Lysistrata*, 36.

THE REV. DR. FOLLIOTT.

Sir, I will thank you for a leg of that capon.

LORD BOSSNOWL.

But, sir, by the by, how came your footman to be going into your cook's room? It was very providential to be sure, but—

THE REV. DR. FOLLIOTT.

Sir, as good came of it, I shut my eyes, and asked no questions. I suppose he was going to study hydrostatics, and he found himself under the necessity of practising hydraulics.

MR. FIREDAMP.

Sir, you seem to make very light of science.

THE REV. DR. FOLLIOTT.

Yes, sir, such science as the learned friend deals in: every thing for every body, science for all, schools for all, rhetoric for all, law for all, physic for all, words for all, and sense for none.[22] I say, sir, law for lawyers, and cookery for cooks: and I wish the learned friend, for all his life, a cook that will pass her time in studying his works; then every dinner he sits down to at home, he will sit on the stool of repentance.[23]

LORD BOSSNOWL.

Now really that would be too severe: my cook should read nothing but Ude.[24]

THE REV. DR. FOLLIOTT.

No, sir! let Ude and the learned friend singe fowls together; let both avaunt from my kitchen. Θύρας δ' ἐπίθεσθε βεβήλοις.* [25] Ude says an elegant supper may be given with sandwiches. *Horresco referens.*[26] An elegant supper. *Di meliora piis.*[27] No Ude for me. Conviviality went out with punch and suppers. I cherish their memory. I sup when I can, but not

---

* "Shut the doors against the profane." ORPHICA, *passim.*

upon sandwiches. To offer me a sandwich, when I am looking for a supper, is to add insult to injury. Let the learned friend, and the modern Athenians, sup upon sandwiches.

MR. MAC QUEDY.

Nay, sir; the modern Athenians know better than that. A literary supper in sweet Edinbroo' would cure you of the prejudice you seem to cherish against us.

THE REV. DR. FOLLIOTT.

Well, sir, well; there is cogency in a good supper; a good supper in these degenerate days, bespeaks a good man; but much more is wanted to make up an Athenian. Athenians, indeed! where is your theatre? who among you has written a comedy?[28] where is your attic salt?[29] which of you can tell who was Jupiter's great grandfather?[30] or what metres will successively remain, if you take off the three first syllables, one by one, from a pure antispastic acatalectic tetrameter?[31] Now, sir, there are three questions for you; theatrical, mythological, and metrical; to every one of which an Athenian would give an answer that would lay me prostrate in my own nothingness.

MR. MAC QUEDY.

Well, sir, as to your metre and your mythology, they may e'en wait a wee. For your comedy, there is the Gentle Shepherd of the divine Allan Ramsay.[32]

THE REV. DR. FOLLIOTT.

The Gentle Shepherd! It is just as much a comedy as the book of Job.

MR. MAC QUEDY.

Well, sir, if none of us have written a comedy, I cannot see that it is any such great matter, any more than I can conjecture what business a man can have at this time of day with Jupiter's great grandfather.

THE REV. DR. FOLLIOTT.

The great business is, sir, that you call yourselves Athenians, while you know nothing that the Athenians thought worth knowing, and dare not show your noses before the civilized world in the practice of any one art in which they were excellent. Modern Athens, sir! the assumption is a personal affront to every man who has a Sophocles in his library. I will thank you for an anchovy.

MR. MAC QUEDY.

Metaphysics, sir; metaphysics. Logic and moral philosophy. There we are at home. The Athenians only sought the way, and we have found it; and to all this we have added political economy, the science of sciences.

THE REV. DR. FOLLIOTT.

A hyperbarbarous[33] technology, that no Athenian ear could have borne. Premises assumed without evidence, or in spite of it; and conclusions drawn from them so logically, that they must necessarily be erroneous.[34]

MR. SKIONAR.

I cannot agree with you, Mr. Mac Quedy, that you have found the true road of metaphysics, which the Athenians only sought. The Germans have found it, sir: the sublime Kant, and his disciples.[35]

MR. MAC QUEDY.

I have read the sublime Kant, sir, with an anxious desire to understand him, and I confess I have not succeeded.

THE REV. DR. FOLLIOTT.
He wants the two great requisites of head and tail.[36]

MR. SKIONAR.

Transcendentalism is the philosophy of intuition, the development of universal convictions; truths which are inherent in the organization of mind, which cannot be obliterated, though they may be obscured, by superstitious prejudice on the one hand, and by the Aristotelian logic[37] on the other.

MR. MAC QUEDY.

Well, sir, I have no notion of logic obscuring a question.

MR. SKIONAR.

There is only one true logic, which is the transcendental; and this can prove only the one true philosophy, which is also the transcendental. The logic of your Modern Athens can prove every thing equally; and that is, in my opinion, tantamount to proving nothing at all.

MR. CROTCHET.

The sentimental against the rational, the intuitive against the inductive, the ornamental against the useful, the intense against the tranquil, the romantic against the classical; these are great and interesting controversies, which I should like, before I die, to see satisfactorily settled.[38]

MR. FIREDAMP.

There is another great question, greater than all these, seeing that it is necessary to be alive in order to settle any question; and this is the question of water against human life. Wherever there is water, there is malaria,[39] and wherever there is malaria, there are the elements of death. The great object of a wise man should be to live on a gravelly hill, without so much as a duck-pond within ten miles of him, eschewing cisterns and water-butts, and taking care that there be no gravel-pits for lodging the rain. The sun sucks up infection from water, wherever it exists on the face of the earth.[40]

THE REV. DR. FOLLIOTT.

Well, sir, you have for you the authority of the ancient mystagogue, who said: Ἔστιν ὕδωρ ψυχῇ θάνατος*.[41] For

* Literally, which is sufficient for the present purpose, "Water is death to the soul."

ORPHICA: *Fr.* XIX.

my part I care not a rush (or any other aquatic and inesculent[42] vegetable) who or what sucks up either the water or
the infection. I think the proximity of wine a matter of much
more importance than the longinquity[43] of water. You are here
within a quarter of a mile of the Thames, but in the cellar of
my friend, Mr. Crotchet, there is the talismanic antidote of
a thousand dozen of old wine; a beautiful spectacle, I assure
you, and a model of arrangement.

MR. FIREDAMP.

Sir, I feel the malignant influence of the river in every part of
my system. Nothing but my great friendship for Mr. Crotchet
would have brought me so nearly within the jaws of the lion.

THE REV. DR. FOLLIOTT.

After dinner, sir, after dinner, I will meet you on this question. I shall then be armed for the strife. You may fight like
Hercules against Achelous, but I shall flourish the Bacchic
thyrsus, which changed rivers into wine: as Nonnus sweetly
sings, Οἴνῳ κυματόεντι μέλας κελάρυζεν Ὑδάσπης.*[44]

MR. CROTCHET, JUN.

I hope, Mr. Firedamp, you will let your friendship carry
you a little closer into the jaws of the lion. I am fitting up
a flotilla of pleasure-boats, with spacious cabins, and a good
cellar, to carry a choice philosophical party up the Thames and
Severn, into the Ellesmere canal, where we shall be among the
mountains of North Wales; which we may climb or not, as
we think proper; but we will, at any rate, keep our floating
hotel well provisioned, and we will try to settle all the questions over which a shadow of doubt yet hangs in the world of
philosophy.[45]

---

* Hydaspes gurgled, dark with billowy wine.

Dionysiaca, XXV. 280.

MR. FIREDAMP.

Out of my great friendship for you, I will certainly go; but I do not expect to survive the experiment.

THE REV. DR. FOLLIOTT.

Alter erit tum Tiphys, et altera quæ vehat Argo Delectos Heroas.* [46] I will be of the party, though I must hire an officiating curate, and deprive poor dear Mrs. Folliott, for several weeks, of the pleasure of combing my wig.

LORD BOSSNOWL.

I hope, if I am to be of the party, our ship is not to be the ship of fools:[47] He! He!

THE REV. DR. FOLLIOTT.

If you are one of the party, sir, it most assuredly will not: Ha! Ha!

LORD BOSSNOWL.

Pray sir, what do you mean by Ha! Ha!?

THE REV. DR. FOLLIOTT.

Precisely, sir, what you mean by He! He!

MR. MAC QUEDY.

You need not dispute about terms; they are two modes of expressing merriment, with or without reason; reason being in no way essential to mirth. No man should ask another why he laughs, or at what, seeing that he does not always know, and that, if he does, he is not a responsible agent. Laughter is an involuntary action of certain muscles, developed in the human species by the progress of civilization. The savage never laughs.[48]

---

* "Another Tiphys on the waves shall float,
  And chosen heroes freight his glorious boat."
                                                    VIRG *Ecl.* IV.

THE REV. DR. FOLLIOTT.

No, sir, he has nothing to laugh at. Give him Modern Athens, the "learned friend," and the Steam Intellect Society. They will develope his muscles.

CHAPTER III.

THE ROMAN CAMP.

> He loved her more then seven yere,
> Yet was he of her love never the nere;
> He was not ryche of golde and fe,
> A gentyll man forsoth was he.
> *The Squyr of Lowe Degre.*[1]

THE Reverend Doctor Folliott having promised to return to dinner, walked back to his vicarage, meditating whether he should pass the morning in writing his next sermon, or in angling for trout, and had nearly decided in favor of the latter proposition, repeating to himself, with great unction, the lines of Chaucer:

> And as for me, though that I can but lite,
> On bokis for to read I me delite,
> And to 'hem yeve I faithe and full credence,
> And in mine herte have 'hem in reverence,
> So hertily, that there is gamē none,
> That fro my bokis makith me to gone,
> But it be seldome, on the holie daie;
> Save certainly whan that the month of Maie
> Is comin, and I here the foulis sing,
> And that the flouris ginnin for to spring,
> Farwell my boke and my devocion:[2]

when his attention was attracted by a young gentleman who was sitting on a camp stool with a portfolio on his knee, taking a sketch of the Roman Camp, which, as has been already said, was within the enclosed domain of Mr. Crotchet. The young stranger, who had climbed over the fence, espying the portly divine, rose up, and hoped that he was not trespassing. "By no means, sir," said the divine, "all the arts and sciences are welcome here; music, painting, and poetry; hydrostatics, and political economy; meteorology, transcendentalism, and fish for breakfast."

THE STRANGER.

A pleasant association, sir, and a liberal and discriminating hospitality. This is an old British camp, I believe, sir.

THE REV. DR. FOLLIOTT.

Roman, sir; Roman: undeniably Roman. The vallum is past controversy. It was not a camp, sir, a *castrum*, but a *castellum*, a little camp, or watch-station,[3] to which was attached, on the peak of the adjacent hill, a beacon for transmitting alarms. You will find such here and there, all along the range of chalk hills, which traverses the country from north-east to south-west, and along the base of which runs the ancient Ikenild road, whereof you may descry a portion in that long strait white line.[4]

THE STRANGER.

I beg your pardon, sir: do I understand this place to be your property?

THE REV. DR. FOLLIOTT.

It is not mine, sir: the more is the pity; yet is it so far well, that the owner is my good friend, and a highly respectable gentleman.

THE STRANGER.

Good and respectable, sir, I take it, mean rich?

THE REV. DR. FOLLIOTT.

That is their meaning, sir.

THE STRANGER.

I understand the owner to be a Mr. Crotchet. He has a handsome daughter, I am told.

THE REV. DR. FOLLIOTT.

He has, sir. Her eyes are like the fish-pools of Heshbon, by the gate of Bethrabbim;[5] and she is to have a handsome fortune, to which divers disinterested gentlemen are paying their addresses. Perhaps you design to be one of them.

THE STRANGER.

No, sir; I beg pardon if my questions seem impertinent; I have no such design. There is a son too, I believe, sir, a great and successful blower of bubbles.

THE REV. DR. FOLLIOTT.

A hero, sir, in his line. Never did angler in September hook more gudgeons.

THE STRANGER.

To say the truth, two very amiable young people, with whom I have some little acquaintance, Lord Bossnowl, and his sister, Lady Clarinda, are reported to be on the point of concluding a double marriage with Miss Crotchet and her brother; by way of putting a new varnish on old nobility. Lord Foolincourt, their father, is terribly poor for a lord who owns a borough.[6]

THE REV. DR. FOLLIOTT.

Well, sir, the Crotchets have plenty of money, and the old gentleman's weak point is a hankering after high blood. I saw your acquaintance, Lord Bossnowl, this morning, but I did not see his sister. She may be there, nevertheless, and doing fashionable justice to this fine May morning, by lying in bed till noon.

THE STRANGER.

Young Mr. Crotchet, sir, has been, like his father, the architect of his own fortune, has he not? An illustrious example of the reward of honesty and industry?

THE REV. DR. FOLLIOTT.

As to honesty, sir, he made his fortune in the city of London, and if that commodity be of any value there, you will find it in the price current. I believe it is below par, like the shares of young Crotchet's fifty companies. But his progress has not been exactly like his father's. It has been more rapid, and he started with more advantages. He began with a fine capital from his father. The old gentleman divided his fortune into three not exactly equal portions; one for himself, one for his daughter, and one for his son, which he handed over to him, saying, "Take it once for all, and make the most of it; if you lose it where I won it, not another stiver[7] do you get from me during my life." But, sir, young Crotchet doubled, and trebled, and quadrupled it, and is, as you say, a striking example of the reward of industry; not that I think his labor has been so great as his luck.

THE STRANGER.

But, sir, is all this solid? is there no danger of reaction? no day of reckoning to cut down in an hour prosperity that has grown up like a mushroom?

THE REV. DR. FOLLIOTT.

Nay, sir, I know not. I do not pry into these matters. I am, for my own part, very well satisfied with the young gentleman. Let those who are not so look to themselves. It is quite enough for me that he came down last night from London, and that he had the good sense to bring with him a basket of lobsters. Sir, I wish you a good morning.

The stranger having returned the reverend gentleman's good morning, resumed his sketch, and was intently employed on it when Mr. Crotchet made his appearance, with Mr. Mac Quedy and Mr. Skionar, whom he was escorting round his grounds, according to his custom with new visitors; the principal pleasure of possessing an extensive domain being that of showing it to other people. Mr. Mac Quedy, according also to the laudable custom of his countrymen, had been appraising every thing that fell under his observation; but, on arriving at the Roman camp, of which the value was purely imaginary, he contented himself with exclaiming: "Eh! this is just a curiosity, and very pleasant to sit in on a summer day."

MR. SKIONAR.

And call up the days of old, when the Roman eagle spread its wings in the place of that beechen foliage. It gives a fine idea of duration, to think that that fine old tree must have sprung from the earth ages after this camp was formed.

MR. MAC QUEDY.

How old, think you, may the tree be?

MR. CROTCHET.

I have records which show it to be three hundred years old.

MR. MAC QUEDY.

That is a great age for a beech in good condition. But you see the camp is some fifteen hundred years, or so, older; and three times six being eighteen, I think you get a clearer idea of duration[8] out of the simple arithmetic, than out of your eagle and foliage.

MR. SKIONAR.

That is a very unpoetical, if not unphilosophical, mode of viewing antiquities. Your philosophy is too literal for our imperfect vision. We cannot look directly into the nature of things; we can only catch glimpses of the mighty shadow in the camera obscura of transcendental intelligence. These six and eighteen are only words to which we give conventional meanings. We can reason, but we cannot feel, by help of them. The tree and the eagle, contemplated in the ideality of space and time, become subjective realities, that rise up as landmarks in the mystery of the past.[9]

MR. MAC QUEDY.

Well, sir, if you understand that, I wish you joy. But I must be excused for holding that my proposition, three times six are eighteen, is more intelligible than yours. A worthy friend of mine, who is a sort of amateur in philosophy, criticism, politics, and a wee bit of many things more, says: "Men never begin to study antiquities till they are saturated with civilization."*

MR. SKIONAR.

What is civilization?

MR. MAC QUEDY.

It is just respect for property. A state in which no man takes wrongfully what belongs to another, is a perfectly civilized state.

MR. SKIONAR.

Your friend's antiquaries must have lived in El Dorado,[10] to have had an opportunity of being saturated with such a state.

MR. MAC QUEDY.

It is a question of degree. There is more respect for property here than in Angola.[11]

MR. SKIONAR.

That depends on the light in which things are viewed.

Mr. Crotchet was rubbing his hands, in hopes of a fine discussion, when they came round to the side of the camp where the picturesque gentleman was sketching. The stranger was rising up, when Mr. Crotchet begged him not to disturb himself, and presently walked away with his two guests.

Shortly after, Miss Crotchet and Lady Clarinda, who had breakfasted by themselves, made their appearance at the same spot, hanging each on an arm of Lord Bossnowl, who very much preferred their company to that of the philosophers, though he would have preferred the company of the latter, or

* Edinburgh Review, somewhere.

any company, to his own. He thought it very singular that so agreeable a person as he held himself to be to others, should be so exceedingly tiresome to himself: he did not attempt to investigate the cause of this phenomenon, but was contented with acting on his knowledge of the fact, and giving himself as little of his own private society as possible.

The stranger rose as they approached, and was immediately recognised by the Bossnowls as an old acquaintance, and saluted with the exclamation of "Captain Fitzchrome!" The interchange of salutation between Lady Clarinda and the Captain was accompanied with an amiable confusion on both sides, in which the observant eyes of Miss Crotchet seemed to read the recollection of an affair of the heart.

Lord Bossnowl was either unconscious of any such affair, or indifferent to its existence. He introduced the Captain very cordially to Miss Crotchet; and the young lady invited him, as the friend of their guests, to partake of her father's hospitality, an offer which was readily accepted.

The Captain took his portfolio under his right arm, his camp stool in his right hand, offered his left arm to Lady Clarinda, and followed at a reasonable distance behind Miss Crotchet and Lord Bossnowl, contriving, in the most natural manner possible, to drop more and more into the rear.

LADY CLARINDA.

I am glad to see you can make yourself so happy with drawing old trees and mounds of grass.

CAPTAIN FITZCHROME.

Happy, Lady Clarinda! oh, no! How can I be happy when I see the idol of my heart about to be sacrificed on the shrine of Mammon?

LADY CLARINDA.

Do you know, though Mammon has a sort of ill name, I really think he is a very popular character; there must be at the bottom something amiable about him. He is certainly one of those pleasant creatures whom every body abuses, but without whom no evening party is endurable. I dare say, love in a cottage[12] is very pleasant; but then it positively must be a cottage ornée:[13] but would not the same love be a great deal safer in a castle, even if Mammon furnished the fortification?

CAPTAIN FITZCHROME.[14]

Oh, Lady Clarinda! there is a heartlessness in that language that chills me to the soul.

LADY CLARINDA.

Heartlessness! No: my heart is on my lips. I speak just what I think. You used to like it, and say it was as delightful as it was rare.

CAPTAIN FITZCHROME.

True, but you did not then talk as you do now, of love in a castle.

LADY CLARINDA.

Well, but only consider: a dun[15] is a horridly vulgar creature; it is a creature I cannot endure the thought of: and a cottage lets him in so easily. Now a castle keeps him at bay. You are a half-pay officer,[16] and are at leisure to command the garrison: but where is the castle? and who is to furnish the commissariat?

CAPTAIN FITZCHROME.

Is it come to this, that you make a jest of my poverty? Yet is my poverty only comparative. Many decent families are maintained on smaller means.

LADY CLARINDA.

Decent families: aye, decent is the distinction from respectable. Respectable means rich, and decent means poor. I should die if I heard my family called decent. And then your decent family always lives in a snug little place: I hate a little place; I like large rooms and large looking-glasses, and large parties, and a fine large butler, with a tinge of smooth red in his face; an outward and visible sign[17] that the family he serves is respectable; if not noble, highly respectable.

CAPTAIN FITZCHROME.

I cannot believe that you say all this in earnest. No man is less disposed than I am to deny the importance of the substantial comforts of life. I once flattered myself that in our estimate of these things we were nearly of a mind.

LADY CLARINDA.

Do you know, I think an opera-box a very substantial comfort, and a carriage. You will tell me that many decent people walk arm in arm through the snow, and sit in clogs and bonnets[18] in the pit[19] at the English theatre. No doubt it is very pleasant to those who are used to it; but it is not to my taste.

CAPTAIN FITZCHROME.

You always delighted in trying to provoke me; but I cannot believe that you have not a heart.

LADY CLARINDA.

You do not like to believe that I have a heart, you mean. You wish to think I have lost it, and you know to whom; and when I tell you that it is still safe in my own keeping, and that I do not mean to give it away, the unreasonable creature grows angry.

CAPTAIN FITZCHROME.

Angry! far from it: I am perfectly cool.

LADY CLARINDA.

Why you are pursing your brows, biting your lips, and lifting up your foot as if you would stamp it into the earth. I must say anger becomes you; you would make a charming Hotspur.[20] Your every-day-dining-out face is rather insipid:

but I assure you my heart is in danger when you are in the heroics. It is so rare too, in these days of smooth manners, to see any thing like natural expression in a man's face.[21] There is one set form for every man's face in female society: a sort of serious comedy, walking gentleman's[22] face: but the moment the creature falls in love, he begins to give himself airs, and plays off all the varieties of his physiognomy from the Master Slender to the Petruchio;[23] and then he is actually very amusing.

CAPTAIN FITZCHROME.

Well, Lady Clarinda, I will not be angry, amusing as it may be to you: I listen more in sorrow than in anger. I half believe you in earnest: and mourn as over a fallen angel.

LADY CLARINDA.

What, because I have made up my mind not to give away my heart when I can sell it? I will introduce you to my new acquaintance, Mr. Mac Quedy: he will talk to you by the hour about exchangeable value,[24] and shew you that no rational being will part with any thing, except to the highest bidder.

CAPTAIN FITZCHROME.

Now, I am sure you are not in earnest. You cannot adopt such sentiments in their naked deformity.

LADY CLARINDA.

Naked deformity: why Mr. Mac Quedy will prove to you that they are the cream of the most refined philosophy. You live a very pleasant life as a bachelor, roving about the country with your portfolio under your arm. I am not fit to be a poor man's wife. I cannot take any kind of trouble, or do any one thing that is of any use. Many decent families roast a bit of mutton on a string; but if I displease my father I shall not have as much as will buy the string, to say nothing of the meat; and the bare idea of such cookery gives me the horrors.

By this time, they were near the Castle, and met Miss Crotchet and her companion, who had turned back to meet them. Captain Fitzchrome was shortly after heartily welcomed by Mr. Crotchet, and the party separated to dress for dinner, the Captain being by no means in an enviable state of mind, and full of misgivings as to the extent of belief that he was bound to accord to the words of the lady of his heart.

CHAPTER IV.

THE PARTY.

En quoi cognoissez-vous la folie anticque? En quoi
cognoissez-vous la sagesse présente?

RABELAIS.[1]

"IF I were sketching a bandit who had just shot his last pursuer,
having outrun all the rest, that is the very face I would give
him," soliloquised the Captain, as he studied the features of
his rival in the drawing-room, during the miserable half-hour
before dinner, when dullness reigns predominant[2] over the
expectant company, especially when they are waiting for some
one last comer, whom they all heartily curse in their hearts,
and whom, nevertheless, or indeed therefore-the-more, they
welcome as a sinner, more heartily than all the just persons
who had been punctual to their engagement.[3] Some new visitors had arrived in the morning, and, as the company dropped
in one by one, the Captain anxiously watched the unclosing
door for the form of his beloved: but she was the last to make
her appearance, and on her entry gave him a malicious glance,
which he construed into a telegraphic communication that she
had stayed away to torment him. Young Crotchet escorted her
with marked attention to the upper end of the drawing-room,
where a great portion of the company was congregated around
Miss Crotchet. These being the only ladies in the company, it
was evident that old Mr. Crotchet would give his arm to Lady
Clarinda, an arrangement with which the Captain could not
interfere. He therefore, took his station near the door, studying his rival from a distance, and determined to take advantage
of his present position, to secure the seat next to his charmer.
He was meditating on the best mode of operation for securing
this important post with due regard to *bienséance*,[4] when he

was twitched by the button by Mr. Mac Quedy, who said to him: "Lady Clarinda tells me, sir, that you are anxious to talk with me on the subject of exchangeable value, from which I infer that you have studied political economy, and as a great deal depends on the definition of value,[5] I shall be glad to set you right on that point." "I am much obliged to you, sir," said the Captain, and was about to express his utter disqualification for the proposed instruction, when Mr. Skionar walked up and said: "Lady Clarinda informs me that you wish to talk over with me the question of subjective reality. I am delighted to fall in with a gentleman who duly appreciates the transcendental philosophy." "Lady Clarinda is too good," said the Captain; and was about to protest that he had never heard the word transcendental[6] before, when the butler announced dinner. Mr. Crotchet led the way with Lady Clarinda: Lord Bossnowl followed with Miss Crotchet: the economist and transcendentalist pinned in the Captain, and held him, one by each arm, as he impatiently descended the stairs in the rear of several others of the company, whom they had forced him to let pass; but the moment he entered the dining-room he broke loose from them, and at the expense of a little *brusquerie*, secured his position.

"Well, Captain," said Lady Clarinda, "I perceive you can still manœuvre."

"What could possess you," said the Captain, "to send two unendurable and inconceivable bores, to intercept me with rubbish about which I neither know nor care any more than the man in the moon?"

"Perhaps," said Lady Clarinda, "I saw your design, and wished to put your generalship to the test. But do not contradict any thing I have said about you, and see if the learned will find you out."

"There is fine music, as Rabelais observes, in the *cliquetis d'assiettes*, a refreshing shade in the *ombre de salle à manger*, and an elegant fragrance in the *fumée de rôti*,"[7] said a voice at the Captain's elbow. The Captain turning round, recognised his clerical friend of the morning, who knew him again immediately, and said he was extremely glad to meet him there; more especially as Lady Clarinda had assured him that he was an enthusiastic lover of Greek poetry.

"Lady Clarinda," said the Captain, "is a very pleasant young lady."

THE REV. DR. FOLLIOTT.

So she is, sir: and I understand she has all the wit of the family to herself, whatever that *totum* may be.[8] But a glass of wine after soup is, as the French say, the *verre de santé*.[9] The current of opinion sets in favor of Hock:[10] but I am for Madeira;[11] I do not fancy Hock till I have laid a substratum of Madeira. Will you join me?

CAPTAIN FITZCHROME.

With pleasure.

THE REV. DR. FOLLIOTT.

Here is a very fine salmon before me: and May is the very *point nommé*[12] to have salmon in perfection. There is a fine turbot close by, and there is much to be said in his behalf: but salmon in May is the king of fish.

MR. CROTCHET.

That salmon before you, doctor, was caught in the Thames, this morning.

THE REV. DR. FOLLIOTT.

Παπαπαῖ![13] Rarity of rarities! A Thames salmon caught this morning. Now, Mr. Mac Quedy, even in fish your Modern Athens must yield. *Cedite Graii*.[14]

MR. MAC QUEDY.

Eh! sir, on its own ground, your Thames salmon has two virtues over all others; first, that it is fresh; and, second, that it is rare; for I understand you do not take half a dozen in a year.

THE REV. DR. FOLLIOTT.

In some years, sir, not one. Mud, filth, gas-dregs, lock-wiers, and the march of mind, developed in the form of poaching, have ruined the fishery. But, when we do catch a salmon, happy the man to whom he falls.[15]

MR. MAC QUEDY.

I confess, sir, this is excellent: but I cannot see why it should be better than a Tweed salmon at Kelso.[16]

THE REV. DR. FOLLIOTT.

Sir, I will take a glass of Hock with you.

MR. MAC QUEDY.

With all my heart, sir. There are several varieties of the salmon genus: but the common salmon, the *salmo salar*,[17] is only one species, one and the same every where, just like the human mind. Locality and education make all the difference.

THE REV. DR. FOLLIOTT.

Education! Well, sir, I have no doubt schools for all are just as fit for the species *salmo salar* as for the *genus homo*. But you must allow that the specimen before us has finished his education[18] in a manner that does honor to his college. However, I doubt that the *salmo salar* is only one species, that is to say, precisely alike in all localities. I hold that every river has its own breed, with essential differences; in flavor especially. And as for the human mind, I deny that it is the same in all men. I hold that there is every variety of natural capacity from the idiot to Newton and Shakspeare; the mass of mankind, midway between these extremes, being blockheads of different degrees; education leaving them pretty nearly as it found them, with this single difference, that it gives a fixed direction to their stupidity, a sort of incurable wry neck to the thing they call their understanding. So one nose[19] points always east, and another always west, and each is ready to swear that it points due north.

MR. CROTCHET.

If that be the point of truth, very few intellectual noses point due north.

MR. MAC QUEDY.

Only those that point to the Modern Athens.

THE REV. DR. FOLLIOTT.

Where all native noses point southward.

MR. MAC QUEDY.

Eh, sir, northward for wisdom, and southward for profit.

MR. CROTCHET, JUN.

Champagne, doctor?

THE REV. DR. FOLLIOTT.

Most willingly. But you will permit my drinking it while it sparkles. I hold it a heresy to let it deaden in my hand, while the glass of my *compotator*[20] is being filled on the opposite side of the table. By the by, Captain, you remember a passage in Athenæus, where he cites Menander on the subject of fish-sauce: ὀψάριον ἐπὶ ἰχθύος.[21] (*The Captain was aghast for an answer that would satisfy both his neighbours, when he was relieved by the divine continuing.*) The science of fish-sauce, Mr. Mac Quedy, is by no means brought to perfection; a fine field of discovery still lies open in that line.

MR. MAC QUEDY.

Nay, sir, beyond lobster-sauce, I take it, ye cannot go.

THE REV. DR. FOLLIOTT.

In their line, I grant you, oyster and lobster sauce are the pillars of Hercules.[22] But I speak of the cruet sauces, where the quintessence of the sapid[23] is condensed in a phial. I can taste in my mind's palate a combination, which, if I could give it reality, I would christen with the name of my college, and hand it down to posterity as a seat of learning indeed.

MR. MAC QUEDY.

Well, sir, I wish you success, but I cannot let slip the question we started just now. I say, cutting off idiots, who have no minds at all, all minds are by nature alike. Education (which begins from their birth) makes them what they are.[24]

THE REV. DR. FOLLIOTT.

No, sir, it makes their tendencies, not their power. Cæsar would have been the first wrestler on the village common.[25] Education might have made him a Nadir Shah;[26] it might also have made him a Washington;[27] it could not have made him a merry-andrew,[28] for our newspapers to extol as a model of eloquence.

MR. MAC QUEDY.

Now, sir, I think education would have made him just any thing, and fit for any station, from the throne to the stocks; saint or sinner, aristocrat or democrat, judge, counsel, or prisoner at the bar.

THE REV. DR. FOLLIOTT.

I will thank you for a slice of lamb, with lemon and pepper. Before I proceed with this discussion,—Vin de Grave,[29] Mr. Skionar,—I must interpose one remark. There is a set of persons in your city, Mr. Mac Quedy, who concoct every three or four months, a thing, which they call a review: a sort of sugar-plum manufacturers to the Whig aristocracy.[30]

MR. MAC QUEDY.

I cannot tell, sir, exactly, what you mean by that; but I hope you will speak of those gentlemen with respect, seeing that I am one of them.

THE REV. DR. FOLLIOTT.

Sir, I must drown my inadvertence in a glass of Sauterne[31] with you. There is a set of gentlemen in your city—

39

MR. MAC QUEDY.

Not in our city, exactly; neither are they a set. There is an editor, who forages for articles in all quarters, from John O'Groat's house to the Land's End. It is not a board,[32] or a society: it is a mere intellectual bazaar, where A. B. and C. bring their wares to market.

THE REV. DR. FOLLIOTT.

Well, sir, these gentlemen among them, the present company excepted, have practised as much dishonesty as, in any other department than literature, would have brought the practitioner under the cognizance of the police. In politics, they have run with the hare, and hunted with the hound. In criticism, they have, knowingly and unblushingly given false characters, both for good and for evil: sticking at no art of misrepresentation, to clear out of the field of literature all who stood in the way of the interests of their own click. They have never allowed their own profound ignorance of any thing, (Greek, for instance,) to throw even an air of hesitation into their oracular decision on the matter. They set an example of profligate contempt for truth,[33] of which the success was in proportion to the effrontery; and when their prosperity had filled the market with competitors, they cried out against their own reflected sin, as if they had never committed it, or were entitled to a monopoly of it. The latter, I rather think, was what they wanted.

MR. CROTCHET.

Hermitage, doctor?

THE REV. DR. FOLLIOTT.

Nothing better, sir. The father who first chose the solitude of that vineyard, knew well how to cultivate his spirit in retirement.[34] Now, Mr. Mac Quedy, Achilles was distinguished above all the Greeks for his inflexible love of truth:[35] could education have made Achilles one of your reviewers?

MR. MAC QUEDY.

No doubt of it, even if your character of them were true to the letter.

THE REV. DR. FOLLIOTT.

And I say, sir—chicken and asparagus—Titan had made him of better clay.* [36] I hold with Pindar: "All that is most excellent is so by nature." *Τὸ δὲ φυᾷ κράτιστον ἅπαν.*† [37] Education can give purposes, but not powers; and whatever purpose had been given him, he would have gone strait forward to them; strait forward, Mr. Mac Quedy.

MR. MAC QUEDY.

No, sir, education makes the man, powers, purposes, and all.

THE REV. DR. FOLLIOTT.

There is the point, sir, on which we join issue.

Several others of the company now chimed in with their opinions, which gave the divine an opportunity to degustate[38] one or two side dishes, and to take a glass of wine with each of the young ladies.

* Juv. XIV. 35.   † *Ol.* IX. 152.

CHARACTERS.

Ay imputé a honte plus que médiocre être vu
spectateur ocieux de tant vaillans, disertz, et
chevalereux personnaiges.   RABELAIS.[2]

LADY CLARINDA (*to the Captain.*)[3]

I DECLARE the creature has been listening to all this
rigmarole, instead of attending to me. Do you ever expect
forgiveness? But now that they are all talking together, and
you cannot make out a word they say, nor they hear a word
that we say, I will describe the company to you. First, there is
the old gentleman on my left hand, at the head of the table,
who is now leaning the other way to talk to my brother. He
is a good tempered, half-informed person, very unreasonably
fond of reasoning, and of reasoning people; people that talk
nonsense logically: he is fond of disputation himself, when
there are only one or two,[4] but seldom does more than listen
in a large company of *illuminés*.[5] He made a great fortune in
the city, and has the comfort of a good conscience. He is very
hospitable, and is generous in dinners; though nothing would
induce him to give sixpence to the poor, because he holds that
all misfortune is from imprudence, that none but the rich ought
to marry, and that all ought to thrive by honest industry,[6] as
he did. He is ambitious of founding a family, and of allying
himself with nobility; and is thus as willing as other grown
children, to throw away thousands for a gew-gaw,[7] though he
would not part with a penny for charity. Next to him is my
brother, whom you know as well as I do. He has finished his
education with credit, and as he never ventures to oppose me
in anything, I have no doubt he is very sensible. He has good
manners, is a model of dress, and is reckoned ornamental in

all societies. Next to him is Miss Crotchet, my sister-in-law that is to be. You see she is rather pretty, and very genteel. She is tolerably accomplished, has her table always covered with new novels, thinks Mr. Mac Quedy an oracle, and is extremely desirous to be called "my lady." Next to her is Mr. Firedamp, a very absurd person, who thinks that water is the evil principle. Next to him is Mr. Eavesdrop, a man who, by dint of a certain something like smartness, has got into good society. He is a sort of bookseller's tool, and coins all his acquaintance in reminiscences and sketches of character. I am very shy of him, for fear he should print me.[8]

CAPTAIN FITZCHROME.

If he print you in your own likeness, which is that of an angel, you need not fear him. If he print you in any other, I will cut his throat. But proceed—

LADY CLARINDA.

Next to him is Mr. Henbane, the toxicologist,[9] I think he calls himself. He has passed half his life in studying poisons and antidotes. The first thing he did on his arrival here, was to kill the cat; and while Miss Crotchet was crying over her, he brought her to life again. I am more shy of him than the other.

CAPTAIN FITZCHROME.

They are two very dangerous fellows, and I shall take care to keep them both at a respectful distance. Let us hope that Eavesdrop will sketch off Henbane, and that Henbane will poison him for his trouble.

LADY CLARINDA.

Well, next to him, sits Mr. Mac Quedy, the Modern Athenian, who lays down the law about every thing, and therefore may be taken to understand every thing. He turns all the affairs of this world into questions of buying and selling. He is the Spirit of the Frozen Ocean[10] to every thing like romance

43

and sentiment. He condenses their volume of steam into a drop of cold water in a moment. He has satisfied me that I am a commodity in the market, and that I ought to set myself at a high price. So you see, he who would have me must bid for me.

CAPTAIN FITZCHROME.

I shall discuss that point with Mr. Mac Quedy.

LADY CLARINDA.

Not a word for your life. Our flirtation is our own secret. Let it remain so.

CAPTAIN FITZCHROME.

Flirtation, Clarinda! Is that all that the most ardent—

LADY CLARINDA.

Now, don't be rhapsodical here. Next to Mr. Mac Quedy is Mr. Skionar, a sort of poetical philosopher, a curious compound of the intense and the mystical. He abominates all the ideas of Mr. Mac Quedy, and settles every thing by sentiment and intuition.

CAPTAIN FITZCHROME.

Then, I say, he is the wiser man.

LADY CLARINDA.

They are two oddities, but a little of them is amusing, and I like to hear them dispute. So you see I am in training for a philosopher myself.

CAPTAIN FITZCHROME.

Any philosophy, for heaven's sake, but the pound-shilling-and-pence philosophy of Mr. Mac Quedy.

LADY CLARINDA.

Why they say that even Mr. Skionar, though he is a great dreamer, always dreams with his eyes open, or with one eye at any rate, which is an eye to his gain:[11] but I believe that in this respect the poor man has got an ill name by keeping bad company. He has two dear friends, Mr. Wilful Wontsee, and Mr. Rumblesack Shantsee,[12] poets of some note, who used to see visions of Utopia, and pure republics beyond the Western deep: but, finding that these El Dorados brought them no revenue, they turned their vision-seeing faculty into the more profitable channel of espying all sorts of virtues in the high and the mighty, who were able and willing to pay for the discovery.

CAPTAIN FITZCHROME.

I do not fancy these virtue-spyers.

LADY CLARINDA.

Next to Mr. Skionar, sits Mr. Chainmail,[13] a good-looking young gentleman, as you see, with very antiquated tastes. He is fond of old poetry, and is something of a poet himself. He is deep in monkish literature, and holds that the best state of society was that of the twelfth century, when nothing was going forward but fighting, feasting, and praying, which he says are the three great purposes for which man was made. He laments bitterly over the inventions of gunpowder, steam, and gas,[14] which he says have ruined the world. He lives within two or three miles, and has a large hall, adorned with rusty pikes, shields, helmets, swords, and tattered banners, and furnished with yew-tree chairs, and two long old worm-eaten oak tables, where he dines with all his household, after the fashion of his favorite age. He wants us all to dine with him, and I believe we shall go.

CAPTAIN FITZCHROME.

That will be something new at any rate.

LADY CLARINDA.

Next to him is Mr. Toogood, the co-operationist, who will have neither fighting nor praying; but wants to parcel out the world into squares like a chess-board, with a community on each, raising everything for one another, with a great steam-engine to serve them in common for tailor and hosier, kitchen and cook.[15]

CAPTAIN FITZCHROME.

He is the strangest of the set, so far.

LADY CLARINDA.

This brings us to the bottom of the table, where sits my humble servant, Mr. Crotchet the younger. I ought not to describe him.

CAPTAIN FITZCHROME.

I entreat you do.

LADY CLARINDA.

Well, I really have very little to say in his favor.

CAPTAIN FITZCHROME.

I do not wish to hear any thing in his favor; and I rejoice to hear you say so, because—

LADY CLARINDA.

Do not flatter yourself. If I take him, it will be to please my father, and to have a town and country-house,[16] and plenty of servants, and a carriage and an opera-box, and make some of my acquaintance who have married for love, or for rank, or for any thing but money, die for envy of my jewels. You do not think I would take him for himself. Why he is very smooth and spruce, as far as his dress goes; but as to his face, he looks as if he had tumbled headlong into a volcano, and been thrown up again among the cinders.

CAPTAIN FITZCHROME.

I cannot believe, that, speaking thus of him, you mean to take him at all.

LADY CLARINDA.

Oh! I am out of my teens. I have been very much in love; but now I am come to years of discretion, and must think, like other people, of settling myself advantageously. He was in love with a banker's daughter, and cast her off on her father's bankruptcy, and the poor girl has gone to hide herself in some wild place.

CAPTAIN FITZCHROME.

She must have a strange taste, if she pines for the loss of him.

LADY CLARINDA.

They say he was good-looking, till his bubble-schemes, as they call them, stamped him with the physiognomy of a desperate gambler. I suspect he has still a *penchant* towards his first flame. If he takes me, it will be for my rank and connexion, and the second seat of the borough of Rogueingrain. So we shall meet on equal terms, and shall enjoy all the blessedness of expecting nothing from each other.

CAPTAIN FITZCHROME.

You can expect no security with such an adventurer.

LADY CLARINDA.

I shall have the security of a good settlement, and then if *andare al diavolo*[17] be his destiny, he may go, you know, by himself. He is almost always dreaming and *distrait*.[18] It is very likely that some great reverse is in store for him: but that will not concern me, you perceive.

CAPTAIN FITZCHROME.

You torture me, Clarinda, with the bare possibility.

LADY CLARINDA.

Hush! Here is music to sooth your troubled spirit. Next to him, on this side, sits the dilettante composer, Mr. Trillo; they say his name was O'Trill, and he has taken the O from the beginning, and put it at the end. I do not know how this may be. He plays well on the violoncello, and better on the piano; sings agreeably; has a talent at verse-making, and improvises a song with some felicity. He is very agreeable company in the evening, with his instruments and music-books. He maintains that the sole end of all enlightened society is to get up a good opera, and laments that wealth, genius, and energy, are squandered upon other pursuits, to the neglect of this one great matter.[19]

CAPTAIN FITZCHROME.

That is a very pleasant fancy at any rate.

LADY CLARINDA.

I assure you he has a great deal to say for it. Well, next to him again, is Dr. Morbific,[20] who has been all over the world to prove that there is no such thing as contagion; and has inoculated himself with plague, yellow fever, and every variety of pestilence, and is still alive to tell the story. I am very shy of him, too; for I look on him as a walking phial of wrath, corked full of all infections, and not to be touched without extreme hazard.

CAPTAIN FITZCHROME.

This is the strangest fellow of all.

LADY CLARINDA.

Next to him sits Mr. Philpot,* the geographer, who thinks of nothing but the heads and tails of rivers, and lays down the streams of Terra Incognita as accurately as if he had been there. He is a person of pleasant fancy, and makes a sort of fairy land of every country he touches, from the Frozen Ocean to the Deserts of Zahara.[21]

CAPTAIN FITZCHROME.

How does he settle matters with Mr. Firedamp?

LADY CLARINDA.

You see Mr. Firedamp has got as far as possible out of his way. Next to him is Sir Simon Steeltrap,[22] of Steeltrap

---

* ΦΙΛοΠΟΤαμος. *Fluviorum amans.*

Lodge, Member for Crouching-Curtown, Justice of Peace for
the county, and Lord of the United Manors of Springgun-
and-Treadmill; a great preserver of game and public morals.
By administering the laws which he assists in making, he
disposes, at his pleasure, of the land and its live stock, including all the two-legged varieties, with and without feathers,
in a circumference of several miles round Steeltrap Lodge.
He has enclosed commons and woodlands; abolished cottage-
gardens; taken the village cricket-ground into his own park,
out of pure regard to the sanctity of Sunday;[23] shut up footpaths and alehouses, (all but those which belong to his electioneering friend, Mr. Quassia, the brewer;)[24] put down fairs
and fiddlers; committed many poachers; shot a few; convicted
one third of the peasantry; suspected the rest; and passed nearly
the whole of them through a wholesome course of prison discipline, which has finished their education at the expense of
the county.[25]

CAPTAIN FITZCHROME.

He is somewhat out of his element here: among such a
diversity of opinions he will hear some he will not like.

LADY CLARINDA.

It was rather ill-judged in Mr. Crotchet to invite him today.
But the art of assorting company is above these *parvenus*.[26]
They invite a certain number of persons without considering
how they harmonise with each other. Between Sir Simon and
you is the Reverend Doctor Folliott. He is said to be an excellent scholar, and is fonder of books than the majority of his
cloth; he is very fond, also, of the good things of this world.
He is of an admirable temper, and says rude things in a pleasant half-earnest manner, that nobody can take offence with.
And next to him again is one Captain Fitzchrome, who is
very much in love with a certain person that does not mean

to have any thing to say to him, because she can better her fortune by taking somebody else.

CAPTAIN FITZCHROME.

And next to him again is the beautiful, the accomplished, the witty, the fascinating, the tormenting, Lady Clarinda,[27] who traduces herself to the said Captain by assertions which it would drive him crazy to believe.

LADY CLARINDA.

Time will show, sir. And now we have gone the round of the table.

CAPTAIN FITZCHROME.

But I must say, though I know you had always a turn for sketching characters, you surprise me by your observation, and especially by your attention to opinions.

LADY CLARINDA.

Well, I will tell you a secret: I am writing a novel.

CAPTAIN FITZCHROME.

A novel!

LADY CLARINDA.

Yes, a novel. And I shall get a little finery by it: trinkets and fal-lals,[28] which I cannot get from papa. You must know I had been reading several fashionable novels, the fashionable this, and the fashionable that; and I thought to myself, why I can do better than any of these myself. So I wrote a chapter or two, and sent them as a specimen to Mr. Puffall, the bookseller,[29] telling him they were to be a part of the fashionable something or other, and he offered me, I will not say how much, to finish it in three volumes, and let him pay all the newspapers for recommending it as the work of a lady of quality, who had made very free with the characters of her acquaintance.[30]

CAPTAIN FITZCHROME.

Surely you have not done so?

LADY CLARINDA.

Oh, no! I leave that to Mr. Eavesdrop. But Mr. Puffall made it a condition that I should let him say so.

CAPTAIN FITZCHROME.

A strange recommendation.

LADY CLARINDA.

Oh, nothing else will do. And it seems you may give yourself any character you like, and the newspapers will print it as if it came from themselves. I have commended you to three of our friends here, as an economist, a transcendentalist, and a classical scholar; and if you wish to be renowned through the world for these, or any other accomplishments, the newspapers will confirm you in their possession for half-a-guinea a piece.

CAPTAIN FITZCHROME.

Truly, the praise of such gentry must be a feather in any one's cap.

LADY CLARINDA.

So you will see, some morning, that my novel is "the most popular production of the day." This is Mr. Puffall's favorite phrase. He makes the newspapers say it of every thing he publishes. But "the day," you know, is a very convenient phrase; it allows of three hundred and sixty-five "most popular productions" in a year. And in leap-year one more.

CHAPTER VI.

THEORIES.

But when they came to shape the model,
Not one could fit the other's noddle.

BUTLER.[1]

Meanwhile, the last course, and the dessert, past by. When the ladies had withdrawn, young Crotchet addressed the company.

MR. CROTCHET, JUN.

There is one point in which philosophers of all classes seem to be agreed; that they only want money to regenerate the world.

MR. MAC QUEDY.

No doubt of it. Nothing is so easy as to lay down the outlines of perfect society. There wants nothing but money to set it going. I will explain myself clearly and fully by reading a paper. *(Producing a large scroll.)* "In the infancy of society— "

THE REV. DR. FOLLIOTT.

Pray, Mr. Mac Quedy, how is it that all gentlemen of your nation begin every thing they write with the "infancy of society?"

MR. MAC QUEDY.

Eh, sir, it is the simplest way to begin at the beginning. "In the infancy of society, when government was invented to save a percentage;[2] say two and a half per cent—."

THE REV. DR. FOLLIOTT.

I will not say any such thing.

MR. MAC QUEDY.

Well, say any percentage you please.

THE REV. DR. FOLLIOTT.

I will not say any percentage at all.

MR. MAC QUEDY.

"On the principle of the division of labor—"[3]

THE REV. DR. FOLLIOTT.

Government was invented to spend a percentage.

MR. MAC QUEDY.

To save a percentage.

THE REV. DR. FOLLIOTT.

No, sir, to spend a percentage; and a good deal more than two and a half per cent. Two hundred and fifty per cent.: that is intelligible.

MR. MAC QUEDY.

"In the infancy of society"—

MR. TOOGOOD.

Never mind the infancy of society. The question is of society in its maturity. Here is what it should be. *(Producing a paper.)* I have laid it down in a diagram.[4]

MR. SKIONAR.

Before we proceed to the question of government, we must nicely discriminate the boundaries of sense, understanding, and reason. Sense is a receptivity—[5]

MR. CROTCHET, JUN.

We are proceeding too fast. Money being all that is wanted to regenerate society, I will put into the hands of this company a large sum for the purpose. Now let us see how to dispose of it.

MR. MAC QUEDY.

We will begin by taking a committee-room in London, where we will dine together once a week, to deliberate.

THE REV. DR. FOLLIOTT.

If the money is to go in deliberative dinners, you may set me down for a committee man and honorary caterer.

MR. MAC QUEDY.

Next, you must all learn political economy, which I will teach you, very compendiously, in lectures over the bottle.

THE REV. DR. FOLLIOTT.

I hate lectures over the bottle. But pray, sir, what is political economy?

MR. MAC QUEDY.

Political economy is to the state what domestic economy is to the family.[6]

THE REV. DR. FOLLIOTT.

No such thing, sir. In the family there is a *paterfamilias*, who regulates the distribution, and takes care that there shall be no such thing in the household as one dying of hunger, while another dies of surfeit. In the state it is all hunger at one end, and all surfeit at the other. Matchless Claret, Mr. Crotchet.

MR. CROTCHET.

Vintage of fifteen, Doctor.

MR. MAC QUEDY.

The family consumes, and so does the state.[7]

THE REV. DR. FOLLIOTT.

Consumes, sir! Yes: but the mode, the proportions: there is the essential difference between the state and the family. Sir, I hate false analogies.

MR. MAC QUEDY.

Well, sir, the analogy is not essential. Distribution will come under its proper head.

THE REV. DR. FOLLIOTT.

Come where it will, the distribution of the state is in no respect analogous to the distribution of the family. The *pater-familias*, sir: the *paterfamilias*.

MR. MAC QUEDY.

Well, sir, let that pass. The family consumes, and in order to consume, it must have supply.

THE REV. DR. FOLLIOTT.

Well, sir, Adam and Eve knew that, when they delved and span.[8]

MR. MAC QUEDY.

Very true, sir, *(reproducing his scroll,)* "In the infancy of society—"

MR. TOOGOOD.

The reverend gentleman has hit the nail on the head. It is the distribution that must be looked to: it is the *paterfamilias* that is wanting in the state. Now here I have provided him. *(Reproducing his diagram.)*

MR. TRILLO.

Apply the money, sir, to building and endowing an opera house, where the ancient altar of Bacchus[9] may flourish, and justice may be done to sublime compositions. *(Producing a part of a manuscript opera.)*

MR. SKIONAR.

No, sir, build *sacella*[10] for transcendental oracles to teach the world how to see through a glass darkly.[11] *(Producing a scroll.)*

MR. TRILLO.

See through an opera-glass brightly.

THE REV. DR. FOLLIOTT.

See through a wine-glass, full of Claret: then you see both darkly and brightly. But, gentlemen, if you are all in the humor for reading papers, I will read you the first half of my next Sunday's sermon. *(Producing a paper.)*

OMNES.
No sermon! No sermon!

THE REV. DR. FOLLIOTT.
Then I move that our respective papers be committed to our respective pockets.

MR. MAC QUEDY.
Political economy is divided into two great branches, production and consumption.

THE REV. DR. FOLLIOTT.
Yes, sir; there are two great classes of men: those who produce much and consume little; and those who consume much and produce nothing. The *fruges consumere nati*,[12] have the best of it. Eh, Captain! You remember the characteristics of a great man according to Aristophanes: ὅστις γε πίνειν οἶδε καὶ βίνειν μόνον. Ha! ha! ha! Well, Captain, even in these tight-laced days, the obscurity of a learned language allows a little pleasantry.[13]

CAPTAIN FITZCHROME.
Very true, sir: the pleasantry and the obscurity go together: they are all one, as it were;—to me at any rate. *(aside.)*

MR. MAC QUEDY.
Now, sir—

THE REV. DR. FOLLIOTT.
Pray, sir, let your science alone, or you will put me under the painful necessity of demolishing it bit by bit, as I have done your exordium.[14] I will undertake it any morning; but it is too hard exercise after dinner.

MR. MAC QUEDY.

Well, sir, in the mean time I hold my science established.

THE REV. DR. FOLLIOTT.

And I hold it demolished.

MR. CROTCHET, JUN.

Pray, gentlemen, pocket your manuscripts; fill your glasses; and consider what we shall do with our money.

MR. MAC QUEDY.

Build lecture rooms, and schools for all.

MR. TRILLO.

Revive the Athenian theatre; regenerate the lyrical drama.[15]

MR. TOOGOOD.

Build a grand co-operative parallelogram, with a steam-engine in the middle for a maid of all work.

MR. FIREDAMP.

Drain the country, and get rid of *malaria*, by abolishing duck-ponds.

DR. MORBIFIC.

Found a philanthropic college of anti-contagionists, where all the members shall be inoculated with the virus of all known diseases. Try the experiment on a grand scale.

MR. CHAINMAIL.

Build a great dining-hall: endow it with beef and ale, and hang the hall round with arms to defend the provisions.

MR. HENBANE.

Found a toxicological institution for trying all poisons and antidotes. I myself have killed a frog twelve times and brought him to life eleven; but the twelfth time he died. I have a phial of the drug, which killed him, in my pocket, and shall not rest till I have discovered its antidote.

THE REV. DR. FOLLIOTT.

I move that the last speaker be dispossessed of his phial, and that it be forthwith thrown into the Thames.

MR. HENBANE.

How, sir? my invaluable, and, in the present state of human knowledge, infallible poison?

THE REV. DR. FOLLIOTT.

Let the frogs have all the advantage of it.[16]

MR. CROTCHET.

Consider, Doctor, the fish might participate. Think of the salmon.

THE REV. DR. FOLLIOTT.

Then let the owner's right-hand neighbour swallow it.

MR. EAVESDROP.

Me, sir! What have I done, sir, that I am to be poisoned, sir?

THE REV. DR. FOLLIOTT.

Sir, you have published a character of your facetious friend, the Reverend Doctor F., wherein you have sketched off me; me, sir, even to my nose and wig. What business have the public with my nose and wig?

MR. EAVESDROP.

Sir, it is all good humored: all in *bonhommie*:[17] all friendly and complimentary.

THE REV. DR. FOLLIOTT.

Sir, the bottle, *la Dive Bouteille*,[18] is a recondite oracle, which makes an Eleusinian temple of the circle in which it moves. He who reveals its mysteries must die.[19] Therefore, let the dose be administered. *Fiat experimentum in animâ vili.*[20]

MR. EAVESDROP.

Sir, you are very facetious at my expense.

THE REV. DR. FOLLIOTT.

Sir, you have been very unfacetious,[21] very inficete[22] at mine. You have dished me up, like a savory omelette, to gratify the appetite of the reading rabble for gossip. The next time, sir, I will respond with the *argumentum baculinum*.[23] Print that, sir: put it on record as a promise of the Reverend Doctor F., which shall be most faithfully kept, with an exemplary bamboo.

MR. EAVESDROP.

Your cloth protects you, sir.

THE REV. DR. FOLLIOTT.

My bamboo shall protect me, sir.

MR. CROTCHET.

Doctor, Doctor, you are growing too polemical.

THE REV. DR. FOLLIOTT.

Sir, my blood boils. What business have the public with my nose and wig?

MR. CROTCHET.

Doctor! Doctor!

MR. CROTCHET, JUN.

Pray, gentlemen, return to the point. How shall we employ our fund?

MR. PHILPOT.

Surely in no way so beneficially as in exploring rivers. Send a fleet of steam-boats down the Niger, and another up the Nile. So shall you civilize Africa, and establish stocking factories in Abyssinia and Bambo.[24]

THE REV. DR. FOLLIOTT.

With all submission, breeches and petticoats must precede stockings. Send out a crew of tailors. Try if the King of Bambo will invest inexpressibles.[25]

MR. CROTCHET, JUN.

Gentlemen, it is not for partial, but for general benefit, that this fund is proposed: a grand and universally applicable scheme for the amelioration of the condition of man.

SEVERAL VOICES.

That is my scheme. I have not heard a scheme but my own that has a grain of common sense.

MR. TRILLO.

Gentlemen, you inspire me. Your last exclamation runs itself into a chorus, and sets itself to music. Allow me to lead, and to hope for your voices in harmony.[26]

> After careful meditation,
> And profound deliberation,

On the various pretty projects which have just been shown,

> Not a scheme in agitation,
> For the world's amelioration,

Has a grain of common sense in it, except my own.

SEVERAL VOICES.

We are not disposed to join in any such chorus.

THE REV. DR. FOLLIOTT.

Well, of all these schemes, I am for Mr. Trillo's. Regenerate the Athenian theatre. My classical friend here, the Captain, will vote with me.

CAPTAIN FITZCHROME.

I, sir? oh! of course, sir.

MR. MAC QUEDY.

Surely, Captain, I rely on you to uphold political economy.

CAPTAIN FITZCHROME.

Me, sir! oh, to be sure, sir.

THE REV. DR. FOLLIOTT.

Pray, sir, will political economy uphold the Athenian theatre?

MR. MAC QUEDY.

Surely not. It would be a very unproductive investment.

THE REV. DR. FOLLIOTT.

Then the Captain votes against you. What, sir, did not the
Athenians, the wisest of nations, appropriate to their theatre
their most sacred and intangible fund? Did not they give to
melopœia, choregraphy, and the sundry forms of didascalics,[27]
the precedence of all other matters, civil and military? Was it
not their law, that even the proposal to divert this fund to
any other purpose should be punished with death? But, sir, I
further propose that the Athenian theatre being resuscitated,
the admission shall be free to all who can expound the Greek
choruses, constructively, mythologically, and metrically, and
to none others.[28] So shall all the world learn Greek: Greek,
the Alpha and Omega of all knowledge. At him who sits not
in the theatre, shall be pointed the finger of scorn: he shall be
called in the highway of the city, "a fellow without Greek."

MR. TRILLO.

But the ladies, sir, the ladies.

THE REV. DR. FOLLIOTT.

Every man may take in a lady: and she who can construe and
metricise[29] a chorus, shall, if she so please, pass in by herself.[30]

MR. TRILLO.

But, sir, you will shut me out of my own theatre. Let there
at least be a double passport, Greek and Italian.

THE REV. DR. FOLLIOTT.

No, sir; I am inexorable. No Greek, no theatre.

MR. TRILLO.

Sir, I cannot consent to be shut out from my own theatre.

THE REV. DR. FOLLIOTT.

You see how it is, Squire Crotchet the younger; you can scarcely find two to agree on a scheme, and no two of those can agree on the details. Keep your money in your pocket. And so ends the fund for regenerating the world.[31]

MR. MAC QUEDY.

Nay, by no means. We are all agreed on deliberative dinners.[32]

THE REV. DR. FOLLIOTT.

Very true; we will dine and discuss. We will sing with Robin Hood, "If I drink water while this doth last;"[33] and while it lasts we will have no adjournment, if not to the Athenian theatre.

MR. TRILLO.

Well, gentlemen, I hope this chorus at least will please you:

> If I drink water while this doth last,
> May I never again drink wine:
> For how can a man, in his life of a span,
> Do any thing better than dine?
> We'll dine and drink, and say if we think
> That any thing better can be,
> And when we have dined, wish all mankind
> May dine as well as we.
> And though a good wish will fill no dish
> And brim no cup with sack,
> Yet thoughts will spring, as the glasses ring,
> To illume our studious track.
> On the brilliant dreams of our hopeful schemes
> The light of the flask shall shine;

And we'll sit till day, but we'll find the way
To drench the world with wine.

The schemes for the world's regeneration evaporated in a tumult of voices.

CHAPTER VII.

THE SLEEPING VENUS.

Quoth he: In all my life till now,
I ne'er saw so profane a show.

BUTLER.[1]

THE library of Crotchet castle was a large and well-furnished apartment, opening on one side into an anti-room, on the other into a music-room.[2] It had several tables stationed at convenient distances; one consecrated[3] to the novelties of literature, another to the novelties of embellishment; others unoccupied, and at the disposal of the company. The walls were covered with a copious collection of ancient and modern books; the ancient having been selected and arranged by the Reverend Doctor Folliott.[4] In the anti-room were card-tables; in the music-room were various instruments, all popular operas, and all fashionable music. In this suite of apartments, and not in the drawing-room, were the evenings of Crotchet castle usually passed.[5]

The young ladies were in the music-room; Miss Crotchet at the piano, Lady Clarinda at the harp, playing and occasionally singing, at the suggestion of Mr. Trillo, portions of *Matilde di Shabran*.[6] Lord Bossnowl was turning over the leaves for Miss Crotchet; the Captain was performing the same office for Lady Clarinda, but with so much more attention to the lady than the book, that he often made sad work with the harmony, by turning over two leaves together. On these occasions Miss Crotchet paused, Lady Clarinda laughed, Mr. Trillo scolded, Lord Bossnowl yawned, the Captain apologised, and the performance proceeded.

In the library, Mr. Mac Quedy was expounding political economy to the Reverend Doctor Folliott, who was *pro more* demolishing its doctrines *seriatim*.[7]

Mr. Chainmail was in hot dispute with Mr. Skionar, touching the physical and moral well-being of man. Mr. Skionar was enforcing his friend Mr. Shantsee's views of moral discipline; maintaining that the sole thing needful for man in this world, was loyal and pious education; the giving men good books to read, and enough of the hornbook[8] to read them; with a judicious interspersion of the lessons of Old Restraint, which was his poetic name for the parish stocks.[9] Mr. Chainmail, on the other hand, stood up for the exclusive necessity of beef and ale, lodging and raiment, wife and children, courage to fight for them all, and armour wherewith to do so.

Mr. Henbane had got his face scratched, and his finger bitten, by the cat, in trying to catch her for a second experiment in killing and bringing to life; and Doctor Morbific was comforting him with a disquisition, to prove that there were only four animals having the power to communicate hydrophobia, of which the cat was one; and that it was not necessary that the animal should be in a rabid state, the nature of the wound being everything, and the idea of contagion a delusion. Mr. Henbane was listening very lugubriously to this dissertation.

Mr. Philpot had seized on Mr. Firedamp, and pinned him down to a map of Africa, on which he was tracing imaginary courses of mighty inland rivers, terminating in lakes and marshes, where they were finally evaporated by the heat of the sun; and Mr. Firedamp's hair was standing on end at the bare imagination of the mass of *malaria* that must be engendered by the operation. Mr. Toogood had begun explaining his diagrams to Sir Simon Steeltrap; but Sir Simon grew testy, and told Mr. Toogood that the promulgators of such doctrines ought to be consigned to the treadmill. The philanthropist walked off from the country gentleman, and proceeded to hold forth to young Crotchet, who stood silent, as one who listens, but in reality without hearing a syllable. Mr. Crotchet senior, as the master of the house, was left to entertain himself with his own meditations, till the Reverend Doctor Folliott tore himself from Mr. Mac Quedy, and proceeded to expostulate with Mr. Crotchet on a delicate topic.

There was an Italian painter, who obtained the name of *Il Bragatore*, by the superinduction of inexpressibles[10] on the naked Apollos and Bacchuses of his betters.[11] The fame of this worthy remained one and indivisible, till a set of heads, which had been, by a too common mistake of nature's journeymen, stuck upon magisterial shoulders, as the Corinthian capitals of "fair round bellies with fat capon lined,"[12] but which nature herself had intended for the noddles of porcelain mandarins,[13] promulgated simultaneously from the east and the west of London, an order that no plaster-of-Paris Venus should appear in the streets without petticoats.[14] Mr. Crotchet, on reading this order in the evening paper, which, by the postman's early arrival, was always laid on his breakfast-table, determined to fill his house with Venuses of all sizes and kinds.[15] In pursuance of this resolution, came packages by water-carriage, containing an infinite variety of Venuses. There were the Medicean Venus, and the Bathing Venus; the Uranian Venus, and the Pandemian Venus; the Crouching Venus, and the Sleeping Venus; the Venus rising from the sea, the Venus with the apple of Paris, and the Venus with the armour of Mars.

The Reverend Doctor Folliott had been very much astonished at this unexpected display. Disposed, as he was, to hold, that whatever had been in Greece, was right;[16] he was more than doubtful of the propriety of throwing open the classical *adytum*[17] to the illiterate profane. Whether, in his interior mind, he was at all influenced, either by the consideration, that it would be for the credit of his cloth, with some of his vice-suppressing neighbours, to be able to say that he had expostulated; or by curiosity, to try what sort of defence his city-bred friend, who knew the classics only by translations, and whose reason was always a little a-head of his knowledge, would make for his somewhat ostentatious display of liberality in matters of taste; is a question, on which the learned may differ: but, after having duly deliberated on two full-sized casts of the Uranian and Pandemian Venus, in niches on each side of the chimney, and on three alabaster figures, in glass cases, on the mantelpiece, he proceeded, peirastically,[18] to open his fire.

THE REV. DR. FOLLIOTT.

These little alabaster figures on the mantelpiece, Mr. Crotchet, and those large figures in the niches,—may I take the liberty to ask you what they are intended to represent?

MR. CROTCHET.

Venus, sir; nothing more, sir; just Venus.

THE REV. DR. FOLLIOTT.

May I ask you, sir, why they are there?

MR. CROTCHET.

To be looked at, sir; just to be looked at: the reason for most things in a gentleman's house being in it at all; from the paper on the walls, and the drapery of the curtains, even to the books in the library, of which the most essential part is the appearance of the back.

THE REV. DR. FOLLIOTT.

Very true, sir. As great philosophers hold that the *esse* of things is *percipi*,[19] so a gentleman's furniture exists to be looked at. Nevertheless, sir, there are some things more fit to be looked at than others; for instance, there is nothing more fit to be looked at than the outside of a book. It is, as I may say, from repeated experience, a pure and unmixed pleasure to have a goodly volume lying before you, and to know that you may open it if you please, and need not open it unless you please. It is a resource against *ennui*,[20] if *ennui* should come upon you. To have the resource and not to feel the *ennui*, to enjoy your bottle in the present, and your book in the indefinite future, is a delightful condition of human existence. There is no place, in which a man can move or sit, in which the outside of a book can be otherwise than an innocent and becoming spectacle. Touching this matter, there cannot, I think, be two opinions. But with respect to your Venuses there can be, and indeed there are, two very distinct opinions. Now, sir, that little figure in the centre of the mantelpiece,—as a grave *paterfamilias*, Mr. Crotchet, with a fair nubile[21] daughter, whose eyes are like the fish-pools of Heshbon,[22]—I would ask you if you hold that figure to be altogether delicate?

MR. CROTCHET.

The Sleeping Venus, sir? Nothing can be more delicate than the entire contour of the figure, the flow of the hair on the shoulders and neck, the form of the feet and fingers. It is altogether a most delicate morsel.

THE REV. DR. FOLLIOTT.

Why, in that sense, perhaps, it is as delicate[23] as whitebait in July.[24] But the attitude, sir, the attitude.

MR. CROTCHET.

Nothing can be more natural, sir.

THE REV. DR. FOLLIOTT.

That is the very thing, sir. It is too natural: too natural, sir: it lies for all the world like —— I make no doubt, the pious cheesemonger, who recently broke its plaster fac-simile over the head of the itinerant vendor, was struck by a certain similitude to the position of his own sleeping beauty, and felt his noble wrath thereby justly aroused.[25]

MR. CROTCHET.

Very likely, sir. In my opinion, the cheesemonger was a fool, and the justice who sided with him was a greater.

THE REV. DR. FOLLIOTT.

Fool, sir, is a harsh term: call not thy brother a fool.

MR. CROTCHET.

Sir, neither the cheesemonger nor the justice is a brother of mine.

THE REV. DR. FOLLIOTT.

Sir, we are all brethren.

MR. CROTCHET.

Yes, sir, as the hangman is of the thief; the 'squire of the poacher; the judge of the libeller; the lawyer of his client; the statesman of his colleague; the bubble-blower of the bubble-buyer; the slave-driver of the negro; as these are brethren, so am I and the worthies in question.

THE REV. DR. FOLLIOTT.

To be sure, sir, in these instances, and in many others, the term brother must be taken in its utmost latitude of interpretation: we are all brothers, nevertheless. But to return to the point. Now these two large figures, one with drapery on the lower half of the body, and the other with no drapery at all; upon my word, sir, it matters not what godfathers and godmothers may have promised and vowed for the children of this world, touching the devil and other things to be renounced, if such figures as those are to be put before their eyes.

MR. CROTCHET.

Sir, the naked figure is the Pandemian Venus, and the half-draped figure is the Uranian Venus; and I say, sir, that figure realizes the finest imaginings of Plato,[26] and is the personification of the most refined and exalted feeling of which the human mind is susceptible; the love of pure, ideal, intellectual beauty.

THE REV. DR.FOLLIOTT.

I am aware, sir, that Plato, in his Symposium, discourseth very eloquently touching the Uranian and Pandemian Venus: but you must remember that, in our Universities, Plato is held to be little better than a misleader of youth; and they have shewn their contempt for him, not only by never reading him, (a mode of contempt in which they deal very largely,) but even by never printing a complete edition of him;[27] although they have printed many ancient books, which nobody suspects to have been ever read on the spot, except by a person attached to the press, who is therefore emphatically called "the reader."[28]

MR. CROTCHET.

Well, sir?

THE REV. DR. FOLLIOTT.

Why, sir, to "the reader" aforesaid, (supposing either of our Universities to have printed an edition of Plato,)[29] or to any one else who can be supposed to have read Plato, or indeed to be ever likely to do so, I would very willingly shew these figures; because to such they would, I grant you, be the outward and visible signs[30] of poetical and philosophical ideas: but, to the multitude, the gross carnal multitude, they are but two beautiful women, one half undressed, and the other quite so.

MR. CROTCHET.

Then, sir, let the multitude look upon them and learn modesty.

THE REV. DR. FOLLIOTT.

I must say that, if I wished my footman to learn modesty, I should not dream of sending him to school to a naked Venus.

MR. CROTCHET.

Sir, ancient sculpture is the true school of modesty. But where the Greeks had modesty, we have cant; where they had poetry, we have cant; where they had patriotism, we have cant; where they had any thing that exalts, delights, or adorns humanity, we have nothing but cant, cant, cant.[31] And, sir, to shew my contempt for cant in all its shapes, I have adorned my house with the Greek Venus, in all her shapes, and am ready to fight her battle, against all the societies that ever were instituted for the suppression of truth and beauty.[32]

THE REV. DR. FOLLIOTT.

My dear sir, I am afraid you are growing warm. Pray be cool. Nothing contributes so much to good digestion as to be perfectly cool after dinner.

MR. CROTCHET.

Sir, the Lacedæmonian virgins wrestled naked with young men; and they grew up, as the wise Lycurgus had foreseen, into the most modest of women, and the most exemplary of wives and mothers.[33]

THE REV. DR. FOLLIOTT.

Very likely, sir; but the Athenian virgins did no such thing, and they grew up into wives who stayed at home,—stayed at home, sir; and looked after their husbands' dinner,—his dinner, sir, you will please to observe.

MR. CROTCHET.

And what was the consequence of that, sir? that they were such very insipid persons that the husband would not go home to eat his dinner, but preferred the company of some Aspasia, or Lais.

THE REV. DR.FOLLIOTT.

Two very different persons, sir, give me leave to remark.

MR.CROTCHET.

Very likely, sir; but both too good to be married in Athens.

THE REV. DR. FOLLIOTT.

Sir, Lais was a Corinthian.[34]

MR. CROTCHET.

Od's vengeance, sir, some Aspasia and any other Athenian name of the same sort of person you like—

THE REV. DR. FOLLIOTT.

I do not like the sort of person at all: the sort of person I like, as I have already implied, is a modest woman, who stays at home and looks after her husband's dinner.

MR.CROTCHET.

Well, sir, that was not the taste of the Athenians. They preferred the society of women who would not have made any scruple about sitting as models to Praxiteles;[35] as you know, sir, very modest women in Italy did to Canova: one of whom, an Italian countess, being asked by an English lady, "how she could bear it?" answered "Very well; there was a good fire in the room."[36]

THE REV. DR. FOLLIOTT.

Sir, the English lady should have asked how the Italian lady's husband could bear it. The phials of my wrath would overflow if poor dear Mrs. Folliott ——: sir, in return for your story, I will tell you a story of my ancestor, Gilbert Folliott.[37] The devil haunted him, as he did Saint Francis, in the likeness of a beautiful damsel; but all he could get from the exemplary Gilbert was an admonition to wear a stomacher and longer petticoats.

MR. CROTCHET.

Sir, your story makes for my side of the question. It proves that the devil, in the likeness of a fair damsel, with short petticoats and no stomacher, was almost too much for Gilbert Folliott. The force of the spell was in the drapery.

THE REV. DR. FOLLIOTT.

Bless my soul, sir!

MR. CROTCHET.

Give me leave, sir. Diderot—

THE REV. DR. FOLLIOTT.

Who was he, sir?

MR. CROTCHET.

Who was he, sir? the sublime philosopher, the father of the encyclopædia, of all the encyclopædias that have ever been printed.[38]

THE REV. DR. FOLLIOTT.

Bless me, sir, a terrible progeny: they belong to the tribe of *Incubi*.[39]

MR. CROTCHET.

The great philosopher, Diderot,—

THE REV. DR. FOLLIOTT.

Sir, Diderot is not a man after my heart. Keep to the Greeks, if you please; albeit this Sleeping Venus is not an antique.

MR. CROTCHET.

Well, sir, the Greeks: why do we call the Elgin marbles[40] inestimable? Simply because they are true to nature. And why are they so superior in that point to all modern works, with all our greater knowledge of anatomy? Why, sir, but because the Greeks, having no cant, had better opportunities of studying models?

THE REV. DR. FOLLIOTT.

Sir, I deny our greater knowledge of anatomy. But I shall take the liberty to employ, on this occasion, the *argumentum ad hominem.*[41] Would you have allowed Miss Crotchet to sit for a model to Canova?

MR. CROTCHET.

Yes, sir.

"God bless my soul, sir!" exclaimed the Reverend Doctor Folliott, throwing himself back into a chair, and flinging up his heels, with the premeditated design of giving emphasis to his exclamation: but by miscalculating his *impetus,*[42] he overbalanced his chair, and laid himself on the carpet in a right angle, of which his back was the base.

CHAPTER VIII.

SCIENCE AND CHARITY.[1]

Chi sta nel mondo un par d'ore contento,
Nè gli vien tolta, ovver contaminata,
Quella sua pace in veruno momento,
Può dir che Giove drittamente il guata.

FORTEGUERRI.[2]

THE Reverend Doctor Folliott took his departure about ten o'clock, to walk home to his vicarage. There was no moon, but the night was bright and clear, and afforded him as much light as he needed. He paused a moment by the Roman camp,[3] to listen to the nightingale; repeated to himself a passage of Sophocles;[4] proceeded through the park gate, and entered the narrow lane that led to the village. He walked on in a very pleasant mood of the state called *reverie*;[5] in which fish and wine, Greek and political economy, the Sleeping Venus he had left behind, and poor dear Mrs. Folliott, to whose fond arms he was returning, passed as in a *camera obscura*,[6] over the tablets of his imagination. Presently the image of Mr. Eavesdrop, with a printed sketch of the Reverend Doctor F., presented itself before him, and he began mechanically to flourish his bamboo. The movement was prompted by his good genius,[7] for the uplifted bamboo received the blow of a ponderous[8] cudgel, which was intended for his head. The reverend gentleman recoiled two or three paces, and saw before him a couple of ruffians, who were preparing to renew the attack, but whom, with two swings of his bamboo, he laid with cracked sconces[9] on the earth, where he proceeded to deal with them like corn beneath the flail of the thresher. One of them drew a pistol, which went off in the very act of being struck aside by the bamboo, and lodged a bullet in the brain

75

of the other. There was then only one enemy, who vainly struggled to rise, every effort being attended with a new and more signal prostration. The fellow roared for mercy. "Mercy, rascal!" cried the divine; "what mercy were you going to shew me, villain? What! I warrant me, you thought it would be an easy matter, and no sin, to rob and murder a parson on his way home from dinner. You said to yourself, doubtless, "We'll waylay the fat parson, (you irreverent knave,) as he waddles home, (you disparaging ruffian,) half-seas-over, (you calumnious vagabond.)" And with every dyslogistic term,[10] which he supposed had been applied to himself, he inflicted a new bruise on his rolling and roaring antagonist. "Ah, rogue!" he proceeded, "you can roar now, marauder; you were silent enough when you devoted my brains to dispersion[11] under your cudgel. But seeing that I cannot bind you, and that I intend you not to escape, and that it would be dangerous to let you rise, I will disable you in all your members, I will contund you as Thestylis did strong-smelling herbs,*[12] in the quality whereof you do most gravely partake, as my nose beareth testimony, ill weed that you are. I will beat you to a jelly, and I will then roll you into the ditch, to lie till the constable comes for you, thief."

"Hold! hold! reverend sir," exclaimed the penitent culprit, "I am disabled already in every finger, and in every joint. I will roll myself into the ditch, reverend sir."

"Stir not, rascal," returned the divine, "stir not so much as the quietest leaf above you, or my bamboo rebounds on your body, like hail in a thunder-storm. Confess, speedily, villain; are you simple thief, or would you have manufactured me into

---

* Thestylis . . . . .
     . . . . herbas contundit olentes.

VIRG. *Ecl.* II. 10, 11.

a subject, for the benefit of science? Aye, miscreant caitiff,[13] you would have made me a subject for science,[14] would you? You are a schoolmaster abroad,[15] are you? You are marching with a detachment of the march of mind, are you? You are a member of the Steam Intellect Society, are you? You swear by the learned friend, do you?"

"Oh, no! reverend sir," answered the criminal, "I am innocent of all these offences, whatever they are, reverend sir. The only friend I had in the world is lying dead beside me, reverend sir."

The reverend gentleman paused a moment, and leaned on his bamboo. The culprit, bruised as he was, sprang on his legs, and went off in double quick time. The Doctor gave him chace, and had nearly brought him within arm's length, when the fellow turned at right angles, and sprang clean over a deep dry ditch. The divine, following with equal ardour, and less dexterity, went down over head and ears into a thicket of nettles. Emerging with much discomposure, he proceeded to the village, and roused the constable; but the constable found, on reaching the scene of action, that the dead man was gone, as well as his living accomplice.

"Oh, the monster!" exclaimed the Reverend Doctor Folliott, "he has made a subject for science of the only friend he had in the world." "Aye, my dear," he resumed, the next morning at breakfast, "if my old reading, and my early gymnastics, (for as the great Hermann says, before I was demulced by the Muses, I was *ferocis ingenii puer, et ad arma quam ad literas paratior,**)[16] had not imbued me indelibly with some of the holy rage of *Frère Jean des Entommeures,*[17] I should be, at this moment, lying on the table of some flinty-hearted anatomist,

---

* "A boy of fierce disposition, more inclined to arms than to letters."— HERMANN'S *Dedication of Homer's Hymns to his Preceptor Ilgen.*

who would have sliced and disjointed me as unscrupulously as I do these remnants of the capon and chine, wherewith you consoled yourself yesterday for my absence at dinner. Phew! I have a noble thirst upon me, which I will quench with floods of tea."

The reverend gentleman was interrupted by a messenger, who informed him that the Charity Commissioners[18] requested his presence at the inn, where they were holding a sitting.

"The Charity Commissioners!" exclaimed the reverend gentleman, "who on earth are they?"

The messenger could not inform him, and the reverend gentleman took his hat and stick, and proceeded to the inn.

On entering the best parlour, he saw three well-dressed and bulky gentlemen sitting at a table, and a fourth officiating as clerk, with an open book before him, and a pen in his hand. The churchwardens, who had been also summoned, were already in attendance.

The chief commissioner politely requested the Reverend Doctor Folliott to be seated, and after the usual meteorological preliminaries had been settled by a resolution, *nem. con.*,[19] that it was a fine day but very hot, the chief commissioner stated, that in virtue of the commission of Parliament, which they had the honor to hold, they were now to inquire into the state of the public charities of this village.

THE REV. DR. FOLLIOTT.

The state of the public charities, sir, is exceedingly simple. There are none. The charities here are all private, and so private, that I for one know nothing of them.

FIRST COMMISSIONER.

We have been informed, sir, that there is an annual rent charged on the land of Hautbois, for the endowment and repair of an almshouse.

THE REV. DR. FOLLIOTT.

Hautbois! Hautbois!

FIRST COMMISSIONER.

The manorial farm of Hautbois, now occupied by Farmer Seedling, is charged with the endowment and maintenance of an almshouse.

THE REV. DR. FOLLIOTT.
(to the Churchwarden.)

How is this, Mr. Bluenose?

FIRST CHURCHWARDEN.

I really do not know, sir. What say you, Mr. Appletwig?

MR. APPLETWIG.
(parish-clerk and schoolmaster; an old man.)

I do remember, gentlemen, to have been informed, that there did stand, at the end of the village, a ruined cottage, which had once been an almshouse, which was endowed and maintained, by an annual revenue of a mark and a half, or one pound sterling, charged some centuries ago on the farm of Hautbois; but the means, by the progress of time, having become inadequate to the end, the almshouse tumbled to pieces.

FIRST COMMISSIONER.

But this is a right which cannot be abrogated by desuetude,[20] and the sum of one pound per annum is still chargeable for charitable purposes on the manorial farm of Hautbois.

THE REV. DR. FOLLIOTT.

Very well, sir.

MR. APPLETWIG.

But sir, the one pound per annum is still received by the parish, but was long ago, by an unanimous vote in open vestry,[21] given to the minister.

79

THE THREE COMMISSIONERS.
(unâ voce.)

The minister!

FIRST COMMISSIONER.

This is an unjustifiable proceeding.

SECOND COMMISSIONER.

A misappropriation of a public fund.

THIRD COMMISSIONER.

A flagrant perversion of a charitable donation.

THE REV. DR. FOLLIOTT.

God bless my soul, gentlemen! I know nothing of this matter. How is this, Mr. Bluenose? Do I receive this one pound per annum?

FIRST CHURCHWARDEN.

Really, sir, I know no more about it than you do.

MR. APPLETWIG.

You certainly receive it, sir. It was voted to one of your predecessors. Farmer Seedling lumps it in with his tithes.

FIRST COMMISSIONER.

Lumps it in, sir! Lump in a charitable donation!

SECOND AND THIRD COMMISSIONER.

Oh-oh-oh-h-h!

FIRST COMMISSIONER.

Reverend sir, and gentlemen, officers of this parish, we are under the necessity of admonishing you that this is a most improper proceeding; and you are hereby duly admonished accordingly. Make a record, Mr. Milky.

MR. MILKY, *(writing.)*

The clergyman and churchwardens of the village of Hm-m-m-m- gravely admonished. Hm-m-m-m.

THE REV. DR. FOLLIOTT.

Is that all, gentlemen?

THE COMMISSIONERS.

That is all, sir; and we wish you a good morning.

THE REV. DR. FOLLIOTT.

A very good morning to you, gentlemen.

"What in the name of all that is wonderful, Mr. Bluenose," said the Reverend Doctor Folliott, as he walked out of the inn, "what in the name of all that is wonderful, can those fellows mean? They have come here in a chaise and four, to make a fuss about a pound per annum, which, after all, they leave as it was: I wonder who pays them for their trouble, and how much."

MR. APPLETWIG.

The public pay for it, sir. It is a job of the learned friend whom you admire so much. It makes away with public money in salaries, and private money in lawsuits, and does no particle of good to any living soul.

THE REV. DR. FOLLIOTT.

Aye, aye, Mr. Appletwig; that is just the sort of public service to be looked for from the learned friend. Oh, the learned friend! the learned friend! He is the evil genius of every thing that falls in his way.

The Reverend Doctor walked off to Crotchet Castle, to narrate his misadventures, and exhale his budget of grievances[22] on Mr. Mac Quedy, whom he considered a ringleader of the march of mind.

CHAPTER IX.

THE VOYAGE.

Οἱ μὲν ἔπειτ᾽ ἀναβάντες ἐπέπλεον ὑγρὰ κέλευθα.

Mounting the bark, they cleft the watery ways.

HOMER.[1]

Four beautiful cabined pinnaces,[2] one for the ladies, one for the gentlemen, one for kitchen and servants, one for a dining-room and band of music, weighed anchor, on a fine July morning, from below Crotchet Castle, and were towed merrily, by strong trotting horses, against the stream of the Thames. They passed from the district of chalk, successively into the districts of clay, of sand-rock, of oolite,[3] and so forth. Sometimes they dined in their floating dining-room, sometimes in tents, which they pitched on the dry smooth-shaven green of a newly-mown meadow: sometimes they left their vessels to see sights in the vicinity; sometimes they passed a day or two in a comfortable inn.

At Oxford, they walked about to see the curiosities of architecture, painted windows, and undisturbed libraries. The Reverend Doctor Folliott laid a wager with Mr. Crotchet "that in all their perlustrations[4] they would not find a man reading," and won it.[5] "Aye, sir," said the reverend gentleman, "this is still a seat of learning, on the principle of—once a captain, always a captain.[6] We may well ask, in these great reservoirs of books whereof no man ever draws a sluice, *Quorsum pertinuit stipare Platona Menandro?** [7] What is done here for the classics? Reprinting German editions on better paper. A great

---

* Wherefore is Plato on Menander piled?

HOR. *Sat.* II. 3, 11.

boast, verily! What for mathematics? What for metaphysics? What for history? What for any thing worth knowing?[8] This was a seat of learning in the days of Friar Bacon. But the Friar is gone, and his learning with him. Nothing of him is left but the immortal nose, which, when his brazen head had tumbled to pieces, crying "Time's Past," was the only palpable fragment among its minutely pulverized atoms, and which is still resplendent over the portals of its cognominal college.[9] That nose, sir, is the only thing to which I shall take off my hat, in all this Babylon of buried literature.[10]

MR. CROTCHET.

But, doctor, it is something to have a great reservoir of learning, at which some may draw if they please.

THE REV. DR. FOLLIOTT.

But, here, good care is taken that nobody shall please. If even a small drop from the sacred fountain, πίδακος ἐξ ἱερῆς ὀλίγη λιβάς,[11] as Callimachus has it, were carried off by any one, it would be evidence of something to hope for. But the system of dissuasion from all good learning is brought here to a pitch of perfection that baffles the keenest aspirant.[12] I run over to myself the names of the scholars of Germany, a glorious catalogue: [13] but ask for those of Oxford,—Where are they? The echoes of their courts, as vacant as their heads, will answer, Where are they? The tree shall be known by its fruit: and seeing that this great tree, with all its specious seeming, brings forth no fruit, I do denounce it as a barren fig.[14]

MR. MAC QUEDY.

I shall set you right on this point. We do nothing without motives. If learning get nothing but honor, and very little of that; and if the good things of this world, which ought to be the rewards of learning, become the mere gifts of self-interested patronage; you must not wonder if, in the finishing of education, the science which takes precedence of all others, should be the science of currying favor.

THE REV. DR. FOLLIOTT.

Very true, sir. Education is well finished, for all worldly purposes, when the head is brought into the state whereinto I am accustomed to bring a marrow-bone, when it has been set before me on a toast, with a white napkin wrapped round it. Nothing trundles along the high road of preferment so trimly as a well-biassed sconce, picked clean within and polished without; *totus teres atque rotundus.** [15] The perfection of the finishing lies in the bias, which keeps it trundling in the given direction. There is good and sufficient reason for the fig being barren, but it is not therefore the less a barren fig.

At Godstow, they gathered hazel on the grave of Rosamond;[16] and, proceeding on their voyage, fell into a discussion on legendary histories.

LADY CLARINDA.

History is but a tiresome thing in itself:[17] it becomes more agreeable the more romance is mixed up with it. The great enchanter has made me learn many things which I should never have dreamed of studying, if they had not come to me in the form of amusement.

THE REV. DR. FOLLIOTT.

What enchanter is that? There are two enchanters: he of the north,[18] and he of the south.

MR. TRILLO.

Rossini?

THE REV. DR. FOLLIOTT.

Aye, there is another enchanter. But I mean the great enchanter of Covent Garden:[19] he who, for more than a

---

* All smooth and round.

quarter of a century, has produced two pantomimes a year, to the delight of children of all ages; including myself at all ages. That is the enchanter for me. I am for the pantomimes. All the northern enchanter's romances put together, would not furnish materials for half the southern enchanter's pantomimes.

LADY CLARINDA.

Surely you do not class literature with pantomime?

THE REV. DR. FOLLIOTT.

In these cases, I do. They are both one, with a slight difference. The one is the literature of pantomime, the other is the pantomime of literature.[20] There is the same variety of character, the same diversity of story, the same copiousness of incident, the same research into costume, the same display of heraldry, falconry, minstrelsy, scenery, monkery, witchery, devilry, robbery, poachery, piracy, fishery, gipsy-astrology, demonology, architecture, fortification, castrametation,[21] navigation; the same running base of love and battle. The main difference is, that the one set of amusing fictions is told in music and action; the other in all the worst dialects of the English language. As to any sentence worth remembering,[22] any moral or political truth, any thing having a tendency, however remote, to make men wiser or better, to make them think, to make them ever think of thinking; they are both precisely alike: *nuspiam, nequaquam, nullibi, nullimodis.*[23]

LADY CLARINDA.

Very amusing, however.

THE REV. DR. FOLLIOTT.

Very amusing, very amusing.

MR. CHAINMAIL.

My quarrel with the northern enchanter is, that he has grossly misrepresented the twelfth century.[24]

THE REV. DR. FOLLIOTT.

He has misrepresented every thing, or he would not have been very amusing. Sober truth is but dull matter to the reading rabble. The angler, who puts not on his hook the bait that best pleases the fish, may sit all day on the bank without catching a gudgeon.*

MR. MAC QUEDY.

But how do you mean that he has misrepresented the twelfth century? By exhibiting some of its knights and ladies in the colors of refinement and virtue, seeing that they were all no better than ruffians, and something else that shall be nameless?

MR. CHAINMAIL.

By no means. By depicting them as much worse than they were, not, as you suppose, much better. No one would infer from his pictures, that theirs was a much better state of society[25] than this which we live in.

MR. MAC QUEDY.

No, nor was it. It was a period of brutality, ignorance, fanaticism, and tyranny; when the land was covered with castles, and every castle contained a gang of banditti, headed by a titled robber, who levied contributions with fire and sword; plundering, torturing, ravishing, burying his captives in loathsome dungeons, and broiling them on gridirons, to force from them the surrender of every particle of treasure which he suspected them of possessing; and fighting every now and then with the neighbouring lords, his conterminal[26] bandits, for the right of marauding on the boundaries. This was the twelfth century, as depicted by all contemporary historians and poets.[27]

---

* Eloquentiæ magister, nisi, tamquam piscator, eam imposuerit hamis escam, quam scierit appetituros esse pisciculos, sine spe prædæ moratur in scopulo.

PETRONIUS ARBITER.

MR. CHAINMAIL.

No, sir. Weigh the evidence of specific facts; you will find
more good than evil. Who was England's greatest hero; the
mirror of chivalry, the pattern of honor, the fountain of generosity, the model to all succeeding ages of military glory?
Richard the First. There is a king of the twelfth century.
What was the first step of liberty? Magna Charta. That was
the best thing ever done by lords. There are lords of the twelfth
century. You must remember, too, that these lords were petty
princes, and made war on each other as legitimately as the
heads of larger communities did or do. For their system of
revenue, it was, to be sure, more rough and summary than that
which has succeeded it, but it was certainly less searching and
less productive. And as to the people, I content myself with
these great points: that every man was armed, every man was a
good archer, every man could and would fight effectively, with
sword or pike, or even with oaken cudgel; no man would live
quietly without beef and ale; if he had them not, he fought till
he either got them, or was put out of condition to want them.
They were not, and could not be, subjected to that powerful
pressure of all the other classes of society, combined by gunpowder, steam, and *fiscality*,[28] which has brought them to that
dismal degradation in which we see them now. And there are
the people of the twelfth century.[29]

MR. MAC QUEDY.

As to your king, the enchanter has done him ample justice,
even in your own view.[30] As to your lords and their ladies,
he has drawn them too favorably, given them too many of
the false colors of chivalry, thrown too attractive a light on
their abominable doings. As to the people, he keeps them so
much in the background, that he can hardly be said to have
represented them at all, much less misrepresented them, which
indeed he could scarcely do, seeing that, by your own showing,

they were all thieves, ready to knock down any man for what they could not come by honestly.

MR. CHAINMAIL.

No, sir. They could come honestly by beef and ale, while they were left to their simple industry. When oppression interfered with them in that, then they stood on the defensive, and fought for what they were not permitted to come by quietly.

MR. MAC QUEDY.

If A., being aggrieved by B., knocks down C., do you call that standing on the defensive?

MR. CHAINMAIL.

That depends on who or what C. is.

THE REV. DR. FOLLIOTT.

Gentlemen, you will never settle this controversy, till you have first settled what is good for man in this world; the great question, *de finibus*,[31] which has puzzled all philosophers. If the enchanter has represented the twelfth century too brightly for one, and too darkly for the other of you, I should say, as an impartial man, he has represented it fairly. My quarrel with him is, that his works contain nothing worth quoting; and a book that furnishes no quotations, is *me judice*,[32] no book,—it is a plaything. There is no question about the amusement,— amusement of multitudes; but if he who amuses us most, is to be our enchanter κατ᾽ ἐξοχήν,[33] then my enchanter is the enchanter of Covent Garden.

CHAPTER X

THE VOYAGE, CONTINUED.

Continuant nostre routte, navigasmes par trois jours
sans rien descouvrir.   RABELAIS.[1]

"THERE is a beautiful structure," said Mr. Chainmail, as they glided by Lechlade church;[2] "a subject for the pencil, Captain. It is a question worth asking, Mr. Mac Quedy, whether the religious spirit which reared these edifices, and connected with them everywhere an asylum for misfortune, and a provision for poverty, was not better than the commercial spirit, which has turned all the business of modern life into schemes of profit, and processes of fraud and extortion. I do not see, in all your boasted improvements, any compensation for the religious charity of the twelfth century. I do not see any compensation for that kindly feeling which, within their own little communities, bound the several classes of society together, while full scope was left for the development of natural character, wherein individuals differed as conspicuously as in costume. Now, we all wear one conventional dress, one conventional face; we have no bond of union, but pecuniary interest; we talk any thing that comes uppermost, for talking's sake, and without expecting to be believed; we have no nature, no simplicity, no picturesqueness:[3] everything about us is as artificial and as complicated as our steam-machinery:[4] our poetry is a caleidoscope of false imagery, expressing no real feeling, portraying no real existence.[5] I do not see any compensation for the poetry of the twelfth century."

MR. MAC QUEDY.

I wonder to hear you, Mr. Chainmail, talking of the religious charity of a set of lazy monks, and beggarly friars, who were much more occupied with taking than giving; of whom, those who were in earnest did nothing but make themselves, and every body about them, miserable, with fastings, and penances, and other such trash; and those who were not, did nothing but guzzle and royster, and, having no wives of their own, took very unbecoming liberties with those of honester men. And as to your poetry of the twelfth century, it is not good for much.

MR. CHAINMAIL.

It has, at any rate, what ours wants, truth to nature, and simplicity of diction. The poetry, which was addressed to the people of the dark ages, pleased in proportion to the truth with which it depicted familiar images, and to their natural connexion with the time and place to which they were assigned. In the poetry of our enlightened times, the characteristics of all seasons, soils, and climates, may be blended together, with much benefit to the author's fame as an original genius. The cowslip of a civic poet is always in blossom, his fern is always in full feather; he gathers the celandine, the primrose, the heath-flower, the jasmine, and the chrysanthemum, all on the same day, and from the same spot; his nightingale sings all the year round, his moon is always full, his cygnet is as white as his swan, his cedar is as tremulous as his aspen, and his poplar as embowering as his beech.[6] Thus all nature marches with the march of mind; but, among barbarians, instead of mead and wine, and the best seat by the fire, the reward of such a genius would have been, to be summarily turned out of doors in the snow, to meditate on the difference between day and night, and between December and July. It is an age of liberality, indeed, when not to know an oak from a burdock is no disqualification for sylvan minstrelsy. I am for truth and simplicity.

THE REV. DR. FOLLIOTT.

Let him who loves them read Greek: Greek, Greek, Greek.

MR. MAC QUEDY.

If he can, sir.

THE REV. DR. FOLLIOTT.

Very true, sir; if he can. Here is the Captain who can. But I think he must have finished his education at some very rigid college, where a quotation, or any other overt act, shewing acquaintance with classical literature, was visited with a severe penalty. For my part, I make it my boast that I was not to be so subdued. I could not be abated of a single quotation by all the bumpers in which I was fined.[7]

In this manner they glided over the face of the waters, discussing every thing and settling nothing.[8] Mr. Mac Quedy and the Reverend Doctor Folliott had many digladiations[9] on political economy: wherein, each in his own view, Doctor Folliott demolished Mr. Mac Quedy's science, and Mr. Mac Quedy demolished Doctor Folliott's objections.

We would print these dialogues if we thought any one would read them: but the world is not yet ripe for this *haute sagesse Pantagrueline*.[10] We must therefore content ourselves with an *échantillon*[11] of one of the Reverend Doctor's perorations.

"You have given the name of a science to what is yet an imperfect inquiry:[12] and the upshot of your so-called science is this: that you increase the wealth of a nation by increasing in it the quantity of things which are produced by labor: no matter what they are, no matter how produced, no matter how distributed. The greater the quantity of labor that has gone to the production of the quantity of things in a community, the richer is the community.[13] That is your doctrine. Now, I say, if this be so, riches are not the object for a community to aim at. I say, the nation is best off, in relation to other nations, which has the greatest quantity of the common necessaries of life distributed among the greatest number of persons; which has the greatest number of honest hearts and stout arms united in a common interest, willing to offend no one, but ready to fight in defence of their own community, against all the rest of the world, because they have something in it worth fighting for. The moment you admit that one class of things, without any reference to what they respectively cost, is better worth having than another; that a smaller commercial value, with one mode of distribution, is better than a greater commercial value, with another mode of distribution; the whole of that curious fabric of postulates and dogmas, which you call the science of political economy, and which I call *politicæ œconomiæ inscientia*, tumbles to pieces."[14]

Mr. Toogood agreed with Mr. Chainmail against Mr. Mac Quedy, that the existing state of society was worse than that of the twelfth century; but he agreed with Mr. Mac Quedy against Mr. Chainmail, that it was in progress to something much better than either,—to which "something much better"[15] Mr. Toogood and Mr. Mac Quedy attached two very different meanings.

Mr. Chainmail fought with Doctor Folliott, the battle of the romantic against the classical in poetry;[16] and Mr. Skionar contended with Mr. Mac Quedy for intuition and synthesis, against analysis and induction in philosophy.[17]

Mr. Philpot would lie along for hours, listening to the gurgling of the water round the prow, and would occasionally edify the company with speculations on the great changes that would be effected in the world by the steam-navigation of rivers: sketching the course of a steam-boat up and down some mighty stream which civilization had either never visited, or long since deserted; the Missouri and the Columbia, the Oroonoko and the Amazon, the Nile and the Niger, the Euphrates[18] and the Tigris, the Oxus and the Indus, the Ganges and the Hoangho;[19] under the overcanopying forests of the new, or by the long-silent ruins of the ancient, world;

through the shapeless mounds of Babylon, or the gigantic temples of Thebes.[20]

Mr. Trillo went on with the composition of his opera, and took the opinions of the young ladies on every step in its progress; occasionally regaling the company with specimens; and wondering at the blindness of Mr. Mac Quedy, who could not, or would not, see that an opera in perfection, being the union of all the beautiful arts,[21]—music, painting, dancing, poetry,—exhibiting female beauty in its most attractive aspects, and in its most becoming costume,— was, according to the well-known precept, *Ingenuas didicisse, &c.,*[22] the most efficient instrument of civilization, and ought to take precedence of all other pursuits in the minds of true philanthropists. The Reverend Doctor Folliott, on these occasions, never failed to say a word or two on Mr. Trillo's side, derived from the practice of the Athenians, and from the combination, in their theatre, of all the beautiful arts, in a degree of perfection unknown to the modern world.[23]

Leaving Lechlade, they entered the canal that connects the Thames with the Severn; ascended by many locks; passed by a tunnel three miles long, through the bowels of Sapperton Hill; agreed unanimously that the greatest pleasure derivable from visiting a cavern of any sort was that of getting out of it;[24] descended by many locks again, through the valley of Stroud into the Severn; continued their navigation into the Ellesmere canal; moored their pinnaces in the Vale of Llangollen by the aqueduct of Pontycysyllty;[25] and determined to pass some days in inspecting the scenery, before commencing their homeward voyage.

The Captain omitted no opportunity of pressing his suit on Lady Clarinda, but could never draw from her any reply but the same doctrines of worldly wisdom, delivered in a tone of *badinage*,[26] mixed with a certain kindness of manner that induced him to hope she was not in earnest.

But the morning after they had anchored under the hills of the Dee,[27]—whether the lady had reflected more seriously than usual, or was somewhat less in good humor than usual, or the Captain was more pressing than usual,—she said to him: "It must not be, Captain Fitzchrome; 'the course of true love never did run smooth:'[28] my father must keep his borough, and I must have a town house and a country house, and an opera box, and a carriage. It is not well for either of us that we should flirt any longer: 'I must be cruel only to be kind.'[29] Be satisfied with the assurance that you alone, of all men, have ever broken my rest. To be sure, it was only for about three nights in all; but that is too much."

The Captain had *le cœur navré*.[30] He took his portfolio under his arm, made up the little *valise*[31] of a pedestrian, and, without saying a word to any one, wandered off at random among the mountains.

After the lapse of a day or two, the Captain was missed, and every one marvelled what was become of him. Mr. Philpot thought he must have been exploring a river, and fallen in and got drowned in the process. Mr. Firedamp had no doubt he had been crossing a mountain bog, and had been suddenly deprived of life by the exhalations of marsh miasmata.[32] Mr. Henbane deemed it probable that he had been tempted in some wood by the large black brilliant berries of the *Atropa Belladonna*, or Deadly Nightshade; and lamented that he had not been by, to administer an infallible antidote. Mr. Eavesdrop hoped the particulars of his fate would be ascertained; and asked if any one present could help him to any authentic anecdotes of their departed friend.[33] The Reverend Doctor Folliott proposed that an inquiry should be instituted as to whether the march of intellect had reached that neighbourhood, as, if so, the Captain had probably been made a subject for science.[34] Mr. Mac Quedy said it was no such great matter, to ascertain the precise mode in which the surplus population[35] was diminished by one. Mr. Toogood asseverated[36] that there was no such thing as surplus population, and that the land properly managed, would maintain twenty times its present inhabitants: and hereupon they fell into a disputation.

Lady Clarinda did not doubt that the Captain had gone away designedly: she missed him more than she could have anticipated; and wished she had at least postponed her last piece of cruelty, till the completion of their homeward voyage.

CHAPTER XI.

CORRESPONDENCE.

"Base is the slave that pays."

ANCIENT PISTOL.[1]

THE Captain was neither drowned nor poisoned, neither miasmatised[2] nor anatomised. But, before we proceed to account for him, we must look back to a young lady, of whom some little notice was taken in the first chapter; and who, though she has since been out of sight, has never with us been out of mind; Miss Susannah Touchandgo, the forsaken of the junior Crotchet, whom we left an inmate of a solitary farm, in one of the deep vallies under the cloudcapt summits of Meirion, comforting her wounded spirit with air and exercise, rustic cheer, music, painting, and poetry, and the prattle of the little Ap Llymrys.

One evening, after an interval of anxious expectation, the farmer, returning from market, brought for her two letters,[3] of which the contents were these:

> *Dotandcarryonetown,*
> *State of Apodidraskiana:*[4]
> *April* 1,[5] 18..

MY DEAR CHILD,[6]

I am anxious to learn what are your present position, intention, and prospects. The fairies who dropped gold in your shoe, on the morning when I ceased to be a respectable man in London, will soon find a talismanic channel for transmitting you a stocking full of dollars,[7] which will fit the shoe, as well as the foot of Cinderella fitted her slipper. I am happy to say, I am again become a respectable man. It was always my ambition to be a respectable man, and I am a very respectable man here, in this new township of a new state, where I have purchased five thousand acres of land, at two dollars an acre, hard cash, and established a very flourishing bank. The notes of Touchandgo and Company, soft cash, are now the exclusive currency of all this vicinity. This is the land, in which all men flourish;[8] but there are three classes of men who flourish especially,—methodist preachers,[9] slave-drivers,[10] and paper-money manufacturers;[11] and as one of the latter, I have just painted the word BANK, on a fine slab of maple, which was green and growing when I arrived,[12] and have discounted[13] for the settlers, in my own currency, sundry bills, which are to be paid when the proceeds of the crop they have just sown shall return from New Orleans; so that my notes are the representatives of vegetation that is to be, and I am accordingly a capitalist of the first magnitude. The people here know very well that I ran away from London; but the most of them have run away from some place or other;[14] and they have a great respect for me, because they think I ran away with something worth taking, which few of them had the luck or the wit to do. This gives them confidence in my resources, at the same time that, as there is nothing portable in the settlement except my own notes, they have no fear that I shall run away with them. They know I am thoroughly conversant with the principles of banking, and as they have plenty of industry, no lack of sharpness, and abundance of land, they wanted nothing but capital to organize a flourishing settlement; and this capital I have manufactured to the extent required, at the expense of a small importation of pens, ink, and paper, and two or three inimitable copper plates. I have abundance here of all good things, a good conscience included; for I really cannot see that I have done any wrong. This was my position: I owed half a million of money; and I had a trifle in my pocket. It was clear that this trifle could never find its way to the right owner. The question was, whether I should keep it, and live like a gentleman; or hand it over to lawyers and commissioners of bankruptcy, and die like a dog on a dunghill. If I could have thought that the said lawyers, &c., had a better title to it than myself, I might have hesitated; but, as such title was not apparent to my satisfaction, I decided the question in my own favor; the right owners, as I have already said, being out of the question altogether. I have always taken scientific views of morals and politics,[15] a habit from which I derive much comfort under existing circumstances.

I hope you adhere to your music, though I cannot hope again to accompany your harp with my flute. My last *andante* movement was too *forte* for those whom it took by surprise. Let not your *allegro vivace*[16] be damped by young Crotchet's desertion, which, though I have not heard it, I take for granted. He is, like myself, a scientific politician, and has an eye as keen as a needle, to his own interest.[17] He has had good luck so far, and is gorgeous in the spoils of many gulls;[18] but I think the Polar Basin and Walrus Company[19] will be too much for him yet. There has been a splendid outlay on credit, and he is the only man, of the original parties concerned, of whom his Majesty's sheriffs could give any account.

I will not ask you to come here. There is no husband for you. The men smoke, drink, and fight, and break more of their own heads than of girls' hearts. Those among them who are musical, sing nothing but psalms. They are excellent fellows in their way, but you would not like them.

Au reste,[20] here are no rents, no taxes, no poor-rates, no tithes, no church-establishment, no routs, no clubs, no rotten boroughs, no operas, no concerts, no theatres, no beggars, no thieves, no king, no lords, no ladies,[21] and only one gentleman, videlicet,[22] your loving father,

TIMOTHY TOUCHANDGO.

P. S. I send you one of my notes; I can afford to part with it. If you are accused of receiving money from me, you may pay it over to my assignees. Robthetill continues to be my factotum; I say no more of him in this place: he will give you an account of himself.

Dotandcarryonetown, &c.

DEAR MISS,

Mr. Touchandgo will have told you of our arrival here, of our setting up a bank, and so forth. We came here in a tilted waggon,[23] which served us for parlour, kitchen, and all. We soon got up a log-house; and, unluckily, we as soon got it down again, for the first fire we made in it, burned down house and all. However, our second experiment was more fortunate; and we are pretty well lodged in a house of three rooms on a floor; I should say the floor, for there is but one.

This new state is free to hold slaves; all the new states have not this privilege:[24] Mr. Touchandgo has bought some, and they are building him a villa.[25] Mr. Touchandgo is in a thriving way, but he is not happy here: he longs for parties and concerts, and a seat in Congress. He thinks it very hard that he cannot buy one with his own coinage, as he used to do in England.[26] Besides, he is afraid of the Regulators,[27] who, if they do not like a man's character, wait upon him and flog him, doubling the dose at stated intervals, till he takes himself off. He does not like this system of administering justice: though I think he has nothing to fear from it. He has the character of having money, which is the best of all characters here, as at home. He lets his old English prejudices influence his opinions of his new neighbours; but I assure you they have many virtues. Though they do keep slaves, they are all ready to fight for their own liberty; and I should not like to be an enemy within reach of one of their rifles. When I say enemy, I include bailiff in the term. One was shot not long ago. There was a trial; the jury gave two dollars damages; the judge said they must find guilty or not guilty; but the counsel for the defendant (they would not call him prisoner,) offered to fight the judge upon the point: and as this was said literally, not metaphorically, and the counsel was a stout fellow, the judge gave in. The two dollars damages were not paid after all; for the defendant challenged the foreman to box for double or quits, and the foreman was beaten. The folks in New York made a great outcry about it, but here it was considered all as it should be. So you see, Miss, justice, liberty, and every thing else of that kind, are different in different places, just as suits the convenience of those who have the sword in their own hands. Hoping to hear of your health and happiness, I remain,

Dear Miss, your dutiful servant,

RODERICK ROBTHETILL.

Miss Touchandgo replied as follows, to the first of these letters:

MY DEAR FATHER,[28]

I am sure you have the best of hearts, and I have no doubt you have acted with the best intentions. My lover, or I should rather say, my fortune's lover, has indeed forsaken me. I cannot say I did not feel it; indeed, I cried very much; and the altered looks of people who used to be so delighted to see me, really annoyed me so, that I determined to change the scene altogether. I have come into Wales, and am boarding with a farmer and his wife. Their stock of English is very small; but I managed to agree with them, and they have four of the sweetest children I ever saw, to whom I teach all I know, and I manage to pick up some Welsh. I have puzzled out a little song, which I think very pretty; I have translated it into English, and I send it you, with the original air. You shall play it on your flute at eight o'clock every Saturday evening, and I will play and sing it at the same time, and I will fancy that I hear my dear papa accompanying me.

The people in London said very unkind things of you: they hurt me very much at the time; but now I am out of their way, I do not seem to think their opinion of much consequence. I am sure, when I recollect, at leisure, every thing I have seen and heard among them, I cannot make out what they do that is so virtuous, as to set them up for judges of morals. And I am sure they never speak the truth about any thing, and there is no sincerity in either their love or their friendship. An old Welsh bard here, who wears a waistcoat embroidered with leeks, and is called the Green Bard of Cadair Idris,[29] says the Scotch would be the best people in the world, if there was nobody but themselves to give them a character: and so I think would the Londoners. I hate the very thought of them, for I do believe they would have broken my heart, if I had not got out of their way. Now I shall write you another letter very soon, and describe to you the country, and the people, and the children, and how I amuse myself, and every thing that I think you will like to hear about: and when I seal this letter, I shall drop a kiss on the cover.

Your loving daughter,

SUSANNAH TOUCHANDGO.[30]

P. S. Tell Mr. Robthetill I will write to him in a day or two. This is the little song I spoke of:

> Beyond the sea, beyond the sea,
> My heart is gone, far, far from me;
> And ever on its track will flee
> My thoughts, my dreams, beyond the sea.

Beyond the sea, beyond the sea,
The swallow wanders fast and free:
Oh, happy bird! were I like thee,
I, too, would fly beyond the sea.

Beyond the sea, beyond the sea,
Are kindly hearts and social glee:
But here for me they may not be;
My heart is gone beyond the sea.[31]

CHAPTER XII.

THE MOUNTAIN INN.

Ὡς ἡδὺ τῷ μισοῦντι τοὺς φαύλους τρόπους
Ἐρημία.

How sweet to minds that love not sordid ways
Is solitude!   MENANDER.[1]

THE Captain wandered despondingly up and down hill for several days, passing many hours of each in sitting on rocks; making, almost mechanically, sketches of waterfalls, and mountain
pools; taking care, nevertheless, to be always before night-fall
in a comfortable inn, where, being a temperate man, he wiled
away the evening with making a bottle of sherry into negus.[2]
His rambles brought him at length into the interior of Merionethshire, the land of all that is beautiful in nature, and all
that is lovely in woman.[3]

Here, in a secluded village, he found a little inn, of small
pretension and much comfort. He felt so satisfied with his
quarters, and discovered every day so much variety in the scenes
of the surrounding mountains, that his inclination to proceed
farther, diminished progressively.

It is one thing to follow the high road through a country,
with every principally remarkable object carefully noted down
in a book, taking, as therein directed, a guide, at particular
points, to the more recondite sights:[4] it is another to sit down
on one chosen spot, especially when the choice is unpremedi-
tated, and from thence, by a series of explorations, to come day
by day on unanticipated scenes. The latter process has many
advantages over the former; it is free from the disappointment
which attends excited expectation, when imagination has out-
stripped reality, and from the accidents that mar the scheme

of the tourist's[5] single day, when the valleys may be drenched with rain, or the mountains shrouded with mist.

The Captain was one morning preparing to sally forth on his usual exploration, when he heard a voice without, inquiring for a guide to the ruined castle. The voice seemed familiar to him, and going forth into the gateway, he recognised Mr. Chainmail. After greetings and inquiries for the absent; "You vanished very abruptly, Captain," said Mr. Chainmail, "from our party on the canal."

CAPTAIN FITZCHROME.

To tell you the truth, I had a particular reason for trying the effect of absence from a part of that party.

MR. CHAINMAIL.

I surmised as much: at the same time, the unusual melancholy of an in general most vivacious young lady made me wonder at your having acted so precipitately. The lady's heart is yours, if there be truth in signs.

CAPTAIN FITZCHROME.

Hearts are not now what they were in the days of the old song; "Will love be controlled by advice?"[6]

MR. CHAINMAIL.

Very true; hearts, heads, and arms have all degenerated, most sadly.[7] We can no more feel the high impassioned love of the ages, which some people have the impudence to call dark, than we can wield King Richard's battleaxe, bend Robin Hood's bow, or flourish the oaken graff of the Pindar of Wakefield.[8] Still we have our tastes and feelings, though they deserve not the name of passions;[9] and some of us may pluck up spirit to try to carry a point, when we reflect that we have to contend with men no better than ourselves.

CAPTAIN FITZCHROME.

We do not now break lances for ladies.

MR. CHAINMAIL.

No, nor even bulrushes. We jingle purses for them, flourish paper-money banners, and tilt with scrolls of parchment.

CAPTAIN FITZCHROME.

In which sort of tilting I have been thrown from the saddle. I presume it was not love that led you from the flotilla.

MR. CHAINMAIL.

By no means. I was tempted by the sight of an old tower, not to leave this land of ruined castles, without having collected a few hints for the adornment of my baronial hall.

CAPTAIN FITZCHROME.

I understand you live *en famille* with your domestics.[10] You will have more difficulty in finding a lady who would adopt your fashion of living, than one who would prefer you to a richer man.

MR. CHAINMAIL.

Very true. I have tried the experiment on several as guests; but once was enough for them: so, I suppose, I shall die a bachelor.

CAPTAIN FITZCHROME.

I see, like some others of my friends, you will give up anything except your hobby.[11]

MR. CHAINMAIL.

I will give up anything but my baronial hall.

CAPTAIN FITZCHROME.

You will never find a wife for your purpose, unless in the daughter of some old-fashioned farmer.

MR. CHAINMAIL.

No, I thank you. I must have a lady of gentle blood; I shall not marry below my own condition: I am too much of a herald;[12] I have too much of the twelfth century in me for that.

CAPTAIN FITZCHROME.

Why then your chance is not much better than mine. A well-born beauty would scarcely be better pleased with your baronial hall, than with my more humble offer of love in a cottage.[13] She must have a town-house, and an opera-box, and roll about the streets in a carriage; especially if her father has a rotten borough,[14] for the sake of which he sells his daughter, that he may continue to sell his country. But you were inquiring for a guide to the ruined castle in this vicinity; I know the way, and will conduct you.

The proposal pleased Mr. Chainmail, and they set forth on their expedition.

CHAPTER XIII.

THE LAKE. THE RUIN.

Or vieni, Amore, e quà meco t'assetta.
ORLANDO INNAMORATO.[1]

MR. CHAINMAIL.

WOULD it not be a fine thing, Captain, you being picturesque,[2] and I poetical; you being for the lights and shadows of the present, and I for those of the past;[3] if we were to go together over the ground which was travelled in the twelfth century by Giraldus de Barri, when he accompanied Archbishop Baldwin to preach the crusade?[4]

CAPTAIN FITZCHROME.

Nothing, in my present frame of mind, could be more agreeable to me.

MR. CHAINMAIL.

We would provide ourselves with his *Itinerarium;* compare what has been, with what is; contemplate in their decay the castles and abbeys, which he saw in their strength and splendor; and, while you were sketching their remains, I would dispassionately inquire what has been gained by the change.

CAPTAIN FITZCHROME.

Be it so.

But the scheme was no sooner arranged, than the Captain was summoned to London by a letter on business, which he did not expect to detain him long. Mr. Chainmail, who, like the Captain, was fascinated with the inn and the scenery,[5] determined to await his companion's return; and, having furnished him with a list of books, which he was to bring with

him from London, took leave of him, and began to pass his
days like the heroes of Ariosto, who

> — tutto il giorno, al bel oprar intenti,
> Saliron balze, e traversar torrenti.[6]

One day Mr. Chainmail traced upwards the course of a
mountain-stream, to a spot where a small waterfall threw
itself over a slab of perpendicular rock, which seemed to bar
his farther progress. On a nearer view, he discovered a flight
of steps, roughly hewn in the rock, on one side of the fall.
Ascending these steps, he entered a narrow winding pass,
between high and naked rocks, that afforded only space for a
rough footpath, carved on one side, at some height above the
torrent.[7]

The pass opened on a lake, from which the stream issued,
and which lay like a dark mirror, set in a gigantic frame of
mountain precipices. Fragments of rock lay scattered on the
edge of the lake, some half-buried in the water: Mr. Chainmail
scrambled some way over these fragments, till the base of a rock
sinking abruptly in the water, effectually barred his progress.
He sat down on a large smooth stone; the faint murmur of the
stream he had quitted, the occasional flapping of the wings
of the heron, and at long intervals, the solitary springing of a
trout, were the only sounds that came to his ear. The sun shone
brightly half-way down the opposite rocks, presenting, on their
irregular faces, strong masses of light and shade. Suddenly
he heard the dash of a paddle, and, turning his eyes, saw a
solitary and beautiful girl gliding over the lake in a coracle:[8] she
was proceeding from the vicinity of the point he had quitted,
towards the upper end of the lake. Her apparel was rustic,
but there was in its style something more *recherchée*,[9] in its
arrangement something more of elegance and precision, than
was common to the mountain peasant girl. It had more of the

contadina[10] of the opera, than of the genuine mountaineer; so at least thought Mr. Chainmail; but she passed so rapidly, and took him so much by surprise, that he had little opportunity for accurate observation. He saw her land, at the farther extremity, and disappear among the rocks: he rose from his seat, returned to the mouth of the pass, stepped from stone to stone across the stream, and attempted to pass round by the other side of the lake; but there again the abruptly sinking precipice closed his way.

Day after day he haunted the spot, but never saw again either the damsel or the coracle. At length, marvelling at himself for being so solicitous about the apparition of a peasant girl in a coracle, who could not, by any possibility, be anything to him, he resumed his explorations in another direction.

One day he wandered to the ruined castle, on the sea-shore, which was not very distant from his inn; and sitting on the rock, near the base of the ruin, was calling up the forms of past ages on the wall of an ivied tower, when on its summit appeared a female figure, whom he recognised in an instant for his nymph of the coracle. The folds of the blue gown pressed by the sea-breeze against one of the most symmetrical of figures, the black feather of the black hat, and the ringleted hair beneath it fluttering in the wind; the apparent peril of her position, on the edge of the mouldering wall, from whose immediate base the rock went down perpendicularly to the sea, presented a singularly interesting combination to the eye of the young antiquary.

Mr. Chainmail had to pass half round the castle, on the land side, before he could reach the entrance: he coasted the dry and bramble-grown moat, crossed the unguarded bridge, passed the unportcullised arch of the gateway, entered the castle court, ascertained the tower, ascended the broken stairs, and stood on the ivied wall. But the nymph of the place was gone. He searched the ruins within and without, but he found not what he sought: he haunted the castle day after day, as he had done the lake, but the damsel appeared no more.[11]

CHAPTER XIV

THE DINGLE.

The stars of midnight shall be dear
To her, and she shall lean her ear
In many a secret place,
Where rivulets dance their wayward round,
And beauty, born of murmuring sound,
Shall pass into her face.

WORDSWORTH.[1]

Miss Susannah Touchandgo had read the four great poets
of Italy,[2] and many of the best writers of France. About the
time of her father's downfall, accident threw into her way
Les Rêveries du Promeneur Solitaire;[3] and from the impression
which these made on her, she carried with her into retirement
all the works of Rousseau. In the midst of that startling light,
which the conduct of old friends on a sudden reverse of fortune
throws on a young and inexperienced mind, the doctrines
of the philosopher of Geneva struck with double force upon
her sympathies: she imbibed the sweet poison,[4] as somebody
calls it, of his writings, even to a love of truth; which, every
wise man knows, ought to be left to those who can get any
thing by it. The society of children, the beauties of nature, the
solitude of the mountains, became her consolation, and, by
degrees, her delight. The gay society from which she had been
excluded, remained on her memory[5] only as a disagreeable
dream. She imbibed her new monitor's ideas of simplicity of
dress, assimilating her own with that of the peasant-girls in
the neighbourhood: the black hat, the blue gown, the black
stockings, the shoes, tied on the instep.

Pride was, perhaps, at the bottom of the change: she was
willing to impose in some measure on herself, by marking a

contemptuous indifference to the characteristics of the class of society from which she had fallen.

> "And with the food of pride sustained her soul
> In solitude."[6]

It is true that she somewhat modified the forms of her rustic dress: to the black hat she added a black feather, to the blue gown she added a tippet,[7] and a waistband fastened in front with a silver buckle; she wore her black stockings very smooth and tight on her ancles, and tied her shoes in tasteful bows, with the nicest possible ribbon. In this apparel, to which, in winter, she added a scarlet cloak, she made dreadful havoc among the rustic mountaineers, many of whom proposed to "keep company"[8] with her in the Cambrian fashion, an honor which, to their great surprise, she always declined. Among these, Harry Ap-Heather,[9] whose father rented an extensive sheepwalk, and had a thousand she-lambs wandering in the mountains, was the most strenuous in his suit, and the most pathetic in his lamentations for her cruelty.

Miss Susannah often wandered among the mountains alone, even to some distance from the farm-house. Sometimes she descended into the bottom of the dingles, to the black rocky beds of the torrents, and dreamed away hours at the feet of the cataracts. One spot in particular, from which she had at first shrunk with terror, became by degrees her favorite haunt.[10] A path turning and returning at acute angles, led down a steep wood-covered slope to the edge of a chasm, where a pool, or resting-place of a torrent, lay far below. A cataract fell in a single sheet into the pool; the pool boiled and bubbled at the base of the fall, but through the greater part of its extent, lay calm, deep, and black, as if the cataract had plunged through it to an unimaginable depth, without disturbing its eternal repose. At the opposite extremity of the pool, the rocks almost met at their summits, the trees of the opposite banks intermingled their leaves, and another cataract plunged from the pool into a chasm, on which the sunbeams never gleamed.[11] High above, on both sides, the steep woody slopes of the dingle soared into the sky; and from a fissure in the rock, on which the little path terminated, a single gnarled and twisted oak stretched itself over the pool, forming a fork with its boughs at a short distance from the rock. Miss Susannah often sat on the rock, with her feet resting on this tree: in time, she made her seat on the tree itself, with her feet hanging over the abyss; and at length, she accustomed herself to lie along upon its trunk, with her side on the mossy bole of the fork, and an arm round one of the branches. From this position a portion of the sky and the woods was reflected in the pool, which, from its bank, was but a mass of darkness.[12] The first time she reclined in this manner, her heart beat audibly; in time, she lay down as calmly as on the mountain heather; the perception of the sublime was probably heightened by an intermingled sense of danger;[13] and perhaps that indifference to life, which early disappointment forces upon sensitive minds, was necessary to the first experiment. There was, in the novelty and strangeness of the position, an excitement which never wholly passed away, but which became gradually subordinate to the influence, at once tranquillising and elevating, of the mingled eternity of motion, sound, and solitude.

One sultry noon, she descended into this retreat with a mind more than usually disturbed by reflections on the past. She lay in her favorite position, sometimes gazing on the cataract; looking sometimes up the steep sylvan acclivities,[14] into the narrow space of the cloudless ether; sometimes down into the abyss of the pool, and the deep bright-blue reflections that opened another immensity below her. The distressing recollections of the morning, the world and all its littlenesses, faded from her thoughts like a dream; but her wounded and wearied spirit drank in too deeply the tranquillising power of the place, and she dropped asleep upon the tree like a ship-boy on the mast.

At this moment Mr. Chainmail emerged into daylight, on a projection of the opposite rock, having struck down through the woods in search of unsophisticated scenery. The scene he discovered filled him with delight: he seated himself on the rock, and fell into one of his romantic reveries;[15] when suddenly the semblance of a black hat and feather caught his eye among the foliage of the projecting oak. He started up, shifted his position, and got a glimpse of a blue gown. It was his lady of the lake,[16] his enchantress of the ruined castle, divided from him by a barrier, which, at a few yards below, he could almost overleap, yet unapproachable but by a circuit perhaps of many hours. He watched with intense anxiety. To listen if she breathed was out of the question: the noses of a dean and chapter would have been soundless in the roar of the torrent. From her extreme stillness, she appeared to sleep: yet what creature, not desperate, would go wilfully to sleep in such a place? Was she asleep then? Nay, was she alive? She was as motionless as death. Had she been murdered, thrown from above, and caught in the tree? She lay too regularly, and too composedly for such a supposition. She was asleep then, and, in all probability, her waking would be fatal. He shifted his position. Below the pool two beetle-browed rocks nearly overarched the chasm,[17] leaving just such a space at the summit as was within the possibility of a leap; the torrent roared below in a fearful gulph. He paused some time on the brink, measuring the practicability and the danger, and casting every now and then an anxious glance to his sleeping beauty.[18] In one of these glances he saw a slight movement of the blue gown, and, in a moment after, the black hat and feather dropped into the pool. Reflection was lost for a moment, and, by a sudden impulse, he bounded over the chasm.

He stood above the projecting oak; the unknown beauty[19] lay like the nymph of the scene;[20] her long black hair, which the fall of her hat had disengaged from its fastenings, drooping through the boughs: he saw that the first thing to be done, was to prevent her throwing her feet off the trunk, in the first movements of waking. He sat down on the rock, and placed his feet on the stem, securing her ankles between his own: one of her arms was round a branch of the fork, the other lay loosely on her side. The hand of this arm he endeavoured to reach, by leaning forward from his seat; he approximated, but could not touch it: after several tantalising efforts, he gave up the point in despair. He did not attempt to wake her, because he feared it might have bad consequences, and he resigned himself to expect the moment of her natural waking, determined not to stir from his post, if she should sleep till midnight.

In this period of forced inaction, he could contemplate at leisure the features and form of his charmer. She was not one of the slender beauties of romance; she was as plump as a partridge;[21] her cheeks were two roses, not absolutely damask, yet verging thereupon; her lips twin-cherries, of equal size; her nose regular, and almost Grecian; her forehead high, and delicately fair; her eyebrows symmetrically arched; her eyelashes long, black, and silky, fitly corresponding with the beautiful tresses that hung among the leaves of the oak, like clusters of wandering grapes.* [22] Her eyes were yet to be seen; but how could he doubt that their opening would be the rising of the sun, when all that surrounded their fringy portals[23] was radiant as "the forehead of the morning sky?"[24]

---

* Ἀλήμονα βότρυν ἐθείρας.

NONNUS.

CHAPTER XV.

THE FARM.

Da ydyw'r gwaith, rhaid d'we'yd y gwir,
Ar fryniau Sîr Meirionydd;
Golwg oer o'r gwaela gawn
Mae hi etto yn llawn llawenydd.

Though Meirion's rocks, and hills of heath,
  Repel the distant sight,
Yet where, than those bleak hills beneath,
  Is found more true delight?[1]

AT length the young lady awoke. She was startled at the sudden sight of the stranger, and somewhat terrified at the first perception of her position. But she soon recovered her self-possession, and, extending her hand to the offered hand of Mr. Chainmail, she raised herself up on the tree, and stepped on the rocky bank.

Mr. Chainmail solicited permission to attend her to her home, which the young lady graciously conceded. They emerged from the woody dingle, traversed an open heath, wound along a mountain road by the shore of a lake, descended to the deep bed of another stream, crossed it by a series of stepping-stones, ascended to some height on the opposite side, and followed upwards the line of the stream, till the banks opened into a spacious amphitheatre, where stood, in its fields and meadows, the farm-house of Ap Llymry.

During this walk, they had kept up a pretty animated conversation. The lady had lost her hat, and, as she turned towards Mr. Chainmail, in speaking to him, there was no envious[2] projection of brim to intercept the beams of those radiant eyes he had been so anxious to see unclosed. There was in them a mixture of softness and brilliancy, the perfection of the beauty of female eyes, such as some men have passed through life without seeing, and such as no man ever saw, in any pair of eyes, but once; such as can never be seen and forgotten.[3] Young Crotchet had seen it; he had not forgotten it; but he had trampled on its memory, as the renegade tramples on the emblems of a faith, which his interest only, and not his heart or his reason, has rejected.

Her hair streamed over her shoulders; the loss of the black feather had left nothing but the rustic costume, the blue gown, the black stockings, and the ribbon-tied shoes. Her voice had that full soft volume of melody which gives to common speech the fascination of music. Mr. Chainmail could not reconcile the dress of the damsel, with her conversation and manners. He threw out a remote question or two, with the hope of solving the riddle, but, receiving no reply, he became satisfied that she was not disposed to be communicative respecting herself, and, fearing to offend her, fell upon other topics. They talked of the scenes of the mountains, of the dingle, the ruined castle, the solitary lake. She told him, that lake lay under the mountains behind her home, and the coracle and the pass at the extremity, saved a long circuit to the nearest village, whither she sometimes went to inquire for letters.

Mr. Chainmail felt curious to know from whom these letters might be; and he again threw out two or three fishing questions, to which, as before, he obtained no answer.

The only living biped they met in their walk, was the unfortunate Harry Ap-Heather, with whom they fell in by the stepping-stones, who, seeing the girl of his heart hanging on another man's arm, and, concluding at once that they were "keeping company," fixed on her a mingled look of surprise, reproach, and tribulation; and, unable to control his feelings under the sudden shock, burst into a flood of tears, and blubbered till the rocks re-echoed.[4]

They left him mingling his tears with the stream, and his lamentations with its murmurs.[5] Mr. Chainmail inquired who that strange creature might be, and what was the matter with him. The young lady answered, that he was a very worthy young man, to whom she had been the innocent cause of much unhappiness.

"I pity him sincerely," said Mr. Chainmail; and, nevertheless, he could scarcely restrain his laughter, at the exceedingly original[6] figure which the unfortunate rustic lover had presented by the stepping-stones.

The children ran out to meet their dear Miss Susan, jumped all round her, and asked what was become of her hat. Ap Llymry came out in great haste, and invited Mr. Chainmail to walk in and dine: Mr. Chainmail did not wait to be asked twice. In a few minutes the whole party, Miss Susan and Mr. Chainmail, Mr. and Mrs. Ap Llymry, and progeny, were seated over a clean homespun tablecloth, ornamented with fowls and bacon, a pyramid of potatoes, another of cabbage, which Ap Llymry said "was poiled with the pacon, and as coot as marrow,"[7] a bowl of milk for the children, and an immense brown jug of foaming ale, with which Ap Llymry seemed to delight in filling the horn[8] of his new guest.

Shall we describe the spacious apartment, which was at once kitchen, hall, and dining room,—the large dark rafters, the pendent bacon and onions, the strong old oaken furniture, the bright and trimly arranged utensils? Shall we describe the cut of Ap Llymry's coat, the colour and tie of his neckcloth, the number of buttons at his knees,—the structure of Mrs. Ap Llymry's cap, having lappets[9] over the ears, which were united under the chin, setting forth especially whether the bond of union were a pin or a ribbon? We shall leave this tempting field of interesting expatiation[10] to those whose brains are high-pressure steam engines for spinning prose by the furlong,[11] to be trumpeted in paid-for paragraphs in the quack's corner of newspapers: modern literature having attained the honorable distinction of sharing with blacking[12] and Macassar oil,[13] the space which used to be monopolized by razor-strops[14] and the lottery; whereby that very enlightened community, the reading public,[15] is tricked into the perusal of much exemplary nonsense; though the few who see through the trickery have no reason to complain, since as "good wine needs no bush,"[16] so, *ex vi oppositi*,[17] these bushes of venal panegyric point out very clearly that the things they celebrate are not worth reading.

The party dined very comfortably in a corner most remote from the fire; and Mr. Chainmail very soon found his head swimming with two or three horns of ale, of a potency to which even he was unaccustomed. After dinner, Ap-Llymry made him finish a bottle of mead, which he willingly accepted, both as an excuse to remain, and as a drink of the dark ages, which he had no doubt was a genuine brewage, from uncorrupted tradition.

In the meantime, as soon as the cloth was removed, the children had brought out Miss Susannah's harp. She began, without affectation, to play and sing to the children, as was her custom of an afternoon, first in their own language, and their national melodies, then in English; but she was soon interrupted by a general call of little voices for "Ouf! di giorno." She complied with the request, and sang the ballad from Paër's Camilla: *Un dì carco il mulinaro.** The children were very

---

* In this ballad, the terrors of the Black Forest are narrated to an assemblage of domestics and peasants, who, at the end of every stanza, dance in a circle round the narrator. The second stanza is as follows:

> Una notte in un stradotto
> Un incauto s'inoltrò;
> E uno strillo udì di botto
> Che l'orecchio gl'intronò:
> Era l'ombra di sua nonna,
> Che pel naso lo pigliò.

familiar with every syllable of this ballad, which had been often fully explained to them. They danced in a circle with the burden of every verse, shouting out the chorus with good articulation and joyous energy; and at the end of the second stanza, where the traveller has his nose pinched by his grandmother's ghost, every nose in the party was nipped by a pair of little fingers. Mr. Chainmail, who was not prepared for the process, came in for a very energetic tweak, from a chubby girl that sprang suddenly on his knees for the purpose, and made the roof ring with her laughter.

So passed the time till evening, when Mr. Chainmail moved to depart. But it turned out on inquiry, that he was some miles from his inn, that the way was intricate, and that he must not make any difficulty about accepting the farmer's hospitality till morning. The evening set in with rain: the fire was found agreeable; they drew around it. The young lady made tea; and afterwards, from time to time, at Mr. Chainmail's special request, delighted his ear with passages of ancient music. Then came a supper of lake trout, fried on the spot, and thrown, smoking hot, from the pan to the plate. Then came a brewage, which the farmer called his nightcap, of which he insisted on Mr. Chainmail's taking his full share. After which, the gentleman remembered nothing, till he awoke, the next morning, to the pleasant consciousness, that he was under the same roof with one of the most fascinating creatures under the canopy of heaven.

> Ouf! di giorno nè di sera,
> Non passiam la selva nera.
>
> *(Ballano in giro.)*

CHAPTER XVI.

THE NEWSPAPER.[1]

Ποίας δ' ἀποσπασθεῖσα φύτλας
Ὀρέων κευθμῶνας ἔχει σκιοέντων;

Sprung from what line, adorns the maid
These vallies deep in mountain-shade?
PIND. Pyth. IX.[2]

MR. CHAINMAIL forgot the Captain and the route of Giraldus de Barri.[3] He became suddenly satisfied that the ruined castle in his present neighbourhood was the best possible specimen of its class, and that it was needless to carry his researches further.

He visited the farm daily: found himself always welcome; flattered himself that the young lady saw him with pleasure, and dragged a heavier chain at every new parting[4] from Miss Susan, as the children called his nymph of the mountains.[5] What might be her second name, he had vainly endeavoured to discover.

Mr. Chainmail was in love: but the determination he had long before formed and fixed in his mind, to marry only a lady of gentle blood, without a blot in her escutcheon,[6] repressed the declarations of passion which were often rising to his lips. In the meantime, he left no means untried, to pluck out the heart of her mystery.[7]

The young lady soon divined his passion, and penetrated his prejudices. She began to look on him with favorable eyes; but she feared her name and parentage would present an insuperable barrier to his feudal pride.

Things were in this state when the Captain returned, and unpacked his maps and books in the parlour of the inn.

MR. CHAINMAIL.

Really, Captain, I find so many objects of attraction in this neighbourhood, that I would gladly postpone our purpose.

CAPTAIN FITZCHROME.

Undoubtedly, this neighbourhood has many attractions; but there is something very inviting in the scheme you laid down.

MR. CHAINMAIL.

No doubt, there is something very tempting in the route of Giraldus de Barri. But there are better things in this vicinity even than that. To tell you the truth, Captain, I have fallen in love.

CAPTAIN FITZCHROME.

What! while I have been away?

MR. CHAINMAIL.

Even so.

CAPTAIN FITZCHROME.

The plunge must have been very sudden, if you are already over head and ears.

MR. CHAINMAIL.

As deep as Llyn-y-dreiddiad-vrawd.

CAPTAIN FITZCHROME.

And what may that be?

MR. CHAINMAIL.

A pool not far off: a resting-place of a mountain stream, which is said to have no bottom. There is a tradition connected with it; and here is a ballad on it,[8] at your service.

LLYN-Y-DREIDDIAD-VRAWD.
THE POOL OF THE DIVING FRIAR.[9]

GWENWYNWYN withdrew from the feasts of his hall:
He slept very little, he prayed not at all:
He pondered, and wandered, and studied alone;
And sought, night and day, the philosopher's stone.[10]

He found it at length, and he made its first proof
By turning to gold all the lead of his roof:
Then he bought some magnanimous heroes, all fire,
Who lived but to smite and be smitten for hire.

With these, on the plains like a torrent he broke;
He filled the whole country with flame and with smoke;
He killed all the swine, and he broached all the wine;
He drove off the sheep, and the beeves, and the kine;[11]

He took castles and towns; he cut short limbs and lives;
He made orphans and widows of children and wives:
This course many years he triumphantly ran,
And did mischief enough to be called a great man.[12]

When, at last, he had gained all for which he had striven,
He bethought him of buying a passport to heaven;
Good and great as he was, yet he did not well know,
How soon, or which way, his great spirit might go.

He sought the grey friars, who, beside a wild stream,
Refected[13] their frames on a primitive scheme;
The gravest and wisest Gwenwynwyn found out,
All lonely and ghostly, and angling for trout.

Below the white dash of a mighty cascade,
Where a pool of the stream a deep resting-place made,
And rock-rooted oaks stretched their branches on high,
The friar stood musing, and throwing his fly.

To him said Gwenwynwyn: "Hold, father, here's store,
For the good of the church, and the good of the poor;"

Then he gave him the stone; but, ere more he could speak,
Wrath came on the friar, so holy and meek:

He had stretched forth his hand to receive the red gold,
And he thought himself mocked by Gwenwynwyn the Bold;
And in scorn of the gift, and in rage at the giver,
He jerked it immediately into the river.

Gwenwynwyn, aghast, not a syllable spake;
The philosopher's stone made a duck and a drake:[14]
Two systems of circles a moment were seen,
And the stream smoothed them off, as they never had been.

Gwenwynwyn regained, and uplifted his voice:
"Oh friar, grey friar, full rash was thy choice;
The stone, the good stone, which away thou hast thrown,
Was the stone of all stones, the philosopher's stone!"

The friar looked pale, when his error he knew;
The friar looked red, and the friar looked blue;
And heels over head, from the point of a rock,
He plunged, without stopping to pull off his frock.

He dived very deep, but he dived all in vain,
The prize he had slighted he found not again:
Many times did the friar his diving renew,
And deeper and deeper the river still grew.

Gwenwynwyn gazed long, of his senses in doubt,
To see the grey friar a diver so stout:
Then sadly and slowly his castle he sought,
And left the friar diving, like dabchick[15] distraught.

Gwenwynwyn fell sick with alarm and despite,
Died, and went to the devil, the very same night:
The magnanimous heroes he held in his pay,
Sacked his castle, and marched with the plunder away.

No knell on the silence of midnight was rolled,
For the flight of the soul of Gwenwynwyn the Bold:

The brethren, unfeed, let the mighty ghost pass,
Without praying a prayer, or intoning a mass.

The friar haunted ever beside the dark stream;
The philosopher's stone was his thought and his dream:
And day after day, ever head under heels
He dived all the time he could spare from his meals.

He dived, and he dived, to the end of his days,
As the peasants oft witnessed with fear and amaze:
The mad friar's diving-place long was their theme,
And no plummet[16] can fathom that pool of the stream.

And still, when light clouds on the midnight winds ride,
If by moonlight you stray on the lone river-side,
The ghost of the friar may be seen diving there,
With head in the water, and heels in the air.

CAPTAIN FITZCHROME.

Well, your ballad is very pleasant: you shall shew me the
scene, and I will sketch it; but just now I am more interested
about your love. What heroine of the twelfth century has risen
from the ruins of the old castle, and looked down on you from
the ivied battlements?

MR. CHAINMAIL.

You are nearer the mark than you suppose. Even from those
battlements, a heroine of the twelfth century has looked down
on me.

CAPTAIN FITZCHROME.

Oh! some vision of an ideal beauty. I suppose the whole will
end in another tradition and a ballad.

MR. CHAINMAIL.

Genuine flesh and blood;[17] as genuine as Lady Clarinda. I
will tell you the story.

Mr. Chainmail narrated his adventures.

CAPTAIN FITZCHROME.

Then you seem to have found what you wished. Chance has thrown in your way what none of the gods would have ventured to promise you.[18]

MR. CHAINMAIL.

Yes, but I know nothing of her birth and parentage. She tells me nothing of herself, and I have no right to question her directly.

CAPTAIN FITZCHROME.

She appears to be expressly destined for the light of your baronial hall. Introduce me: in this case, two heads are better than one.

MR. CHAINMAIL.

No, I thank you. Leave me to manage my chance of a prize, and keep you to your own chance of a —

CAPTAIN FITZCHROME.

Blank. As you please. Well, I will pitch my tent here, till I have filled my portfolio, and shall be glad of as much of your company as you can spare from more attractive society.

Matters went on pretty smoothly for several days, when an unlucky newspaper threw all into confusion. Mr. Chainmail received newspapers by the post, which came in three times a week. One morning, over their half-finished breakfast, the Captain had read half a newspaper very complacently, when suddenly he started up in a frenzy, hurled over the breakfast table, and, bouncing from the apartment, knocked down Harry Ap-Heather, who was coming in at the door to challenge his supposed rival to a boxing-match.

Harry sprang up, in a double rage, and intercepted Mr. Chainmail's pursuit of the Captain, placing himself in the doorway, in a pugilistic attitude. Mr. Chainmail, not being disposed for this mode of combat, stepped back into the parlour, took the poker in his right hand, and displacing the loose bottom of a large elbow chair, threw it over his left arm, as a shield.[19] Harry, not liking the aspect of the enemy in this imposing attitude, retreated with backward steps into the kitchen, and tumbled over a cur, which immediately fastened on his rear.

Mr. Chainmail, half-laughing, half-vexed, anxious to overtake the Captain, and curious to know what was the matter with him, pocketed the newspaper, and sallied forth, leaving Harry roaring for a doctor and tailor, to repair the lacerations of his outward man.[20]

Mr. Chainmail could find no trace of the Captain. Indeed, he sought him but in one direction, which was that leading to the farm; where he arrived in due time, and found Miss Susan alone. He laid the newspaper on the table, as was his custom, and proceeded to converse with the young lady: a conversation of many pauses, as much of signs as of words. The young lady took up the paper, and turned it over and over, while she listened to Mr. Chainmail, whom she found every day more and more agreeable, when, suddenly, her eye glanced on something which made her change colour, and dropping the paper on the ground, she rose from her seat, exclaiming: "Miserable must she be who trusts any of your faithless sex! never, never, never, will I endure such misery twice." And she vanished up the stairs. Mr. Chainmail was petrified.[21] At length, he cried aloud: "Cornelius Agrippa[22] must have laid a spell on this accursed newspaper;" and was turning it over, to look for the source of the mischief, when Mrs. Ap-Llymry made her appearance.

MRS. AP-LLYMRY.

What have you done to poor dear Miss Susan? she is crying ready to break her heart.

MR. CHAINMAIL.

So help me the memory of Richard Cœur-de-Lion,[23] I have not the most distant notion of what is the matter.

MRS. AP-LLYMRY.

Oh, don't tell me, sir; you must have ill-used her. I know how it is. You have been keeping company with her, as if you wanted to marry her; and now, all at once, you have been trying to make her your mistress. I have seen such tricks more than once, and you ought to be ashamed of yourself.

MR. CHAINMAIL.

My dear madam, you wrong me utterly. I have none but the kindest feelings, and the most honorable purposes towards her. She has been disturbed by something she has seen in this rascally paper.

MRS. AP-LLYMRY.

Why, then, the best thing you can do is to go away, and come again tomorrow.

MR. CHAINMAIL.

Not I, indeed, madam. Out of this house I stir not, till I have seen the young lady, and obtained a full explanation.

MRS. AP-LLYMRY.

I will tell Miss Susan what you say. Perhaps she will come down.

Mr. Chainmail sate with as much patience as he could command, running over the paper, from column to column. At length, he lighted on an announcement of the approaching marriage of Lady Clarinda Bossnowl with Mr. Crotchet the younger. This explained the Captain's discomposure, but the cause of Miss Susan's was still to be sought: he could not know that it was one and the same.

Presently, the sound of the longed-for step was heard on the stairs; the young lady reappeared, and resumed her seat:

her eyes showed that she had been weeping. The gentleman was now exceedingly puzzled how to begin, but the young lady relieved him by asking, with great simplicity: "What do you wish to have explained, sir?"

MR. CHAINMAIL.

I wish, if I may be permitted, to explain myself to you. Yet could I first wish to know what it was that disturbed you in this unlucky paper. Happy should I be if I could remove the cause of your inquietude!

MISS SUSANNAH.

The cause is already removed. I saw something that excited painful recollections; nothing that I could now wish otherwise than as it is.

MR. CHAINMAIL.

Yet, may I ask why it is that I find one so accomplished, living in this obscurity, and passing only by the name of Miss Susan?

MISS SUSANNAH.

The world and my name are not friends. I have left the world, and wish to remain for ever a stranger to all whom I once knew in it.

MR. CHAINMAIL.

You can have done nothing to dishonor your name.

MISS SUSANNAH.

No, sir. My father has done that of which the world disapproves, in matters of which I pretend not to judge. I have suffered for it as I will never suffer again. My name is my own secret: I have no other, and that is one not worth knowing. You see what I am, and all I am. I live according to the condition of my present fortune, and here, so living, I have found tranquillity.

MR. CHAINMAIL.

Yet, I entreat you, tell me your name.

MISS SUSANNAH.

Why, sir?

MR. CHAINMAIL.

Why, but to throw my hand, my heart, my fortune, at your feet, if—

MISS SUSANNAH.

If my name be worthy of them.

MR. CHAINMAIL.

Nay, nay, not so; if your hand and heart are free.

MISS SUSANNAH.

My hand and heart are free; but they must be sought from myself, and not from my name.

She fixed her eyes on him, with a mingled expression of mistrust, of kindness, and of fixed resolution, which the far-gone *innamorato*[24] found irresistible.

MR. CHAINMAIL.

Then from yourself alone I seek them.

MISS SUSANNAH.

Reflect. You have prejudices on the score of parentage. I have not conversed with you so often, without knowing what they are. Choose between them and me. I too have my own prejudices on the score of personal pride.[25]

MR. CHAINMAIL.

I would choose you from all the world, were you even the daughter of the *exécuteur des hautes œuvres*, as the heroine of a romantic story I once read, turned out to be.[26]

MISS SUSANNAH.

I am satisfied. You have now a right to know my history, and if you repent, I absolve you from all obligations.

She told him her history; but he was out of the reach of repentance. "It is true," as at a subsequent period he said to the Captain, "she is the daughter of a money-changer; one who, in the days of Richard the First, would have been plucked by the beard in the streets: but she is, according to modern notions, a lady of gentle blood. As to her father's running away, that is a minor consideration: I have always understood, from Mr. Mac Quedy, who is a great oracle in this way, that promises to pay ought not to be kept; the essence of a safe and economical currency being an interminable series of broken promises.[27] There seems to be a difference among the learned as to the way in which the promises ought to be broken; but I am not deep enough in their casuistry to enter into such nice distinctions."

In a few days there was a wedding, a pathetic leave-taking of the farmer's family, a hundred kisses from the bride to the children, and promises twenty times reclaimed and renewed, to visit them in the ensuing year.

CHAPTER XVII.

THE INVITATION.

A cup of wine, that's brisk and fine,
And drink unto the leman[1] mine.
Master Silence.[2]

THIS veridicous[3] history began in May, and the occurrences already narrated have carried it on to the middle of autumn. Stepping over the interval to Christmas, we find ourselves in our first locality, among the chalk hills of the Thames; and we discover our old friend, Mr. Crotchet, in the act of accepting an invitation, for himself, and any friends who might be with him, to pass their Christmas-day at Chainmail Hall, after the fashion of the twelfth century.[4] Mr. Crotchet had assembled about him, for his own Christmas festivities, nearly the same party which was introduced to the reader in the spring. Three of that party were wanting. Dr. Morbific, by inoculating himself once too often with non-contagious matter, had explained himself out of the world. Mr. Henbane had also departed, on the wings of an infallible antidote. Mr. Eavesdrop, having printed in a magazine some of the after-dinner conversations of the castle, had had sentence of exclusion passed upon him, on the motion of the Reverend Doctor Folliott, as a flagitious[5] violator of the confidences of private life.

Miss Crotchet had become Lady Bossnowl, but Lady Clarinda had not yet changed her name to Crotchet. She had, on one pretence and another, procrastinated the happy event, and the gentleman had not been very pressing; she had, however, accompanied her brother and sister-in-law, to pass Christmas at Crotchet Castle. With these, Mr. Mac Quedy, Mr. Philpot, Mr. Trillo, Mr. Skionar, Mr. Toogood, and

Mr. Firedamp, were sitting at breakfast, when the Reverend Doctor Folliott entered and took his seat at the table.

THE REV. DR. FOLLIOTT.

Well, Mr. Mac Quedy, it is now some weeks since we have met: how goes on the march of mind?

MR. MAC QUEDY.

Nay, sir; I think you may see that with your own eyes.

THE REV. DR. FOLLIOTT.

Sir, I have seen it, much to my discomfiture. It has marched into my rick-yard, and set my stacks on fire, with chemical materials, most scientifically compounded. It has marched up to the door of my vicarage, a hundred and fifty strong; ordered me to surrender half my tithes; consumed all the provisions I had provided for my audit feast,[6] and drunk up my old October.[7] It has marched in through my back-parlour shutters, and out again with my silver spoons, in the dead of the night.[8] The policeman[9] who has been down to examine, says my house has been broken open on the most scientific principles. All this comes of education.[10]

MR. MAC QUEDY.

I rather think it comes of poverty.

THE REV. DR. FOLLIOTT.

No, sir. Robbery perhaps comes of poverty, but scientific principles of robbery come of education. I suppose the learned friend has written a sixpenny treatise on mechanics, and the rascals who robbed me have been reading it.[11]

MR. CROTCHET.

Your house would have been very safe, Doctor, if they had had no better science than the learned friend's to work with.

THE REV. DR. FOLLIOTT.

Well, sir, that may be. Excellent potted char. The lord deliver me from the learned friend.

MR. CROTCHET.

Well, Doctor, for your comfort, here is a declaration of the learned friend's that he will never take office.

THE REV. DR. FOLLIOTT.

Then, sir, he will be in office next week.[12] Peace be with him. Sugar and cream.

MR. CROTCHET.

But, Doctor, are you for Chainmail Hall on Christmas-day?

THE REV. DR. FOLLIOTT.

That am I, for there will be an excellent dinner, though, peradventure, grotesquely served.

MR. CROTCHET.

I have not seen my neighbour since he left us on the canal.

THE REV. DR. FOLLIOTT.

He has married a wife, and brought her home.

LADY CLARINDA.

Indeed! If she suits him, she must be an oddity: it will be amusing to see them together.

LORD BOSSNOWL.

Very amusing. He! He!

MR. FIREDAMP.

Is there any water about Chainmail Hall?

THE REV. DR. FOLLIOTT.

An old moat.

MR. FIREDAMP.

I shall die of *malaria*.

MR. TRILLO.

Shall we have any music?

THE REV. DR. FOLLIOTT.

An old harper.

MR. TRILLO.

Those fellows are always horridly out of tune. What will he play?

THE REV. DR. FOLLIOTT.

Old songs and marches.

MR. SKIONAR.

Amongst so many old things, I hope we shall find Old Philosophy.[13]

THE REV. DR. FOLLIOTT.

An old woman.

MR. PHILPOT.

Perhaps an old map of the river in the twelfth century.

THE REV. DR. FOLLIOTT.

No doubt.

MR. MAC QUEDY.

How many more old things?

THE REV. DR. FOLLIOTT.

Old hospitality; old wine; old ale; all the images of old England; an old butler.

MR. TOOGOOD.

Shall we all be welcome?

THE REV. DR. FOLLIOTT.

Heartily; you will be slapped on the shoulder, and called Old boy.

LORD BOSSNOWL.

I think we should all go in our old clothes. He! He!

THE REV. DR. FOLLIOTT.

You will sit on old chairs, round an old table, by the light of old lamps, suspended from pointed arches, which, Mr. Chainmail says, first came into use in the twelfth century;[14] with old armour on the pillars, and old banners in the roof.

LADY CLARINDA.

And what curious piece of antiquity is the lady of the mansion?

THE REV. DR. FOLLIOTT.

No antiquity there; none.

LADY CLARINDA.

Who was she?

THE REV. DR. FOLLIOTT.

That I know not.

LADY CLARINDA.

Have you seen her?

THE REV. DR. FOLLIOTT.

I have.

LADY CLARINDA.

Is she pretty?

THE REV. DR. FOLLIOTT.

More,—beautiful. A subject for the pen of Nonnus, or the pencil of Zeuxis. Features of all loveliness, radiant with all virtue and intelligence. A face for Antigone. A form at once plump and symmetrical, that, if it be decorous to divine it by externals, would have been a model for the Venus of Cnidos.[15] Never was any thing so goodly to look on, the present company excepted, and poor dear Mrs. Folliott. She reads moral philosophy, Mr. Mac Quedy, which indeed she might as well let alone; she reads Italian poetry, Mr. Skionar; she sings Italian music, Mr. Trillo; but, with all this, she has the greatest of female virtues, for she superintends the household, and looks after her husband's dinner. I believe she was a mountaineer: παρθένος ὀυρεσίφοιτος, ἐρήμαδι σύντροφος ὕλη,* as Nonnus sweetly sings.[16]

* A mountain-wandering maid,
Twin-nourished with the solitary wood.

CHAPTER XVIII.

CHAINMAIL HALL.

Vous autres dictes que ignorance est mere de tous maulx, et dictes vray: mais toutesfoys vous ne la bannissez mye de vos entende-mens, et vivez en elle, avecques elle, et par elle. C'est pourquoy tant de maulx vous meshaignent de jour en jour.

RABELAIS, l. 5. c. 7.[1]

THE party which was assembled on Christmas-day in Chain-mail Hall, comprised all the guests of Crotchet Castle, some of Mr. Chainmail's other neighbours, all his tenants and domes-tics, and Captain Fitzchrome. The hall was spacious and lofty; and with its tall fluted pillars and pointed arches, its windows of stained glass, its display of arms and banners intermingled with holly and misletoe, its blazing cressets[2] and torches, and a stupendous fire in the centre, on which blocks of pine were flaming and crackling, had a striking effect on eyes unaccus-tomed to such a dining-room. The fire was open on all sides, and the smoke was caught and carried back, under a funnel-formed canopy, into a hollow central pillar. This fire was the line of demarcation between gentle and simple, on days of high festival.[3] Tables extended from it on two sides, to nearly the end of the hall.

Mrs. Chainmail was introduced to the company. Young Crotchet felt some revulsion of feeling at the unexpected sight of one whom he had forsaken, but not forgotten, in a condition apparently so much happier than his own. The lady held out her hand to him with a cordial look of more than forgiveness; it seemed to say that she had much to thank him for. She was the picture of a happy bride, *rayonnante de joie et d'amour*.[4]

Mr. Crotchet told the Reverend Doctor Folliott the news of the morning. "As you predicted," he said, "your friend, the learned friend, is in office; he has also a title; he is now Sir Guy de Vaux."[5]

THE REV. DR. FOLLIOTT.

Thank heaven for that! he is disarmed from further mischief. It is something, at any rate, to have that hollow and wind-shaken reed rooted up for ever from the field of public delusion.[6]

MR. CROTCHET.

I suppose, Doctor, you do not like to see a great reformer in office; you are afraid for your vested interests.[7]

THE REV. DR. FOLLIOTT.

Not I, indeed, sir; my vested interests are very safe from all such reformers as the learned friend. I vaticinate[8] what will be the upshot of all his schemes of reform. He will make a speech of seven hours' duration,[9] and this will be its quintessence: that, seeing the exceeding difficulty of putting salt on the bird's tail,[10] it will be expedient to consider the best method of throwing dust in the bird's eyes. All the rest will be

> *Τ πππτιμπρό.*
> *Ποποποί, ποποποί.*
> *Τιοτιοτιοτιοτιοτιοτίγξ.*
> *Κικκαβαῦ, κικκαβαῦ.*
> *Τοροτοροτοροτορολιλιλίγξ.* *

as Aristophanes[11] has it; and so I leave him, in Nephelococcygia.† [12]

Mr. Mac Quedy came up to the divine as Mr. Crotchet left him, and said: "There is one piece of news which the old gentleman has not told you. The great firm of Catchflat and

---

* Sounds without meaning; imitative of the voices of birds. From the Ὄρνιθες of Aristophanes.

† "Cuckoo-city-in-the-clouds." From the same comedy.

Company, in which young Crotchet is a partner, has stopped payment."

THE REV. DR. FOLLIOTT.

Bless me! that accounts for the young gentleman's melancholy. I thought they would overreach themselves with their own tricks. The day of reckoning, Mr. Mac Quedy, is the point which your paper-money science always leaves out of view.[13]

MR. MAC QUEDY.

I do not see, sir, that the failure of Catchflat and Company has any thing to do with my science.

THE REV. DR. FOLLIOTT.

It has this to do with it, sir, that you would turn the whole nation into a great paper-money shop, and take no thought of the day of reckoning. But the dinner is coming. I think you, who are so fond of paper promises, should dine on the bill of fare.[14]

The harper at the head of the hall struck up an ancient march, and the dishes were brought in, in grand procession.

The boar's head, garnished with rosemary, with a citron in its mouth, led the van.[15] Then came tureens[16] of plum-porridge; then a series of turkeys, and, in the midst of them, an enormous sausage, which it required two men to carry. Then came geese and capons, tongues and hams, the ancient glory of the Christmas pie, a gigantic plum-pudding, a pyramid of minced pies, and a baron of beef bringing up the rear.[17]

"It is something new under the sun," said the divine, as he sat down, "to see a great dinner without fish."

MR. CHAINMAIL.

Fish was for fasts, in the twelfth century.

THE REV. DR. FOLLIOTT.

Well, sir, I prefer our reformed system of putting fasts and feasts together. Not but here is ample indemnity.[18]

Ale and wine flowed in abundance. The dinner passed off merrily: the old harper playing all the while the oldest music in his repertory. The tables being cleared, he indemnified himself for lost time at the lower end of the hall, in company with the old butler and the other domestics, whose attendance on the banquet had been indispensable.

The scheme of Christmas gambols, which Mr. Chainmail had laid for the evening, was interrupted by a tremendous clamor without.[19]

THE REV. DR. FOLLIOTT.

What have we here? Mummers?[20]

MR. CHAINMAIL.

Nay, I know not. I expect none.

"Who is there?" he added, approaching the door of the hall.

"Who is there?" vociferated the divine, with the voice of Stentor.[21]

"Captain Swing,"[22] replied a chorus of discordant voices.

THE REV. DR. FOLLIOTT.

Ho, ho! here is a piece of the dark ages we did not bargain for. Here is the Jacquerie.[23] Here is the march of mind with a witness.

MR. MAC QUEDY.

Do you not see that you have brought disparates together?[24] the Jacquerie and the march of mind.

THE REV. DR. FOLLIOTT.

Not at all, sir. They are the same thing, under different names. Πολλῶν ονομάτων μορφὴ μία.* [25] What was Jacquerie in the dark ages, is the march of mind in this very enlightened one—very enlightened one.

---

* "One shape of many names."

ÆSCHYLUS: *Prometheus.*

MR. CHAINMAIL.

The cause is the same in both; poverty in despair.[26]

MR. MAC QUEDY.

Very likely; but the effect is extremely disagreeable.

THE REV. DR. FOLLIOTT.

It is the natural result, Mr. Mac Quedy, of that system of state seamanship which your science upholds. Putting the crew on short allowance, and doubling the rations of the officers, is the sure way to make a mutiny on board[27] a ship in distress, Mr. Mac Quedy.

MR. MAC QUEDY.

Eh! sir, I uphold no such system as that. I shall set you right as to cause and effect. Discontent increases with the increase of information.* That is all.

THE REV. DR. FOLLIOTT.

I said it was the march of mind. But we have not time for discussing cause and effect now. Let us get rid of the enemy.

And he vociferated at the top of his voice, "What do you want here?"

"Arms, arms," replied a hundred voices, "Give us the arms."[28]

THE REV. DR. FOLLIOTT.

You see, Mr. Chainmail, this is the inconvenience of keeping an armoury, not fortified with sand bags, green bags,[29] and old bags of all kinds.

---

* This looks so like caricature, (a thing abhorrent to our candour,) that we must give authority for it. "We ought to look the evil manfully in the face, and not amuse ourselves with the dreams of fancy. The discontent of the laborers in our times is rather a proof of their superior information than of their deterioration."—*Morning Chronicle: December* 20, 1830.

MR. MAC QUEDY.

Just give them the old spits and toasting irons, and they will go away quietly.

MR. CHAINMAIL.

My spears and swords! not without my life. These assailants are all aliens to my land and house. My men will fight for me, one and all. This is the fortress of beef and ale.

MR. MAC QUEDY.

Eh! sir, when the rabble is up, it is very indiscriminating. You are e'en suffering for the sins of Sir Simon Steeltrap, and the like, who have pushed the principle of accumulation a little too far.

MR. CHAINMAIL.

The way to keep the people down, is kind and liberal usage.

MR. MAC QUEDY.

That is very well, (where it can be afforded,) in the way of prevention; but in the way of cure, the operation must be more drastic. *(Taking down a battle-axe.)* I would fain have a good blunderbuss[30] charged with slugs.

MR. CHAINMAIL.

When I suspended these arms for ornament, I never dreamed of their being called into use.

MR. SKIONAR.

Let me address them. I never failed to convince an audience that the best thing they could do was to go away.[31]

MR. MAC QUEDY.

Eh! sir, I can bring them to that conclusion in less time than you.

MR. CROTCHET.

I have no fancy for fighting. It is a very hard case upon a guest, when the latter end of a feast is the beginning of a fray.[32]

MR. MAC QUEDY.

Give them the old iron.

THE REV. DR. FOLLIOTT.

Give them the weapons! *Pessimo, medius fidius, exemplo.** [33] Forbid it the spirit of *Frere Jean des Entommeures!* [34] No! let us see what the church militant,[35] in the armour of the twelfth century, will do against the march of mind. Follow me who will, and stay who list. Here goes: *Pro aris et focis!* [36] that is, for tithe pigs and fires to roast them!

He clapped a helmet on his head, seized a long lance, threw open the gates, and tilted out on the rabble,[37] side by side with Mr. Chainmail, followed by the greater portion of the male inmates of the hall, who had armed themselves at random.

The rabble-rout, being unprepared for such a sortie, fled in all directions, over hedge and ditch.

Mr. Trillo stayed in the hall, playing a march on the harp, to inspirit the rest to sally out. The water-loving Mr. Philpot had diluted himself with so much wine, as to be quite *hors de combat.*[38] Mr. Toogood, intending to equip himself in purely defensive armour, contrived to slip a ponderous coat of mail over his shoulders, which pinioned his arms to his sides; and in this condition, like a chicken trussed for roasting, he was thrown down behind a pillar, in the first rush of the sortie. Mr. Crotchet seized the occurrence as a pretext for staying with him, and passed the whole time of the action in picking him out of his shell.

"Phew!" said the divine, returning; "an inglorious victory: but it deserves a devil[39] and a bowl of punch."

MR. CHAINMAIL.

A wassail-bowl.[40]

---

* A most pernicious example, by Hercules!

PETRONIUS ARBITER.

THE REV. DR. FOLLIOTT.

No, sir. No more of the twelfth century for me.

MR. CHAINMAIL.

Nay, Doctor. The twelfth century has backed you well. Its manners and habits, its community of kind feelings between master and man, are the true remedy for these ebullitions.

MR. TOOGOOD.

Something like it: improved by my diagram: arts for arms.

THE REV. DR. FOLLIOTT.

No wassail-bowl for me. Give me an unsophisticated bowl of punch, which belongs to that blissful middle period, after the Jacquerie was down, and before the march of mind was up. But, see, who is floundering in the water?

Proceeding to the edge of the moat, they fished up Mr. Firedamp, who had missed his way back, and tumbled in. He was drawn out, exclaiming, "that he had taken his last dose of *malaria* in this world."

THE REV. DR. FOLLIOTT.

Tut, man; dry clothes, a turkey's leg and rump, well devilled, and a quart of strong punch, will set all to rights.

"Wood embers," said Mr. Firedamp, when he had been accommodated with a change of clothes, "there is no antidote to *malaria* like the smoke of wood embers; pine embers." And he placed himself, with his mouth open, close by the fire.

THE REV. DR. FOLLIOTT.

Punch, sir, punch: there is no antidote like punch.

MR. CHAINMAIL.

Well, Doctor, you shall be indulged. But I shall have my wassail-bowl, nevertheless.

An immense bowl of spiced wine, with roasted apples hissing on its surface, was borne into the hall by four men, followed by an empty bowl of the same dimensions, with all the materials of arrack punch,[41] for the divine's especial brewage. He accinged[42] himself to the task, with his usual heroism, and having finished it to his entire satisfaction, reminded his host to order in the devil.

THE REV. DR. FOLLIOTT.

I think, Mr. Chainmail, we can amuse ourselves very well here all night. The enemy may be still excubant:[43] and we had better not disperse till daylight. I am perfectly satisfied with my quarters. Let the young folks go on with their gambols; let them dance to your old harper's minstrelsy; and if they please to kiss under the misletoe, whereof I espy a goodly bunch suspended at the end of the hall, let those who like it not, leave it to those who do. Moreover, if among the more sedate portion of the assembly, which, I foresee, will keep me company, there were any to revive the good old custom of singing after supper, so to fill up the intervals of the dances, the steps of night would move more lightly.

MR. CHAINMAIL.

My Susan will set the example, after she has set that of joining in the rustic dance, according to good customs long departed.

After the first dance, in which all classes of the company mingled, the young lady of the mansion took her harp, and following the reverend gentleman's suggestion, sang a song of the twelfth century.

FLORENCE AND BLANCHFLOR.*

Florence and Blanchflor, loveliest maids,
　　Within a summer grove,

* Imitated from the Fabliau, *De Florance et de Blanche Flor, alias Jugement d'Amour.*

Amid the flower-enamelled shades
    Together talked of love.

A clerk sweet Blanchflor's heart had gain'd;
    Fair Florence loved a knight:
And each with ardent voice maintained,
    She loved the worthiest wight.

Sweet Blanchflor praised her scholar dear,
    As courteous, kind, and true;
Fair Florence said her chevalier
    Could every foe subdue.

And Florence scorned the bookworm vain,
    Who sword nor spear could raise;
And Blanchflor scorned the unlettered brain
    Could sing no lady's praise.

From dearest love, the maidens bright
    To deadly hatred fell,
Each turned to shun the other's sight,
    And neither said farewell.

The king of birds, who held his court
    Within that flowery grove,
Sang loudly: "'Twill be rare disport
    To judge this suit of love."

Before him came the maidens bright,
    With all his birds around,
To judge the cause, if clerk or knight
    In love be worthiest found.

The falcon and the sparrow-hawk
    Stood forward for the fight:
Ready to do, and not to talk,
    They voted for the knight.

And Blanchflor's heart began to fail,
   Till rose the strong-voiced lark,
And, after him, the nightingale,
   And pleaded for the clerk.

The nightingale prevailed at length,
   Her pleading had such charms;
So eloquence can conquer strength,
   And arts can conquer arms.

The lovely Florence tore her hair,
   And died upon the place;
And all the birds assembled there,
   Bewailed the mournful case.

They piled up leaves and flowerets rare.
   Above the maiden bright,
And sang: "Farewell to Florence fair,
   Who too well loved her knight."

Several others of the party sang in the intervals of the dances. Mr. Chainmail handed to Mr. Trillo another ballad of the twelfth century, of a merrier character than the former. Mr. Trillo readily accommodated it with an air, and sang

THE PRIEST AND THE MULBERRY TREE.*

Did you hear of the curate who mounted his mare,
And merrily trotted along to the fair?
Of creature more tractable none ever heard;
In the height of her speed she would stop at a word,
And again with a word, when the curate said Hey,
She put forth her mettle, and galloped away.

As near to the gates of the city he rode,
While the sun of September all brilliantly glowed,
The good priest discovered, with eyes of desire,

* Imitated from the Fabliau, *Du Provoire qui mengea des Môres.*

A mulberry tree in a hedge of wild briar,
On boughs long and lofty, in many a green shoot,
Hung large, black, and glossy, the beautiful fruit.

The curate was hungry, and thirsty to boot;
He shrunk from the thorns, though he longed for the fruit;
With a word he arrested his courser's keen speed,
And he stood up erect on the back of his steed;
On the saddle he stood, while the creature stood still,
And he gathered the fruit, till he took his good fill.

"Sure never," he thought, "was a creature so rare,
So docile, so true, as my excellent mare.
Lo, here, how I stand" (and he gazed all around,)
"As safe and as steady as if on the ground,
Yet how had it been, if some traveller this way,
Had, dreaming no mischief, but chanced to cry Hey?"

He stood with his head in the mulberry tree,
And he spoke out aloud in his fond reverie:
At the sound of the word, the good mare made a push,
And down went the priest in the wild-briar bush.
He remembered too late, on his thorny green bed,
Much that well may be thought, cannot wisely be said.

Lady Clarinda, being prevailed on to take the harp in her turn, sang the following stanzas.

> In the days of old,
> Lovers felt true passion,
> Deeming years of sorrow
> By a smile repaid.
> Now the charms of gold,
> Spells of pride and fashion,
> Bid them say good morrow
> To the best-loved maid.
>
> Through the forests wild,
> O'er the mountains lonely,

They were never weary
Honor to pursue:
If the damsel smiled
Once in seven years only,
All their wanderings dreary,
Ample guerdon[44] knew.

Now one day's caprice
Weighs down years of smiling,
Youthful hearts are rovers,
Love is bought and sold:
Fortune's gifts may cease,
Love is less beguiling;
Wiser were the lovers,
In the days of old.

The glance which she threw at the Captain, as she sang the last verse, awakened his dormant hopes. Looking round for his rival, he saw that he was not in the hall; and, approaching the lady of his heart, he received one of the sweetest smiles of their earlier days.

After a time, the ladies, and all the females of the party, retired. The males remained on duty with punch and wassail, and dropped off one by one into sweet forgetfulness; so that when the rising sun of December looked through the painted windows on mouldering embers and flickering lamps, the vaulted roof was echoing to a mellifluous concert of noses, from the clarionet of the waiting-boy at one end of the hall, to the double bass of the Reverend Doctor, ringing over the empty punch-bowl, at the other.

CONCLUSION.[45]

FROM this eventful night, young Crotchet was seen no more on English mould.[46] Whither he had vanished, was a question that could no more be answered in his case, than in that of King Arthur, after the battle of Camlan.[47] The great firm of Catchflat and Company figured in the Gazette, and paid sixpence in the pound; and it was clear that he had shrunk from exhibiting himself on the scene of his former greatness, shorn of the beams of his paper prosperity. Some supposed him to be sleeping among the undiscoverable secrets of some barbel-pool in the Thames;[48] but those who knew him best were more inclined to the opinion that he had gone across the Atlantic, with his pockets full of surplus capital, to join his old acquaintance, Mr. Touchandgo, in the bank of Dotandcarry-onetown.

Lady Clarinda was more sorry for her father's disappointment than her own; but she had too much pride to allow herself to be put up a second time in the money-market; and when the Captain renewed his assiduities, her old partiality for him, combining with a sense of gratitude for a degree of constancy which she knew she scarcely deserved, induced her, with Lord Foolincourt's hard-wrung consent, to share with him a more humble, but less precarious fortune, than that to which she had been destined as the price of a rotten borough.[49]

THE END.

Peacock's Preface of 1837

PREFACE

TO THE
VOLUME OF "STANDARD NOVELS"
CONTAINING
"HEADLONG HALL," "NIGHTMARE ABBEY," "MAID
MARIAN," AND "CROTCHET CASTLE."

ALL these little publications appeared originally without prefaces. I left them to speak for themselves; and I thought I might very fitly preserve my own impersonality, having never intruded on the personality of others, nor taken any liberties but with public conduct and public opinions.[1] But an old friend assures me, that to publish a book without a preface is like entering a drawing-room without making a bow. In deference to this opinion, though I am not quite clear of its soundness, I make my prefatory bow at this eleventh hour.[2]

---

[1] **my own impersonality . . . public conduct and public opinions**: TLP makes a similar claim in his Preface to the 1856 edition of *Mel*: 'Of the disputants whose opinions and public characters (for I never trespassed on private life) were shadowed in some of the persons of the story, almost all have passed from the diurnal scene.'

[2] **In deference to this opinion . . . this eleventh hour**: Cf. Anthony Ashley Cooper, Third Earl of Shaftesbury's Preface to his *Characteristicks of Men, Manners, Opinions, Times* [1711], ed. Philip Ayres, 2 vols. (Oxford: Clarendon Press, 1999), vol. 1, p. 3: '*If the Author of these united Tracts had been any Friend to* PREFACES, *he wou'd probably have made his Entrance after that manner, in one or other of the Five Treatises formerly publish'd apart . . . Being satisfy'd, however, that there are many Persons who esteem these* Introductory Pieces *as very essential in the Constitution of a Work; he has thought fit, in behalf of his honest* Printer, *to substitute these Lines, under the Title of* A PREFACE.'

"Headlong Hall" was written in 1815; "Nightmare Abbey," in 1817;[3] "Maid Marian," with the exception of the last three chapters, in 1818; "Crotchet Castle," in 1830. I am desirous to note the intervals, because, at each of those periods, things were true, in great matters and in small, which are true no longer. "Headlong Hall" begins with the Holyhead Mail, and "Crotchet Castle" ends with a rotten borough. The Holyhead mail no longer keeps the same hours, nor stops at the Capel Cerig Inn, which the progress of improvement has thrown out of the road;[4] and the rotten boroughs of 1830 have ceased to exist, though there are some very pretty pocket properties, which are their worthy successors.[5] But the classes of tastes, feelings, and opinions, which are successively brought into play in these little tales, remain substantially the same. Perfectibilians, deteriorationists, statu-quo-ites, phrenologists, transcendentalists, political economists, theorists in all sciences, projectors in all arts, morbid visionaries, romantic enthusiasts, lovers of music, lovers of the picturesque, and lovers of good dinners, march, and will march for ever, *pari passu*[6] with the march of mechanics, which some facetiously call the march of intellect. The fastidious in old wine are a race that does not decay. Literary violators of the confidences of private life still gain a disreputable livelihood and an unenviable notoriety.

---

[3] **1817**: *NA* was actually written in the spring of 1818. See the account of its composition in the Introduction.

[4] **The Holyhead mail ... out of the road**: The mail coach road from London to Holyhead was realigned and reconstructed by Thomas Telford from 1815 to 1819.

[5] **rotten boroughs ... worthy successors**: Although the Reform Act of 1832 disenfranchised fifty-seven of the most notorious 'rotten boroughs' of the sort that TLP had satirized in *Mel*, a number of 'pocket boroughs' – ones with so few constituents that their parliamentary representation could be controlled by a single landowning individual or family – survived until the Reform Act of 1867. Cf. TLP's comment in his Preface to the 1856 edition of *Mel*: 'The boroughs of Onevote and Threevotes have been extinguished: but there remain boroughs of Fewvotes, in which Sir Oran Haut-ton might still find a free and enlightened constituency.'

[6] *pari passu*: 'Side by side; simultaneously and equally; at an equal rate of progress' (*OED*).

Match-makers from interest, and the disappointed in love and in friendship, are varieties of which specimens are extant. The great principle of the Right of Might is as flourishing now as in the days of Maid Marian: the array of false pretensions, moral, political, and literary, is as imposing as ever: the rulers of the world still feel things in their effects, and never foresee them in their causes; and political mountebanks continue, and will continue, to puff nostrums[7] and practise legerdemain[8] under the eyes of the multitude; following, like the "learned friend" of Crotchet Castle,[9] a course as tortuous as that of a river, but in a reverse process; beginning by being dark and deep, and ending by being transparent.

THE AUTHOR OF "HEADLONG HALL."

March 4, 1837.

---

[7] **nostrums**: 'A means or device for accomplishing something; a pet scheme or favourite remedy, esp. for bringing about some social or political reform or improvement' (*OED*).

[8] **legerdemain**: 'Trickery, deception, hocus-pocus' (*OED*).

[9] **the "learned friend" of Crotchet Castle**: The Reverend Doctor Folliott's sobriquet for Henry Brougham, first Baron Brougham and Vaux. Opposing barristers traditionally referred to each other, in the law courts or in parliamentary debates, as 'my learned friend'.

Holograph fragment of Chapter 4 (c. 1830)

HOLOGRAPH fragment of a draft of Chapter 4 of *Crotchet Castle* (c. 1830).

A single leaf torn from notebook. The text is almost illegible in places where the pencil is fading and rubbing off.

Location: Pforzheimer Collection, New York Public Library (TLP 151).

over the expectant company especially when they
are waiting for some one last comer whom
they all heartily curse in their hearts and
whom they welcome ~~with~~ as a sinner more
heartily than all the just persons who had
been punctual to their engagement: in which
welcome they are by no means insincere seeing
that though they had cursed him but the
minute before they sincerely rejoice in his
arrival as the removal of the last impediment
between themselves and their dinner.

Philosophie d'amateur. (Sain[t] Paul & learned
friend: Quackery)[1]

---

[1] **Philosophie... Quackery**: The last sentence, set off from the preceding section, perhaps shows TLP beginning to sketch out a new dialogue or chapter. On 'Philosophy d'amateur' and Brougham, see Appendix A, n. 9 (p. 154) and *CC*, ch. 3: 'A worthy friend of mine, who is a sort of amateur in philosophy, criticism, politics, and a wee bit of many things more' (p. 28). Philosophers aligned to the utilitarian and materialist causes were routinely accorded the status of 'amateurs'. In 'The Fate of a Broom' (Appendix G), TLP satirizes Brougham for 'Pouring on king, lords, church, and rabble, / Long floods of favour-currying gabble' (p. 171). He may have been irreverently associating Brougham's conduct with 'Saint Paul's precept of being all things to all men' (*Mel*, ch. 1). St Paul is also mentioned in *ME*, ch. 6, and his words are invoked in *GG*, ch. 7.

Holograph fragment of Chapter 5 (c. 1830)

HOLOGRAPH fragment of an early draft of Chapter 5 of *Crotchet Castle* (c. 1830).

One page, folded down the middle.

Location: Pierpont Morgan Library, Literary and Historical Manuscripts (MA 4361).

> The next neighbour[1] of Mr Crotchet was
> ~~Squire Steeltrap~~ Steeltrap Fitz-Treadmill
> Esquire a great game-preserver and justice
> of peace. ~~This~~ worthy with ~~his~~ the help of his
> clerk Maresnest and his ^head^ gamekeeper Dogspike
> and his solicitor Kiteclaw contrived to be the
> terror of the peasantry whom he had stripped of
> their common rights & stopped out of their old
> ~~footpaths~~ paths, not even leaving them a strip of
> green for cricket: in return for which kindness they
> never lost an opportunity of pulling down his
> fences cutting off the heads of his young plantations
> & treading on the eggs of his birds. ~~and s~~ Dogspike
> had been several times grievously ~~bat~~ beaten and
> Kiteclaw had even been waylaid and left ~~haff~~

---

[1] **The next neighbour**: The phrasing suggests that *CC*, ch. 5 was conceived as a third-person roundtable survey of the characters, whereas in the published version of the text each description comes from Lady Clarinda and is given to Captain Fitzchrome. This draft is not quite the basis for the dialogue between Lady Clarinda and Captain Fitzchrome in the published 1831 version of ch. 5 (although it comes close to a section of that text, pp. 48–9); it must therefore represent a fairly early version of this part of the novel.

~~haf~~ half-dead in a ditch.[2] ~~The S~~ Somebody
was always punished for these outrages: generally
somebody who was not guilty: which added to
the number of the aggrieved and emboldened the
former perpetrators to a repetition of their exploits.[3]

[2] **Kiteclaw... half-dead in a ditch**: This fragment spells out and extends
some of the criticisms of landowners and Enclosure Acts made in earlier
chapters; the mention of what happens to Kiteclaw is perhaps transposed
into or partly reflected in the attack on Folliott in *CC*, ch. 8 (pp. 75–8).

[3] **The next neighbour... their exploits**: Cf. *CC*, ch. 5: 'Next to him is Sir
Simon Steeltrap, of Steeltrap Lodge, Member for Crouching-Curtown,
Justice of Peace for the county, and Lord of the United Manors of
Springgun-and-Treadmill; a great preserver of game and public morals.
By administering the laws which he assists in making, he disposes, at his
pleasure, of the land and its live stock, including all the two-legged varieties,
with and without feathers, in a circumference of several miles round
Steeltrap Lodge. He has enclosed commons and woodlands; abolished
cottage-gardens; taken the village cricket-ground into his own park, out of
pure regard to the sanctity of Sunday; shut up footpaths and alehouses, (all
but those which belong to his electioneering friend, Mr. Quassia, the
brewer;) put down fairs and fiddlers; committed many poachers; shot a few;
convicted one third of the peasantry; suspected the rest; and passed nearly
the whole of them through a wholesome course of prison discipline, which
has finished their education at the expense of the county' (p. 49).

Holograph manuscript of 'Touchandgo'
(watermark 1827)

HOLOGRAPH manuscript of 'Touchandgo', on three pages of a double quarto sheet of blue-grey Whatman paper, dated 1827 in watermark, tipped in at the back of a bound manuscript copy of *Paper Money Lyrics*. The poem is reprinted in Halliford , 7.242–4 (see also 7.496–7).

Location: Pforzheimer Collection, New York Public Library (TLP 18).

pray who can show
Hoho! hoho! ~~and do you know~~
Whither has fled great Touchandgo?
He's gone off in a chaise and pair[1]
And not a man on earth knows where.

In his own chariot off he ran
And there was not a turnpike man
~~His   In his own chariot he has gone~~
Twixt London and the western channel
Could see his arms upon the pannel
~~He set off with the morning-dawn~~

Some say he took the road to Bristol[2]

---

[1] **chaise and pair**: A carriage drawn by a pair of horses.

[2] **Some say he took the road to Bristol**: '[Rowland] Stephenson arrived in Bristol seven or eight days before [George] Ledbetter was despatched in pursuit of him. This officer traced him from the Gloucester-hotel at Clifton, to the Lamplighter's-hall at Pill, where Stephenson remained for one night. Whilst he was there, it was pretended he was in a very delicate state of

Equipped with sixpence and ^ ᵃ pistol
Some say with ~~plen~~ᵍᵒˡᵈ he' ˢ ~~was~~ ʷᵉˡˡ apparelled
And blunderbusses double-barrelled³

Others affirm he strove to pop
His brains out in my uncle's shop
And missing fire set off to Milford⁴
With lots of sovereigns which he pilfered

Some say he beat about all Sunday
I' th' wind's eye off the isle of Lundy⁵
Showered on them pails to [for of] gold like manna⁶

---

health, and that, all other remedies having failed, the wretched invalid was recommended to try, as a last resort, a short voyage, in the hope that sea-sickness might afford him some relief' (*The Times* (22 Jan. 1829), p. 2).

3 **pistol . . . blunderbusses double-barrelled**: 'Some suspicion was from the first excited by their exhibition of three brace of pistols, added to their great anxiety to avoid notice, and their profuse expenditure of money' (*The Times* (13 Jan. 1829), p. 3).

4 **Milford**: The Port of Milford Haven in Wales; 'on the 2d instant, Stephenson and his companion took a skiff and arrived at Milford, from whence they went into Angle Bay (a small inlet on the south side of Milford) next day, Saturday' (*The Times* (13 Jan. 1829), p. 3).

5 **isle of Lundy**: 'The boat in which Stephenson and Lloyd embarked had not proceeded far from the shore, when Stephenson began to justify the prediction of his physician: the sea-voyage was already working his cure, he raised himself in the boat, and astonished the crew by a sudden accession of health and strength. He soon satisfied the doubts and scruples of the boatmen. They sailed to Lundy Island, and there met the *Ranger*, of Bideford, on board which Stephenson and Lloyd got. The *Ranger* beat about the Channel for some time without falling in with a single outward-bound ship. Lee, the captain, being unable to continue any longer at sea, offered to take Stephenson and Lloyd to Clovelly, where his brother, who had a fine pilot-boat (the *Sally*), lived, and having assured them that Clovelly was a retiring and unfrequented place, they consented to be put on shore there' (*The Times* (22 Jan. 1829), p. 2).

6 **Showered on them . . . gold like manna**: 'In the evening [Stephenson] sent two guineas to the pilots, with a request that they would drink his health. This piece of liberality quite won their hearts, and determined them to do all

And there was shipped off for Savannah.[7]

Others aver he still doth dwell
Deep in a fishing vessel's well
And there chin-deep in Milford Haven
Takes cold and croaks like any raven.

They add
~~Some say~~ his assignée's[8] attorney
Has ~~fl~~ waited on Sir Richard Birnie[9]
With a request that Mr Bishop[10]

Him
~~The culprit~~ from said ^fishing^ smack may fish up.

in their power for a gentleman who had proved himself, as one of them
said, "a real *genman*." . . . Towards the evening the Captain of the *Sally*
informed them that the wind had considerably lulled, and in a few minutes
everything was got ready for sea. Stephenson paid the bill, giving a very
liberal allowance to all the servants; he even thought the charges too
moderate. The landlady was quite delighted with his generosity' (*The Times*,
22 Jan. 1829), p. 2).

[7] **And there was shipped off for Savannah**: Stephenson and Lloyd took
passage on a ship to Savannah, Georgia.

[8] **assignée's**: An 'assignée' is a person to whom a right or liability is legally
transferred, or a person appointed to act for someone else.

[9] **Sir Richard Birnie**: Scottish police magistrate in London. In Feb. 1820,
he headed the Bow-Street Runners in apprehending the Cato Street
conspirators. They were plotting to assassinate a number of British cabinet
ministers and the Prime Minister, Lord Liverpool, in the hope of sparking a
revolution.

[10] **Mr Bishop**: Daniel Bishop, an officer of Bow Street. 'A communication
having been forwarded to Bow-street, Sir R. Birnie immediately sent for
[James] Ellis and [George] Ruthven, who were directed to proceed with all
despatch for Bristol. They left town accordingly on Sunday afternoon,
having received orders to scour the coast from Bristol to Biddeford, and to
examine all the intermediate ports. On Monday afternoon [Daniel] Bishop
was despatched to Falmouth, his instructions being to proceed onwards
until he met his colleagues. Fast-sailing vessels were in the mean time
despatched by the Admiralty to intercept and search every ship coming
down the Channel' (*The Times* (7 Jan. 1829), p. 3).

~~Others declare that~~
Some say a fleet has just weighed anchor

To chace ~~this wildgoose of a~~ the flying clerk and banker
With
~~Or~~ picked men guns and comrades

       or
To take ~~and~~ sink or burn the blades.

Well done Britannia rules the waves
A fleet to catch the brace of knaves

       coinage[11]
This paper-~~money~~ sets in motion
All England and the Atlantic ocean.

Now hark away you Bow-street runners
Whistle you boatswains swear you gunners

       all your canvas
~~Hoist~~ Spread ~~every rag~~ seamen loyal
Gib[12] studding-sail[13] and top-gallant-royal[14]

Jack Tar[15] has found a worthy foe
~~Old England's tars are well employed~~
To chace in mighty Touchandgo
~~In hunting Stevenson and Lloyd~~

---

[11] **paper-coinage**: On 'the sacred thirst of paper-money', cf. *CC*, ch. 1 (p. 6), 2 (p. 51), 11 (p. 97), 12 (p. 105), 18 (p. 108).

[12] **Gib**: 'A piece of wood or metal employed to keep something else, e.g. some part of a machine, in place' (*OED*).

[13] **studding-sail**: 'A sail set beyond the leeches of any of the principal sails during a fair wind' (*OED*).

[14] **top-gallant-royal**: 'Gallant' is 'often used as an admiring epithet for a ship' (*OED*); cf. *The Tempest*, act 5, scene 1, line 237: 'Our royal, good, and gallant ship'.

[15] **Jack Tar**: A common nickname for sailors of the Royal Navy.

Who'll back the "Victory" 'gainst the "Funny"?[16]
Huzza! St George and paper-money.

---

[16] **the "Victory" 'gainst the "Funny"**: HMS Victory, a 104-gun first-rate ship of the line of the Royal Navy, was launched in 1765 and is best known as Lord Nelson's flagship at the Battle of Trafalgar in 1805. A 'funny' is 'A narrow, clinker-built pleasure-boat for a pair of sculls. Also loosely, any light boat' (*OED*).

2 Holograph manuscript fragment of 'Touchandgo'
(watermark 1828)

Holograph manuscript of 'Touchandgo'
(watermark 1828)

HOLOGRAPH manuscript of 'Touchandgo', with numerous corrections, on a double folio sheet of blue-grey Whatman paper (dated
1828 in watermark). The first page is numbered '199' and the third
'201'. The poem is reprinted in Halliford, 7.494–6.

Location: Pforzheimer Collection, New York Public Library (TLP
55).

> My feelings have
> been very much hurt
> by reading some wicked
> verses about you in a
> newspaper. I could not
> help copying them, because
> they were about you; and
> so I send them to you;
> but it is very inconsiderate
> and cruel in people, to
> amuse themselves in this
> way with other people's
> misfortunes. To be sure there
> is some comfort in the last verse.[1]

Ho ho! ho ho! pray who can shew,
Whither has fled great Touchandgo?
He's gone off in a chaise and pair,
And not a soul on earth knows where.

In his own chariot off he ran,
And there was not a turnpike man

---

[1] **My feelings . . . last verse**: The wording of this paragraph resembles *CC*,
ch. 11 (p. 101): 'The people in London said very unkind things of you: they
hurt me very much at the time; but now I am out of their way, I do not seem
to think their opinion of much consequence.'

'Twixt London and the western channel,
Could see his arms upon the pannel.
Some say~~s he took the road to Bris~~
       he took the road to Milford,[2]
With lots ~~to~~ of sovereigns which he pilfered,
With hidden jewels well apparelled
~~And others swear he's gone to Bristol~~
~~Equipped with~~ And blunderbusses double-barrelled.
~~With only sixpence and a pistol.~~

Others aver, he tried to pop
His brains out in my uncle's shop,
         set off for
And, missing fire, ~~went post~~ Bristol,
Equipped with sixpence and a pistol.[3]

Others affirm, he still doth dwell
Deep in a fishing-vessel's well,
Croaking, while cold his utterance clogs,
Like Aristophanes's frogs.[4]

Some say, his assignée's attorney,
Has sailed on Sir Richard Birnie,
With a request that Mr. Bishop[5]
Him from said fishing-smack may fish up.[6]

Some say, his creditors are frantic,
      halfw~~ay~~ seas o'er
To think he's ~~safe across~~ th' Atlantic:
Some say, a fleet has just weighed anchor,
      moon-shooting
To chase the great ~~sky-scraping~~ banker.

[2] **Milford**: See Appendix D, n. 4 (p. 159).
[3] **Bristol . . . pistol**: See Appendix D, nn. 2 and 3.
[4] **Aristophanes's frogs**: The frogs are said to sing while Dionysus is ferried across the lake to Hades. Cf. references to Aristophanes' *Frogs* in *CC*, ch. 6 (pp. 56, 58).
[5] **assignée's . . . Birnie . . . Bishop**: See Appendix D, nn. 8–10.
[6] **Others affirm . . . fish up**: Stanzas 5 and 6 are lightly cancelled with a cross-hatching in ink.

Where'er he be, on land or sea,
~~I own~~ Is, after all, all one to me:
~~I wis,~~ In London town there ˄ ^surely^ be
Five hundred rogues as great as he.*

_____

_____

* I trust there are within this realm
    Five hundred good as he.
        King Henry in Chevy Chase.[7]

        ~~As a set-off~~
      ~~against~~ Now to drive
      this piece of cruelty out
      of your mind I send
      you the ~~ballad founded~~
      ~~I spoke of. It is founded~~
      on a tradition connected
          spot
      with a ~~stream~~ in
      this neighbourhood which
      I visit every-day. –

      ~~Llyaydreiddiadriawd~~

      little song I spoke of.
          ~~Tros y Mor.~~[8]

---

[7] **Chevy Chase**: This famous ballad probably originated in the early fifteenth century, undergoing many corruptions and alterations before it was first printed in Thomas Percy's *Reliques of Ancient English Poetry* (1765) in two different versions. On being told of the death of Lord Percy, King Henry IV ('King Harry') responds 'I've a hundred captains in England . . . / As good as ever was he' (stanza 58, lines 245–6).

[8] **As a set-off . . . Tros y Mor**: The last paragraph anticipates Susannah's introduction of the song that she sends to her father in *CC*, ch. 11; in her postscript in the novel, she uses the phrase: 'This is the little song I spoke of' (p. 108).

Holograph fragment of Chapter 16 (c. 1830)

HOLOGRAPH fragment of an advanced draft of Chapter 16 of *Crotchet Castle* (c. 1830).

One small quarto leaf, folded twice, numbered 263 (altered from 253), possibly from a notebook. The text is written on both sides in a single column down the right-hand half of the page, the speakers' names extending into the left-hand column.

Location: British Library (RP 6769).

M͟r Chainmail
could find no trace of the
Captain. ~~He~~ Indeed he
sought him but in one
direction which was that
leading to the farm: where
he arrived in due time and
found Miss Susan alone.
He laid the newspaper on
the table as was his custom
and proceeded to converse
with the young lady: a
conversation of many pauses
as much of signs as of
words. The young lady
took up the paper and
turned it over and over
while she listened to M͟r
Chainmail whom she found

every day more and more
agreeable when suddenly
her eye glanced on ~~a passage~~
something which made her
change colour and dropping [page break]
on
the paper ~~from~~ on the ground
she ~~star~~ rose from her
seat exclaiming: ~~It is~~
~~not yet too~~[1] "Miserable must
she be who trusts any of
your faithless sex. = Never
never never will I endure
such misery twice." And
she vanished up the stairs
Mͬ Chainmail was petrified
At length he ~~exclaimed~~ cried
aloud: Cornelius Agrippa
must have laid ~~up~~ a spell
on this accursed newspaper
and was turning ~~out~~ it over
to look for the source of
the mischief when Mͬˢ
      Llymry
Ap – ~~Flummery~~[2] made her
appearance.

---

[1] ~~It is not yet too~~: There is the suggestion of a plot twist in Susan's cancelled
words; it is perhaps 'not yet too' late for something. She cannot be expecting
to rekindle her old romance with Crotchet, given that he is now married.
Perhaps she was originally intended to say that it is not yet too late to escape
her budding romance with Chainmail, and thus protect herself from further
injury.

[2] **Llymry ... ~~Flummery~~**: Cf. TLP's footnote to *CC*, ch. 1, in which he
explains that 'flummery' is an English translation of 'llymry' (p. 10).

M^{rs} Ap~~Flummery~~ Llymry.[3]
What have you done to
poor dear Miss Susan? She
is crying ready to break
her heart.

[3] **M^{rs} Ap~~Flummery~~ Llymry**: Mrs Ap-Llymry's speech is presented without speech marks, as is Chainmail's brief speech on Cornelius Agrippa, though a closing set may have been cut off by a page break. Mrs Ap-Llymry's speech is not indented, but the fact that TLP gives her name alone, followed by a full stop, and then her speech beneath it, suggests the play-script layout (with names in small capitals) that is given to extended passages of dialogue in the published text of *CC*. 'Mrs Ap-' has been added on the indented left margin as if it is a second thought; the name was originally 'Flummery' alone. This also suggests the way of recording characters' names in drama, as cues to identify them before they give their speeches. It might also indicate that TLP did not at first intend Mrs Ap-Llymry, but Mr Ap-Llymry, to make this speech (and hence the challenge to Chainmail): this could explain his initial reference to the character by surname only. Perhaps TLP changed his mind because he had already made Chainmail suffer the attentions of one Welsh male aggressor in this chapter, the infatuated Harry Ap-Heather.

APPENDIX G

'The Fate of a Broom: An Anticipation' (1831, 1837)

THESE lines, with an introductory comment from the author, were added by Peacock as a footnote to Chapter 18 in 1837.

I may here insert, as somewhat germane to the matter, some lines which were written by me, in March, 1831, and printed in *The Examiner* of August 14. 1831. They were then called 'An Anticipation:' they may now (1837), be fairly entitled 'A Prophecy fulfilled.'

THE FATE OF A BROOM: AN ANTICIPATION.
    Lo! in Corruption's lumber-room,
    The remnants of a wondrous broom;[1]
    That walking, talking, oft was seen,
    Making stout promise to sweep clean;[2]
    But evermore, at every push,
    Proved but a stump[3] without a brush.
    Upon its handle-top, a sconce,[4]

---

[1] **broom**: A pun on Brougham's name, pronounced 'broom'.
[2] **promise to sweep clean**: Brougham was renowned for his political
    opportunism. Having passionately defended many liberal causes
    in the 1810s and 20s, he backtracked on some of them during the 1830s.
    Having championed the abolition of slavery, for example, he then showed
    little interest in the Slavery Abolition Bill of 1833. In educational reform, he
    ended up opposing the levying of a compulsory rate, which had originally
    been his idea.
[3] **stump**: A pun, '"a place or an occasion of political oratory" (*Century
    Dictionary*); *to go on the stump*, *to take the stump*: to go about the country
    making political speeches, whether as a candidate or as the advocate of a
    cause' (*OED*; first instance 1816); recalling Brougham's breaking of electoral
    promises earlier in his career.
[4] **sconce**: The figure of a head. A 'sconce' is 'A Jocular term for: The head; esp.
    the crown or top of the head' (*OED*). Cf. sconces in *CC*, ch. 8 (p. 75) and
    9 (p. 84).

Like Brahma's,[5] looked four ways at once,
Pouring on king, lords, church, and rabble,
Long floods of favour-currying gabble;[6]
From four-fold mouth-piece always spinning
Projects of plausible beginning,
Whereof said sconce did ne'er intend
That any one should have an end;[7]
Yet still, by shifts and quaint inventions,[8]
Got credit[9] for its good intentions,
Adding no trifle to the store,
Wherewith the devil paves his floor.
Worn out at last,[10] found bare and scrubbish,
And thrown aside with other rubbish,
We'll e'en hand o'er the enchanted stick,
As a choice present for Old Nick,[11]
To sweep, beyond the Stygian lake,[12]
The pavement it has helped to make.

---

[5] **Brahma's . . . at once**: Each head in the four-faced representation of Brahma represents one of the four Vedas, or scriptures. Cf. *CC*, ch. 1, on 'Brahma, the Maker' (p. 6).

[6] **Pouring . . . gabble**: See Appendix B, n. 1.

[7] **an end**: A pun, meaning both 'finishing-point' and 'objective in view'.

[8] **inventions**: Another reference to Brougham's oratory; see 'invention' (*OED*): '*Rhetoric*. The finding out or selection of topics to be treated, or arguments to be used.'

[9] **credit**: Another pun, hinting at Brougham's financial gain as well as his good repute.

[10] **Worn out at last**: Brougham was forced to give up the Chancellorship in 1834, with the fall of the Whig government.

[11] **Old Nick**: Satan.

[12] **Stygian lake**: One of the rivers beyond the underworld in Greek and Roman mythology. The wording may also recall another oratorical debate, in Milton's *Paradise Lost*: 'The Stygian council thus dissolved; and forth, / In order came the grand infernal Peers' (book 2, lines 506–7).

NOTE ON THE TEXT

We have collated the first edition of *Crotchet Castle* (1831) against the second lifetime edition (1837), incorporating into our copytext some of the corrections made in the latter. Our rationale for doing so is outlined here.

It is the policy of the Cambridge Edition of the Novels of Thomas Love Peacock to employ as copytexts the first editions, in book-length form, of Peacock's fictions. In the case of *Crotchet Castle*, this policy makes good sense for several reasons. The first edition of 1831, in all likelihood set from Peacock's manuscript, was printed by J. and C. Adlard of Bartholomew Close, London. The Adlards had an established connection with Peacock and his novels, having already printed the first editions of *Nightmare Abbey* (1818) and *The Misfortunes of Elphin* (1829), and the third edition of *Headlong Hall* (1822). *Crotchet Castle* was minimally revised in preparation for Richard Bentley's Standard Novels edition of 1837, which was printed by A. Spottiswoode of New Street Square.

There are few errors or misprints in 1831; the text is consistent in its formatting, spellings, capitalizations and treatment of names. By contrast, Bentley's 1837 Standard Novels edition of *Headlong Hall*, *Nightmare Abbey*, *Maid Marian* and *Crotchet Castle*, a cheap, sparingly altered reprint, shows evidence of haste and carelessness. It was advertised on the title page as appearing 'WITH CORRECTIONS, AND A PREFACE, BY THE AUTHOR'. Some corrections are indeed apparent – to Greek and Latin quotations, for instance – and are presumably authorial. On several occasions, we have emended the text accordingly; all such changes are recorded in the combined list of emendations and variants. But dozens of further variations enter the text in 1837. *Crotchet Castle* was a late addition to Bentley's volume; he was keen to see the book in print with minimal delay. The text was most probably set, at speed, from a marked copy of 1831. There are more slips in 1837 than in 1831: in Chapter 3, 'putting' has become 'putitng' and 'eighteen' is 'eighten'; in Chapter 9, 'fight' has turned into 'fiight' and 'industry' is 'imdustry'.

Whilst there are only three substantive changes in the main body of the text – from 'life' (1831) to 'woe' (1837) in Chapter 2, from 'reasons' (1831) to 'reason' (1837) in Chapter 7, and from 'who has been' (1831) to 'who was sent' (1837) in Chapter 17 – nearly every page reveals discrepancies in spelling and punctuation between the two editions. There are further small differences in the presentation of epigraphs, songs and passages of dialogue, and in lineation. In keeping with fashions in orthography and in the formal appearance of printed books, the 1831 text is more lavishly punctuated, keener on capital letters, and prefers a different system of spelling ('shew', 'civilise', 'realise', 'honor', 'favor', 'color') from 1837's ('show', 'civilize', 'realize', 'honour', 'favour', 'colour'). The 1831 edition, published as a freestanding volume, has each chapter start on a fresh page, whilst the 1837 edition, in which *Crotchet Castle* is one of four novels in the same book, runs them together and therefore saves on space. The 1837 text tends to make dashes longer and to render what were hyphenated words in 1831 as unhyphenated. There is one major addition in 1837: Peacock's lines on Brougham ('Lo! in Corruption's lumber-room, / The remnants of a wondrous broom . . . '), originally published in *The Examiner* (14 August 1831), are reprinted as a footnote to Folliott's satirical remarks on a defecting politician (Chapter 18). These lines appear in Appendix G of the present volume.

Our copytext for *Crotchet Castle* (1831) is that of the English Faculty Library Rare Book Room, Oxford, XM60.1 [Cro] 400217606. This has been checked against another copy of 1831, also in the English Faculty Library Rare Book Room [XM60.1 [Cro] 400217605], against three copies in the Bodleian Library [31.193,

Dunston B 1428a and B 1428b], and against a copy in the British Library [N.859(1)]. Four copies of Richard Bentley's 1837 Standard Novels edition of *Headlong Hall, Nightmare Abbey, Maid Marian* and *Crotchet Castle* have been consulted; their locations are as follows: the English Faculty Library Rare Book Room, Oxford [XM60.1 [Hea] 400309745], the Bodleian Library [Dunston B 1430 and 256 e.15834], and the British Library [W4 / 7498].

Some account of the conjugate relation and disputed order of the two pairs of preliminary leaves of *Crotchet Castle* has been provided in our Introduction, pp. lxx–lxxii. In our copytext, the prelims are arranged as follows: (1) title, (2) advertisement, (3) contents, (4) half-title.[1] When deciding how to order these materials in the present

---

[1] In copies of the first edition that survive in the United Kingdom and North America and have been consulted or referred to by the present editors, the prelims appear in various configurations:

(1) advertisement, (2) half-title, (3) title, (4) contents; [as in The Pennsylvania State University Library, PR5162.C7 1831 (La Fayette Butler's copy, in original dark blue-grey boards)]

(1) title, (2) contents, (3) advertisement, (4) half-title; [as in The Pennsylvania State University Library, PR5162.C7 1831 (John A. Spoor's copy, rebound)]

(1) title, (2) contents, (3) half-title, (4) advertisement; [as in Cambridge University Library Rare Books Room, Syn.7.83.48 (rebound)]

(1) advertisement, (2) title, (3) contents, (4) half-title; [as in a copy presently in the ownership of Antiquitates (rebound)]

(1) title, (2) contents, (3) no half-title, (4) no advertisement; [as in the Bodleian Library 31.193 (rebound)]

(1) title, (2) contents, (3) half-title, (4) no advertisement [as in the Carl H. Pforzheimer Collection, New York Public Library, Pforz (Peacock, T. L. Crotchet Castle. 1831), possibly rebound; in a copy presently owned by James Burmester: Rare Books; in the Bodleian Library Dunston B 1428a (rebound) and B 1428b (rebound); and in the English Faculty Library Rare Book Room, Oxford XM60.1 [Cro] 400217605 – in original dark blue-grey boards]

(1) title, (2) advertisement, (3) contents, (4) half-title [as in English Faculty Library (Oxford) Rare Book Room XM60.1 [Cro] 400217606 (rebound)]

edition, we have borne in mind that the printer's imprint originally appeared on the verso of the title page, an arrangement which clearly demonstrates that the title leaf was intended to be the first leaf. In early editions of Peacock's books, the printer's imprint appears either in this location or on the verso of the half-title (where there is one). We have therefore chosen to follow our copytext in placing the title page first and the so-called 'half-title' (which normally precedes the title page) after the contents leaf, rather than to follow the Halliford editors' suggestion that the correct order of the preliminary leaves of *Crotchet Castle* is (1) advertisement, (2) half-title, (3) title, (4) contents.

No attempt has been made to reproduce our copytext's spacing between a quotation mark and a word, or between a word and an exclamation mark, or to indicate variations in this kind of spacing between 1831 and 1837: such features are not textually significant. Nor has this spacing been reproduced in our transcriptions of Peacock's manuscript material. Spacing has, however, been respected where it might be said to contribute to meaning or to reflect the passage of time – in portions of dialogue, for instance, or in the amount of white space left on the page between Chapter 18 and the Conclusion. Dashes and their varying lengths have been reproduced as they appear in the copytext.

Ambiguous line-end hyphenations have been resolved with reference, where possible, to other instances of the same or a related compound in *Crotchet Castle*, and to the general pattern of hyphenation in the copytext: 1831 has more hyphens than 1837. Holograph fragments of the novel, as well as Peacock's letters and other published and unpublished texts, have been consulted in order to determine a resolution.

Peacock's footnotes remain, as he intended, at the bottom of the page; as in the copytext, they are indicated with daggers and asterisks. The presence of editorial endnotes is contrastingly indicated by superscript numbers in the text. However, Peacock's footnotes typically necessitate their own editorial endnotes. This means that the reader will sometimes have to behave like Mr Facing-bothways of *Pilgrim's Progress*, looking to the bottom of the page for the author's typically brief and sometimes cryptic indication of his source material and to the editors' explanatory note at the back of the volume, where more information (such as a translation and some context for the quotation) is provided. Within our editorial endnotes and list of emendations and variants annotations of this type are prefaced by '[Footnote:]'.

Peacock's Greek, Latin, Italian and French are printed so as to conform as closely as possible to their typographical appearance in the copytext, except where this might impede comprehension. As a young man Peacock regularly omitted accents and smooth breathings in his handwritten Greek, but he changed his mind and began including them some time in the middle of the 1820s. The early editions of his novels generally reflect his changing preferences in this matter, and his present editors have followed suit other than when there was good reason to think that a compositor failed to follow his known preferences at the time of writing. For the most part, then, Peacock's Greek has been reproduced as it appears in the copytext. However, a few minor adjustments have been necessary. As in Nicholas A. Joukovsky's edition of Peacock's letters, obsolete Greek abbreviations for $ου$ and $στ$ – common in early nineteenth-century printing, but very difficult to reproduce now – have been expanded. In order to avoid confusion, the placing of Greek accents and breathings has also been standardized (for more information on Peacock's Greek and its idiosyncrasies, see *Letters*, 1.cxii–cxiii). The combined list of emendations and variants records all instances of such standardization.

EMENDATIONS AND VARIANTS

The word or phrase as emended appears first, before the bracket. The emendation is located, its source identified, and the rejected reading of the copytext follows. A semicolon is used to separate the source of the emendation from the copytext reading. Two symbols indicate changes in punctuation. The swung dash (~) stands for the word previously cited when the variant is not in that word but in associated punctuation. The caret (^) stands for the absence of punctuation at a given point. A dropped letter or number or punctuation mark is indicated by square brackets [ ].

For a description of variants in the title page and preliminary materials, please see the Introduction, pp. lxx–lxxii and Note on the text, pp. 183–4. In the list below, variants are recorded only between the copytext of 1831 and the Standard Novels edition of 1837; details of the various copies consulted are given in the Note on the text. In two of the entries below, discrepancies exist between copies of the 1837 text as regards dropped letters; these have been noted in square brackets. All variants in substantives are listed, as are all variants in the spelling or capitalization of proper names. Variants in punctuation that affect the meaning of a passage or significantly alter the sentence structure, including all changes involving full stops, question marks, or exclamation points, have been listed; variants in hyphenation have not, other than when they occur within proper names (in 1837, Ap Llymry becomes Ap-Llymry). Variants in spacing between a word and a punctuation mark are not recorded.

Emendations show the date of an edition (1837) directly after the square bracket; variants incorporate a reading followed by the date of an edition (1837). If a word is emended on the editors' judgement only, that is apparent from the absence of a source. Where Peacock's Greek has been standardized, the change has been marked by a siglum (∗) after the entry.

CHAPTER I

page 5 line 1	CHAPTER] 1837; CHAP. 1831
page 6 line 11	Maker] maker 1837
page 6 line 12	Preserver] preserver 1837
page 6 line 13	Destroyer] destroyer 1837
page 6 line 17	they] They 1837
page 6 footnote	II. 2, 26.] II. 2. 26. 1837
page 7 line 3	honors] honours 1837
page 7 lines 5–6	ceremonies (payment being the principal), he] 1837; ceremonies,(payment being the principal,) he 1831
page 7 line 18	Castle] castle 1837
page 7 line 21	Castle] castle 1837
page 7 line 29	Castle:] castle; 1837
page 8 footnote	I. 10, 24.] 1. 10. 24. 1837
page 9 line 5	honors] honours 1837
page 9 line 6	honor] honour 1837
page 10 footnote	Anglicè] Anglicé 1837
page 11 line 21	Castle] castle 1837
page 11 line 28	Follē] Folle 1837
page 12 line 1	Bishop] bishop 1837
page 12 line 2	Devil] devil 1837
page 12 line 3	Devil] devil 1837
page 12 footnote	Folliot] Folliott 1837

CHAPTER 2

page 13 line 1	CHAPTER] 1837; CHAP. 1831
page 13 line 8	"I am] 1837; ^~ 1831

page 13 line 10	Hydrostatics] hydrostatics 1837
page 14 line 13	πρόϛωπον] πρόσωπον 1837
page 14 line 14	τηλαυγὲϛ] τηλαυγές 1837
page 14 line 14	πρόϛωπον] πρόσωπον 1837
page 14 line 16	fowl,] ~,—1837
page 16 line 28	supper.] ~! 1837
page 18 lines 4–5	civilized] civilised 1837
page 18 line 32	organization] organisation 1837
page 19 line 8	Modern] modern 1837
page 19 line 20	life] woe 1837
page 19 line 30	Ἐστιν] Ἔστιν 1837
page 20 line 18	Οἴνῳ] 1837; Οἴνω 1831
page 20 line 18	Ὑδάσπης] 1837; Ὑδάσπης 1831
page 21 line 7	dear] *om.* 1837
page 21 line 26	civilization] civilisation 1837

CHAPTER 3

page 23 line 1	CHAPTER] 1837; CHAP. 1831
page 23 line 7	*Lowe*] *Low* 1837
page 23 line 11	favor] favour 1837
page 23 line 13	Chaucer:] Chaucer:—
page 23 line 18	gamē] gamé 1837
page 23 line 24	Farwell] Farewell 1837
page 24 line 7	sir.] ~? 1837
page 25 line 18	putting] putitng 1837
page 26 line 6	father's. It] father's: it 1837
page 26 line 15	labor] labour 1837
page 27 line 28	eighteen] eighten 1837
page 28 line 7	civilization] civilisation 1837
page 28 line 9	civilization] civilisation 1837
page 28 line 11	property. A] property: a 1837
page 28 line 12	civilized] civilised 1837
page 29 line 22	natural] []atural 1837

page 32 line 18	shew] show 1837
page 33 line 1	Castle] castle 1837
page 33 line 5	Captain] captain 1837

CHAPTER 4

page 34 line 1	CHAPTER] 1837; CHAP. 1831
page 34 line 8	Captain] captain 1837
page 34 line 10	dullness] dulness 1837
page 34 line 17	Captain] captain 1837
page 34 line 26	Captain] captain 1837
page 35 line 6	point."] ~."—1837
page 35 line 7	Captain] captain 1837
page 35 line 12	philosophy."] ~."—1837
page 35 line 13	Captain] captain 1837
page 35 line 17	Captain] captain 1837
page 35 line 23	Captain] captain 1837
page 35 line 25	Captain] captain 1837
page 36 line 2	Captain's] captain's 1837
page 36 line 2	Captain] captain 1837
page 36 line 7	Captain] captain 1837
page 36 line 13	favor] favour 1837
page 36 line 27	Παπαπαῖ] Παπαπᾶι *
page 37 line 18	the] []he 1837
page 37 line 20	honor] honour 1837
page 37 line 23	flavor] flavour 1837
page 38 line 16	by] bye 1837
page 38 line 16	Captain] captain 1837
page 38 line 18	*Captain] captain* 1837
page 40 line 11	cognizance] cognisance 1837
page 40 line 16	click] clique 1837
page 41 line 3	letter.] ~^ 1837
page 41 line 9	strait] straight 1837
page 41 line 9	strait] straight 1837

page 41 [footnote:]	35.] 1837; ~^ 1831
page 41 [footnote:]	*Ol.* IX] Ol. ix 1837

CHAPTER 5

page 42 line 1	CHAPTER] 1837; CHAP. 1831
page 42 line 3	médiocre] mediocre 1837
page 42 line 30	anything] any thing 1837
page 45 line 4	El] []l 1837 [Bodleian 256.e.15834 and B1430]
page 45 line 24	favorite] favourite 1837
page 45 line 32	everything] every thing 1837
page 46 line 12	favor] favour 1837
page 46 line 14	favor] favour 1837
page 47 line 11	connexion] connection 1837
page 47 line 26	sooth] soothe 1837
page 47 line 30	piano;] ~: 1837
page 50 line 6	Captain] captain 1837
page 50 line 21	had] have 1837
page 51 line 4	no!] ~; 1837
page 51 line 21	favorite] favourite 1837

CHAPTER 6

page 52 line 1	CHAPTER] 1837; CHAP. 1831
page 52 line 6	past] passed 1837
page 52 line 25	cent—."] cent.—" 1837
page 53 line 4	labor] labour 1837
page 53 line 11	than] []han 1837
page 54 line 18	Claret] claret 1837
page 54 line 21	Doctor] doctor 1837
page 55 line 30	Claret] claret 1837
page 56 line 1	humor] humour 1837
page 56 line 15	Captain] captain 1837
page 56 line 15	You] you 1837

page 56 line 16	οἶδε] οιδε *
page 56 line 17	Captain] captain 1837
page 56 linc 18	obscurity 1837; obscur[]lity 1831
page 57 line 2	mean time] meantime 1837
page 58 line 10	Doctor] doctor 1837
page 58 line 23	humored] humoured 1837
page 59 line 13	Doctor] doctor 1837
page 59 line 25	civilize] civilise 1837
page 59 line 29	King] king 1837
page 60 line 22	Captain] captain 1837
page 60 line 27	Captain] captain 1837
page 60 line 30	sir!] ~? 1837
page 60 line 30	oh,] ~! 1837
page 61 line 7	Captain] captain 1837

CHAPTER 7

page 64 line 1	CHAPTER] 1837; CHAP. 1831
page 64 line 7	anti-room] anteroom 1837
page 64 line 14	anti-room] anteroom 1837
page 64 line 23	Captain] captain 1837
page 64 line 28	Captain] captain 1837
page 65 line 22	everything] every thing 1837
page 67 line 21	reason] 1837; reasons 1831
page 69 line 30	realizes] realises 1837
page 70 line 8	shewn] shown 1837
page 70 line 21	shew] show 1837
page 71 line 7	shew] show 1837
page 71 line 23	their] the 1837
page 71 line 23	husbands'] husband's 1837
page 73 line 17	progeny:] ~! 1837
page 74 line 4	Miss] Mis[] 1837
page 74 line 10	his] hi[] 1837 [Bodleian 256e.15834 and B1430]

CHAPTER 8

page 75 line 1	CHAPTER] 1837; CHAP. 1831
page 76 line 4	shew] show 1837
page 76 footnote	*Ecl.* II] *Ecl.* ii
page 77 line 1	Aye] Ay 1837
page 77 line 13	Doctor] doctor 1837
page 77 line 14	chace] chase 1837
page 77 line 24	Aye] Ay 1837
page 77 footnote	letters."] ~.^ 1837
page 78 line 19	Reverend] reverend 1837
page 78 line 24	honor] honour 1837
page 79 line 7	FOLLIOTT.] 1837; ~, 1831
page 79 line 12	APPLETWIG.] 1837; ~, 1831
page 80 line 1	COMMISSIONERS.] 1837; ~; 1831
page 81 line 12	was:] ~. 1837
page 81 line 20	Aye, aye] Ay, ay 1837
page 81 line 24	Reverend Doctor] reverend doctor 1837

CHAPTER 9

page 82 line 1	CHAPTER] 1837; CHAP. 1831
page 82 line 3	ἀναβάντες] 1837; ἀναβάντες 1831
page 82 line 22	Aye] Ay 1837
page 82 line 26	*stipare*] 1837; *stipere* 1831
page 82 footnote	II.] ii.
page 83 line 3	the Friar] the friar 1837
page 83 line 6	Past] past 1837
page 83 line 7	pulverized] pulverised 1837
page 83 line 13	learning] []earning 1837
page 83 line 22	catalogue:] ~! 1837
page 83 line 29	honor] honour 1837
page 84 line 2	favor] favour 1837

page 84 line 25	north] North 1837
page 84 line 25	south] South 1837
page 84 line 29	Aye] Ay 1837
page 85 line 24	ever] even 1837
page 86 line 10	colors] colours 1837
page 86 footnote	quam] []uam 1837
page 87 line 4	honor] honour 1837
page 87 line 16	fight] fiight 1837
page 87 line 19	of] *om.* 1837
page 87 line 28	favorably] favourably 1837
page 87 line 29	colors] colours 1837
page 88 line 5	industry] imdustry 1837

CHAPTER 10

page 89 line 1	CHAPTER] 1837; CHAP. 1831
page 89 line 23	everything] every thing 1837
page 89 line 25	caleidoscope] kaleidoscope 1837
page 90 line 11	the truth] she truth 1837
page 90 lines 12–13	connexion] connection 1837
page 90 line 20	spot;] spot: 1837
page 91 line 4	Captain] captain, 1837
page 91 line 6	shewing] showing 1837
page 91 line 24	labor] labour 1837
page 91 line 26	labor] labour 1837
page 92 line 28	civilization] civilisation 1837
page 93 line 12	civilization] civilisation 1837
page 93 line 31	Captain] captain 1837
page 94 line 5	humor] humour 1837
page 94 line 15	Captain] captain 1837
page 94 line 19	Captain] captain 1837
page 95 line 1	Captain] captain 1837
page 95 line 8	Captain] captain 1837

CHAPTER 11

page 96 line 1	CHAPTER] 1837; CHAP. 1831
page 96 line 5	Captain] captain 1837
page 96 line 12	vallies] valleys 1837
page 96 line 18	these:] ~: —1837
page 97 line 8	methodist] Methodist 1837
page 97 line 27	organize] organise 1837
page 98 line 7	favor] favour 1837
page 98 line 22	Majesty's] majesty's 1837
page 99 line 1	P. S.] ~—1837
page 99 line 20	Congress] congress 1837
page 99 line 22	Regulators] regulators 1837
page 100 line 18	letters:] ~: —1837
page 101 line 26	P. S.] ~—1837
page 101 line 27	of:] ~: —1837

CHAPTER 12

page 103 line 1	CHAPTER] 1837; CHAP. 1831
page 103 line 3	ὡϛ] ὡϛ 1837
page 103 line 7	Captain] captain 1837
page 103 line 29	expectation,] ~. 1837
page 104 line 3	Captain] captain 1837
page 104 line 8	Captain] captain 1837
page 104 line 26	Pindar] Pinder 1837
page 105 lines 21–2	anything] any thing 1837

CHAPTER 13

page 107 line 1	CHAPTER] 1837; CHAP. 1831
page 107 line 2	LAKE. THE] LAKE.—THE 1831
page 107 line 6	Captain,] captain,—1837
page 107 line 8	past;] ~,—1837
page 107 lines 18–19	splendor] splendour 1837

page 107 line 23	Captain] captain 1837
page 107 line 26	Captain] captain 1837
page 108 line 30	*recherchée*] *recherché* 1837
page 109 line 13	anything] any thing 1837

CHAPTER 14

page 111 line 1	CHAPTER] 1837; CHAP. 1831
page 111 line 15	light,] ~^ 1837
page 112 line 2	fallen.] ~, 1837
page 112 line 13	honor] honour 1837
page 112 line 24	favorite] favourite 1837
page 113 line 11	bole] boll 1837
page 113 line 12	the branches] theb ranches 1837
page 113 line 27	favorite] favourite 1837
page 114 line 27	gulph] gulf 1837
page 115 footnote	ἐθείρας] ἐθειρας 1837

CHAPTER 15

page 116 line 1	CHAPTER] 1837; CHAP. 1831
page 116 line 25	Ap Llymry] Ap-Llymry 1837
page 118 line 13	Ap Llymry] Ap-Llymry 1837
page 118 line 16	Ap Llymry] Ap-Llymry 1837
page 118 line 19	Ap Llymry] Ap-Llymry 1837
page 118 line 21	Ap Llymry] Ap-Llymry 1837
page 118 line 27	Ap Llymry's] Ap-Llymry's 1837
page 118 lines 28–9	Ap Llymry's] Ap-Llymry's 1837
page 119 line 1	honorable] honourable 1837
page 119 line 2	Macassar] macassar 1837
page 120 footnote	*Ballano in giro*] ~ *Giro* 1837

CHAPTER 16

| page 121 line 1 | CHAPTER] 1837; CHAP. 1831 |
| page 121 line 6 | vallies] valleys 1837 |

page 121 line 8   Captain] captain 1837
page 121 line 21   in] on 1837
page 121 line 26   favorable] favourable 1837
page 121 line 29   Captain] captain 1837
page 122 line 2   Captain] captain 1837
page 122 line 10   Captain] captain 1837
page 122 line 16   FITZCHROME] FITZCHORME 1837
page 122 line 23   CHAINMAIL] 1837; CHAINMAL 1831
page 122 line 26   service.] ~: —1837
page 125 line 16   shew] show 1837
page 126 line 24   Captain] captain 1837
page 126 line 30   Captain] captain 1837
page 127 line 9   Captain] captain 1837
page 127 line 13   Captain] captain 1837
page 127 line 25   never, never, never] Never, never, never
                       1837
page 127 line 32   she] She 1837
page 128 line 3   matter.] ~! 1837
page 128 line 12   honorable] honourable 1837
page 128 line 15   AP-LLYMRY] AP-LLYRMY 1837
page 128 line 28   Captain's] captain's 1837
page 129 line 23   dishonor] dishonour 1837
page 131 line 6   Captain] captain 1837

CHAPTER 17

page 132 line 1   CHAPTER] 1837; CHAP. 1831
page 133 line 9   to] *om.* 1837
page 133 line 13   me] my 1837
page 133 line 13   my] me 1837
page 133 line 17   has been down] was sent down 1837
page 133 line 28   Doctor] doctor 1837
page 134 line 2   lord] Lord 1837
page 134 line 5   Doctor] doctor 1837

page 134 line 9	him.] ~! 1837
page 134 line 11	Doctor] doctor 1837
page 134 line 23	He] he 1837
page 135 line 26	Old] old 1837
page 135 line 28	He! He!] ~ he! 1837
page 137 line 2	ὁυρεσίφοιτος] οὑρεσίφοιτος 1837

CHAPTER 18 AND CONCLUSION

page 138 line 1	CHAPTER] 1837; CHAP. 1831
page 138 line 15	misletoe] mistletoe 1837
page 139 line 9	Doctor] doctor 1837
page 139 line 22	Κικκαβαῦ, κικκαβαῦ] Κικκακαῦ, κικηαβαῦ 1837
page 139 footnote	Ὄρνιθες] Ὀρνιθις 1837
page 141 line 9	clamor] clamour 1837
page 141 line 27	ονομάτων μορφή μία] ὀνομάτων μορφῆμία 1837
page 142 footnote	candour,)]~),
page 142 footnote	laborers] labourers 1837
page 142 footnote	20,] 20. 1837
page 143 line 27	less] 1837; []ess 1831
page 144 line 5	*Frere] Frère* 1837
page 144 line 25	action in] actionin 1837
page 145 line 4	Doctor] doctor 1837
page 145 line 28	Doctor] doctor 1837
page 146 line 1	divine's] divines 1837
page 147 line 3	gain'd] gained 1837
page 148 line 13	rare.] ~, 1837
page 149 line 23	stanzas.] ~: —1837
page 150 line 2	Honor] Honour 1837

AMBIGUOUS LINE-END HYPHENATIONS

The hyphenated word in the copytext appears on the left; the word as it is printed in this edition appears on the right.

page 5 line 22	hand-/kerchief]	handkerchief
page 11 line 24	pre-/eminence]	pre-eminence
page 13 line 11	six-/penny]	sixpenny
page 13 line 23	night-/cap]	night-cap
page 14 line 17	touch-/stone]	touch-stone
page 25 line 2	fish-/pools]	fish-pools
page 45 line 18	gun-/powder]	gunpowder
page 45 line 23	house-/hold]	household
page 49 line 7	Steel-/trap]	Steeltrap
page 69 line 23	god-/fathers]	godfathers
page 78 line 32	Haut-/bois]	Hautbois
page 91 line 13	digla-/diations]	digladiations
page 92 line 30	Oroo-/noko]	Oroonoko
page 93 line 28	Ponty-/cysyllty]	Pontycysyllty
page 139 line 28	Catch-/flat]	Catchflat

EXPLANATORY NOTES

The present edition of *Crotchet Castle* includes fuller cross-referencing to Peacock's verse, drama, letters and essays, and to the works of other writers, than has previously been attempted. A multi-layered and densely allusive structure is one of the most enjoyable and potentially confusing aspects of Peacock's fictional style; when the Reverend Doctor Folliott boasts in Chapter 10 of his refusal to be 'subdued' on the matter of 'quotation' (p. 91), he might be speaking for his author. For the sake of convenience, reference has generally been made to standard scholarly editions of primary works. However, we have also made note of any significant features in the texts we know Peacock owned or which he is likely to have consulted; such features have been cited and briefly discussed in the notes below.

The treatment of quotations from Shakespeare offers a representative example of how we have proceeded with Peacock's sources. His library included *The Plays of William Shakespeare; in twenty-one volumes, with the corrections and illustrations of various commentators, to which are added notes by Samuel Johnson and George Steevens, revised and augmented by Isaac Reed with a Glossarial Index, Sixth Edition* (J. Nichols and Sons, etc., 1813), also known as the Reed Edition (*Sale Catalogue* 562). Some annotations in the Reed Edition of 1813 are relevant to moments in *Crotchet Castle*, and it has been cited in a note to Chapter 2. But we cannot be sure that Peacock was seeking to quote faithfully from this or from any particular edition of Shakespeare; indeed, his playful riffs on a single quotation in Chapter 1 suggest that he was not. References are therefore given to act, scene and line numbers in the second edition of *The Riverside Shakespeare*.

Place of publication, unless otherwise stated, is London.

TITLE PAGE AND PRELIMS

CROTCHET CASTLE: See Introduction, pp. lxx–lxxii on the disputed order of the preliminary materials in *CC*. Halliford suggests that TLP may have known Thomas Hurlstone's *Crotchet Lodge*, first acted in 1795 at Covent Garden (Halliford, 1.cxlix-cl); a spin-off drama, *The New Crotchet Lodge*, appeared in 1799. Hurlstone describes 'the cabin of a *Cognoscenti*, / Who'll give the *Crotchet Science*, in full score, / Such terms as *Amateurs* ne'er heard before'. Miss Crotchet and a Welsh character, Squire Shinken Ap Lloyd, also feature; the action and dialogue, however, are foreign to those of *Crotchet Castle*. See *Crotchet Lodge; A Farce, in two acts* (1795). On the various inflections of 'Crotchet', see ch. 1. Peacock's title may also owe something to Robert Burton's association, in *The Anatomy of Melancholy*, of a 'crotchet' in the sense of a 'whimsie' and a 'fiction' with a 'castle in the ayre' (part 1, section 3, member 1, subsection 2).

AUTHOR OF HEADLONG HALL: The title pages of *Mel*, *NA*, *MM*, *ME* and *GG* also avoid naming TLP and refer to him as 'The Author of *Headlong Hall*'. *HH* itself carried no indication of authorship on the title page. This was common practice in the period. After the anonymous publication of *Waverley* (1814), Walter Scott's novels followed a similar pattern and were signed 'by the Author of Waverley'. In his 'General Preface' to the *Magnum Opus*, Waverley Novels (1829), Scott noted: 'I can render little better reason for choosing to remain anonymous, than by saying with Shylock, that such was my humour' (the Edinburgh Edition of the Waverley Novels, gen. ed. David Hewitt, 30 vols. (Edinburgh: Edinburgh University Press, 1993–), vol. 25a: *Introductions and Notes from The Magnum Opus: Waverley to A Legend of the Wars of Montrose*, ed. J. H. Alexander, with P. D. Garside and Claire Lamont (Edinburgh: Edinburgh University Press, 2012), pp. 8–49 (p. 15)).

Le monde . . . son miroir: 'The world is full of fools and whoever wishes not to see any of them must live alone and break his mirror'. This proverbial couplet derives from *Satyre IV*, on the prevalence of human folly, in [Louis Petit's] *Discours satyriques et moraux, ou*

Satyres générales (Rouen: Richard Lallemant, 1686), later published as *Le nouveau Juvénal satyrique, pour la réformation des moeurs et des abus de notre siècle* (Utrecht: A. Schouten, 1716), where the relevant lines are as follows: 'Que de quelque côté que l'on tourne la vûë, / Il s'en presente aux yeux, & qui n'en veut point voir, / Doit les tenir fermez, & casser son Miroir' (lines 14–16).

Should once the world . . . earnest to: Samuel Butler, *Miscellaneous Thoughts – in Verse*: 'Should once the World resolve t'abolish / All that's ridiculous, and foolish, / It wou'd have nothing left to do, / T'apply in Jest or Earnest to' (lines 1–4). Cf. epigraphs from Butler prefacing chs. 2, 6 and 7 of *CC*, and the titular epigraph to *NA*, which compounds lines from different sections of Butler's *Hudibras* (1662– 78) and his 'Satyr upon the Weakness and Misery of Man'. The latter was first published posthumously, like *Miscellaneous Thoughts*, in *Genuine Remains* (1759). TLP owned this edition (*Sale Catalogue* 97; see also Butler items 96, 98, 99). The titular epigraph to *GG* is also taken from *Miscellaneous Thoughts*. *Hudibras* is cited in chs. 17 and 23 of *Mel* and in ch. 21 of *GG* (see also the notice of *NA* in *Monthly Review*, 90 (Nov. 1819), 327–9, which compares the book to *Hudibras*); in addition, Butler provides the epigraphs to chs. 3 and 4 of *MM*. For further references to Butler, see TLP's Marlow Journal (7 July–26 Sept. 1818), where he mentions reading 'some of Butler's minor poems, on the abuse of learning, on plagiaries, &c, for the fourth or fifth time' (26 July 1818), *Letters*, 1.136 and n.; see also 2.378, 449). TLP cites Butler's *Miscellaneous Thoughts* in a note to *Horæ Dramaticæ*, 'Querolus' (Halliford, 10.12 n.).

CHAPTER I

1 **villa**: A 'country seat' (Johnson's *Dictionary*) or any residence of a superior or handsome type, or of some architectural pretension – as is suggested by 'castellated', even if (as TLP goes on to point out) the remains of a castle really do stand nearby. See *OED* 'villa, n.', 1.d.; cf. Mainchance Villa, 'new residence of Peter Paypaul Paperstamp' in *Mel*, ch. 39.

2 **Captain Jamy... Henry V**: Henry V, act 3, scene 2, lines 118–
19. Captain Jamy is meant to be speaking in a thick Scottish
accent; he is intervening in a blasphemous and heated discussion
between the Irish Captain Macmorris and the Welsh Captain
Fluellen. The moment is appropriate to *CC* because it stresses
national character, and because it invites opposing sides to put
their respective cases and present their opinions. The fact that
each man speaks vociferously and wilfully misunderstands the
other is also relevant to what follows in *CC*.

3 **the Thames**: TLP often invokes the river's progress in order to
register diverse responses to 'progress' more generally (particularly in relation to commercial and financial matters). See e.g.
his letter to Edward Thomas Hookham (6–8 June 1809): 'The
Thames is almost as good a subject for a satire as a panegyric.
—A satirist might exclaim: The rapacity of Commerce, not content with the immense advantages derived from this river in a
course of nearly 300 miles, erects a ponderous engine over the
very place of it's nativity, to suck up it's unborn waters ... A panegyrist ... might say ... this noble river, this beautiful emblem,
and powerful instrument, of the commercial greatness of Britain'
(*Letters*, 1.35). See also TLP's earlier panegyric, *The Genius of
the Thames: A Lyrical Poem, in Two Parts* (1812): in part 2,
'commerce, wealth, and plenty smile / Along the silver-eddying
Thames' (Halliford, 6.155; see also 6.117–19, 6.129).

4 **polluted... streams of Surrey**: Conservancy of the River
Thames was entrusted to the citizens of London by various charters from 1197 and exercised by the Corporation of
London until 1857. Its jurisdiction extended from the River
Colne near Staines to Yantlett Creek and included parts of the
Rivers Medway and Lea and all streams and creeks of tidal
waters within these bounds. No significant legislation to address
pollution by refuse and sewage was passed until 1857, when
jurisdiction over the Thames from Staines to the sea was transferred to the Thames Conservancy Board. An Act of 1866 added

responsibility for the Upper Thames, at the same time increasing the number of Conservators, but the Conservancy Board was not granted full authority until 1874. In later life, TLP refused to visit London on account of its smoke and gas, referred to in *Mel*, ch. 16. The pollution he lamented was intellectual, too: 'Mystic's patent smoke public intellect shall choke' (*Mel*, ch. 39). See TLP's letters to Lord Broughton (22 Feb. 1862), to Thomas Hookham (3 Apr. 1862) and to Lord Broughton (17 May 1862) on air and water pollution (*Letters*, 2.437, 442, 443).

5 **greensward**: Poetic, romantic term for grass-covered ground or turf; cf. Walter Scott, *The Bridal of Triermain, or The Vale of St. John: In Three Cantos* (1813): 'the soft greensward is inlaid / With varied moss and thyme' (*The Poetical Works of Sir Walter Scott*, ed. J. Logie Robertson (London, New York and Toronto: Oxford University Press, 1904), 'Introduction to Canto Third', stanza 5, lines 11–12).

6 **pure and pellucid . . . Bandusium**: Horace, *Odes*, book 3, ode 13, apostrophizes this spring, which he describes as *splendidior vitro* ('more resplendent than glass'). The spring is known only from Horace's poem, and its location is disputed.

7 **wells of Scamander . . . the Greeks**: Scamander is one of the two rivers of the Trojan plain. Its source (the 'wells') is said in the *Iliad* (book 22, lines 147–52) to be two springs, one hot, the other cold. In Homer, Scamander is described as having 'beautiful streams'; like the fountain of Bandusium, the river therefore makes a suitable comparison for a pre-pollution Thames. 'Wells of Scamander . . . coming of the Greeks' is a fairly close translation of *Iliad*, book 22, lines 153–6, a wistful aside in Achilles' pursuit of Hector round the walls of Troy. The fact that its waters could be used for washing clothes further suggests Scamander's cleanliness.

8 **one of those beautiful vallies . . . a retired citizen**: In view of this description and the suggestion that a portion of the Ikenild

road is visible from the estate (ch. 3, p. 24), TLP seems to have in mind a location very near Goring, at the southern extremity of the Chiltern hills, in Oxfordshire, as the site of Crotchet Castle. Cf. Samuel Ireland, *Picturesque Views on the River Thames* (1799) (*Sale Catalogue* 258), a work that might have influenced the character and pursuits of Fitzchrome. TLP owned other volumes of picturesque engravings: William Gilpin's *Picturesque Beauty of the Mountains and Lakes of Cumberland and Westmoreland* (1786), *Observations on the River Wye* (1789) and *Observations on the Western Parts of England* (1798) (*Sale Catalogue* 201).

9 **Ebenezer Mac Crotchet . . . "north countrie"**: Cf. 'the hungry Scot' in *Mel*, ch. 1. Scots are associated with the financial discussions and developments that *CC* satirizes. Several poems in TLP's *Paper Money Lyrics* (wr. 1825–6; pub. 1837) refer to the Scottish: see, for example, 'Mac Fungus', 'a Scotch adept who dined with me last year', 'a Scotchman . . . singing "Prosperity"', and the 'Lament of Scotch Economists' (Halliford, 7.104, 116, 117, 128–31).

10 **handkerchief . . . pilgrimage**: The handkerchief, stick and voyage to London in search of wealth recall Dick Whittington. The first recorded pantomime version of the story dates from 1814; a few years later, George Cruikshank published an illustrated version, *The History of Dick Whittington, Lord Mayor of London: with the Adventures of his Cat* (c. 1820).

11 **Duke's Place**: A large Jewish community had lived in and around Duke's Place, Aldgate, since 1650.

12 **the windy side of the law**: *Twelfth Night*, act 3, scene 4, line 164. The speaker is Olivia's servant, Fabian, commenting on the letter in which Sir Andrew Aguecheek challenges Cesario to a duel. Cf. another likely reference to this scene in *Twelfth Night*, in ch. 2 (p. 13).

13 **the alley**: Exchange or Change Alley, a narrow passage connecting shops and coffeehouses in the City of London. Bounded by

Lombard Street, Cornhill and Birchin Lane, it served as a convenient shortcut from the Royal Exchange to the Post Office. The coffeehouses of Exchange Alley, especially Jonathan's and Garraway's, were early venues for speculation and the trading of shares and commodities.

[Footnote:] **Luculli** . . . *Imitation*: a reference to the story of how a soldier in the army of the Roman general Lucullus lost all his money. His condition of poverty drove him to subsequent deeds of bravery. Horace, *Epistles*, book 2, epistle 2, lines 26–40, to which TLP directs us, is the main source for this story. '*In Anna's wars* . . . *Imitation*': *The Second Epistle of the Second Book of Horace Imitated* (1737), line 53; in Pope's text, 'bold' is 'old' (*Poems*, vol. 4), but TLP likes the word 'bold' and has already used the phrase 'bold round-surfaced lawn' in this chapter (p. 5).

14 **sacred thirst of paper-money**: TLP alludes to Virgil, *Aeneid*, book 2, line 57: 'auri sacra fames' ('the sacred or accursed greed for gold'). Because 'sacra' can mean both 'sacred' and 'accursed', the phrase featured in a long-running debate among economists as well as poets concerning the desirability or not of acquiring wealth. This is the first of many references to paper money in *CC*, and a matter of longstanding concern to TLP. See e.g. his letter to Shelley of 19 July 1818: 'There is nothing new under the political sun except that the forgery of bank notes increases in a compound ratio of progression and that the silver disappears rapidly both symptoms of inextricable disarrangement in the machinery of the omnipotent paper-mill' (*Letters*, 1.145). See also *Paper Money Lyrics*, Halliford, 7.95–146. In his Preface, TLP explained that the poems were written 'during the prevalence of an influenza to which the beautiful fabric of paper-credit is periodically subject; which is called commercial panic by citizens, financial crisis by politicians, and day of reckoning by the profane' (Halliford, 7.99). He refers to the financial crash of late 1825. After an exorbitant period of lending, authorities lost control of

the money supply and alarmed note-holders began to withdraw gold from the banks. Eighty country banks failed during the early months of 1826. Of the 624 companies created from 1824–5, around 500 had disappeared by 1827.

15 **Mr. Ramsbottom, the zodiacal mythologist**: Cf. John Frank Newton (1767–1837), a close friend of Shelley and an acquaintance of TLP, a member of the back-to-nature school, a vegetarian and a Zoroastrian astrologer ('Ramsbottom' alludes to the zodiacal sign of Aries, or the Ram). His views are laid out in *Three Enigmas Attempted to be Explained* (1821). Newton fed into the portrait of Mr Escot in *HH* and of Mr Toobad in *NA*. See *Memoirs of Percy Bysshe Shelley*, where TLP notes of Newton that 'he was the absolute impersonation of a single theory . . . He saw the Zodiac in everything' (Halliford, 8.71–3).

16 **Uranus . . . Seva, the Destroyer**: Brahma, Vishnu and Sive are the Trimurti (triad) of Hindu mythology; Uranus, Saturn and Jupiter are their counterparts in Roman mythology. A poetic treatment of this aspect of Jupiter is found in Shelley's *Prometheus Unbound* (1820). The whole passage corresponds with the description of Newton's zodiacal theory in *Memoirs of Percy Bysshe Shelley* (Halliford, 8.71–2). See also Petronius, *Satyricon*, 35; TLP recalled the specific detail about the zodiacal interests of Trimalchio in his essay on 'Gastronomy and Civilization' (Halliford, 9.354).

17 **a Scotchman returning home . . . going back**: The source of this possibly proverbial story is untraced, but such phrases are common in Scots: 'hanna': do not have; 'ower muckle': over much; 'unco braw': truly excellent.

18 **essential . . . arms**: The practice of buying a coat of arms began at least as early as the sixteenth century; arms could be obtained from the College of Arms by anyone who could afford the fee.

19 **videlicet**: 'That is to say; namely; to wit' (*OED*). TLP prefers this form to the common abbreviation *viz*. See also *HH*, ch. 10; *Mel*, ch. 19; *NA*, ch. 1.

20 **rampant . . . swallowed**: This heraldic terminology is a mixture of real ('rampant', 'pendent') and nonce terms. 'Rampant': erect; 'turgescent': turgid, bloated; 'pendent': hanging or drooping; 'tranchant': adapted for cutting; sharp; 'gaspant': gasping. *OED* gives TLP as the only source for 'gaspant'. The musical term 'A sharp' picks up on the fact that 'crotchet' is also the symbol for a note of half the value of a minim; 'crotchet rampant' might be describing a musical score as well as the numerous hobby-horses of *CC* and suggesting erotic comedy. 'Sharp' could also mean, in this context, 'satirical'. The turgescent bladders perhaps indicate bloated, impractical opinions, which in turn resemble the bubble of financial speculation. On 'rampant', see also the epigraph to 'Caledonian War Whoop' in *Paper Money Lyrics*: 'By the Coat of our House, which is an ass rampant, I am ready to fight under this banner' ('Shadwell's *Humourists*' (Halliford, 7.131)).

21 **He . . . people**: On other structures named after something they are not, see TLP's 'Recollections of Childhood: The Abbey House' (1837): 'The house derived its name from standing near, though not actually on, the site of one of those rich old abbeys' (Halliford, 8.29).

22 **vallum**: Rampart or wall, set with stakes or a palisade.

23 **prætorium**: Location of the commanding officer's tent.
 [Footnote:] **Naturam . . . 24**: Horace, *Epistles*, book 1, no. 10, line 24. TLP has provided a translation in the text: 'though you expel nature with a pitchfork, she will yet always come back' (p. 8).

24 **barley-giving earth**: The phrasing is reminiscent of *Odyssey*, book 3, line 3, and book 12, line 386.

25 **game-bagging**: From the later fourteenth century the right to hunt game was legally restricted to a select minority. The legal position was strengthened in 1671 in an effort to prevent anyone from hunting hares, partridges and moor fowl, unless they had freeholds of at least £100 a year, or long leaseholds valued at £150. Sons and heirs of esquires and others 'of higher degree'

were permitted by the 1671 Act to participate, while all lords of manors 'not under the degree of an esquire' were authorized to appoint gamekeepers with the right to seize guns and goods. The 1671 legislation also excluded non-landed wealth from the ranks of sportsmen, and turned the hunting of game into a socially exclusive pastime. Efforts to repeal the laws began in the 1770s, but came to a successful conclusion only in 1831. However, poaching remained an offence, and as a result an undeclared state of war persisted in the countryside.

26 **common-enclosing**: Obtaining, by act of Parliament, the right to fence in open fields and common land, in order to appropriate it to individual use. The Enclosure Acts removed previously existing rights of local people to carry out activities in these areas, such as cultivation, cutting hay, grazing animals, sharing resources such as small timber, fish and turf or sometimes living on the land. Enclosure or Inclosure Acts for small areas had been passed sporadically since the twelfth century, but most were passed between 1750 and 1860. Much larger areas were also enclosed during this time; in 1801, the Inclosure (Consolidation) Act was passed to tidy up previous acts. In 1845 another General Inclosure Act allowed for the appointment of Inclosure Commissioners who could enclose land without submitting a request to Parliament. For TLP's criticisms of enclosure, see 'The Last Day of Windsor Forest' (1862), Halliford, 8.148–9.

27 **rack-renting**: Charging 'a very high, excessive, or extortionate rent; spec. a rent equal (or nearly equal) to the annual value of the land' (*OED*). See also Maria Edgeworth, *Castle Rackrent* (1800).

28 **King Nebuchadnezzar . . . grass**: Daniel, chapter 4, verses 32–3: 'And they shall drive thee from men, and thy dwelling *shall be* with the beasts of the field: they shall make thee to eat grass as oxen, and seven times shall pass over thee, until thou know that the most High ruleth in the kingdom of men, and giveth it to whomsoever he will. The same hour was the thing fulfilled upon Nebuchadnezzar: and he was driven from me, and did eat

grass as oxen, and his body was wet with the dew of heaven, till his hairs were grown like eagles' *feathers*, and his nails like birds' *claws*.'

29 **Captain Jamy ... tway**: Cf. epigraph to this chapter (p. 5) and n. 2. Here, 'question' has become 'airgument', and ''tween you tway' has become 'betwixt ony tway'.

30 **march of intellect**: A phrase coined by Edmund Burke in his *Speech on Conciliation with America* (1775) and henceforth applied by its supporters and detractors to the cult of progress in the nineteenth century; see TLP's 'The Four Ages of Poetry' (1820): 'A poet in our times is a semi-barbarian in a civilized community ... The march of his intellect is like that of a crab, backward' (*NA*, Appendix C). The British Library's database of nineteenth-century newspapers for the years 1826–34 contains over a thousand examples of the phrase 'march of intellect'. In December 1828, Walter Scott described the Burke and Hare murders, recently uncovered in Edinburgh, as 'a horrid example how men may stumble and fall in the full march of intellect' (*The Letters of Sir Walter Scott*, ed. H. J. C. Grierson, 12 vols. (London and Toronto: Constable and Macmillan, 1932–7), vol. 11, p. 72).

31 **exhibitors ... lecturers**: The first decades of the nineteenth century saw a growth in lecturing institutions, including the Royal Institution (1800), the London Institution (1806), the Surrey Institution (1807) and the Russell Institution (1809). Humphry Davy, Michael Faraday, Sydney Smith, Samuel Taylor Coleridge, William Hazlitt and many other luminaries of the age gave lectures, and the Utilitarians adopted the model to found the Mechanics' Institutes in the middle of the 1820s. The popularity of the form often led to sneers from the Tory journals; see, for example, Lockhart's reference to Hazlitt as a mere 'lecture manufacturer' (*Blackwood's Edinburgh Magazine*, Aug. 1818). In this context, TLP's narrator is thinking primarily of the political economists; see *Paper Money Lyrics*, where reference is made to

'our brawl chiel lacture: / His ecoonoomic science Wad silence a' your clanking' and to 'the lecturing Scots' (Halliford, 7.104, 124).

32 **political economy**: The 'branch of economics dealing with the economic problems of government' or 'The branch of knowledge . . . that deals with the production, distribution, consumption, and transfer of wealth; the application of this discipline to a particular sphere; (also) the condition of a state, etc., as regards material prosperity; the financial considerations attaching to a particular activity, commodity, etc.' (*OED*). Political economy evolved in the early nineteenth century, through the writings of Jeremy Bentham, James Mill, David Ricardo, John Ramsay McCulloch and others, into a specific discipline. The first sentence of McCulloch's popular textbook, *Principles of Political Economy, with a Sketch of the Rise and Progress of the Science* (Edinburgh: William and Charles Tait, 1825) states that: 'Political Economy *is the science of the laws which regulate the production, distribution, and consumption of those articles or products which have exchangeable value, and are either necessary, useful, or agreeable to man*', p. 1. In *Paper Money Lyrics*, TLP refers to 'that arch class of quacks, who call themselves political economists' (Halliford, 7.99).

33 **boxed**: 'To box' is to memorize and/or repeat a series of facts in their proper order, respective classifications, and so on; 'to box the compass' is to repeat the thirty-two points of the compass in order (*OED*).

34 **mania . . . biting**: Cf. *OED* 'To bite', 15.a.: '*trans.* (*colloq.*) To deceive, to overreach, "take in".'

35 **loan-jobbing**: Serving as a middle-man in the discounting of loans. This is the *OED*'s only instance of the word as an adjective.

36 **Catchflat and Company**: In the *Lexicon Balatronicum: A Dictionary of Buckish Slang, University Wit, and Pick Pocket Eloquence* (C. Chappel, 1811), a revised and enlarged version of

Francis Grose's *Classical Dictionary of the Vulgar Tongue* (1785), a 'FLAT' is 'A bubble, gull, or silly fellow'. TLP owned a copy of Grose's *Provincial Glossary; with a collection of local proverbs and popular superstitions* (first published in 1787); see *Sale Catalogue* 80 (it should be numbered 81).

37 **paper prosperity... blowing of bubbles**: See *OED* 'bubble', 3.a.: 'Anything fragile, unsubstantial, empty, or worthless; a deceptive show. From 17th c. onwards often applied to delusive commercial or financial schemes, as *the Mississippi bubble, the South Sea bubble.*'

38 **Mr. Touchandgo, the great banker**: For full details of this affair, see Introduction, pp. lix–lxi and ch. 13.

39 **gudgeons**: 'GUDGEON. One easily imposed on. To gudgeon; to swallow the bait, or fall into a trap: from the fish of that name, which is easily taken' (*Lexicon Balatronicum*). See also ch. 3.

40 **Ap-Llymry's**: 'Ap' is 'son of' (*OED*).

41 **dingles**: 'A deep dell or hollow; now usually applied (app. after Milton) to one that is closely wooded or shaded with trees; but, according to Ray and in mod. Yorkshire dialect, the name of a deep narrow cleft between hills' (*OED*). Cf. ch. 14.

42 **nymph... faithless Strephon**: Conventional terms for lovers in pastoral; see e.g. William Hawkins, *The Faithless Shepherd: A Pastoral Inscribed to the Fair Sex*, published in the *Morning Chronicle and London Advertiser* (24 July 1778): the shepherd is called Strephon; the stock figures of a nymph and a shepherd called Strephon are satirized in Swift's urban pastorals 'Strephon and Chloe' (1734) and 'The Lady's Dressing Room' (1732). Susannah is again described as a nymph in ch. 13.

43 **melancholy... white and red**: *Twelfth Night*, act 2, scene 4, line 113 (Viola is indirectly describing to Orsino her own love for him); 'white and red' may allude to *Love's Labour's Lost*, act 1, scene 2, line 90, where the phrase occurs in a discussion of love between Don Armado and Moth, and immediately after a

reference to green as the 'colour of lovers'. But it could also refer to (for instance) *Twelfth Night*, act 1, scene 5, line 239, where the common pairing of 'red and white' describes Olivia's beauty, 'truly blent', a comment which would also apply to the salutary effects of Susannah's Welsh environment and activities on her appearance.

[Footnote:] **Llymry. Anglicè flummery**: 'Anglicè': In plain English, in other words; 'flummery': 'A kind of food made by coagulation of wheatflour or oatmeal' (Johnson's *Dictionary*), or 'A name given to various sweet dishes made with milk, flour, eggs, etc.', or 'Mere flattery or empty compliment; nonsense, humbug, empty trifling' (*OED*). In the *Lexicon Balatronicum*, 'flummery' is 'Oatmeal and water boiled to a jelly; also compliments, neither of which are over-nourishing'. See Appendix F on Llymry and Flummery in *CC* (pp. 168–9).

44 **double X**: Probably double porter (beer), the X used popularly to indicate strength and purity.

45 **the Wrekin**: A large, isolated hill in east Shropshire, associated with legend and folklore.

46 **physiognomy**: The science which attempts to correlate physical features with character or disposition. See e.g. Johann Kaspar Lavater, *Physiognomische Fragmente*, translated as *Essays on Physiognomy* (1789–98), and Alexander Walker, *Physiognomy Founded on Physiology* (1834).

47 **sallowed**: This is the *OED*'s earliest recorded usage of 'sallow' as a verb.

48 **scathed by . . . thunderbolts of Heaven**: The German romance is Shelley's novel *St Irvyne; or, The Rosicrucian: A Romance* (published 1810, dated 1811) which TLP is misquoting, presumably from memory. The exact phrase is 'the inerasible traces of the thunderbolts of God'. Percy Bysshe Shelley, *Zastrozzi: A Romance, and, St. Irvyne: or, The Rosicrucian: A Romance*, ed. Stephen C. Behrendt, Broadview Literary Texts (Peterborough, ON: Broadview Press, 2002), ch. 10, p. 237.

49 **Lemma**: From the Greek λῆμμα: 'profit, gain'. The word often has connotations of unjust gain, and this may be intended still further to undermine the 'ingenuous dealings' mentioned earlier in this chapter. The idolization of wealth loosely recalls Trimalchio in Petronius' *Satyricon*, especially since Crotchet plays host to the decadent gathering. Possibly, however, TLP was not aware of this sinister nuance of the word λῆμμα.

50 **march of mind**: A common phrase, in TLP and elsewhere; cf. instances in chs. 2 (p. 13), 4 (p. 37), 8 (p. 77), 17 (p. 133), 18 (pp. 141, 145); see also 'march of intellect', above, n. 30 (p. 200). Mary Russell Mitford's ode, 'The March of Mind', was recited at the first anniversary celebrations of the British and Foreign Schools Society in 1815. Cf. TLP's poem, 'The Lament of Scotch Economists' (wr. 1826–7): 'Improvements vast will then be past: / The march of mind will backward lead; / For how can mind be left behind, / When we march back across the Tweed?' (Halliford, 7.129). See also William Thomas Moncrieff's poem, 'The March of Intellect, or, Mechanical Academics' (1830). The phrase was often associated with Brougham and his reputation as a modernizer – see e.g. the *Morning Post* (28 Feb. 1828): 'The day is at hand when he shall stand forth the Great Captain of the Age, and at the head of his legions begin the march of intellect.' [Footnote:] **Let him . . . suprà**: Pope, *The Second Epistle of the Second Book of Horace Imitated*, line 51; Pope capitalizes 'Castles' and 'Groat' (Pope, *Poems*, vol. 4).

51 **squires expectant**: TLP is continuing to spoof heraldic terminology and word order.

52 **"astounding progress" of intelligence**: 'Progress' was becoming a key refrain of the period, particularly in Utilitarian circles; James Mill's essay on 'Education' (first published in the *Encyclopedia Britannica* and republished throughout the 1820s) claimed: 'That he is a progressive being is the grand distinction of Man. He is the only *progressive* being upon this globe' (*Political Writings*, ed. Terence Ball (Cambridge: Cambridge University Press,

1992), p. 189). See also James Mill's claim in *Elements of Political Economy* (1821), ch. 2, section 2, that 'that grand and distinguishing attribute of our nature' is its 'progressiveness'.

53 **rear . . . van**: TLP's military language is inspired by the image of a 'march'; 'van' means 'The foremost division or detachment of a military or naval force when advancing or set in order for doing so' (*OED*). Cf. ch. 18, in which the boar's head 'led the van' (p. 140).

54 **the tower . . . Damascus**: Song of Solomon, ch. 7, v. 4: 'thy nose *is* as the tower of Lebanon which looketh toward Damascus'. Cf. allusions to the Song of Solomon in chs. 3 (p. 25) and 7 (p. 68).

55 **etymologists**: Etymological study in the modern sense emerged in the late eighteenth century, and was an increasingly fashionable interest; see, for example, John Horne Tooke (1736–1812), Επεα Πτεροεντα, *or, The Diversions of Purley*, the first part of which was published in 1786 and revised in 1798; part 2 appeared in 1805. TLP read and loved the work (*Letters*, 1.45).

56 **Follis Optimus**: 'An excellent bellows', as TLP explains later in the paragraph. 'Latin *follem, follis*, lit. "bellows", but in late popular Latin employed in the sense of "windbag," empty-headed person, fool' (*OED*).

57 **Gilbert Folliott**: Folliott or Foliot died in 1186 or 1188. A strong opponent of Thomas Becket, he was known for his eloquence and (unlike his fictional descendant) for his austere habits. [Footnote:] **The devil began . . . the devil's head**: Folliott's exchange with the devil seems to derive from Matthew Paris (c. 1200–59). It is recounted in, among other places, T. C. Banks, *The Dormant and Extinct Baronage of England*, 3 vols. (J. White, 1807), vol. 1, p. 86. The story is also discussed in *Critical Review*, 3rd ser., 40 (1808), p. 396 (a review of Banks's book). Since TLP read editions of this periodical published in 1805 and 1809 (see *Letters*, 1.38, 40, 48, 53), it is possible that he first found a reference to the story here. In Banks, the poem appears in a slightly different form. Possibly TLP was encouraged to attempt his own versification (if such it is) by the statement in the *Critical Review*

that 'subsequent writers who have added the bishop's reply, give them both [the devil's taunt and Folliott's retort] in a poetical shape' – meaning that one man's versification of this story would have as much validity as the next man's. 'Astarot': Eastern equivalent of Aphrodite, Greek goddess of love; 'posed': Cf. *OED* 'to pose', 2.a.: 'To put (a person) at a loss; to confuse, perplex, puzzle, nonplus'; '"the heroic student", as Mr. Coleridge calls him': Coleridge uses the phrase 'heroic Luther' in Essay 8 of *The Friend* (Coleridge, *Works*, vol. 4, 1.63). '*voies de fait*': violence.

58 **a smattering of many things . . . knowledge of none**: Loosely recalls a line about Margites, a buffoon who was the subject of a pseudo-Homeric poem which now survives only in a few fragments. Cf. fr. 3 of the *Margites* in M. L. West (ed.), *Homeric Hymns. Homeric Apocrypha. Lives of Homer* (2003), p. 246. πόλλ' ἠπίστατο ἔργα, κακῶς δ' ἠπίστατο πάντα ('He knew a lot of things, but he knew them all badly'). More pertinently, perhaps, given TLP's admiration of Petronius' *Satyricon*, the characterization of the parvenu Crotchet resembles that of Trimalchio, a man who also retires on his ill-gotten wealth and invites guests to his house for dinners and disquisitions. Petronius makes comic capital of the fact that Trimalchio too is 'eminently jolly, but by no means eminently learned'. In 'Gastronomy and Civilization' (1851), TLP observes: 'Trimalchio is . . . a very absurd and exaggerated person, bearing about the same proportion to one of the nobles of his time, as a new city lord of these days does to the cultivated gentleman' (Halliford, 9.360).

59 **intellectual harlequin's jacket . . . bright and prominent**: The bright motley jacket traditionally worn by Harlequin, the stock clown of the *commedia dell'arte* and of nineteenth-century pantomime. See TLP's description of Trimalchio's antics in the *Satyricon*, antics which resemble scenes in early nineteenth-century pantomime (Halliford, 9.360–1). TLP was a keen admirer of pantomime; see his letter to Shelley (of 13 Jan. 1819): 'There is a very splendid pantomime at Covent Garden founded

on the adventures of Baron Munchausen: I have seen it twice'
(*Letters*, 1.164). He refers to the Covent Garden pantomime
Harlequin Munchausen; or, The Fountain of Love (first performed
on 26 Dec. 1818). Given the shadiness of Crotchet's financial
dealings, see also TLP's 'A Border Ballad' in *Paper Money Lyrics*:
'Their promise to pay is as Harlequin's wand' (Halliford, 7.126).

CHAPTER 2

1 **Quoth Ralpho . . . BUTLER:** Samuel Butler, *Hudibras*, part 1,
canto 3, lines 1337–8: 'Quoth *Ralpho*, Nothing but th'abuse / Of
Humane Learning you produce'. Ralpho is attacking Hudibras's
parade of learned terms and much-vaunted logic, arguing that
the knight is absurd, fraudulent, and profane; his wilful errors,
says Ralpho, obstruct the path to truth.

2 **one fine May morning:** Ch. 1 (p. 6) has already alluded to
Twelfth Night, act 3, scene 4, a scene in which Fabian notes:
'More matter for a May morning' (line 142). The time of year
suggests fun and games, as George Steevens noted in the edition
of Shakespeare owned by TLP: 'It was usual on the first of
May to exhibit metrical interludes of the comic kind, as well as
the *morris-dance*' (*The Plays of Shakespeare*, ed. Samuel Johnson,
George Steevens and Isaac Reed, 6th edn (J. Nichols and Sons,
1813), vol. 5, p. 364 n.). The allusion to *Twelfth Night* is made
explicit later in this chapter.

3 **Hydrostatics . . . learned friend:** The 'learned friend' (a term
used in parliament for those MPs who were lawyers) refers
to Henry Brougham (1778–1868). Brougham was a tireless
reformer (an advocate of law reform, the abolition of slavery,
the extension of education, among many other things) and a
renowned public figure: according to Macaulay, by the early
1830s Brougham was, next to the King, the most popular
man in England. See Robert Stewart, *Henry Brougham, 1778–
1868: His Public Career* (Bodley Head, 1986), pp. 230–84. The
'Steam Intellect Society' is Folliott's name for the Society for the

Diffusion of Useful Knowledge (SDUK), set up by Brougham in 1826 to publish cheap and accessible works on scientific and artistic subjects. The 'sixpenny tract' refers to SDUK treatises brought out from early 1827 in the Library of Useful Knowledge series; Brougham wrote the introductory treatise (*Discourse on the Objects, Advantages and Pleasures of Science*), which sold 39,000 copies. It included an extended description of the workings of the steam engine. Several other pamphlets were published on hydrostatics, hydraulics, pneumatics, electricity and galvanism.

4 *triformis*, **like Hecate**: *triformis*: 'three-form'. Hecate was a Graeco-Roman goddess of witchcraft; she is frequently depicted in Greek art with three heads, or sometimes even as being three goddesses.

5 *bifrons*, **like Janus**: *bifrons*: 'with two faces'. Janus, the Roman god of passage and transition, was normally depicted in Roman art with two faces. TLP is referring to Brougham's habit of courting both liberal and conservative political factions.

6 **Mr. Facing-both-ways of Vanity Fair**: Mr *Facing-bothways*, of the wealthy town of Fair-Speech, appears in *Pilgrim's Progress* (1678), part 1. Christian meets him after he has in fact left Vanity Fair. His companions are *By-ends*, Lord *Turn-about*, Lord *Timeserver*, Lord *Fair-speech*, Mr *Smooth-man*, Mr *Any-thing* and Mr *Two-tongues*. See John Bunyan, *Grace Abounding to the Chief of Sinners and The Pilgrim's Progress from this World to that which is to come*, ed. Roger Sharrock (Oxford University Press, 1966), p. 219. See *GG*, ch. 18, for a passing reference to 'the next meeting of the Pantopragmatic Society, under the presidency of Lord Facing-both-ways, and the vice-presidency of Lord Michin Malicho'. The Pforzheimer Collection (New York Public Library) includes a holograph fragment (watermark 1842) in TLP's hand on Lord Facing-both-ways (TLP 149).

7 **short mould**: A type of candle, made in a mould, as opposed to one made by dipping.

8 **exhaled his grievance**: Cf. 'exhale his budget of grievances' (again with reference to Folliott) in ch. 8 (p. 81).

[Footnote:] **Quasi Mac Q. E. D., son of a demonstration**: TLP thus explains the origins of 'Mac Quedy': 'Quasi': almost; 'Mac': son of; 'Q. E. D.', or quod erat demonstrandum: '"Which was to be demonstrated"': placed at the end of a mathematical proof (originally, one in Euclid) to indicate that a previously stated theorem is thereby proved; (in extended use) used to convey that a fact or situation demonstrates the truth of a person's theory or claim' (*OED*).

9 **Mr. Mac Quedy, the economist**: TLP's readers would have recognized Mac Quedy's resemblance to John Ramsay McCulloch (1789–1864), the best-known political economist of the day. He was chief economic writer for the *Edinburgh Review* from 1818, and a popular lecturer and disseminator of Ricardian political economy. He wrote the first substantive article on political economy to appear in the *Encyclopaedia Britannica*, later expanded into *Principles of Political Economy* (1825). In 1828 he published a best-selling annotated version of Adam Smith's *Inquiry into the Nature and Causes of the Wealth of Nations*, and took up the first Chair of Political Economy at the newly founded University of London. The *ODNB* claims: 'In his own time he was probably more famous, more widely read by those engaged in making or debating economic policy, and more often singled out for attack by critics of the "dismal science" than any other economist.' Ricardo's other chief disciple at this time, James Mill (1773–1836), also informs the portrait of Mac Quedy. Mill was TLP's colleague at the India House. He founded the Political Economy Club in 1821, at which Ricardo, Malthus, Torrens and many others debated the fundamental propositions of their science. Mill's *Essay on Government* (1820), subsequently reprinted in editions of his *Essays* in 1823, 1825 and 1828, informs many of the debates which follow.

[Footnote:] **ΣΚΙᾶς ONAP.** *Umbræ somnium*: As TLP tells us, Skionar's name is derived from σκιᾶς ὄναρ (*skiās onar*), 'a dream of a shadow'. The metaphor is common in Greek literature; see I. L. Pfeijffer, *Three Aeginetan Odes of Pindar* (Leiden and Boston: Brill, 1999), pp. 598–9. But σκιᾶς ὄναρ is derived specifically from Pindar, *Pythian* 8.95–6: σκιᾶς ὄναρ / ἄνθρωπος ('man is a dream of a shadow'). Although the precise sense of this is disputed, it clearly denotes mankind's ephemerality. TLP was a keen reader of Pindar, as can be seen from the number of times he is quoted in *CC*; there is also evidence in his *Letters* of a deep interest in the writer as early as the 1810s (see *Letters*, index s.v. 'Pindar'). This particular passage of *Pythian* 8 must have made an impression upon TLP, for he quotes it again in a letter to Lord Broughton (13 Jan. 1860), referring to the death of Macaulay (*Letters*, 2.386). Shelley transcribed the relevant lines from *Pythian* 8 in a notebook and used a phrase echoing them in line 12 of the Conclusion of 'The Sensitive Plant': 'And we, the shadows of the dream' (*The Poems of Shelley*, vol. 3, ed. Jack Donovan, Cian Duffy, Kelvin Everest and Michael Rossington (Harlow: Longman-Pearson, 2011), p. 315 and n.).

10 **Mr. Skionar, the transcendental poet**: Skionar may be read, in part, as a parodic representation of Samuel Taylor Coleridge (1772–1834), who espoused the transcendental idealism of Immanuel Kant (1724–1804): the view that human knowledge (although not illusory) extends only to things as they appear to us and not to things as they are in themselves, and is accordingly confined to phenomena (see Coleridge's *Biographia Literaria* (1817), chs. 9, 13, 22). Skionar is the consummate foil to Mac Quedy's Benthamite view of human behaviour and motivation, in response to which Skionar echoes Coleridge's more recondite criticisms of political economy and of the mechanical systems of thought from which he considered it to derive. TLP is not only mocking Coleridge; he also sympathized with the queries he posed to modern thinkers. Mac Quedy and Skionar

together comprise one of the more extreme examples of intellectual incompatibility in TLP.

11 **Mr. Firedamp, the meteorologist**: 'Firedamp': 'A miner's term for carburetted hydrogen or marsh-gas, which is given off by coal and is explosive when mixed in certain proportions with atmospheric air' (*OED*). Not in Johnson's *Dictionary*.

12 **Lord Bossnowl ... Rogueingrain**: A 'boss' is 'A stud; an ornament raised above the rest of the work; a shining prominence' (Johnson's *Dictionary*); 'A protuberance or swelling on the body of an animal or plant; a convex or knob-like process or excrescent portion of an organ or structure' (*OED*); 'noll' is 'A head; a noddle' (Johnson's *Dictionary*); 'The top or crown of the head; the head itself' (*OED*); hence, 'Bossnowl': 'knob-head'. 'Rogueingrain': Someone rotten to the core; one whose villainy is deep-seated.

13 **demulcent**: 'Softening; mollifying; assuasive' (Johnson's *Dictionary*); 'Soothing, lenitive, mollifying, allaying irritation' (*OED*). Johnson and the *OED* both cite a work of popular medicine, directly relevant to this moment in *CC*, by the physician John Arbuthnot: *An Essay Concerning the Nature of Aliments, and the Choice of Them, According to the Different Constitutions of Human Bodies*, 2nd edn (J. Tonson, 1732).

14 **man ... breakfast-table**: 'Man of taste' is a typical TLP pun; the link between civilized behaviour and gustatory pleasure is also widespread in the period (esp. in essays by William Hazlitt and Charles Lamb). See e.g. Hazlitt's 'On Table Companions and the Art of Dining', in *The Atlas* (29 Aug. 1830). Folliott's sense of the relationship between ingesting, imbibing and refined debate has a classical inflection (from Plato's *Symposium* and beyond), as his subsequent comments make clear. (See also 'deliberative dinners' in ch. 6 (pp. 54, 62)).

[Footnote:] **Far shining ... PIND. Ol. vi**: Pindar, *Olympian* 6.3–4. TLP's translation is accurate. πρόσωπον, reused in the next sentence of the main text, means 'face' (TLP omits the connecting particle δ' after ἀρχομένου, in order that the maxim should be able to stand alone syntactically). TLP is known to have used Christian Gottlob Heyne's 1807–9 editions of Pindar: see *Letters*, 1.74, n. 22; 1.141, n. 14. As Heyne knew, ἀρχομένου is read nearly unanimously by ancient and modern editions. The variant printed by Heyne barely affects the meaning, but he champions it on stylistic grounds. TLP admired Heyne's scholarship immensely (see *Letters*, 2.446); in opting for the standard ἀρχομένου, he perhaps felt confident enough in his Greek to take issue with the eminent German editor on this textual point. August Boeckh's and Christian Wilhelm Ahlwardt's editions of Pindar (published respectively in 1811–21 and 1820), which TLP also owned (*Sale Catalogue* 661 and 497), print ἀρχομένου, so TLP may have consulted one of them on this point. But he venerated Heyne's edition and the line-divisions of Pindar's text as printed in *CC* suggest that he consulted Heyne rather than Boeckh or Ahlwardt when quoting *Pythian* 9 there. On the other hand, the orthography and punctuation of the quotation of ἀρχομένου . . . τηλαυγές are marginally closer to Ahlwardt than to Heyne.

15 **the foot of Hercules**: To judge of Hercules by his foot is to judge the whole by the part. It is possible to extrapolate a man's character, in this case, from his breakfast-table. The expression derives from the account of how the Greek mathematician and philosopher Pythagoras calculated all of Hercules' other physical attributes from the supposed size of the hero's foot. See e.g. Aulus Gellius, *Noctes Atticae* (*Attic Nights*), trans. John C. Rolfe (1927), book 1, ch. 1.

16 **but the touch-stone is fish . . . progression**: Folliott above all others in *CC* is a devotee of classical learning. His comment on the various grades of fish is cast in the form of a priamel, a literary device which is widespread among the ancients. See the opening of Pindar, *Olympian* 1; this is probably the most relevant parallel, given the quotation of another ode of Pindar earlier in Folliott's

speech. TLP quotes the opening of *Olympian* 1 in a letter to Thomas Jefferson Hogg (26 Sept. 1817), and refers to it in his Marlow journal entry for 23 July 1818 (*Letters*, 1.116, 135 and n. 33).

17 **matter for a May morning**: *Twelfth Night*, act 3, scene 4, line 142.

18 **eximious**: 'Famous; eminent; conspicuous; excellent' (Johnson's *Dictionary*); cf. *ME*, ch. 7: 'the most eximious and transcendent persons and things of the superficial garniture of the earth'.

19 **Be content, sir . . .** *ἐγχέλεις*: TLP alludes to a passage in Aristophanes' comedy *Lysistrata*. The women of Athens are plotting how they may end the Peloponnesian War and bring about the destruction of 'all the Boeotians', the enemies of Athens. At this suggestion one of the Athenian women present worriedly intercedes on a trivial matter – to safeguard Boeotia's culinary delicacy of eels. The 'scholiast' refers to the ancient commentaries, of varying dates and authorship, on works of classical literature (the commentaries are known as 'scholia'), and the scholiast on this passage of Aristophanes explains the allusion to eels by informing us that Boeotia's Lake Copais was famed for them. Reading and citing scholia is emphatically a scholarly practice, so Folliott's reference to them presents him as a learned, rather finicky, man. The edition of the Aristophanes scholia used by TLP was Dindorf (*Sale Catalogue* 43). The Edinburghians had been styled the 'modern Athenians'; in July 1761, Alexander Carlyle wrote to Gilbert Elliot that Thomas Sheridan had told him that 'Edinburgh is the Athens of Great Britain . . . and we believe him' (National Library of Scotland, MS. 11015, 106). The Boeotians were not Athenians – Boeotia was a cultural backwater in comparison with Athens – so telling Mac Quedy to be content to rival the *Boeotians* is a condescending and deprecatory remark.

[Footnote:] **Calonice . . . Lysistrata, 36**: TLP's footnote misattributes the parts in the dialogue: it is Lysistrata who wishes destruction to all Boeotians and Calonice who interrupts 'Except the eels'.

20 **those who have . . . metrical quantity**: On Greek metre, TLP counted himself among the learned number whom a Folliott would respect. His interest in the subject is shown in a letter to Thomas Forster (15 Jan. 1812): 'You will find much information περι μετρων ['on metre'] in the Enchiridion of Hephæstio; and Herman [sic] has treated largely on the subject, in the third volume of Heyne's Pindar' (*Letters*, 1.73). TLP owned Gaisford's edition of Hephaestion (Oxford, 1810) (*Sale Catalogue* 153). The debate between the ancients and the moderns as it is staged here also played out in the pages of the utilitarian *Westminster Review* via recourse to metrics. See, for example, John Bowring's wry take on the issue: 'We admit that . . . the moral and religious duties of a people must be inculcated by means of dactyls, anapaests, and iambics . . . nothing but a due intimacy with the deep profundities of longs and shorts can render ten thousand men in black coats the exclusively proper persons to teach the rising generation how to make laws, practice physic, govern colonies, and spin cotton . . . but who teaches men to make steam engines and dye scarlet cloth for the army? Does this knowledge come by scanning?' ('The Library of Useful Knowledge', *Westminster Review*, 7 (Apr. 1827), pp. 269–317 (p. 277)).

21 **principles . . . nutshell**: Folliott's tone and position here mirror Macaulay's in his celebrated attack on James Mill's *Essay on Government* in the *Edinburgh Review*, 49 (1829): 'men always act from self-interest. This truism the Utilitarians proclaim with as much pride as if it were new, and as much zeal as if it were important. But, in fact, when explained, it means only that men, if they can, will do as they choose' (repr. in Mill, *Political Writings*, ed. Ball, p. 299).

22 **Yes . . . none**: A further allusion to Brougham's educational projects. In addition to his efforts on behalf of the charity schools, Brougham became involved with Birkbeck's London

Mechanics' Institute in 1824 and used his influence to encourage the growth of similar institutes across England. He played a key role in the establishment of London University in 1826, contributing to the design of a curriculum that was strongly secular in nature (featuring several branches of science and medicine, geography, languages and other subjects that had not been taught before). Folliott's scepticism echoes that of many contemporary satirists of the university; see e.g. an article in *John Bull*: 'it is proposed to instruct butchers in geometry, and tallow-chandlers in Hebrew – tailors are to be perfected in Oriental literature, and shoemakers finished up in mathematics' (14 Feb. 1825). Several leading Utilitarians were on the committee of the University, including TLP's colleague James Mill; 'schools for all' echoes Mill's pamphlet, *Schools for All* (1812), part of his longstanding commitment to educational reform. See also TLP's satirical squib 'Inscription Placed Under the First Stone of the London-University' (wr. 1826), Halliford, 7.240–1.

23 **stool of repentance**: A low stool used in Presbyterian churches, mostly in Scotland, on which a transgressor against morality (typically, anyone who had committed fornication or adultery, including e.g. Robert Burns) was made to sit during divine service and receive public rebuke from the minister.

24 **Ude**: Louis Eustache Ude (1769–1846), celebrated chef, author of *The French Cook* (1813), which reached its 14th edition in 1841. Ude introduced the light sandwich supper during the regency. Stanzas 62 to 74 of canto 15 of *Don Juan* (1819–24) contain numerous references to Ude's recipes. (See TLP's praise of *Don Juan* as his favourite poem of the age in *Letters*, 1.186: 'I have read nothing else in recent literature that I think good for anything'.)

25 θύρας δ' ἐπίθεσθε βεβήλοις: TLP derives this phrase, which he translates accurately in his footnote, from 'ORPHICA, *passim*'. The *Orphica* are a collection of poems attributed to the legendary Greek sage Orpheus. Their subject is the Orphic

Mysteries, and 'Shut the doors against the profane' is the proclamation preceding ritual activity: the uninitiated must be excluded from the cult's secret rites. TLP quotes from Gottfried Hermann's edition (1805), which he owned and admired, despite his tempered enthusiasm for Orphic poetry itself; see his letter to Thomas Forster of 13 Feb. 1812 (*Letters*, 1.81; *Sale Catalogue* 468).

26 *Horresco referens*: 'I shudder to tell it'; from Virgil, *Aeneid*, book 2, line 204. In this passage Aeneas is recounting to Dido the destruction of Troy. One episode – the devouring of Laocoon and his sons by a sea-serpent – is so horrific that Aeneas recoils at the recollection of it.

27 *Di meliora piis*: 'May the gods grant a better fate to the pious'; from Virgil, *Georgics*, book 3, line 513, in a passage describing the sufferings of plague-victims. TLP had earlier used this line in a letter to Thomas Forster (6 Apr. 1810, *Letters*, 1.51).

28 **comedy**: 'The days of Comedy are gone, alas!', wrote Byron in canto 13, stanza 94, line 749 of *Don Juan* (Byron, *Works*, vol. 5). TLP recalled his attempts to 'reconcile' Shelley 'to comedy' in *Memoirs of Percy Bysshe Shelley* (Halliford, 8.82). On comedy, see also TLP's 'French Comic Romances' (Halliford, 9.255–87).

29 **attic salt**: Literary refinement (*OED* 'Attic', A.2., whose closest parallel is from *Tristram Shandy*). Appropriately enough for Folliott, the 'attic salt' is a calque of Latin *sal Atticum* (*sal*: 'salt' and 'wit'). TLP uses the phrase in a punning compliment to Thomas Jefferson Hogg (7 Sept. 1818, *Letters*, 1.150).

30 **Jupiter's great grandfather**: Uranus is grandfather of Jupiter, but in mainstream mythology Uranus has no father himself. This may be an error on TLP's part, or it may be meant to show the inadequacy of the Reverend Doctor's learning.

31 **a pure antispastic acatalectic tetrameter**: All genuine terms from Greek metrics; see *OED* and Dodson, *Crotchet Castle*, p. 180. However, Folliott's question, whose terms are in any

case ambiguous, is essentially nonsense; it is supposed to epitomize an arcane, esoteric type of knowledge about antiquity. TLP probably had in mind here Hermann's treatise on Pindaric metre, printed in vol. 3 of Heyne's edition of the poet. This essay (in Latin) is replete with recondite technical terms, and Hermann's method of description is to start with the basic metrical form and then catalogue permutations of it; see esp. §XI ('De versibus antispasticis'), which TLP had read by 1812. The rare term 'antispastic' comes ultimately from the ancient metrician Hephaestion, with whose fragmentary treatise TLP was familiar. Hephaestion does in fact record an antispastic acatalectic tetrameter (*Enchiridion*, 10.6, p. 34, lines 11–12, *Hephaestionis Enchiridion*, ed. Max Consbruch (Leipzig: B. G. Teubner, 1906)), but he does not proceed to add or remove syllables in the way that Folliott demands.

32 **the divine Allan Ramsay**: Allan Ramsay (1684–1758), Scottish poet. In *The Gentle Shepherd* (1725), a descendant of John Gay's *The Shepherd's Week* (1714), Ramsay employed the pastoral form to celebrate the return of the royalist exile Sir William Worthy, a thin disguise for James Stuart. The drama was enormously successful, boosting Ramsay's reputation in England as well as north of the border. Following the appearance of Gay's *The Beggar's Opera* (1728), Ramsay's play was converted into a ballad opera. In this form it remained popular into the early nineteenth century; it was performed at least 47 times in Scotland, 101 times in England, and 5 times in the United States before 1837.

33 **hyperbarbarous**: The original sense of the Greek word βάρβαρος (*barbaros*) is 'heterophonous', and possibly Folliott intends this nonce-compound in the sense 'excessively un-Hellenic' (rather than as straightforwardly deprecatory).

34 **premises . . . erroneous**: The argument again echoes Macaulay's renowned critique of James Mill's *Essay on Government* in the *Edinburgh Review*, 49 (1829): 'He reasons *a priori*, because the

phenomena are not what, by reasoning *a priori*, he will prove them to be. In other words, he reasons *a priori*, because, by so reasoning, he is certain to arrive at a false conclusion!' (repr. in Mill, *Political Writings*, ed. Ball, p. 274). See above, n. 22 (pp. 214–15).

35 **The sublime Kant, and his disciples**: Immanuel Kant, German philosopher and proponent, in the *Critique of Pure Reason* (1781), of the doctrine of transcendental idealism; he was highly influential on English Romantic thought, especially that of Coleridge.

36 **head and tail**: Given that Coleridge (as one of Kant's 'disciples') is in the air here, Folliott may be thinking of the satirical verses 'To the author of the Ancient Mariner' – quoted by Coleridge himself in ch. 1 of *Biographia Literaria*: 'Your poem must eternal be, / Dear sir! it cannot fail, / For 'tis incomprehensible / And without head or tail' (Coleridge, *Works*, vol. 7, 1.28). See also Coleridge's comment to Joseph Cottle on 7 Mar. 1815 that 'The common end of all *narrative*, nay, of *all*, poems is to convert a *series* into a *Whole:* to make those events, which in real or imagined History move on in a *strait* Line, assume to our Understandings a *circular* motion – the snake with it's Tail in it's Mouth' (*Collected Letters of Samuel Taylor Coleridge*, ed. Earl Leslie Griggs, 6 vols. (Oxford: Clarendon Press, 1956–71; repr. 2000), vol. 4, p. 545).

37 **Transcendentalism ... Aristotelian logic**: Skionar opposes logic – the formal basis for scientific method – to transcendental philosophy, which pertains to the general theory of knowledge rather than to the evidence of the senses.

38 **controversies ... settled**: But cf. TLP to Thomas Forster in Feb. 1811: 'with respect to philosophy, I am become a complete Academic. I am persuaded, that in all questions purely speculative there is just as much to be said on the one side as the other' (*Letters*, 1.62).

39 *malaria*: 'Originally: an unwholesome condition of the atmosphere attributed to marshy districts of Italy and other hot

countries; any febrile disease thought to be caused by this. Now: *spec.* any of a group of diseases of humans and other vertebrates caused by protozoans of the genus *Plasmodium* (phylum Apicomplexa), which are transmitted by mosquitoes and parasite red blood cells, resulting in haemolysis, periodic fever, and various other symptoms' (*OED*, 'malaria', 1: the earliest citation of the word in English, from 1740, is from Horace Walpole). In its figurative sense of 'malign influence' (*OED*), malaria relates to the sense of intellectual pollution that manifests itself throughout *CC* and TLP's works more generally.

40 **The sun sucks up ... face of the earth**: Cf. 'All the infections that the sun sucks up / From bogs, fens, flats' (*Tempest*, act 2, scene 2, lines 1–2) and 'Infect her beauty, / You fen-sucked fogs' (*King Lear*, act 2, scene 4, lines 166–7).

41 **Ἔστιν ... θάνατος**: This is fr. 19 in Hermann's edition of the *Orphica*. ἐστιν is an error for ἔστιν: the word appears correctly as ἔστιν in Hermann's text and in the 1837 edition of *CC* (see Emendations and variants). In full, the line runs Ἔστιν ὕδωρ ψυχῇ, θάνατος δ' ὑδάτεσσιν ἀμοιβή ('Water is the transformation for the soul, and death is the transformation for water'). The first instance of 'transformation' is not expressed in Greek and must be understood from the second half of the line; this should be obvious enough to anyone as well read in Greek as TLP. However, TLP construes θάνατος ('death') with the preceding phrase, which is impossible, and he understands the first part of the line as 'Water is death to the soul'. Presumably this is TLP's own error, rather than an attempt to characterize Folliott as a sciolist. Or it could be a wilful reinterpretation of the original Greek through selective quotation to suit Firedamp's temperament.

42 **inesculent**: 'Not used for food, inedible' (*OED*). This is the *OED*'s only citation of the word.

43 **longinquity**: Long distance, remoteness. TLP's is the *OED*'s most recent instance of the word in this sense.

44 **You may fight . . .** Ὑδάσπης: The water-god Achelous competed with Hercules for the hand of Deianeira, but Hercules defeated him by force; Firedamp's battle against malaria would, if modelled on this combat, be an intense physical struggle. Folliott suggests a more cerebral path to victory. Nonnus' *Dionysiaca*, a Greek epic poem from the fourth or fifth century AD, gives an account of the conquest of India by Dionysus (Bacchus); TLP read some of Nonnus in July 1818, but stalled at this point for an unknown duration (see *Letters*, 1.149 n. 16). Two years later, in 'The Four Ages of Poetry', he described the *Dionysiaca* as the 'best specimen' of poetry in the age of brass, since it 'contains many passages of exceeding beauty in the midst of masses of amplification and repetition' (*NA*, Appendix C). In 1822, the *London Magazine* published an anonymous article, signed 'Vida', in praise of Nonnus (Oct. 1822, pp. 336–40; Nov. 1822, pp. 440–3). The MS of this article is included in the Pforzheimer Collection, New York Public Library, with an attestation by Richard Garnett on the front cover: 'This essay would seem to be by T. L. Peacock, but the MS is not in his hand' (TLP 132). In books 22–4 of the *Dionysiaca*, the god of wine must contend with the river Hydaspes, who opposes his troops. Eventually, the river is defeated by Bacchus and his waters are metamorphosed into wine. Folliott thus humorously suggests that one could eliminate the threat of stagnant water by changing it to wine. The thyrsus is an ivy-crowned staff brandished by Bacchus and his followers.

45 **I hope . . . philosophy**: Crotchet Junior is proposing a trip similar to those TLP enjoyed; in May 1809 he went on a two-week expedition to trace the course of the Thames on foot from its source to Chertsey, and in late August he took an excursion up the Thames from Old Windsor to beyond Lechlade with Shelley, Mary Godwin and Charles Clairmont.

46 *Alter erit . . . Delectos Heroas*: 'There will then be another Tiphys, and another Argo to carry chosen heroes.' TLP quotes Virgil, *Eclogue* 4, lines 34–5; his translation in the footnote is rather

loose. The *Argo* was the ship that carried Jason and his band of heroes ('the Argonauts') to Colchis on a quest for the Golden Fleece; Tiphys was the *Argo*'s helmsman. Virgil's Fourth Eclogue is the so-called 'Messianic Eclogue', which was believed, from the time of the Church Fathers onwards, to foretell the birth of Christ; it is therefore an appropriate text for the clergyman Folliott to be familiar with. The poem prophesies the coming of a golden age. However, there are warnings that suffering must be endured before that happy time, and seafaring is an element of that hardship. Folliott's allusion to Virgil may therefore cast an ominous atmosphere over the boating expedition. On the other hand, Folliott may just be using it as a moderately apposite learned tag.

47 **ship of fools**: Sebastian Brant, *Daß Narrenschyff ad Narragoniam* (1494), a satire on human nature first translated into English as *The Ship of Fools* in 1509. The work consists of a prologue, 112 brief satires, and an epilogue, all illustrated with woodcuts; it criticizes the state of the church and attacks vice. The book was translated into Latin by Jacob Locher in 1497, into French by Paul Riviere in 1497 and by Jehan Droyn in 1498, into English by Alexander Barclay and by Henry Watson (both in 1509).

48 **You need not ... The savage never laughs**: Debate about the meaning of 'Ha Ha' and 'He He' had been reinvigorated since the publication of Frances Hutcheson's *Reflections Upon Laughter* (1750), which had argued, against Hobbes, that laughter was a non-judgmental response to the perception of an unexpected incongruity. James Beattie's essay *On Laughter and Ludicrous Composition* (1776) became the definitive survey and examination of the competing theories. On the physiological aspect of laughter emphasized by Mac Quedy, see Joseph Priestley, *A Course of Lectures on Oratory and Criticism* (1777), lecture 24; Kant's *Critique of Judgment* (1790), book 2, section 54; and Erasmus Darwin, *Zoonomia; or the Laws of Organic Life*, 2 vols. (1794–6), vol. 1, section 34. The discovery of nitrous oxide (or 'laughing

gas') by Thomas Beddoes Senior and Humphry Davy in 1799 also influenced contemporary debate, and can be felt in Mac Quedy's claim that laughter is an 'involuntary action'. See also William Hazlitt on laughter as involuntary in 'On Wit and Humour', *Lectures on the English Comic Writers* (Taylor and Hessey, 1819).

CHAPTER 3

1 **THE SQUYR OF LOWE DEGRE:** An anonymous late Middle English metrical romance, one of the better known English romances during the Elizabethan and Jacobean eras, and again in the nineteenth century. Unlike practically all other Middle English romances, it is known from printed editions only: there is one complete text, comprising 1132 lines, printed by William Copland around 1560. TLP cites lines 17–20 of the Copland text, which was reprinted by Joseph Ritson in vol. 3 (pp. 145–92 (p.146)) of his *Ancient Engleish Metrical Romanceës*, 3 vols. (1802), a work owned by TLP (*Sale Catalogue* 528); 'nere': closer (i.e. to fulfilment); 'fe': property; 'forsoth': forsooth, truly. See also Thomas Percy, *Bishop Percy's Folio Manuscript: Ballads and Romances*, ed. John W. Hales and Frederick J. Furnivall, 3 vols. (1867–8), vol. 3, pp. 263–8. Walter Scott refers to *The Squyr of Low Degre* in several fictions; in *Quentin Durward* (1823) and *The Fair Maid of Perth* (1828), the hero finds himself in a situation resembling that of the squire and cannot help identifying with him.

2 **the lines of Chaucer . . . my devocion:** Geoffrey Chaucer, *The Legend of Good Women* (F text), Prologue, lines 29–39. In 1862, TLP wrote to Lord Broughton that he was reading the *Canterbury Tales*, 'which I have read and admired before' (*Letters*, 2.438; see also *Sale Catalogue* 120).

3 **vallum . . . watch-station:** Folliott uses terminology from Roman military building; 'vallum': palisade; 'castrum': fortified outpost; 'castellum': diminutive of 'castrum'. His assertion that

the site was a Roman fort is supported by the narrator's remarks
in ch. 1 (p. 7).

4 **the ancient Ikenild road . . . long strait white line**: See *Railroadiana: A New History of England: or, Picturesque, biographical,
historical, legendary and antiquarian sketches descriptive of the vicinity of the railroads: first series, London and Birmingham Railway*
(Simpkin, Marshall and Co., 1838) for a brief account of the
attractions of the 'ancient "Ikenild way"', and of its 'modern
improvements', i.e. 'the Grand Junction Canal and the Railroad'
(p. 44).

5 **Her eyes are like the fish-pools . . . Bethrabbim**: 'Thy neck *is* as
a tower of ivory; thine eyes *like* the fishpools in Heshbon, by the
gate of Bathrabbim' (Song of Solomon, ch. 7, v. 4).

6 **a lord who owns a borough**: A lord who controls, by wealth
and political influence, the selection of a Member of Parliament
from an electoral district. See also *Mel*, esp. ch. 22: 'The Borough
of Onevote'. On 'rotten boroughs' and 'boroughmongers', see
TLP's letters to Shelley in 1818 (*Letters*, 1.130–1, 161).

7 **stiver**: 'Used (like *penny*) as a type of a coin of small value, or of
a small amount of money; *occas.* a small quantity of anything, a
'bit'. *not a stiver* = nothing' (*OED*).

8 **a clearer idea of duration**: see McCulloch, *Principles*: 'But all
inquiries, that have the establishment of general principles for
their object, either are, or ought to be, founded on periods of
average duration' (p. 245).

9 **Your philosophy . . . the past**: An amalgam of Coleridgean allusions; on the 'tree', the 'camera obscura' and the poetical way
of thinking, see Coleridge's discussion of Milton in ch. 22 of
Biographia Literaria; see also ch. 12 for Coleridge's discussion of
the 'subjective' and 'objective'.

[Footnote:] **Edinburgh Review, somewhere**: Although 'antiquities' and 'civilization' are key terms in the *Edinburgh Review* in
the 1820s and early 1830s, there appears to be no precise source
for this quotation; indeed, that may be part of the joke. The

suggestion is that the article in question is penned by Brougham, a frequent contributor to the journal, a 'learned' and 'worthy friend' and an 'amateur' in many fields. See also Appendix B, n. 1 (p. 155).

10 **El Dorado**: A mythical, golden city of perfect happiness. See Voltaire, *Candide, ou l'optimisme* (1759), chs. 17–18, for a depiction of this utopia; the inhabitants have no interest in accumulating wealth or possessions, and the government keeps all inns open for free. There is a further reference to 'El Dorados' in ch. 5 (p. 45).

11 **property . . . Angola**: The Portuguese government in Angola was notorious for exploiting the indigenous population. The export of slaves was banned in Angola in 1836, but the trade did not end until the Brazilian market was closed in the early 1850s.

12 **love in a cottage**: Proverbial; a marriage for love, without sufficient means to maintain one's social status. Cf. *Mel*, ch. 14: 'The Cottage'. In Austen's *Sense and Sensibility* (1811), Willoughby declares that a cottage is 'the only form of building in which happiness is attainable' shortly before abandoning Marianne (vol. 1, ch. 14, p. 85). See also John Keats, *Lamia* (1820): 'Love in a hut, with water and a crust, / Is – Love, forgive us! – cinders, ashes, dust' (part 2, lines 1–2).

13 **cottage ornée**: '"The term cottage has for some time past been in vogue as a particular designation for small country residences and detached suburban houses, adapted to a moderate scale of living, yet with all due attention to comfort and refinement. While, in this sense of it, the name is divested of all associations with poverty, it is convenient, inasmuch as it frees from all pretension and parade and restraint" (*Penny Cycl.* Supp. (1845) I. 426). In this sense, the appellation cottage orné (cottage ornée) was in vogue, when picturesqueness was aimed at' (*OED* 'cottage, n.', 4.a.). The *OED*'s first citation for 'Cottage Orné' dates from 1781; by 1830, as Frederick Marryat implies, the craze was becoming tired: 'The cottage-ornée (as all middle-sized houses

with verandas and French windows are now designated)'. See Frederick Marryat, *The King's Own*, 3 vols. (Henry Colburn and Richard Bentley, 1830), vol. 2, p. 125. A 'tasteful little Cottage Ornèe, on a strip of waste Ground' appears in ch. 3 of Austen's unpublished *Sanditon* (wr. 1817).

14 CAPTAIN FITZCHROME: The narrator does not stop referring to the captain as 'THE STRANGER' until he is known by name to the characters in *CC*.

15 **dun**: 'One who duns; an importunate creditor, or an agent employed to collect debts' (*OED*).

16 **half-pay officer**: An officer in receipt of half the usual or full wages or salary, either because he is not in actual service, or because he has retired after the prescribed time. Cf. Captain Hawltaught in *Mel*, who 'retired on his half-pay and the produce of his prize-money' (ch. 6).

17 **outward and visible sign**: The phrase comes from the Catechism of the Book of Common Prayer (1662), another form of scripted exchange that influences TLP's fictional dialogues. In response to the question 'What meanest thou by this word Sacrament?', the catechist is directed to answer: 'I mean an outward and visible sign of an inward and spiritual grace given unto us, ordained by Christ himself, as a means whereby we receive the same, and a pledge to assure us thereof.' Lady Clarinda's wilfully irreverent use of this source (as well as her flip defiance towards her suitor) may influence Captain Fitzchrome's immediate response: 'I cannot believe that you say all this in earnest' (p. 31).

18 **clogs and bonnets**: Wealthy ladies would have worn delicate, flat or low heeled shoes made of soft kid or cloth; these wore out quickly. Poorer women, female labourers and peasants went barefoot, or wore sandals or hardwearing clogs. Bonnets, however, were a staple of the female wardrobe and do not of themselves denote lower-class status. In *Northanger Abbey* (1817), Catherine Morland's mother wears clogs, indicating her rusticity, but every girl in Bath wears a bonnet (vol. 1, chs. 2 and 10).

19 **the pit**: 'The middle part of the theatre' (Johnson's *Dictionary*); 'The part of a theatre auditorium which is on the floor of the house; (now) esp. the part of this behind the stalls. Also: the people occupying this area' (*OED* 'pit', 10.a.).

20 **a charming Hotspur**: A fiery rebel lord in Shakespeare, *Henry IV, Part I*.

21 **smooth manners . . . natural expression in a man's face**: See Gilbert Austin, *Chironomia: or a Treatise on Rhetorical Delivery: Comprehending Many Precepts, both Ancient and Modern, for the Proper Regulation of the Voice, the Countenance and Gesture* (1806). Other manuals of the period describe the appropriate 'expressions' (facial and vocal) associated with acting and therefore with the 'walking gentleman' and Shakespearean character invoked in this passage; see e.g. Johannes Jelgerhuis, *Lessons on the Principles of Gesticulation and Mimic Expression* (1827).

22 **walking gentleman**: A male actor playing a small part with little or no speaking.

23 **Master Slender . . . Petruchio**: Wooers of ladies in, respectively, *The Merry Wives of Windsor* and *The Taming of the Shrew*; the former is weak and ridiculous, the latter forceful and ultimately successful.

24 **exchangeable value**: 'When it is said that an article or product is possessed of exchangeable value, it is meant that one or more individuals are disposed to give a certain quantity of labour, or a certain quantity of some other article or product, obtainable only by means of labour, in exchange for it' (McCulloch, *Principles*, p. 3; see also pp. 211–14).

CHAPTER 4

1 **En quoi . . . RABELAIS**: Lines from 'Prologue', *Le Cinquiesme et dernier livre des faicts et dicts heroïques du bon Pantagruel* (1564), Rabelais, *Œuvres*, p. 723. 'Pray, how came you to know that Men were formerly Fools? How did you find that they are now

Wise?' (Ozell, vol. 5, p. liv). The two queries cited by TLP occur in the first paragraph of the author's prologue and form part of a series of questions. Cf. epigraphs to chs. 5 (p. 42), 10 (p. 89) and 18 (p. 138). A quotation from the same prologue is given as the epigraph to ch. 1 of *NA*. Cf. also *HH*, ch. 11; *GG*, ch. 12 and ch. 19 (epigraph). TLP owned a copy of *Œuvres de François Rabelais* (Paris: Louis Janet, 1823); see *Sale Catalogue* 512. On Rabelais' importance to him, not least as a writer who uses comedy as a form of critique, see letter to Thomas Jefferson Hogg (7 Sept. 1818): 'Your comparison of Rabelais to the court fool is most correct: he is indeed the court fool of Olympus: the chief jester of Jupiter' (*Letters*, 1.150). See also TLP's 'French Comic Romances': 'Rabelais, one of the wisest and most learned, as well as wittiest of men, put on the robe of the all-licensed fool, that he might, like the court-jester, convey bitter truths under the semblance of simple buffoonery' (Halliford, 9.258–9). TLP associates this form of comic writing with 'freedom of conscience and freedom of enquiry': 'among the most illustrious authors of comic fiction are some of the most illustrious specimens of political honesty and heroic self-devotion'; their central aim is 'the exposure of abuses . . . an intense love of truth, and a clear apprehension of truth, are both essential to comic writing of the first class' (Halliford, 9.261–2).

2 **dullness reigns predominant**: The phrasing is reminiscent of Alexander Pope's *Dunciad* (1728–44). The Argument of Book the Fourth states that the poet *'shews the Goddess coming in her Majesty, to destroy* Order *and* Science, *and to substitute the* Kingdom of the Dull *upon earth'* (Pope, *Poems*, vol. 5, p. 337).

3 **they welcome as a sinner . . . punctual to their engagement**: Cf. Luke, ch. 2, v. 15: 'I say unto you, that likewise joy shall be in heaven over one sinner that repenteth, more than over ninety and nine just persons, which need no repentance'. See Appendix B for a draft fragment of this paragraph (p. 155).

4 *bienséance*: propriety.

5 **the subject of exchangeable value ... definition of value**: Discussions about 'value' were central to political economy. David Ricardo: 'When I last saw him [James Mill] it was his intention to steer clear if possible of the difficult word value' (letter to J. R. McCulloch, 17 Jan. 1821; *The Works and Correspondence of David Ricardo*, ed. Piero Sraffa, with the collaboration of M. H. Dobb, 11 vols. (Cambridge: Cambridge University Press for the Royal Economic Society, 1951–73), vol. 8, p. 337); during the 1820s the word was contentious. After the publication of Thomas Malthus's *The Measure of Value* (1823), Ricardo wrote to Malthus: 'My complaint against you is that you claim to have given us an accurate measure of value, and I object to your claim, not that I have succeeded and you have failed, but that we have both failed' (15 Aug. 1823; *Works and Correspondence of David Ricardo*, vol. 9, p. 352). In 1825, Samuel Bailey's *Dissertation on the Nature, Measures, and Causes of Value* argued that the quantity of labour can be considered neither as the measure nor as the cause of value. See also part 3, section 1 on 'value' in McCulloch, *Principles of Political Economy* (1825), and the 3rd edition of James Mill's *Elements of Political Economy* (1826), which added new material to the chapter on exchange value.

6 **subjective reality ... transcendental**: In this context, 'transcendental' refers to Kant's philosophical approach (according to the *OED*, the adjective is first used in this way in 1798). See also the *Encyclopaedia Britannica* (1801), Supplement 2, p. 355: 'Kant ... calls all knowledge, of which the object is not furnished by the senses, and which concerns the kind and origin of our ideas, transcendental knowledge', and the *Edinburgh Review* (1803), on 'Villers's Philosophy of Kant': 'Philosophy ... is transcendental, when ... it investigates the subjective elements, which ... modify the qualities or elements of the object as perceived' (pp. 253–80 (p. 258)).

7 **the *cliquetis d'assiettes* ... the *ombre de salle à manger* ... the *fumée de rôti***: 'The clatter of plates ... the shade of the dining

room ... the steam from a roast'. No exact source for these phrases has been found in Rabelais, although his works are full of the joys of dining, and of roast meat – perhaps especially evident in *Le Tiers livre des faicts et dicts heroïques du bon Pantagruel*, whose 'Prologue' is cited in ch. 5 (p. 42).

8 **whatever that *totum* may be**: Whatever the sum total of it [the family's wit] may be.

9 *verre de santé*: Glass of health.

10 **Hock**: 'Old strong Rhenish' (Johnson's *Dictionary*); 'The wine called in German *Hochheimer*, produced at Hochheim on the Main; hence, commercially extended to other white German wines' (*OED*).

11 **Madeira**: 'A fortified wine produced on the island of Madeira; a variety of this' (*OED*). See the revised ending to the 1837 edition of *NA*, whose final words become: 'Scythrop, pointing significantly towards the dining-room, said, "Bring some Madeira"'. TLP was fond of the wine; see *Letters*, 2.362 and n.

12 *point nommé*: Perfect time.

13 Παπαπαῖ: An expanded form of παπαῖ, which is an exclamation of surprise.

14 *Cedite Graii*: Propertius, *Elegies*, book 2, 34.65–6. In this passage Propertius offers advance praise of Virgil's *Aeneid*: 'Give way, Roman writers, give way, Greeks: Something greater than the *Iliad* is coming into being.' *Cedite Graii* can stand alone grammatically, and Folliott uses it to mean 'Give way, Greeks', thus extending the sphere of reference of Propertius' original beyond mere writers (it is fish, not literature, that is relevant to Folliott's point). The 'Greeks' here are the 'modern Athenians'.

15 **happy the man to whom he falls**: Cf. John Dryden's celebrated lines, paraphrasing Horace: 'Happy the Man, and happy he alone, / He, who can call to day his own' (1685; 'Horace. Ode 29. Book 3', stanza 8, lines 65–6; *The Works of John Dryden*, 20 vols., gen. eds. E. N. Hooker, H. T. Swedenberg, Jr, and Alan

Roper (Berkeley and Los Angeles: University of California Press, 1956–2000), vol. 3: *Poems, 1685–1692*, ed. Earl Miner and Vinton A. Dearing (1969), p. 83). The poem is transcribed in TLP's hand, with the lines from Horace in Latin, in TLP 87(a), 87(b) (c. 1860) (Pforzheimer Collection, New York Public Library); the first half of line 5 differs from Dryden's translation.

16 **a Tweed salmon at Kelso**: The Scottish Border town of Kelso, on the River Tweed, was and is renowned for its Atlantic salmon.

17 *salmo salar*: The Atlantic salmon.

18 **finished his education**: Such phrasing is always loaded in TLP: cf. *CC*, chs. 5 (p. 42), 9 (pp. 83–4), 10 (p. 91). Folliott summarizes his contempt for a 'finished' modern 'education' in ch. 9: 'Education is well finished, for all worldly purposes, when the head is brought into the state whereinto I am accustomed to bring a marrow-bone, when it has been set before me on a toast, with a white napkin wrapped round it' (p. 84). See also '*finish his education*' in *Mel*, ch. 6, '*finishing* my *education*' in *HH*, ch. 4, and TLP's note to *Sir Proteus: A Satirical Ballad* (1814): 'This must have been something which had *finished* its *education*, as the saying is, at one of our learned universities' (Halliford, 6.286 n.).

19 **nose**: The brief discussion of noses perhaps recalls *Tristram Shandy*, book 3, ch. 5 and elsewhere. Tristram's father has studied several classical and modern authorities on noses, and sets great store by noses as indexes of character.

20 *compotator*: Fellow-drinker.

21 **By the by . . . ἰχθύος**: An allusion to Athenaeus, *The Deipnosophists*, 9.385e, where snippets of Menander's *Carthaginians* and *Ephesian* (frr. 226 and 172 Körte–Thierfelder) are quoted. Neither fragment contains the phrase ὀψάριον ἐπὶ ἰχθύος, which, from the context, TLP must intend to mean 'relish on fish'. In fact, the phrase ἐπὶ τοῦ ἰχθύος occurs only once in this section of Athenaeus (9.385d), and its meaning is 'in reference to the fish'. ὀψάριον is a diminutive of the word for 'fish', and the point of

the interlocutors' discussion in Athenaeus is to determine which writers of the past have used this word for 'little fish' *in reference to the fish*. Neither fragment of Menander is about fish-sauce.

22 **the pillars of Hercules**: These are the rocks that flank what is now referred to as the Straits of Gibraltar. They represented the limits of the known world.

23 **quintessence of the sapid**: Sapid: 'Of food, etc.: Readily perceptible by the organs of taste, having a decided taste or flavour; *esp.* having a pleasant taste, savoury, palatable' (*OED*). This sentence from *CC* is quoted under *OED*, of 'sapid' as 'quasi-*n*. A sapid substance'.

24 **all minds . . . are**: The discussion between Mac Quedy and Folliott draws on a debate about the influence of education on character, and about the need for education for the people. See esp. James Mill's 'Education' for the *Encyclopaedia Britannica* (later incorporated into his *Essays* (1823; repr. 1825, 1828)), where he argued that 'it is education wholly which constitutes the remarkable difference between the Turk and the Englishman, and even that still more remarkable difference between the most cultivated European and the wildest savage . . . this great mass of mankind [is] equally susceptible of mental excellence . . . Enough is ascertained to prove, beyond a doubt, that if education does not perform every thing, there is hardly anything which it does not perform . . . all the difference which exists, or can ever be made to exist, between one class of men, and another, is wholly owing to education' (repr. in Mill, *Political Writings*, ed. Ball, pp. 147, 159, 160, 161). More generally, see Mill's *Schools for All*, alluded to in ch. 2 of *CC* (p. 16), and Jeremy Bentham's *Chrestomathia* (1817), which set out a secondary school curriculum that suppressed classical teaching and emphasised scientific studies.

25 **Cæsar . . . village common**: An image probably inspired by Thomas Gray's *Elegy Written in a Country Churchyard* (1751). Gray's celebrated passage on the unfulfilled greatness of the villagers invokes Hampden, Milton and Cromwell (lines 57–60).

In the Eton manuscript of the *Elegy*, 'Cromwell' is 'Caesar'. See *The Poems of Thomas Gray, William Collins, Oliver Goldsmith*, ed. Roger Lonsdale (Longmans, 1969), pp. 127–8 and n. TLP's reference to 'the petty tyrant of the fields' in *Mel*, ch. 2 also alludes to these lines of the *Elegy*.

26 **Nadir Shah**: Nader or Nadir Shah (1688 or 1698–1747), military genius who usurped the Persian throne in 1736.

27 **Washington**: George Washington (1732–99), first President of the United States of America, commander-in-chief of the Continental Army during the American Revolutionary War, and one of the Founding Fathers.

28 **merry-andrew**: 'A person who entertains people with antics and buffoonery; a clown; a mountebank's assistant' (*OED*).

29 **Vin de Grave**: i.e. wine from Graves, part of the Bordeaux region; Graves is considered to be the birthplace of claret.

30 **a review . . . the Whig aristocracy**: Folliott refers to the *Edinburgh Review*, which promoted Whig opinions and interests; McCulloch was a frequent contributor (his first article was a review of Ricardo's *Principles of Political Economy* in June 1818). See also TLP's 'An Essay on Fashionable Literature': 'The two principal periodical publications of the time – the Edinburgh and Quarterly Reviews are the organs and oracles of the two great political factions the Whigs and Tories' (*NA*, Appendix B).

31 **Sauterne**: Sauternes is a French sweet wine from the Sauternais region of the Graves locale in Bordeaux.

32 **From John O'Groat's . . . board**: i.e. from one end of Britain to the other. See TLP's 'An Essay on Fashionable Literature': 'The *country gentlemen* appear to be in the habit of considering reviews as the joint productions of a body of men who meet at a sort of green board where all new literary productions are laid before them for impartial consideration . . . The mysterious *we* of the invisible assassin converts his poisoned dagger into a host of legitimate broadswords . . . Of the ten or twelve articles which compose the Edinburgh Review one is manufactured on the spot

another comes from Aberdeen another from Islington another from Herefordshire another from the coast of Devon another from bonny Dundee &c &c &c' (*NA*, Appendix B).

33 **contempt for truth**: On TLP's feeling that 'periodical criticism' is 'merely a fraudulent & exclusive tool of party and partiality', see his 'An Essay on Fashionable Literature' (*NA*, Appendix B).

34 **Hermitage . . . retirement**: A French wine named for a ruin, supposedly a hermit's retreat, in the area in which it is produced (the northern Rhône wine region of France, south of Lyon).

35 **Achilles was distinguished . . . love of truth**: A reference to the *Iliad*, book 9, lines 312–13: 'For hateful in my eyes as the gates of Hades is that man who hides one thing in his mind and says another.'

36 **Titan . . . clay**: Juvenal, *Satires*, 14.35: 'meliore luto finxit praecordia Titan'. The Titan is Prometheus, who formed mankind from clay. Juvenal says that most men will tend to vice, except a few who will reject wickedness because they are better by nature. Folliott is presumably referring to the fact that Achilles was half-divine, his mother being the goddess Thetis.

37 **Τὸ δὲ φυᾷ κράτιστον ἅπαν**: In the passage cited by TLP, Pindar champions innate qualities over skills that are learnt.

38 **degustate**: 'To taste; *esp.* to taste attentively, so as to appreciate the savour' (*OED*: there are only two citations, of which this is one). Johnson's *Dictionary* includes only the noun 'DEGUSTATION'.

CHAPTER 5

1 **CHAPTER V**: See Appendix C for a draft fragment of ch. 5 (pp. 156–7).

2 **Ay imputé . . . RABELAIS**: Lines from 'Prologue', *Le Tiers livre des faicts et dicts heroïques du bon Pantagruel*. Rabelais, *Œuvres*, pp. 348–9. '*I held it not a little disgraceful to be only an* Idle Spectator *of so many valorous, eloquent and warlike Persons*' (Ozell, vol. 3, p. xi).

3 LADY CLARINDA (*to the Captain.*): Lady Clarinda's speech, in which she comments for her suitor on the diverse assembly around them, has precedents in writers whom TLP admired. See Carl Dawson: 'Robert Bage lets a character do this in *Barham Downs*; Isaac Disraeli lets one of his characters do it in *Vaurien*; but Peacock's more likely models were Petronius' *Satyricon* and Moliere's *Le Misanthrope*' (*His Fine Wit*, pp. 259–60). See esp. act 2, scene 5 of *Le Misanthrope* (1666).

4 **very unreasonably fond of reasoning . . . one or two**: This description of Crotchet aligns him with the character of Hudibras, another befuddled and disputatious would-be logician.

5 **illuminés**: i.e. one of the Illuminati (plural of Latin *illuminatus*, 'enlightened'), a name given to several groups, real and fictitious. Historically, the name refers to the Bavarian Illuminati, a secret society founded on 1 May 1776 to oppose superstition, prejudice, religious influence over public life and abuses of state power, and to support women's education and gender equality. The Illuminati were outlawed by the Bavarian government, with the encouragement of the Roman Catholic Church, and permanently disbanded in 1785. The group was vilified by conservative and religious critics who claimed they had regrouped and were responsible for the French Revolution. In later use, 'Illuminati' refers to various organizations claiming, more or less plausibly, links to the original Bavarian Illuminati or similar secret societies. See also *NA*, ch. 2: '[Scythrop] now became troubled with the *passion for reforming the world*. He built many castles in the air, and peopled them with secret tribunals, and bands of illuminati, who were always the imaginary instruments of his projected regeneration of the human species . . . Such were the views of those secret associations of illuminati, which were the terror of superstition and tyranny.' Cf. Scott, *Novels*, vol. 3: *The Antiquary* [1816], ed. David Hewitt (1995): 'a simple youth whispered me that he was an *Illuminé*, and carried on an intercourse with the invisible world' (vol. 1, ch. 13, p. 101).

6 **all misfortune . . . honest industry**: A caricature of what Humphry House memorably described as the 'grim alliance between Malthusianism and Nonconformity': 'Let the poor live hard lives, sober, celibate, and unamused; let them eat the plainest food, pinch to save, and save to lower the rates – then "civilization" might win through' (*The Dickens World*, 2nd edn (Oxford: Oxford University Press, 1942), pp. 73–6).

7 **gew-gaw**: 'A gaudy trifle, plaything, or ornament, a pretty thing of little value, a toy or bauble' (*OED* 'gewgaw, n.'). Cf. 'The Four Ages of Poetry', in which the modern poet is depicted as 'raking up the ashes of dead savages to find gewgaws and rattles for the grown babies of the age' (*NA*, Appendix C).

8 **Mr. Eavesdrop . . . print me**: On TLP's displeasure at those who published gossip in the name of reminiscences, see his review of Thomas Moore's *Letters and Journals of Lord Byron* (1830), where he associates that book with Leigh Hunt's *Lord Byron and Some of His Contemporaries* (1828): both are said to belong to the 'eavesdropping genus' (Halliford, 9.76). On TLP's antipathy to 'this system of biographical gossip', see also *Letters*, 2.371, 217–20.

9 **Mr. Henbane, the toxicologist**: 'Henbane' is a poisonous plant. The character recalls the surgeon, anatomist and toxicologist Benjamin Collins Brodie (1783–1862), Professor of Comparative Anatomy and Physiology at the Royal College of Surgeons. Brodie did poison a cat and bring it to life again; the cat lived on as a pet of Joanna Baillie. (Maria Edgeworth told the story when she stayed with Baillie in 1822; see *Maria Edgeworth: Letters from England*, ed. Christina Colvin (Oxford: Oxford University Press, 1971), pp. 316–17.) More generally, 'toxicology' was a relatively recent medical development (the *OED*'s first citation is from 1799). 'Toxicologist' dates back to c. 1829–32.

10 **the Spirit of the Frozen Ocean**: See Matthew Lewis, 'Amorossan, or the spirit of the frozen ocean', in *Romantic Tales*, 4 vols. (1808). This story, an oriental romance of German origin,

was singled out from the rest of Lewis's collection in the *Critical Review* as exhibiting 'in the most powerful colours, the cold and chilling miseries' arising from mistrust (*Critical Review, or, Annals of Literature*, vol. 15 (1808), p. 360). See also *Sale Catalogue* 407 and 408.

11 **A great dreamer... eye to his gain**: Coleridge claimed that *Kubla Khan* came to him in a dream (see Halliford, 8.290 for TLP's wry reflections on this claim). See also TLP's poem *Rhododaphne* (1818), Canto 3: 'The world, oh youth! deems many wise, / Who dream at noon with waking eyes, / While spectral fancy round them flings / Phantoms of unexisting things' (Halliford, 7.34), and *NA* on Flosky: 'He dreamed with his eyes open, and saw ghosts dancing round him at noontide' (ch. 1). Cf. Coleridge's *Biographia Literaria*, ch. 23: 'The poet does not require us to be awake and believe; he solicits us only to yield ourselves to a dream; and this too with our eyes open' (Coleridge, *Works*, vol. 7, 2.218).

12 **Mr. Wilful Wontsee, and Mr. Rumblesack Shantsee**: TLP is gesturing to William Wordsworth and Robert Southey, both of whom had long had reputations as apostates. Each had accepted a government sinecure, Southey as Poet Laureate. 'Rumblesack' alludes to the free butt of sack (i.e. wine) provided by the government to a Laureate every year. See TLP's *Sir Proteus: A Satirical Ballad* for extended commentary on Wordsworth, Southey, Coleridge and 'the apostate train' (Halliford, 6.281–313 (p. 312)). See also TLP to Shelley (19 July 1818): 'The Cumberland poets by their conduct on this occasion have put the finishing stroke to their own disgrace. I am persuaded there is nothing in the way of dirty work that these men are not abject enough to do if the blessed Lord – (Lonsdale) – commanded it, or any other blessed member of the holy and almighty seat-selling aristocracy to which they have sold themselves body and soul' (*Letters*, 1.145). At one stage, Southey and Coleridge had planned to form a utopian society in America, but the reference

to 'visions of Utopia' here casts aspersions on the efficacy of such ideals; see Hazlitt: 'Poetry dwells in a perpetual Utopia of its own, and is, for that reason, very ill calculated to make a Paradise on earth' (*Examiner*, 22 Dec. 1816, p. 802).

13 **Mr. Chainmail**: Chainmail shares several characteristics with Samuel Rush Meyrick (1783–1848). On Meyrick's particular interest in Welsh castles, see Butler, *Peacock*, p. 184. Meyrick was a pioneer in the study of arms and armour; see his *A Critical Enquiry into Ancient Armour* (1824). He also built Goodrich Hall in 1828, where he housed his extensive collection of armour. David Garnett suggests that TLP had Sir Edward Strachey in mind for the portrait of Chainmail, despite the fact that Strachey was only eighteen years old when *CC* was written (see Garnett, *Novels*, 2.680 n.). More generally, Chainmail embodies a growing interest in Britain's medieval past, stimulated in part by Scott's works (novels and ballad collections), by Romantic historiographers, and by researchers and collectors such as Percy and Ritson.

14 **gunpowder, steam, and gas**: Cf. a letter from Lord Broughton to TLP (22 Oct. 1854), in which he asks 'what do you think of printing? What of steam? What of gun powder? Indeed what of any art of which very mischievous use has been made more frequently than any good use?' (*Letters*, 2.351).

15 **Mr. Toogood . . . cook**: Cf. Robert Owen (1771–1858), Welsh industrialist and social reformer, pioneer of utopian socialist thought in England and a founder of the cooperative movement. A pacifist and anti-religionist, Owen believed the society of the future would be divided into small, self-contained, autonomous communities. His own model communities, established in America in 1824, were laid out in squares. The name 'Mr. Toogood' also suggests such semi-allegorical characters as Squire Allworthy in *Tom Jones* and Goodwill in *Pilgrim's Progress*. For further reference to 'Mr. Owen's parallelograms', or 'quadrangular paradises', as they were called, see ch. 6 (p. 57).

16 **town and country-house**: Cf. TLP to Thomas Forster (14 Nov.
1811): 'After all, a happy interchang<e> of town and country,
society and retirement, keeps the mind in its proper tone, and
preserves the relish of both' (*Letters*, 1.67).

17 *andare al diavolo*: Go to the devil.

18 *distrait*: 'Having the attention distracted from what is present;
absent-minded' (*OED* 'distrait, adj.', 2). Cf. Byron, *Don Juan*,
canto 16, stanza 30, lines 238–9: 'So much distrait he was, that all
could see / That something *was* the matter' (Byron, *Works*, vol. 5).

19 **Mr. Trillo ... this one great matter**: TLP's description suggests that the poet Thomas Moore (1779–1852) may have been
one model for Mr Trillo. Moore was approached by two music
publishers, William and James Power, to take part in a ven-
ture which proved astonishingly successful: the series of *Irish
Melodies* (1808–34). He wrote the words for characteristic Irish
airs arranged by Sir John Stevenson, and Moore's performances
recommended the songs to fashionable society. However, as in
the case of Folliott, there is an element of authorial self-parody
at play in Trillo: TLP was an opera buff. As of 1829, he was
music critic for two London periodicals.

20 **Dr. Morbific**: From *morbificus*, disease. Perhaps suggested by
the career of Charles Maclean (fl. 1788–1824), physician and
political writer, an outspoken anti-contagionist and opponent of
quarantine. Maclean, like TLP, entered the service of the East
India Company. He travelled to India, Jamaica and Indonesia.
These postings gave him exceptional facilities for the study of
fevers, and in 1796 he published his results in *Dissertation on the
Source of Epidemic Diseases*, which argued that epidemics arose not
from contagion but from miasmata, atmospheric phenomena,
and the cumulative effects of scarcity and famine.
[Footnote:] *ΦΙΛοΠΟΤαμος*. **Fluviorum amans**: 'Lover of rivers'.
'Philpot' is thus derived fancifully by TLP from φιλοπόταμος.
The word is not attested in Greek. The character was perhaps
suggested by MacGregor Laird (1808-61), Scottish shipbuilder

and explorer, an expert on African and Indian rivers, and TLP's friend. The trip down the Niger, proposed in ch. 6 (p. 59) by Philpot, was being planned by Laird during the period in which *CC* was written. See MacGregor Laird and R. A. K. Oldfield, *Narrative of an Expedition into the Interior of Africa by the River Niger in the Steam-Vessels Quorra and Alburka in 1832, 1833 and 1834* (Richard Bentley, 1837). In 1837, Laird co-founded the British and North American Steam Navigation Company, whose vessel the *Sirius* made the first completely steam-powered Atlantic crossing in 1838. He remained immersed in the problems of iron steamship technology, taking out a number of patents in the field, until 1850. There may be an element of self-parody involved in the character of Philpot, given TLP's love of rivers and of navigation.

21 **Deserts of Zahara**: i.e. the Sahara Desert, the great desert of Libya or northern Africa. The names 'Zahara' and 'Sahara' were both used to identify this desert in the nineteenth century, as were others: 'Saara's' (Henry Brackenridge), 'Zaarras' (Thomas De Quincey) and Saharah (Charles Dickens). See *OED* 'Sahara, n.'.

22 **Sir Simon Steeltrap**: The name 'Steeltrap' implies 'a true-born English squire', committed to the 'game-bagging, poacher-shooting, trespasser-pounding, footpath-stopping, common-enclosing, rack-renting, and all the other liberal pursuits and pastimes which make a country gentleman' (ch. 1, p. 8). In the Pierpont Morgan MS fragment of this chapter, Sir Simon Steeltrap is called Steeltrap Fitz-Treadmill Esquire. See Appendix C (p. 156–7).

23 **Sunday**: An allusion to sabbatarianism (the strict observance of Sunday as a holy day reserved for worship). The Lord's Day Observance Act, drawn up in 1781, forbade the Sunday opening of places of entertainment or debate to which admission was gained by payment.

24 **Mr. Quassia, the brewer**: Quassia: 'The bitter-tasting wood, bark, or root of *Quassia amara*; a medicinal preparation made

from this, usually by infusion, used as an antipyretic or parasiti-
cide' (*OED* 'quassia, n.'). Quassia was sometimes used in brewing
as a substitute for hops.

25 **He has enclosed . . . expense of the county**: This section comes
closest of any passage in *CC* to the draft fragment of ch. 5 transcribed in Appendix C (pp. 156–7). See also E. G. Wakefield,
Swing Unmasked; or, The Causes of Rural Incendiarism (Effingham
Wilson, 1831): 'Speaking generally . . . the privileged classes of
our rural districts take infinite pains to be abhorred by their
poorest neighbours. They inclose commons. They stop footpaths. They wall in their parks. They set spring-guns and man-
traps . . . They superintend alehouses, decry skittles, deprecate
beer-shops, meddle with fairs, and otherwise curtail the already
narrow amusements of the poor' (pp. 14–15).

26 *parvenus*: People from a humble background who have rapidly
gained wealth or an influential social position; upstarts, social
climbers (*OED*).

27 **beautiful . . . Clarinda**: Lady Clarinda's relationship with Captain Fitzchrome echoes that of TLP in 1812 with Clarinda
Knowles, a woman he had hoped to marry. TLP described her as
'of all the girls whom I have ever met with, the most lovely, the
most engaging, the most witty, and the most accomplished . . . so
every way fascinating, that she is to me little less than a spirit
of heaven' (*Letters*, 1.94); 'I doubt if the concentrated attractions of all the nymphs I have e<ver> loved and caressed would
compose a being half so encha<nti>ng as this goddess of my
idolatry' (*Letters*, 1.96).

28 **fal-lals**: 'A piece of finery or frippery, a showy adornment in
dress. Chiefly *pl*' (*OED*).

29 **Mr. Puffall, the bookseller**: 'To puff' in this context means
'To praise, extol, or commend, esp. extravagantly, unduly, or in
inflated or unjustifiable terms; to make the subject of a lauda-
tory advertisement, review, etc.; to make favourable mention of,
promote, publicize' (*OED* 'puff v.'). Mr Puffall will ensure that

there are extravagantly complimentary reviews of Lady Clarinda's book. See also TLP's 'An Essay on Fashionable Literature' (*NA*, Appendix B).

30 **three volumes . . . characters of her acquaintance**: Cf., for instance, John Moore, *Mordaunt. Sketches of Life, Characters, and Manners, of various Countries; including the Memoirs of a French Lady of Quality*, 3 vols. (1800). Lady Caroline Lamb's *Glenarvon*, 3 vols. (1816) popularized this type of thinly veiled triple-decker *roman à clef*. All but one of Austen's published novels appeared in three volumes; *Sense and Sensibility* (1811) was advertised on the title page as 'By a Lady'; other title pages were in the format of TLP's, referring to Austen as the author of other works rather than by name. Cf. also Mary Shelley, *The Last Man* (1826), 3 vols., 'by the Author of Frankenstein' (the work includes characters modelled on Shelley and Byron).

CHAPTER 6

1 **But when they came . . . BUTLER**: *Hudibras*, part 3, canto 2, lines 253–4: 'For when they came to shape the *Model*, / Not one could fit anothers Noddle.' The lines form part of a vigorous, earthy survey of religious fanatics and their imitators at home and abroad.

2 **In the infancy of society . . . to save a percentage**: Cf. Sir Edward Strachey's anecdote in his 'Recollections of Thomas Love Peacock', included in *Calidore and Miscellanea*, ed. Richard Garnett (J. M. Dent, 1891): 'one day [TLP] came to my father's room, and said, with mock indignation, "I will never dine with Mill again, for he asks me to meet only political economists. I dined with him last night, when he had Mushet and MacCulloch, and after dinner, Mushet took a paper out of his pocket, and began to read: 'In the infancy of society, when Government was invented to save a percentage – say, of 3½ per cent.' – on which he was

stopped by MacCulloch with, 'I will say no such thing,' meaning that this was not the proper percentage'" (p. 18). See also Van Doren, *Life*, pp. 197–8.

3 **the division of labor**: A central tenet of Smith's *Wealth of Nations*. 'The effect of the division of labour in increasing the quantity and perfection of the products of industry had been noticed by several of the writers who preceded Dr Smith, and especially by Mr Harris and M. Turgot. But neither of these writers did what Dr Smith has done. None of them has fully traced its operation, or shown that the power of engaging in different employments depends on the power of exchanging; and that, consequently, the advantages derived from the division of labour are necessarily dependent upon, and regulated by, the extent of the market. This is a principle of very great importance, and by establishing it Dr Smith shed a new light on the whole science, and laid the foundation of many important practical conclusions' (McCulloch, *Principles*, pp. 91–2).

4 **a diagram**: Owen liked to use charts, tables and diagrams in his writing; this probably refers to his plan for a 'quadrangular village'. 'Ideally, Owen thought, communities should be constructed in the form of a large quadrangle, with public buildings in the centre. Persons of a particular political or religious persuasion might want to associate with others of their kind, and Owen designed a table showing 140 combinations of such views' (*ODNB*).

5 **sense, understanding, and reason . . . receptivity**: see Coleridge, *Biographia Literaria*, ch. 5, where he writes of 'three separate classes' in which 'Our inward experiences' are 'arranged'. One of them is 'the passive sense, or what the school-men call the merely receptive quality of the mind' (Coleridge, *Works*, vol. 7, 1.90). On 'understanding' and 'reason', see Kant's distinction between reason and understanding in the *Critique of Pure Reason* (1790).

6 **deliberative dinners**: A vital analogue for the 'deliberative dinner' in TLP's work – and in *CC* especially, given the range of
references to food – is the Greek symposium. A symposium typically followed a meal, but the whole occasion could be called 'a
shared meal' (see e.g. Plato, *Symposium*, 172b). It was a serio-
comic institution, linked to Greek notions of play. See Introduction, pp. ci–cix.

7 **Political economy ... the family**: This is the opening sentence
of the Introduction of James Mill's *Elements of Political Economy*.
See also McCulloch, *Principles*: '*Economy*, from οἶκος a house,
or family, and νόμος, a law – *the government of a family*. Hence
Political Economy may be said to be to the State what domestic
economy is to a single family' (p. 1). The analogy of family and
state goes back at least as far as Aristotle; see *Politics*, book 1,
§5, 1–2. Folliott's concern in this discussion about the use of
'false analogies' suggests that he may have in mind the following
passage: 'Some thinkers, however, suppose that statesman, king,
estate manager, and master of a family have a common character. This is a mistake; they think that the distinction between
them is not a difference in kind, but a simple, numerical difference ... mastership and statesmanship are not identical, nor are
all forms of power the same, as some thinkers suppose' (*Politics*,
book 1, §1 and §6).

8 **The family consumes, and so does the state**: Cf. 'The family
consumes; and in order to consume, it must be supplied by
production' (Mill, Introduction, *Elements of Political Economy*,
p. 1).

9 **Adam and Eve ... when they delved and span**: 'When Adam
delved and Eve span / Who was then a gentleman?' Usually
attributed to John Ball (d. 1381), an English Lollard priest who
played a leading role in the Peasants' Revolt of 1381. On 12 June
the Kentish insurgents assembled on Blackheath. Ball preached
to them, taking as his text the words: 'Whanne Adam dalfe and

Eve span, / Who was þanne a gentil man?' Although this couplet has become associated with Ball's name, it was a popular proverb which is recorded from at least the early fourteenth century.

10 **the ancient altar of Bacchus**: The drama began as hymns sung to Bacchus (Dionysus), Greek god of fertility and wine.

11 *sacella*: 'little shrines'. Oracles were not itinerant, but had fixed shrines.

12 **see through a glass darkly**: 1 Corinthians, ch. 13, v. 11: 'For now we see through a glass, darkly; but then face to face: now I know in part; but then shall I know even as I am known.'

13 **The *fruges consumere nati***: Those 'born to consume resources' (Horace, *Epistles*, book 1, epistle 2, line 27). In the original, Horace sets himself against the prudent Odysseus, who knew the virtue of holding back from indulging his appetites.

14 **You remember...pleasantry**: Folliott quotes Aristophanes, *Frogs*, line 740. Xanthias, slave of the wine-god Dionysus, is told that his master is 'noble' (γεννάδας); in reply he says 'How could he not be noble, *given that he knows only how to drink and fuck?*' Folliott amuses himself with the obscenity, which is cloaked by 'the obscurity of a learned language'.

15 **exordium**: 'The beginning of anything; *esp.* the introductory part of a discourse, treatise, etc.; "the proemial part of a composition" (Johnson)' (*OED*).

16 **regenerate the lyrical drama**: TLP might have in mind Shelley's *Prometheus Unbound* (1820) and *Hellas* (1822), both of which are subtitled 'A Lyrical Drama'. Cf. also TLP's review of Lord Mount Edgcumbe's *Musical Reminiscences* (1824): 'Rousseau has admirably described what the lyrical drama ought to be'; 'The business, indeed, of the lyrical dramatist' (Halliford, 9.229, 230).

17 **Let the frogs have all the advantage of it**: Cf. Folliott's quotation, above, from Aristophanes, *Frogs*; see, too, the reference to 'Aristophanes's frogs' in 'Touchandgo' (Appendix E, p. 165).

18 ***bonhommie***: 'Bonhomie' or 'bonhommie': 'Good nature; the quality of being a good fellow' (*OED*).

19 ***la Dive Bouteille***: The divine bottle; proverbial; possibly originating in Jean de la Fontaine or Rabelais. TLP is probably referring to the oracular Holy Bottle consulted by Panurge (Rabelais, *Le Cinquiesme et dernier livre des faicts et dicts heroïques du bon Pantagruel*, chs. 43–5, *Œuvres complètes*, pp. 829–35. The phrase 'la dive Bouteille' appears in the first sentence of ch. 43 (p. 829). See also Ozell, vol. 5, pp. 151–6.

20 **makes an Eleusinian temple . . . must die**: The Eleusinian Mysteries were the highly secretive rites in honour of Demeter and Persephone held at Eleusis (near Athens). Knowledge of the cult's activities was limited to initiates, who in turn were forbidden under pain of death from divulging information to outsiders.

21 ***Fiat experimentum in animâ vili***: 'Let the experiment be performed on a worthless life'. The maxim occurs in Kant's *Der Streit der Fakultäten* (1798), though with the more common *corpore* for *animâ*. It is also used in Thomas De Quincey's *Confessions of an English Opium-Eater* (first published in the *London Magazine*, Sept. and Oct. 1821), reviewed in *Asiatic Journal*, vol. 14 (1822). TLP may well have read De Quincey – and indeed this very review, given his connection with the East India Company from 1819 onwards and his subscription to the *Asiatic Journal* from 1830 to 1844 (*Sale Catalogue* 44).

22 **unfacetious**: This is the *OED*'s only recorded instance of the word.

23 **inficete**: 'Unfacetious; not witty' (*OED*). The *OED* gives only two examples for this word, one of which is this. The other is from the *Westminster Review* for 1830, where TLP might have come across it.

24 ***argumentum baculinum***: The 'argument of the rod', i.e. an 'appeal to force'.

25 **Abyssinia and Bambo**: Abyssinia: Ethiopia; *Bambo* is in Nigeria.

26 **inexpressibles**: '(*colloq.*) Breeches or trousers. (Orig. euphemistic: cf. *ineffables* (INEFFABLE *n.* 1), inexplicables (INEXPLICABLE *n.* 2), *unmentionables* (UNMENTIONABLE *n.* 1a).)' (*OED*).

27 **chorus . . . harmony**: TLP's critical writings on and reviews of opera often single out the importance of the chorus. See e.g. his review of Lord Mount Edgcumbe's *Musical Reminiscences* (1824), where each member of the chorus 'should seem as if he knew that he had some business of his own in the scene, and not as if he were a mere unit among thirty or forty automata' (Halliford, 9.225–6). Conversely, TLP criticizes another chorus as being 'remarkable for nothing, but the heterogeneousness of its composition, and the independence of proceeding asserted by its constituent voices' (Halliford, 9.423). The ideal chorus is a balance of variety and unity.

28 **melopœia, choregraphy . . . didascalics**: Respectively, the arts of musical composition, dancing, and teaching. According to the *OED*, 'didascalics' should be 'didascalies', pl. of 'didascaly', meaning 'In *pl.* The Catalogues of the ancient Greek Dramas'. This is the *OED*'s earliest recorded usage of the word.

29 **What, sir . . . and to none others**: Athenian drama was performed at the religious festival known as the Dionysia, an important event in the civic calendar. The theatre received heavy subsidies, both from private individuals and (at least from the middle of the fourth century BC) from the state treasury. Particularly expensive were the 'choruses' – the sung and danced passages between the scenes of dialogue, here alluded to by 'melopœia' and 'choregraphy'. The Athenian statesman Eubulus (c. 405–c. 335 BC) supposedly created a law whereby even to try to divert the treasury's festival ('theoric') funds to a military purpose was a capital offence. Although modern scholars dispute the veracity of this assertion, it was the orthodoxy in TLP's day (see e.g. Ephraim Chambers' *Cyclopædia* (1728), s.v. 'Theoretic').

30 **metricise**: 'To analyse the metre of, scan' (*OED*). This is the *OED*'s earliest recorded usage of the word.

31 **pass in by herself**: Trillo's objection seems to be that if one were to revert to the theatre of the ancient Greeks, all women would thereby be excluded from attending plays. It was disputed in TLP's lifetime, and still is, whether women had been permitted to attend the theatre in Athens. The most important proponent of the view that women were debarred from the theatre was the German scholar Karl August Böttiger (1760–1835). Although Böttiger's arguments did not convince everyone at the time, TLP apparently here takes the absence of women from Athenian dramatic performances as a given.

32 **regenerating the world**: See *NA*, ch. 2 and ch. 5: 'Scythrop's schemes for regenerating the world, and detecting his seven golden candlesticks, went on very slowly in this fever of his spirit.'

33 **sing with Robin Hood . . . last**: An allusion to the traditional ballad 'Little John a Begging', or 'Little John and the Four Beggars', which ends with Robin and Little John rejoicing over their money: 'Then *Robin Hood* took *Little John* by ye hand, . . . / And danced about the Oak tree; / If we drink water while this doth last / then an il death may we die' (lines 82–5). See Percy, *Bishop Percy's Folio Manuscript*, vol. 1, p. 49 (citing Antony à Wood, ballad 401, fol. 34).

CHAPTER 7

1 **Quoth he . . . BUTLER**: Samuel Butler, *Hudibras*, part 2, canto 2, lines 665–6: 'Quoth he, In all my life till now / I ne'r saw so profane a *Show*.' The lines are spoken by Hudibras in response to a grotesque rabble, led by a triumphant Amazon who sits 'face to tail, and bum to bum' on a horse (line 643); he compares the 'show' to examples from ancient literature (Ralpho, as ever, disputes the knight's interpretation). The episode, given the title

'The Adventure of the Riding', is excerpted in William Hazlitt's *Select British Poets, or New Elegant Extracts from Chaucer to the Present Time* (William C. Hall, 1824), p. 172.

2 **The library of Crotchet castle ... into a music-room**: The library in *HH* is 'interior to the music-room' (ch. 6). In *Mel*, TLP ostentatiously refuses to enter into detail about the library: 'we shall describe [it] no farther than by saying, that the apartment was Gothic and the furniture Grecian' (ch. 2). Of the library in *NA* we know little, other than that it has a view of the sea (ch. 5). Falconer's splendid library in *GG* is on the top floor of his Folly and therefore has the best view of any room in the building, an arrangement whose wisdom Opimian questions; more detail is given regarding the contents and appearance of this galleried library than about any other in TLP (*GG*, ch. 3). See also General Editor's preface, p. xv and n. 5 below (pp. 248–9).

3 **tables ... consecrated**: Another example of TLP's deft and lightly parodic use of religious language in a socially refined and hyper-literary setting, reminiscent of *The Rape of the Lock* and Belinda's 'sacred Rites of Pride' at the dressing table (canto 1, line 128). Cf. Lady Clarinda's delicately mocking echo of the catechism in ch. 3 (p. 31), and the later reference in ch. 7 (p. 66) to Pope's *Essay on Man* (Pope, *Poems*, vol. 2).

4 **the ancient ... selected and arranged by the Reverend Doctor Folliott**: Folliott's selection and arrangement of classical texts, like his frequent allusions to ancient customs and literature, are traits shared with his author; on the resemblances between them, see Introduction, pp. lxxvii, lxxxi–lxxxii.

5 **In this suite of apartments ... usually passed**: In TLP, a library is often a sociable venue as well as a retreat for private reading and reflection. Mr Cranium's lecture (ch. 11 of *HH*) takes place in the library. 'Here is the best of company', says Anthelia in *Mel*, 'pointing to the shelves of the library' (ch. 2); but she allows many people to join her there. In ch. 5 of *NA*, 'the family and

the visitors were assembled' in the library; in ch. 6, 'the whole party met, as usual, in the library'. Tea and coffee are served there in ch. 12 of *NA* and in chs. 2 and 31 of *Mel* – rather than in the drawing-room, as might have been expected. In *GG*, Mr Falconer and Dr Opimian enjoy reading alone in their respective libraries; they also work happily together in Falconer's panoramic library (chs. 9, 12).

6 **Matilde de Shabran**: *Matilde di Shabran, ossia Bellezza e cuor di ferro*, a *melodramma giocoso* in two acts by Gioachino Rossini. The opera was first performed in Rome at the Teatro Apollo, 24 Feb. 1821; this premiere was followed by a street brawl between Rossini's admirers and his detractors. It was presented in London on 3 July 1823. Mr Trillo's choice marks him out as passionate, fashionable and daring in his tastes. TLP reviewed a production of *Matilde di Shabran* at the King's Theatre for *The Examiner* (10 Mar. 1833), p. 150; *CC* itself might be classified as a *melodramma giocoso* of sorts. For further comments on Rossini, see *Letters*, 1.120, 1.122, 2.223–4. In his review of Edgcumbe's *Musical Reminiscences*, TLP wrote: 'There can be no question that Rossini's music is more spirit-stirring than Paësiello's, and more essentially theatrical: more suited to the theatre by its infinite variety of contrast and combination, and more dependent on the theatre for the development of its perfect effect. We were present at the first performance of an opera of Rossini's in England: *Il Barbiere di Siviglia*, in March, 1818. We saw at once that there was a great revolution in dramatic music. Rossini burst on the stage like a torrent, and swept everything before him except Mozart' (Halliford, 9.244).

7 *pro more . . . seriatim*: *pro more*: 'In his customary way'; *seriatim*: 'in sequence'.

8 **hornbook**: 'A leaf of paper containing the alphabet (often with the addition of the ten digits, some elements of spelling, and the Lord's Prayer) protected by a thin plate of translucent horn, and mounted on a tablet of wood with a projecting piece for a handle.

A simpler and later form of this, consisting of the tablet without the horn covering, or a piece of stiff cardboard varnished, was also called a battledore' (*OED* 'horn-book', 1). As is clear from other things he says, Shantsee (via Skionar) is calling for the use of methods that are already obsolescent.

9 **Old Restraint . . . poetic name for the parish stocks**: See 'restraint', 5.b. (*OED*).

10 **inexpressibles**: See ch. 6 (p. 59).

11 *Il Bragatore . . . his betters*: Daniele da Volterra (c. 1509–66), painter and sculptor, employed by Pope Pius IV to add draperies to nude figures in Michelangelo's *Last Judgment* (among other works). He thereby earned the nickname 'Il Braghettone' ('the breeches-maker'); 'Il Bragatore' ('the boaster') may be a corruption. Daniele's work began in 1565, shortly after the Council of Trent had condemned nudity in religious art.

12 **Corinthian capitals of "fair round bellies with fat capon lined"**: In architecture, the capital (from Latin *caput*, or 'head') forms the topmost member of a column; Corinthian capitals are the most ornate, decorated with acanthus leaves and scrolls. See Jaques, 'Fair round belly with fat capon lined', in *As You Like It*, act 2, scene 7, line 154. This combination – of refined heads with gross bellies – echoes in its affront to decorum the library's incongruous mixture of Gothic and Grecian elements in *Mel* (ch. 2).

13 **noddles of porcelain mandarins**: Mandarin porcelain ware was produced in China for export in the late eighteenth century. Groups of figures in mandarin dress appear in the decorative panels – painted mainly in gold, red and rose pink and framed in underglaze blue – that characterize the ware. After 1800, mandarin porcelain was often copied by English potters.

14 **promulgated . . . petticoats**: A possible reference back to the context of the epigraph from *Hudibras*: 'The Adventure of the Riding' also involves a petticoat. See above, n. 1 (pp. 247–8).

15 **Mr. Crotchet . . . Venuses of all sizes and kinds**: Crotchet collects for himself nine types of Venus; for tentative identifications, see Dodson, *Crotchet Castle*, p. 197 n. 8. All have ancient pedigree – except the Sleeping Venus, which is the target of Folliott's subsequent attack.

16 **whatever had been in Greece, was right**: A parodic echo of Pope's *An Essay on Man* (1734–5): 'whatever IS, is RIGHT' (epistle 1, line 292; *Poems*, vol. 3, p. 1). Like the irreverent uses to which religious language is put in *CC*, Pope's line is here directed to purposes mischievously foreign to its original context. *An Essay on Man* served to popularize the optimistic philosophy of Gottfried Wilhelm Leibniz (1646–1716): the claim that the actual world is the best of all possible worlds is the foundation of Leibniz's theodicy. Folliott, however, is arguing pessimistically against the current state of the world, especially of the drive to popularize knowledge, and in favour of the superiority of past civilizations to the present. Voltaire's *Candide, ou L'optimisme*, with its satiric, erratic and fantastical assault on Leibniz, is one likely influence on TLP's response to *An Essay on Man*; for a further reference to *Candide*, see *Letters*, 2.284 and n. 7.

17 *adytum*: 'The innermost or most sacred part of a temple or other place of worship; (*Classical Archit.*) a small sanctuary in the cella reserved for oracles, priests, or priestesses' (*OED*).

18 **peirastically**: 'By experiment, tentatively' (*OED*). Coined by TLP in *Mel* (ch. 18).

19 **As great philosophers . . . *percipi***: A reference to the fundamental tenet of George Berkeley's subjective idealism, *esse est percipi* ('to be is to be perceived'). Kant opposed this idea, so it is perhaps not surprising that Folliott, who in ch. 2 shows hostility to Kant, refers to subjective idealists as 'great philosophers' – although he does not take any kind of philosopher entirely seriously.

20 *ennui*: 'The feeling of mental weariness and dissatisfaction produced by want of occupation, or by lack of interest in present

surroundings or employments' (*OED*). On books as a resource against *ennui*, see Maria Edgeworth, *Moral Tales for Young People*, 5 vols. (Effingham, Wilson, 1801): 'she felt insupportable ennui from the want of books and conversation suited to her taste' ('Angelina; or, L'amie inconnue', vol. 2, p. 14).

21 **nubile**: Marriageable; sexually mature.

22 **eyes are like the fish-pools of Heshbon**: Song of Solomon, ch. 7, v. 4. Folliott has referred to this passage before, in ch. 3, when describing Miss Crotchet; an earlier part of the same verse is applied to her in ch. 1 by the narrator: 'she was perhaps a little too much to the taste of Solomon, and had a nose which rather too prominently suggested the idea of the tower of Lebanon, which looked towards Damascus' (p. 11).

23 **delicate**: Crotchet and Folliott are toying with diametrically opposed senses of delicacy; Folliott uses 'delicate' to indicate something becoming, proper, or modest; Crotchet's 'delicate morsel' suggests, by contrast, something luxurious and voluptuous (*OED* 'delicate', 12.a. and b.; 2.a.).

24 **whitebait in July**: Whitebait, a small silvery-white fish, is caught in large numbers in the estuary of the Thames (as well as elsewhere). It was and is esteemed as a delicacy. Cf. TLP's 'A Whitebait Dinner, at Lovegrove's, at Blackwall. July, 1851', which includes the line 'And whitebait, daintiest of our fishy fare' (Halliford, 7.259). *CC*, like *GG*, is full of references to fish. Like Folliott, TLP loved fish in all its forms, as is evident from the holograph recipes for e.g. salmon, eel (broiled, stewed, and Athenian), bream, sole and perch (c. 1853–60) that survive in the Pforzheimer Collection in New York Public Library (TLP 40, 41).

25 **pious cheesemonger . . . justly aroused**: Perhaps refers to an incident in the life of Joseph Livesey (1794–1884), Baptist, prosperous cheesemonger, a radical champion of municipal reform and public health. Livesey founded the first National Temperance Movement in Preston in 1832.

26 **Pandemian Venus . . . imaginings of Plato**: A reference to the
Symposium, as explained in the following paragraph. In this
Platonic dialogue, each of the guests assembled at the fictional
gathering is called upon to discourse on the nature of Love.
The distinction between Pandemian ('Common') and Uranian
('Heavenly') Love is made in the speech of Pausanias (*Symposium*,
180c–5c). Common Love is merely physical and is felt for women
or boys; Heavenly Love, although still physical, can be directed
only at those who are themselves rational, i.e. adolescent males.
Hence the distinction between Crotchet's fully naked Venus,
representing Common Love, and the partially clothed Heavenly
Venus, embodying a species of Love that is not wholly dependent
on the physical.

27 **Plato . . . edition of him**: On TLP's admiration of Plato's
Symposium, see *Letters*, 1.114, and TLP to Shelley on learning that his friend was translating Plato's text: 'You have done
well in translating the Symposium and I hope you will succeed
in attracting attention to Plato for he certainly wants patronage in these days when philosophy sleeps and classical literature
seems destined to participate its repose' (*Letters*, 1.147). See also
TLP's 'An Essay on Fashionable Literature': 'The period seemed
to promise the revival of philosophy: but it has since fallen into
deeper sleep than ever & even classical literature seems sinking
into the same repose' (*NA*, Appendix B).

28 **a person . . . called "the reader"**: i.e. books published by the
university presses are read by no one other than the presses' own
proofreaders.

29 **(supposing . . . Plato,)**: No complete edition of Plato had yet
been published by either Oxford or Cambridge University Press.
George Burges (1785/6–1864) of Trinity College, Cambridge,
had in 1826 brought out a *variorum* edition of the complete
Plato (*Platonis et quæ vel Platonis esse feruntur vel Platonica solent
comitari scripta Græce omnia . . .*); the publisher, however, was
London-based. The complete edition of Plato owned by TLP

was the Bipontine, published in Zweibrücken in 1781 (*Sale Catalogue* 501).

30 **outward and visible signs**: Cf. Lady Clarinda's reference in ch. 3 to 'an outward and visible sign' (p. 31).

31 **cant, cant, cant**: 'A pet phrase, a trick of words; *esp.* a stock phrase that is much affected at the time, or is repeated as a matter of habit or form'; 'Phraseology taken up and used for fashion's sake, without being a genuine expression of sentiment; canting language'; '*esp.* affected or unreal use of religious or pietistic phraseology; language (or action) implying the pretended assumption of goodness or piety' (*OED* 'cant', 5.b., 6.a., 6.b.). Cf. Byron, who in 1821 identified cant as 'the grand "primum mobile" of England': 'Cant political – Cant poetical – Cant religious – Cant moral – but always *Cant*, multiplied through all the varieties of life' (*Complete Miscellaneous Prose*, ed. Andrew Nicholson (Oxford: Clarendon, 1991), p. 128). See TLP's review of Moore's *Letters and Journals of Lord Byron*: '"The staple commodity of the present age in England," says Lord Byron himself somewhere, "is cant: cant moral, cant religious, cant political; but always cant." How much of this staple commodity there may be in Mr. Moore's lamentations, we shall leave our readers to judge' (Halliford, 9.115). See also Hazlitt, 'On Cant and Hypocrisy', who also quotes Byron's comment approvingly (*London Weekly Review*, 6 Dec. 1828).

32 **societies . . . instituted for the suppression of truth and beauty**: King George III's Royal Proclamation '*For the Encouragement of* PIETY *and* VIRTUE, *and for preventing and punishing of* VICE, PROFANENESS *and* IMMORALITY' (1787) had exhorted the British public to reject sexually explicit material. It called for the suppression of 'all loose and licentious prints, books, and publications, dispersing poison to the minds of the young and unwary, and to punish the publishers and vendors thereof' (*Gentlemen's Magazine: and Historical Chronicle*, 57, Part 1 (1787), 534–5 (p. 534)). Groups which sprang up to

promote this aim included the Proclamation Society, which in 1802 became The Society for the Suppression of Vice. Its efforts to curtail licentious publications had little effect, however, because the Society had no power to destroy the material it condemned. The number of such 'societies' active when TLP was writing was high enough to suggest that his reference is probably unspecific.

33 **Lacedæmonian virgins . . . exemplary of wives and mothers**: The freedom enjoyed by the women of Sparta (Lacedaemon) was unique in Greece, and as girls they took part in athletic training along with the boys. Lycurgus was a legendary law-maker who was supposed to have written the Spartan laws and constitution. The Spartan exemplar was a recurrent theme in socio-political theorising.

34 **Very likely, sir . . . Lais was a Corinthian**: Crotchet argues that Athenian men would not have had to engage prostitutes if their own wives had had a less restrictive and dreary upbringing. Aspasia and Lais were two of the most famous courtesans of fifth-century Athens. Aspasia had dealings with many of the leading men of the day, and above all with Pericles (whom she married, although it was not a full marriage because she was a foreigner). Lais was indeed a Corinthian, but Folliott does not mention that Aspasia was from Miletus, presumably because this would weaken his argument that the reason Lais was not married in Athens was that she was a foreigner. Aspasia was supposed to have been much more politically involved and scheming than Lais, which is presumably what Folliott is referring to when he remarks that they were 'two very different persons'.

35 **sitting as models to Praxiteles**: Praxiteles was an Athenian sculptor active c. 370–320 BC. His most famous work was the Aphrodite of Cnidos, the first nude Aphrodite. It is thought that Phryne – the most celebrated courtesan of the fourth century – sat as the model for the sculptor.

36 **an Italian countess . . . fire in the room**: Napoleon's sister Pauline Bonaparte (1780–1825) was the model for Antonio Canova's 'Venus Victrix', a semi-nude life-size reclining neoclassical portrait sculpture commissioned by her second husband, Camillo Borghese, 6th Prince of Sulmona, and executed between 1805 and 1808. It is a matter of debate whether she posed naked. When asked how she could sit for the sculptor wearing so little, Pauline Bonaparte reputedly answered that there was a stove in the studio that kept her warm; this may be apocryphal, or no more than a provocative quip.

37 **my ancestor, Gilbert Folliott**: See TLP's footnote to ch. 1 (p. 12).

38 **Diderot . . . all the encyclopædias that have ever been printed**: Denis Diderot (1713–84), philosopher, critic, dramatist and novelist, best known for serving as co-founder, chief editor of and contributor (along with Jean le Rond d'Alembert) over a twenty-year period to the monumental, 35-volume *Encyclopédie, ou dictionnaire raisonné des sciences, des arts et des métiers* (1772).

39 ***Incubi***: Feigned evil spirits or demons (originating in personified representations of the nightmare), supposed to descend on people in their sleep, and especially to seek carnal intercourse with women. In the Middle Ages, their existence was legally recognized (see *OED* 'incubus').

40 **Elgin marbles**: The Parthenon Marbles, also known as the Elgin Marbles, a collection of classical Greek marble sculptures, inscriptions and architectural members that originally formed part of the Parthenon and other buildings on the Acropolis of Athens. Thomas Bruce, 7th Earl of Elgin, obtained permission from the Ottoman authorities to remove pieces from the Parthenon while serving as British ambassador to the Ottoman Empire from 1799 to 1803. From 1801 to 1812, Elgin's agents took about half of the remaining sculptures of the Parthenon, as well as architectural members and sculpture from the Propylaea and Erechtheum. The Marbles were transported by sea to

Britain, where the acquisition of these treasures was supported by some; others compared Elgin's actions to vandalism or looting. Following a public debate in Parliament and Elgin's subsequent exoneration, the marbles were purchased by the British government in 1816 and placed on display in the British Museum.

41 *argumentum ad hominem*: An argument made against an individual; shifting an argument from legitimate matters to the feelings or character of the opponent.

42 *impetus* . . . **his back was the base**: *impetus*: 'The force with which a body moves or maintains its velocity and overcomes resistance; energy of motion; impulse, impulsion' (*OED*). Cf. other geometrically precise accidents and falls in TLP, e.g. the account of Mr Cranium in ch. 8 of *HH*: 'His ascent being unluckily a little out of the perpendicular, he descended with a proportionate curve from the apex of his projection.'

CHAPTER 8

1 **SCIENCE AND CHARITY**: The title of this chapter sums up Brougham's twin preoccupations: dissemination of knowledge to the masses, and the investigation of how charitable funds were administered. In 1816, Brougham had formed a committee 'to inquire into the education of the lower orders in the metropolis' (*ODNB*). The committee looked at every charity school in London, and revealed the desperate need for better education as well as the misuse of charitable funds in those schools. In 1818, its remit was extended to all of England and Wales. In the same year, Brougham introduced a bill to appoint a commission which would investigate all charities in England and Wales. This led to the appointment of the first paid Charity Commissioners, to ensure that charitable bequests were correctly and efficiently applied.

2 **Chi sta . . . FORTEGUERRI**: [Niccolò Forteguerri or Fortiguerra] (1674–1735), *Il Ricciardetto* (Paris [Venice]: n. p. 1738), canto

14, stanza 1, lines 1–4: 'Whoever in this world is content for a while and whose peace is neither taken away from him nor spoilt can say that Jove is watching over him directly.' The poem is burlesque and chivalric, complementing the Butlerian and Rabelaisian epigraphs and allusions in *CC*.

3 **He paused . . . Roman camp**: TLP's phrasing and the scenario depicted here – a night expedition, pausing by a camp, prior to a murderous assault by two enemies – are faintly, comically reminiscent of an epic night sortie, see e.g. *Iliad*, book 10 (the so-called 'Doloneia'), in which Odysseus and Diomedes set out on an expedition at night, from the Greek camp, and capture and kill an enemy scout, Dolon, on the Trojan plain. This Homeric echo contributes to the mock-epic flavour of the chapter. Cf. also battle scenes in *Tom Jones*, esp. book 4, ch. 8, entitled '*A Battle sung by the Muse in the* Homerican *Stile, and which none but the classical Reader can taste*' (*The History of Tom Jones, A Foundling*, ed. Martin C. Battestin and Fredson Bowers, 2 vols. (Oxford: Clarendon Press, 1974), vol. 1, pp. 177–84 (p. 177)). See also *CC*, ch. 16 (pp. 126–7).

4 **a passage of Sophocles**: As the Penguin edition of *CC* suggests, TLP probably had in mind *Oedipus at Colonus*, lines 668–80, 'with its reference to leafy valleys thronged with nightingales' (p. 277).

5 **the state called *reverie***: 'A moment or period of being lost, esp. pleasantly, in one's thoughts; a daydream' (*OED* 'reverie'). The word is also associated with revelry, music and deluded ideas or impractical theories, all of which feature in *CC*. Cf. Charles Lamb, 'Dream Children: A Reverie' (1822). Coleridge famously ascribed the origins of his fragmentary poem *Kubla Khan* (first published 1816) to 'a sort of Reverie brought on by two grains of Opium, taken to check a dysentery' (note on the Crewe MS copy of the poem). Lady Clarinda remarks in ch. 5: 'Mr. Skionar, though he is a great dreamer, always dreams with his eyes open, or with one eye at any rate, which is an eye to his gain' (p. 44).

6 ***camera obscura***: 'An instrument comprising a darkened room or box with a convex lens or a pinhole in one side, used for projecting an image of an external object on to a surface inside the instrument so that it can be viewed, drawn, or (in later use) reproduced on a light-sensitive surface. Also *fig.* (now rare)' (*OED*). The term was still in common use in 1830, although Thomas Wedgwood had begun experimenting in the 1790s with the chemical action of light for making pictures, a process that would lead to the modern art of photography.

7 **good genius**: Appropriately for Folliott, the idea of a 'good genius' belongs to pagan and Christian tradition. With reference to classical pagan belief, a 'genius' is the tutelary god or attendant spirit allotted to every person at his birth, to govern his fortunes and determine his character, and to conduct him out of the world. By a person's good and evil genius is also meant the two mutually opposed spirits (in Christian belief, *angels*) by whom every person is attended throughout life.

8 **ponderous**: 'Having great weight; heavy, weighty, massive; clumsy, unwieldy, or slow-moving due to weight or size', but TLP may also be punning on another sense of the word: 'Tending to gravitate towards another body' (*OED*).

9 **sconces**: There is another reference to sconces in ch. 9 (p. 84).

10 **dyslogistic term**: 'Expressing or connoting disapprobation or dispraise; having a bad connotation; opprobrious. (The opposite of *eulogistic*.)' (*OED*). Apparently coined by Jeremy Bentham in *The Elements of the Art of Packing, as applied to special juries, particularly in cases of libel law* (Effingham Wilson 1821), p. 15.

11 **dispersion**: 'The action of dispersing or scattering abroad; the condition or state of being dispersed; scattering, distribution, circulation' (*OED*).

12 **I will contund you as Thestylis did strong-smelling herbs**: A reference to Virgil, Eclogue 2, lines 10–11: 'Thestylis et rapido fessis messoribus aestu / alia serpyllumque herbas

contundit olentis' ('And Thestylis pounds for the reapers tired by the fierce heat / Garlic and thyme, fragrant herbs'). TLP uses the rare verb 'contund' (obsolete in this sense by his own day, according to the *OED*) as a calque of Virgil's *contundit*. Literally, to 'contund' is to pound or beat (in a mortar); it is a pharmaceutical term. It also means 'To bruise (the body), affect with contusions; to pound or thrash (adversaries). *humorous* or *affected*' (*OED*).

13 **miscreant caitiff**: Pleonasm; both words often feature in Shakespeare, although they do not occur together in any of his plays.

14 **a subject for science**: With the growth of medical schools, many wealthy doctors paid for gangs of so-called 'resurrectionists' to steal bodies from graves. In the 1820s, corpses sold for between £10 and £20. Here, the allusion is to the recent case of William Burke and William Hare, Irish immigrants to Edinburgh who committed fifteen murders in 1828. They sold the corpses of their victims to Dr Robert Knox as dissection material for his popular anatomy lectures. The police gave Hare immunity from prosecution in exchange for his confession. Burke was found guilty on Christmas Day 1828, hanged and then publicly dissected (40,000 people queued to see the dismembered corpse). The story was told repeatedly in broadsheets and ballads; William Roughead's collection of documents, *Burke and Hare* (1921) lists twenty-two broadsides, twenty-one ballads and twenty pamphlets and books on the crime in the immediate aftermath of the trial. See ch. 1 (p. 8) and n. 30 (p. 200) on 'march of intellect', a phrase associated by Scott with these murders. Cf. TLP on 'CORPSE-DIGGERS' and '*Resurrection-men*' in *Letters*, 1.88.

15 **a schoolmaster abroad**: An allusion to Brougham's celebrated phrase 'The schoolmaster is abroad', referring to the education of the masses, first used in a speech in Jan. 1828 (*The Times*, 30 Jan. 1828). Brougham's efforts to obtain state-supported education, seen in a bill of 1820 to establish parochial schools and again in a bill in 1837, foundered on sectarian religious divisions.

16 **for as the great Hermann...** *paratior*: TLP quotes G. Hermann, *Homeri Hymni et Epigrammata* (Leipzig: Weidmann, 1806; *Sale Catalogue* 579), p. iii, altering Hermann's Latin in order to fit the grammar of his own sentence. TLP admired Gottfried Hermann, a towering German classicist; writing to Thomas L'Estrange, TLP says: 'I feel especially indebted to Heyne and Hermann' (23 June 1862, *Letters*, 2.446). For biographical details of Heyne and Hermann, see *Letters*, 2.447, nn. 3–4). 'To demulce' is 'To soothe or mollify (a person); to soften or make gentle. Formerly said also of soothing medicines' (*OED*; the verb is now obsolete).

17 *Frère Jean des Entommeures*: Rabelais, *La Vie trés horrificque du grand Gargantua, pere de Pantagruel*, ch. 27 (pp. 77–81). Frère Jean single-handedly routs an army that is pillaging his monastery's vineyard; in English, his name is usually given as Friar John of the Funnels.

18 **Charity Commissioners**: A permanent set of Charity Commissioners was not appointed until 1859.

19 *nem. con.*: *nemine contradicente*, 'with no opposition'.

20 **abrogated by desuetude**: i.e. annulled or repealed, owing to disuse.

21 **open vestry**: Vestry: 'In English parishes: An assembly or meeting of the parishioners... held originally in the vestry of the parish church, for the purpose of deliberating or legislating upon the affairs of the parish or upon certain temporal matters connected with the church' (*OED* 'vestry').

22 **exhale his budget of grievances**: Budget: 'bag'; 'to open one's budget' means 'to speak one's mind' (*OED* 'budget'); 'exhale' gives the phrase an added comic weariness.

CHAPTER 9

1 οἱ μὲν ἔπειτ'... **watery ways.** HOMER: *Iliad*, book 1, line 312; the translation is accurate. The original context in Homer does not contribute to the meaning in *CC*; rather, TLP has used

this line of the *Iliad* as a convenient tag to introduce 'The Voyage'.

2 **pinnaces**: Small sailing vessels.

3 **oolite**: 'Any limestone composed of small rounded granules resembling the roe of a fish, each consisting of calcium carbonate surrounding a grain of sand as a nucleus' (*OED*).

4 **perlustrations**: 'Perlustration' is 'The action or an act of inspecting, surveying, or viewing a place thoroughly; a comprehensive survey or description' (*OED*).

5 **a wager ... and won it**: 'Tuesday, August 6th., 1822. I was at the Library the whole day, and not a single member of the University came into the room, excepting Mr. Eden, the assistant. Oxford Race day' (*Dr Bliss's Memorandum*, in Macray's *Annals of the Bodleian Library*, cited in Garnett, *Novels*, 2.708 n).

6 **once a captain, always a captain**: Proverbial. Cf. W. Hamilton Reid, *Memoirs of the Public Life of John Horne Tooke, Esq.* (Sherwood, Neely and Jones, 1812): 'Is it possible for any one who has once entered into holy orders, again to become one of the laity? Or is it once a captain, and always a captain' (p. 153). See also 'An Essay on Fashionable Literature': 'If philosophy be not dead she is at least sleeping in the country of Bacon & Locke. The seats of learning (as the universities are still called according to the proverb once a captain always a captain) are armed cap-a-pie against her' (*NA*, Appendix B).

7 *Quorsum ... Menandro*: Horace, *Satires*, book 2, satire 3, line 11. In the poem, Damasippus complains about Horace's lack of productivity, asking him to what end he piled up such a stack of books if they were ultimately to be of no use to him. Scholars disagree about whether 'Plato' here is the fourth-century comic poet who preceded Menander, or the more famous philosopher.

8 **What is done here ... anything worth knowing**: German scholars led the world in classical studies during this period; they were frequently engaged by Oxford University Press to produce editions of classical authors. As to the superior production quality

of Oxford books as their one redeeming feature, TLP may have in mind a hostile piece in the *Edinburgh Review*, 14 (1809), pp. 429–41. It is a review of a lavish edition of Strabo published by Oxford and edited by Oxford men. The reviewer, Richard Payne Knight, is not impressed with this 'ponderous monument of operose ignorance and vain expense' (p. 441). He leads with an attack on Oxford University in general, complaining of the inconsequentiality of the output of the institution (cf. esp. Folliott's reference to the barren fig-tree, *CC*, ch. 9 (p. 83)). TLP had probably read the review, for a letter to Edward Thomas Hookham (18 Aug. 1810) evinces a keen interest in this scholar (see also *HH*, chs. 3 and 4): 'Payne Knight is fond of paper war, and trims up the British Critic and the Edinburgh Review most gloriously' (*Letters*, 1.58). During this period Oxford University Press was engaging the services of foreign (esp. German) editors for their classical texts, but it is not quite accurate to say that the University was 'reprinting' German editions: they were originals. Similarly, TLP most likely failed to appreciate the difference between University Press books, those printed at the Press for others, and those published by local firms other than the Press.

9   **the days of Friar Bacon . . . its cognominal college**: Roger Bacon [Bakun] (c. 1214–92?), scholar, philosopher and Franciscan friar, was reputed to have made a brazen head which, except for the nose, collapsed into fragments after uttering the words 'Time is', 'Time was', and 'Time's past'. Bacon, like Folliott, lamented the corruption of knowledge. One possible remedy was, for Bacon, that of experimental science, which may partly explain why Folliott is said, in a word of TLP's invention, to open his argument 'peirastically' (p. 67), i.e. 'by experiment, tentatively', in ch. 7 (and see n. 18 (p. 251)). Both the Latin terms *experientia* and *experimentum*, like the early English 'experience' and 'experiment', covered a wide range of meanings, from active testing (perhaps in a legalistic sense), through experiences of a quasi-mystical kind,

to the knowledge of life recognizable in such phrases as 'long experience'. The most likely of several conflicting explanations of how Brasenose College, Oxford got its name suggests that it is owing to a brass doorknocker, shaped like a nose. Cf. TLP's poem 'Oh Nose of Wax! True Symbol of the Mind' (wr. c. 1826), which ends: 'Thy name to those scholastic bowers shall pass, / And rival Oxford's ancient nose of brass' (Halliford, 7.242).

10 **Babylon of buried literature**: The city of Babylon on the River Euphrates in southern Iraq first came to prominence as the royal city of King Hammurabi (about 1790–50 BC). From around 1500 BC a dynasty of Kassite kings took control in Babylon and unified southern Iraq into the kingdom of Babylonia. The Babylonian cities were centres of great scribal learning and produced writings on divination, astrology, medicine and mathematics.

11 πίδακος . . . λιβάς: Callimachus, *Hymn to Apollo*, 112; the preceding phrase is a translation of the Greek. The choice of this passage of Callimachus is appropriate. It comes from a speech in which Apollo, god of poetry, sets out his poetic manifesto. The god affirms his preference for concise, refined poetry as opposed to verse of overblown proportions which – for all its size – may well be devoid of any real merit. He expresses the difference through a comparison of different types of watercourse: the Euphrates, which carries along much pollution and detritus, is contrasted with 'the trickling stream that springs from a holy fountain, pure and undefiled, the very crown of waters' (tr. A. W. Mair); cf. F. J. Williams, *Callimachus: Hymn to Apollo* (Oxford: Clarendon, 1978), p. 85. In keeping with the spirit of Callimachus' original, Folliott here applies the metaphor of pure water to learning.

12 **But . . . aspirant**: On TLP's antipathy to the universities, see his review of Moore's *Letters and Journals of Lord Byron*: 'If the Universities can make nothing of genius, their discipline, if it were good for anything, might make something of mediocrity or of dulness: but their discipline is mere pretence, and is limited to

the non-essentials of education: they settle down mediocrity into a quiet hatred of literature, and confirm a questionable dunce into a hopeless, incurable, and self-satisfied blockhead' (Halliford, 9.100–1). See also TLP on his own education (letter to Thomas L'Estrange, 23 June 1862): 'I did not go to any University or public school. I was six years and a half at a private school on Englefield Green. I left it before I was thirteen. The master was not much of a scholar; but he had the art of inspiring his pupils with a love of learning, and he had excellent classical and French assistants. I passed many of my best years with my mother, taking more pleasure in reading than in society. I was early impressed with the words of Harris: "To be competently skilled in ancient learning is by no means a work of such insuperable pains. The very progress itself is attended with delight, and resembles a journey through some pleasant country, where, every mile we advance, new charms arise. It is certainly as easy to be a scholar as a gamester, or many other characters equally illiberal and low. The same application, the same quantity of habit, will fit us for one as completely as for the other." Thus encouraged, I took to reading the best books, illustrated by the best critics . . . Such was my education' (*Letters*, 2.446).

13 **I run over . . . a glorious catalogue**: TLP admired German clas-sical scholarship. In a letter to Sir John Cam Hobhouse (15 Oct. 1844), he wrote: 'You do me credit to which I have no title, in setting me down as a German scholar' (*Letters*, 2.284).

14 **barren fig**: For the parable of the barren fig, see Matthew, ch. 12, v. 33 and Luke, ch. 13, vv. 6–9.

15 *totus teres atque rotundus*: See TLP's letter to Sir John Cam Hobhouse (9 Oct. 1846), enclosing 'Ancient Examples of Mod-ern Political Virtue', including the claim that 'The modern' has undergone 'a sort of intellectual planing and polishing; which produces him in a new aspect; neat and trim; smooth and round: *totus teres atque rotundus, Externi quem nil valeat per leve morari*' (*Letters*, 2.292 and n. 7).

16 **the grave of Rosamond**: 'Fair Rosamund' (born before 1140?, died 1175/6), mistress of Henry II. By the fourteenth century she had become a figure of romance and legend, much of it associated with her death. In the earliest account, the mid-fourteenth-century *Croniques de London*, Queen Eleanor causes Rosamund to be bled to death in a hot bath at Woodstock, after which the king has her buried at Godstow. In Higden's *Polychronicon*, Eleanor tracks Rosamund down by following her silken embroidery through the maze. What happened next Higden did not know, only that Rosamund's death ensued. Later sources represent the queen as confronting her beautiful rival and offering her the choice of death by poison or the dagger. Rosamund chose the poisoned bowl, and the grieving king had her body interred at Godstow nunnery. See TLP's *The Genius of the Thames*, part 2, for the legends that had gathered about her name and for his reference to the hazel, 'the fruit of which is always apparently perfect, but is invariably found to be hollow' (Halliford, 6.140–1, 163).

17 **History is but a tiresome thing in itself**: Cf. Catherine Morland's discussion of history as a wearisome duty, and of invention and imagination with the Tilneys, in *Northanger Abbey*, vol. 1, ch. 14.

18 **two enchanters: he of the north**: Sir Walter Scott, often referred to as 'The Enchanter of the North' during his lifetime; in TLP's 'A Border Ballad', he is an 'enchanter' (Halliford, 7.125). In relation to Clarinda's preceding comment – 'The great enchanter has made me learn many things which I should never have dreamed of studying, if they had not come to me in the form of amusement' – see TLP's 'An Essay on Fashionable Literature', where he writes that Scott is 'the most popular writer of his time perhaps the most universally successful in his own day of any writer that ever lived. He has the rare talent of pleasing all ranks and classes of men from the peer to the peasant and all orders and degrees of mind . . . On the arrival of Rob Roy, as formerly on that of Marmion, the scholar lays aside his Plato the statesman suspends

his calculations the young lady deserts her harp the critic smiles as he trims his lamp the lounger thanks god for his good fortune & the weary artisan resigns his sleep for the refreshment of the magic page' (*NA*, Appendix B).

19 **the great enchanter of Covent Garden**: Charles Farley (1771–1859), actor and theatre producer. His most notable pantomime was *Harlequin and Mother Goose* (1806), whose special effects included a chair which rose into the flies when it was sat on, a duck which flew out of a pie, a letter box which changed into a lion's mouth and a sideboard which turned itself into a beehive. TLP may have paired these two particular characters as 'great enchanters' because Farley had adapted Scott's *Old Mortality* as *The Battle of Bothwell Brigg* (1820) – a work outside his usual range, but giving scope to technical wizardry. On TLP's interest in pantomime, see also ch. 1 (p. 12) and n. 59 (pp. 206–7).

20 **literature of pantomime . . . pantomime of literature**: See no. 69 of Friedrich Schlegel's *Athenäums-Fragmente* (1798): 'Die Pantomimen der Alten haben wir nicht mehr. Dagegen ist aber die ganze Poesie jetzt pantomimisch' ('We no longer have the pantomimes of the ancients. On the other hand, all modern poetry resembles pantomime') in *Kritische Friedrich-Schlegel-Ausgabe*, gen. ed. Ernst Behler (Paderborn: Ferdinand Schöningh, 1958–), vol. 2: *Charakteristiken und Kritiken I (1796–1801)*, ed. Hans Eichner (1967), p. 175. During the Regency, the pantomime became hugely popular and its relations with literature were much discussed. See canto 1, stanza 1 of Byron's *Don Juan*: 'I WANT a hero: an uncommon want, / When every year and month sends forth a new one, / Till, after cloying the gazettes with cant, / The age discovers he is not the true one; / Of such as these I should not care to vaunt, / I'll therefore take our ancient friend Don Juan, / We all have seen him in the pantomime / Sent to the devil, somewhat ere his time' (*Works*, vol. 5).

21 **castrametation**: 'The art or science of laying out a camp' (*OED*).

22 **any sentence worth remembering**: Cf. Folliott's argument at
the end of this chapter that Scott's works 'contain nothing worth
quoting' (p. 88).

23 *nuspiam, nequaquam, nullibi, nullimodis*: Never, by no means,
nowhere, in no way. All except *nequaquam* are late, rare
forms.

24 **My quarrel ... twelfth century**: The debate in chs. 9 and 10
regarding the benefits of medieval life quickly moves beyond
the issue of Scott's historical accuracy, although it closely follows the sides taken in reviews of his medieval novels during
the 1820s (see P. D. Garside, 'Scott, the Romantic Past and the
Nineteenth Century', *Review of English Studies*, New Series, 23
(1972), 147–61). Dismissing the Middle Ages as 'a period of brutality, ignorance, fanaticism, and tyranny', Mac Quedy broadly
represents the anti-feudal views of the late eighteenth-century
Scottish Enlightenment school of Hume and Robertson. Chainmail, defending Richard I as 'the mirror of chivalry, the pattern of
honor, the fountain of generosity', takes the opposing position of
William Cobbett, Robert Southey and such nineteenth-century
antiquarians as George Chalmers and Sharon Turner. TLP thus
presents, in broad terms, two different schools of historiography
and philosophy. See James Mulvihill, 'Thomas Love Peacock's
Crotchet Castle: Reconciling the Spirits of the Age', *Nineteenth-
Century Fiction*, vol. 38 (1983), 253–70 (esp. pp. 262–9), and
further below.
[Footnote:] **Eloquentiæ magister ... PETRONIUS ARBITER**:
Petronius, *Satyricon*, 3. 'A master of oratory is like a fisherman;
he must put the particular bait on his hook which he knows the
little fish will make for, or he may sit waiting on his rock with
no hope of a catch.' In other words, the needs of one's potential
clients are to be taken into account. TLP owned several editions
of Petronius by the time he wrote *CC* (*Sale Catalogue* 490–2, 659–
60). The orthography of this quotation precisely matches that of

A. A. Renouard's edition. The *Sale Catalogue* shows that TLP's copy of Renouard was particularly fine, 'printed on rose coloured paper (*very few copies so printed*)' and bound in half morocco. Oddly, however (given that TLP seems to have quoted the text from it in this passage of *CC*), its pages were uncut.

25 **By depicting them ... much better state of society**: TLP may have in mind Scott's *The Fair Maid of Perth*, which dwelt on the harshness and misery of medieval life.

26 **conterminal**: Conterminous, having a common boundary. Not, as stated by Dodson in *Crotchet Castle*, coined by TLP (see *OED* for an earlier instance), but rare.

27 **all contemporary historians and poets**: Mac Quedy echoes several utilitarian commentators on how the feudal and chivalric emphasis of the new medievalism acted as a mask for tyranny. See, for example, John Stuart Mill's speech on the 'Utility of Knowledge' (1823): 'this appeal from the age of civilization to the age of barbarism is made ... by those alone who now, as then, would wish to see the great mass of mankind subject to the despotic sway of nobles, priests, and kings', in *Journals and Debating Speeches Part I*, ed. John M. Robson (Toronto: University of Toronto Press, 1988), p. 261. See also Mill's essay in the *Westminster Review*, vol. 11 (July 1826), pp. 62–103: 'the compound of noble qualities, called the *spirit of chivalry* (a rare combination in all ages) was almost unknown in the age of chivalry ... that age so called was equally distinguished by moral depravity and by physical wretchedness' (p. 66).

28 *fiscality*: 'Exclusive regard to fiscal considerations. Also, fiscal policy; *pl.* fiscal matters' (*OED*); apparently coined by Jeremy Bentham in *The Rationale of Reward* (1825). On gunpowder and steam, see ch. 5 (pp. 43–6).

29 **people of the twelfth century**: Mr Chainmail's invocation of the Middle Ages as a corrective to contemporary social and political developments is a bass note of Romantic medievalism. TLP had

himself made use of this comparative method; see his comment to Shelley (29 Nov. 1818): 'I am writing a comic romance of the 12th century which I shall make the vehicle of much oblique satire on all the oppressions that are done under the sun' (*Letters*, 1.156). Edmund Burke had noted in *Reflections on the Revolution in France* (1790) that 'the age of chivalry is gone. – That of sophisters, oeconomists, and calculators, has succeeded' (*The French Revolution, 1790–1794*, ed. L. G. Mitchell (Oxford: Clarendon Press, 1989), p. 127; vol. 8 of *The Writings and Speeches of Edmund Burke*, gen. ed. Paul Langford, 9 vols. (Oxford: Clarendon Press, 1981–)), and the 1820s saw the publication of several works of eulogistic medievalism. See John Lindgard's *History of England* (1819–30), relied on by William Cobbett in his polemical defence of the Middle Ages in opposition to modern society, *A History of the Protestant Reformation in England and Ireland* (1824–6), and Kenelm Digby's *The Broadstone of Honour, or the True Sense and Practice of Chivalry* (1822–7).

30 **As to your king . . . your own view**: Richard I appeared in Scott's *Ivanhoe* (1819) and *The Talisman* (1825).

31 **de finibus**: sc. *bonorum et malorum*, 'on the ends of good and evil'. *De finibus bonorum et malorum* is the title of an extensive philosophical treatise by Cicero whose subject is the greatest good for man.

32 **me judice**: In my judgement or opinion.

33 **κατ᾽ ἐξοχήν**: *Par excellence*.

CHAPTER 10

1 **Continuant . . . RABELAIS**: The opening sentence of Rabelais, *Le Cinquiesme et dernier livre des faicts et dicts heroïques du bon Pantagruel*, ch. 1. Rabelais, *Œuvres complètes*, p. 729. 'PURSUING our Voyage, we sail'd three Days, without discovering any Thing' (Ozell, vol. 5, p. 1). In Rabelais' continuation of the same sentence, however, the crew sight land. The epigraph may imply that this chapter acts both as an interlude and as a prelude.

2 **Lechlade church**: A fifteenth-century church in Lechlade, or Lechlade-upon-Thames, in south-east Gloucestershire. TLP visited the church with Shelley, Mary Godwin and Charles Clairmont in 1815 (see Shelley's 'A Summer-Evening Church-Yard'). See also the reference to Lechlade in TLP's *The Genius of the Thames*, part 2 (Halliford, 6.139).

3 **picturesqueness**: The picturesque, touched upon throughout *CC*, was an evolving aesthetic category from the late eighteenth century onwards, stressing variety in landscape and its 'capability of being formed into pictures' (*Northanger Abbey*, vol. 1, ch. 14, p. 112). See esp. William Gilpin's *Three Essays: On Picturesque Beauty, On Picturesque Travel and On Sketching Landscape* (1792), which emphasized the picturesque nature of irregularity, ruggedness, intricacy and chiaroscuro – elements which inform the descriptions in this chapter. TLP was a close follower of the debate between Uvedale Price and Richard Payne Knight about the precise qualities of the picturesque; see *Letters*, 1.27 and n. 22 and *HH*, esp. chs. 3 and 4. See also the first sentence of *NA*, where the Abbey is described as being in 'a highly picturesque state of semi-dilapidation'; cf. Radcliffe, *The Italian* (1797), vol. 1, ch. 3 (p. 37). TLP refers to the 'tourist' in ch. 12 (p. 104); he also uses the phrase 'picturesque tourist' several times in his letters (see e.g. *Letters*, 1.34, 43, 96) and in his musical farce 'The Three Doctors' (1813) (*HH*, Appendix). 'The Four Ages of Poetry' touches on 'the principles of picturesque beauty' in painting and poetry (*NA*, Appendix C).

4 **conventional dress . . . steam-machinery**: Chainmail's language echoes Thomas Carlyle's essay, 'Signs of the Times', published in the *Edinburgh Review*, 49 (1829), 439–59. Carlyle denounced 'The Age of Machinery' in which people are 'uniform in dress and movement' and focus on 'money and money's worth': 'We war with rude nature', he noted, 'Men have crossed oceans by steam . . . There is no end to our machinery'. See also ch. 7 of Coleridge's *On the Constitution of the Church and State* (1830),

where he remarks on 'the population mechanized into engines for the manufactory of new rich men' and on a 'Mechanic Philosophy' (Coleridge, *Works*, vol. 10, pp. 63, 64).

5 **no nature . . . no real existence**: The language is similar to that of TLP on 'modern poetry', with its 'exaggerated feeling' and 'factitious sentiment'; he asserted that the 'Lake Poets' had 'contrived, though they had retreated from the world for the express purpose of seeing nature as she was, to see her only as she was not' ('The Four Ages of Poetry', *NA*, Appendix C). See also TLP's criticisms of Moore's poetry in his review of *Letters and Journals of Lord Byron*, where he asserts that Moore's figures appear 'unreal', 'made up of disparates and non-existences', leading to a 'figurative language more than ever chaotic and caleidoscopical' (Halliford, 9.136–7).

6 **cowslip . . . beech**: See TLP's criticism of 'modern English song, in which everything is illustrated by a chaos of images which never met in the organized world', in his review of Edgcumbe's *Musical Reminiscences* (Halliford, 9.230). See also TLP's review of Moore's *The Epicurean* (1827), in Halliford, 9.32–3, for similar concerns.

7 **bumpers . . . fined**: A custom similar to 'sconcing': 'He who commits any of a certain number of *faux pas* may be "sconced" by the senior undergraduate at his table. Either he must supply beverages for the whole table or he must "floor," i.e., drink with one breath, a sconce holding three or four pints of liquid' (*Handbook to the University of Oxford* (Oxford: Oxford University Press, 1946), p. 107). A 'bumper' is 'a cup or glass of wine, etc., filled to the brim' (*OED*). Cf. the portrayal of Oxford in ch. 9 (pp. 82–4).

8 **discussing every thing and settling nothing**: Possibly echoing the endless disputes of the fallen angels in *Paradise Lost* (1667), book 2, lines 555–61 (*Paradise Lost*, ed. Alastair Fowler, rev. 2nd edn, Longman Annotated English Poets (Harlow: Pearson/ Longman, 2007)).

9 **digladiations**: 'Fighting or fencing with swords . . . *fig*. Strife or bickering of words; wrangling, contention, disputation' (*OED*).

10 *haute sagesse Pantagrueline*: Lofty Pantagruelian wisdom.

11 *échantillon*: Specimen.

12 **the name of a science . . . an imperfect inquiry**: Folliott's language recalls Macaulay's review of Mill's *Essays on Government* in the *Edinburgh Review*, vol. 49 (Mar. 1829): 'We believe that it is utterly impossible to deduce the science of government from the principles of human nature' (p. 185).

13 **You . . . community**: Folliott's sense of how political economists define 'the wealth of a nation' is targeting a central emphasis of Smith's *Wealth of Nations*, namely: the equation between increasing population and production and national greatness. (For TLP's reading of Smith, see *Letters*, 1.139.) Folliott is also questioning Ricardo's adoption of Smith's labour theory of value, which claims that the price or value of any product is mainly defined by the amount of labour that goes into its production. See Ricardo's *On the Principles of Political Economy* (John Murray, 1817), and the additional chapter 'On value' in the 3rd edn (1821).

14 **The moment . . . tumbles to pieces**: Folliott is thinking of developments in political economy in the wake of Ricardo's work: 'The "new school" of Ricardo, as it came to be known about 1820, was subjected to criticism for a catalogue of perceived errors, including: over-abstraction and the generation of "noxious" theoretical paradoxes, the use of an absolute concept of value related exclusively to the expenditure of labour, [and] use of a labour theory of value more generally' ('Ricardo, David', *ODNB*). McCulloch was the chief popularizer and champion of Ricardian economics; *politicæ œconomiæ inscientia*: ignorance of political economy.

15 **something much better**: Both the Benthamites and the Owenites envisioned an ideal society run on economic principles; for the Benthamites, though, 'something much better' meant private

ownership and a *laissez-faire* governmental policy, whereas for the Owenite Toogood the emphasis was on communal owner-ship and active governmental involvement.

16 **the romantic against the classical in poetry**: Broadly speak-ing, in this context, the battle of exuberance, passion and excess against reason, tradition and common sense. See *OED* 'classical', 7: 'Characterized by adherence to established stylistic forms, and by harmony, balance, and restraint, believed to be exemplified in the classics of Greek and Roman antiquity. Freq. opposed to *romantic.*'

17 **intuition ... induction in philosophy**: Skionar is arguing along Coleridgean lines. See a note in ch. 12 of *Biographia Literaria*: 'I take this occasion to observe, that here and elsewhere Kant uses the terms intuition, and the verb active (Intueri, *germanice* Anschauen) for which we have unfortunately no correspondent word, exclusively for that which can be represented in space and time ... But as I see no adequate reason for this exclusive sense of the term, I have reverted to its wider signification author-ized by our elder theologians and metaphysicians, according to whom the term comprehends all truths known to us with-out a medium' (Coleridge, *Works*, vol. 7, 1.289). In contrast, Mac Quedy's emphasis on inductive reasoning is a defence of an empirical procedure. See *OED* 'induction', 6: 'The bring-ing forward, adducing, or enumerating of a number of separate facts, particulars, etc., esp. for the purpose of proving a general statement.'

18 **the steam-navigation of rivers ... Euphrates**: In 1829, TLP drew up a *Memorandum Respecting the Application of Steam Nav-igation to the Internal and External Communications of India* (pub. 1837) for the East India Company (the Company was searching for a quicker way of travelling to and from India). Captain F. R. Chesney noted: 'My visits to the India House ... led to an intro-duction to Mr. Peacock, one of the leading people in the Exam-iner's Office. I found that he was deeply versed in the ancient

history of the Euphrates, and that he had not only been the first
to bring this line of communication with India forward, but that
he had collected in a thick book every private notice he could
find of that river, whether contained in Gibbon, Balbi, or any
other work' (Louisa Chesney and Jane O'Donnell, *The Life of the
Late General F. R. Chesney, By his Wife and Daughter*, ed. Stanley
Lane-Poole, 2nd edn (London and Sydney: Eden, Remington
and Co, 1893), p. 261); see Introduction, pp. lix, xcv–xcvii. TLP
became a champion of steam navigation to India, although he
thought it would chiefly benefit the mails, not trade. However,
he became sceptical about the value of Britain's imperial designs,
and told a parliamentary Select Committee: 'I am not sure that
it would be any benefit to the people of India to send Europeans amongst them' (*Report from the Select Committee on Steam
Communication with India: together with the Minutes of Evidence,
Appendix and Index* (House of Commons, 1837), p. 55).

19 **the Missouri . . . the Hoangho**: The pairs of rivers are located,
respectively, in North America, in South America, Africa, the
Middle East and (the final four rivers) in Asia.

20 **shapeless mounds of Babylon . . . gigantic temples of Thebes**:
The ruins of ancient Babylon consisted of a number of very
large mounds. Captain Richard Wilbraham wrote of 'The
shapeless mounds of Babylon' as resembling 'the skeleton' (*Travels in the Trans-Caucasian Provinces of Russia* (John Murray,
1839), p. 291). Thebes: capital of the ancient Egyptian empire,
named by the Greeks after their native Thebes; it flourished in
the fifteenth century BC and was renowned for its complex of
huge temples.

21 **the union of all the beautiful arts**: For TLP's appreciation and
reviews of operatic works, see Halliford, 9.402–45.

22 *Ingenuas didicisse*: Ovid, *Epistulae Ex Ponto*, 2.9.47–8: 'ingenuas didicisse fideliter artes / emollit mores nec sinit esse feros'
('Faithful study of liberal arts / Softens character and does not
allow it to be wild').

23 **the practice of the Athenians . . . the modern world**: TLP's
review of Edgcumbe's *Musical Reminiscences* also moves from
discussion of opera to praise of 'the Athenians' and 'the progress
of freedom and intelligence' (Halliford, 9.226–7). TLP associated modern opera with Greek drama elsewhere, too; see his
comment on Bellini's *La sonnambula* in 1831: 'It came upon us as
a shadow of the Athenian stage' (Halliford, 9.437). A very brief
note in TLP's hand on the same work survives in the Pforzheimer
Collection (TLP 122: (j) [no date]). Shelley expresses a similar
opinion to Folliott's on 'combination' in *A Defence of Poetry*,
where he laments that 'Tragedy becomes a cold imitation of the
form of the great masterpieces of antiquity, divested of all harmonious accompaniment of the kindred arts', and that 'the art itself
never was understood or practised according to the true philosophy of it, as at Athens. For the Athenians employed language,
action, music, painting, the dance, and religious institution to
produce a common effect in the representation of the highest
idealisms of passion and of power' (*Shelley's Poetry and Prose:
Authoritative Texts, Criticism*, ed. Donald H. Reiman and Neil
Fraistat, Norton Critical Edition, 2nd edn (New York: Norton,
2002), pp. 520, 518).

24 **the greatest pleasure . . . getting out of it**: Cf. Samuel Johnson's
verdict on Pope's grotto: 'A grotto is not often the wish or pleasure of an Englishman, who has more frequent need to solicit
than exclude the sun' (*The Lives of the Poets*, ed. Roger Lonsdale,
4 vols. (Oxford: Clarendon Press, 2006), vol. 4, p. 28).

25 **Leaving Lechlade . . . Pontycysyllty**: 'Pontycysyllty' is Pontcy-
syllte, whose spectacular aqueduct was built between 1795 and
1805 to carry the Ellesmere (now Llangollen) Canal across the
Dee Valley. The party sails from south-east England to the west,
ultimately to the north-east of Wales.

26 *badinage*: 'Humorous, witty, or trifling discourse; banter;
frivolous or light-hearted raillery. Also: an instance of this; a
witticism, a sally' (*OED*). In his review of Moore's *Letters and*

Journals of Lord Byron, TLP asserts that Byron spoke to Leigh Hunt, as to Thomas Medwin, 'in the same spirit in which he wrote much of his *badinage* in Don Juan'. In the same review, shortly after associating 'the hundred fountains of the river Hoangho' with Hunt's 'querulous egotisms', TLP describes Byron's letters in terms of 'that spirit of *badinage* which says things not meant or expected to be believed' (Halliford, 9.74, 80, 81). TLP's great admiration for *Don Juan* notwithstanding, given the likely associations between Medwin, Hunt and Eavesdrop, and given that this review appeared shortly before *CC*, it seems that TLP has kept in mind in his fiction as in his journalism a network of relations between the multi-spouting Hoangho, biographical egomania and frothy *badinage*.

27 **the Dee**: The river Dee flows north-east through Merionethshire, past Llangollen and into Cheshire.

28 **The course . . . run smooth**: Lady Clarinda is quoting Lysander's words to Hermia in *A Midsummer Night's Dream* (act 1, scene 1, line 134). Despite Clarinda's claim that 'it must not be', the fact that Lysander and Hermia eventually marry (despite her father Egeus's objections) may give Captain Fitzchrome some cause for hope.

29 **I must . . . be kind**: Hamlet's words to Gertrude in *Hamlet* (act 3, scene 4, line 178). This allusion may temper the hope that has just been raised.

30 *le cœur navré*: A broken heart.

31 *valise*: A travelling case, usually made of leather.

32 **miasmata**: Plural of miasma, 'noxious vapour' (*OED*). See also Mr Firedamp's reference to malaria in ch. 6 (p. 57).

33 **authentic anecdotes of their departed friend**: Such language echoes the title pages of popular contemporary biographies, collections of *ana*, and scandalous narratives of the lives and loves of celebrities ('departed' being a standard euphemism for 'dead'): see e.g. John Cecil, *Sixty Curious and Authentic Narratives and Anecdotes respecting Extraordinary Characters* (1819); Alexander

Kilgour, *Anecdotes of Lord Byron, from authentic sources* (1825); *The Scrap-Book, or a Selection of Interesting and Authentic Anecdotes* (1825). For TLP's opinions of such works, see e.g. his review of Moore's *Letters and Journals of Lord Byron* (Halliford, 9.71–139 (esp. pp. 138–9)).

34 **a subject for science**: In other words, the Captain has probably been murdered in order to be sold on to a surgeon for dissection. Cf. ch. 8, in which Folliott uses the phrase 'subject for science' twice, with this dread fate in mind (p. 77).

35 **surplus population**: Recalling Thomas Malthus, *Essay on the Principle of Population* (1798), and his concerns about how to manage population growth (Malthus does not, however, use the phrase 'surplus population' in the text itself). In ch. 1 of Dickens' *A Christmas Carol* (1843), Scrooge observes that the poor should perish in order to 'decrease the surplus population' (*A Christmas Carol and Other Christmas Books*, ed. Robert Douglas-Fairhurst, Oxford World's Classics (Oxford: Oxford University Press, 2006), p. 14).

36 **asseverated**: 'asseverate': 'to affirm solemnly, assert emphatically' (*OED*).

CHAPTER II

1 **Base . . . ANCIENT PISTOL**: Pistol to Corporal Nym in *Henry V* (act 2, scene 1, line 96). TLP used the same epigraph for 'The Three Little Men', one of his *Paper Money Lyrics* (Halliford, 7.108).

2 **miasmatised**: 'to affect by miasma'; the only instance of this word in the *OED*.

3 **two letters**: In its positive notice of the work, the *Mirror of Literature, Amusement, and Instruction* printed the two American letters and Susannah Touchandgo's response as a representative extract of *CC* (*Mirror*, part 1, vol. 17 (2 Apr. 1831), pp. 234–6).

4 *Apodidraskiana*: TLP's coinage, based on the Greek verb ἀπο-διδράσκω (*apodidraskō*) 'run away'.

5 *April* 1: The date of the letter suggests that someone is being played for a fool.

6 MY DEAR CHILD: The exploits of Touchandgo and Robthetill were modelled on the case of Rowland Stephenson (a Lombard Street banker and Tory MP for Leominster) and his clerk James Lloyd; for further details, see Introduction, pp. lix–lxi, and Appendix D (pp. 158–62). The pair absconded from London in Dec. 1828 when unsecured advances came to light which bankrupted Remington's Bank. Stephenson fled with Lloyd to Savannah, Georgia, and was formally bankrupted under the twelve-month rule on 19 Jan. 1830, thus forfeiting his parliamentary seat. On 'Touchandgo', see TLP's poem of that name (Appendices D and E, and Halliford, 7.242–4), and Nicholas A. Joukovsky, 'The Revision of Peacock's "Touchandgo" and the Composition of *Crotchet Castle*', *Notes and Queries*, 257/New Series, 59 (2012), 386–7.

7 **talismanic channel … dollars**: Cf. 'the talismanic influence of the coin' in *HH*, ch. 9.

8 **land … flourish**: Notwithstanding the satirical take on Touchandgo's new start in America, TLP was attracted to the country as a land of commercial opportunity; see his letter to Shelley (15 Sept. 1818) on Birkbeck's *Notes on America*: 'He has emigrated with his whole family … where he has purchased a *prairie* … Multitudes are following his example even from this neighbourhood … The temptation to agriculturists with a small capital must be irresistible: and the picture he presents of the march of population and cultivation … is one of the most wonderful spectacles ever yet presented to the mind's eye of philosophy' (*Letters*, 1.152). See also Introduction, pp. xcvi–xcvii.

9 **methodist preachers**: Methodism thrived in America during the second Great Awakening (c. 1790–1840). In 1784, though still maintaining his allegiance to Anglicanism, John Wesley

279

had ordained men for the American ministry, so laying the groundwork for the Methodist Episcopal Church. The African Methodist Episcopal Church was formed in 1816.

10 **slave-drivers**: The *OED*'s first British citation of this phrase occurs in an article in the *Athenaeum* (29 Feb. 1828).

11 **paper-money manufacturers**: See *Letters*, 1.145. In his review of Jefferson's *Memoirs* (1829), under the heading 'Paper-Currency and Banks', TLP approvingly quotes Jefferson's criticism of 'juggling tricks and banking dreams . . . All these doubts and fears prove only the extent of all the dominion which the banking institutions have obtained over the minds of our citizens . . . and this dominion must be broken, or it will break us' (Halliford, 9.176–7).

12 **BANK . . . arrived**: See 'A Border Ballad', from TLP's *Paper Money Lyrics*; 'They put in sash-windows where none were before, / And they wrote the word "BANK" o'er the new-painted door' (Halliford, 7.126).

13 **discounted**: A bill not yet due is bought from its holder at less than face value. The buyer hopes to collect the full amount when the bill is due and the seller realises most of the amount of the bill without having to wait for it to be due.

14 **most of them . . . some place or other**: Not all of them 'have run away' for disreputable reasons, as TLP points out in his review of Jefferson's *Memoirs* (1829), in which America is praised as 'beyond the reach of injury from the combined despotisms of the earth . . . an asylum for the oppressed and unfortunate of all nations' (Halliford, 9.145).

15 **scientific views of morals and politics**: Cf. TLP's satirical swipes at 'scientific views', hence at Brougham's morals and politics, in ch. 8 (pp. 76–7).

16 *andante . . . forte . . . allegro vivace*: Moderately slow . . . loud . . . fast and lively (musical terms).

17 **interest**: Touchandgo may be punning on the financial sense of 'interest' here.

18 **gorgeous in the spoils of many gulls**: Luxuriating in the gains he has made from people he has deceived; 'gull': 'a credulous person; one easily imposed upon; a dupe, simpleton, fool' (*OED*).

19 **Polar Basin and Walrus Company**: TLP could have in mind a company speculating in whaling, sealing and fishing at one of the Poles; the London firm of Enderby Bros., for example, sponsored a number of expeditions to the Antarctic in the first four decades of the century.

20 *Au reste*: For the rest, besides.

21 **no rents . . . no ladies**: In his review of Jefferson's *Memoirs*, TLP praises 'the total abolition of internal taxes . . . the rapid extinction of national debt . . . [and] the efficient protection and ample reward of domestic industry' (Halliford, 9.145; see also 9.165).

22 **videlicet**: see ch. 1 (p. 7) and n. 19 (p. 197).

23 **tilted waggon**: In *Notes on a Journey in America, from the Coast of Virginia to the Territory of Illinois*, 3rd edn (James Ridgway, 1818), p. 32, Morris Birkbeck describes this as a small wagon covered with a 'tilt' (i.e., a sheet or blanket).

24 **new state . . . this privilege**: A reference to the terms of the Missouri Compromise (1820); Missouri (1821) was the only slave state admitted to the Union in the decade preceding *CC*.

25 **they are building him a villa**: See ch. 1 on the social implications of building a villa (p. 7).

26 **he cannot buy . . . England**: Cf. the Borough of Onevote in *Mel*, ch. 22.

27 **Regulators**: Vigilantes.

28 **MY DEAR FATHER**: See Appendix E for a draft fragment of this letter (pp. 164–6).

29 **Green . . . Idris**: Cadair (or Cader) Idris is a mountain ridge in western Merionethshire. The Green Bard is fictitious.

30 **SUSANNAH TOUCHANDGO**: Given that Susannah is a forsaken daughter, it may be relevant that, during the composition of *CC*, TLP was almost certainly having an extra-marital affair that

resulted in the birth of a natural daughter, Susan Mary Abbott. See Nicholas A. Joukovsky and Jim Powell, 'A Peacock in the Attic', *Times Literary Supplement* (22 July 2011), 13–15. There is possibly a coded reference to Susan at the beginning of this chapter, where TLP describes Susannah as 'a young lady . . . who, though she has since been out of sight, has never with us been out of mind' (p. 96).

31 **Beyond the sea**: A poem in the style of the 'penillion' (Welsh verses sung to the accompaniment of a harp) which was given the Welsh title 'Tros y Mor' ('Beyond the sea') in an early draft (see Appendix E). See *ME*, ch. 15: 'pennillion, or unconnected stanzas, sung in series by different singers, the stanzas being complete in themselves, simple as Greek epigrams, and presenting in succession moral precepts, pictures of natural scenery, images of war or of festival, the lamentations of absence or captivity, and the complaints or triumphs of love. This pennillion-singing long survived among the Welsh peasantry almost every other vestige of bardic customs, and may still be heard among them on the few occasions on which rack-renting, tax-collecting, common-enclosing, methodist-preaching, and similar developments of the light of the age, have left them either the means or inclination of making merry.'

CHAPTER 12

1 **'Ὡς ἡδὺ . . . MENANDER**: Menander fr. 401.1–2 Körte–Thierfelder. The translation is accurate. Cf. TLP's declared twin loves of 'solitude and navigation' in a letter to Mary Shelley (13 Sept. 1847), *Letters*, 2.301.

2 **negus**: A mixture of wine, hot water, sugar and other flavouring. Named after its inventor, Col. Francis Negus (*OED*).

3 **Merionethshire . . . all that is beautiful in nature, and all that is lovely in woman**: Cf. TLP's description of 'beauteous Merion' in *The Philosophy of Melancholy* (1812): 'The mighty cataracts burst

and thunder down: / The rock-set ash, with tortuous branches grey, / Veils the deep glen, and drinks the flying spray; / And druid oaks extend their solemn shades / O'er the fair forms of Britain's loveliest maids' (Halliford, 6.194); see also chs. 13 and 14 (pp. 107–15).

4 **It is . . . sights**: A glancing reference to the fairly recent development of British tourism. The relative inaccessibility of the continent as a result of Napoleonic wars led to a rise in domestic tours, and to an increased demand for guidebooks. See, for example, *A Picturesque Description of North Wales, Embellished with Twenty Select Views from Nature* (1823).

5 **tourist's**: The word 'tourist' was a recent coinage. See, for example, Samuel Pegge, *Anecdotes of the English language: chiefly regarding the local dialect of London* (Nichols, Son, and Bentley, 1814), p. 313: 'a Traveller now-a-days is called a Tour-*ist*'. See ch. 10, n. 3 (p. 271).

6 **Will . . . advice**: Slightly misquoted from Air no. 8 in John Gay's *The Beggar's Opera* (1728), act 1, scene 8, lines 48–57. The allusion is apposite, given that both men are in search of a wife. In answer to Peachum's comment, 'Why, *Polly*, I shall soon know if your [sic] are married', Polly sings: '*Can Love be controul'd by Advice? / Will Cupid our Mothers obey? / Though my Heart were as frozen as Ice, / At his Flame 'twould have melted away. // When he kist me so closely he prest, / 'Twas so sweet that I must have comply'd; / So I thought it both safest and best / To marry, for fear you should chide*' (*Dramatic Works*, ed. John Fuller, 2 vols. (Oxford: Clarendon Press, 1983), vol. 2, p. 14).

7 **hearts, heads, and arms . . . degenerated, most sadly**: In his emphasis on degeneracy and deterioration, Chainmail echoes Escot in *HH*; see e.g. ch. 10: 'Such is the lamentable progress of degeneracy and decay. In the course of ages, a boot of the present generation would form an ample chateau for a large family of our remote posterity. The mind, too, participates in the contraction of the body. Poets and philosophers of all ages

and nations have lamented this too visible process of physical and moral deterioration.'

8 **the oaken graff of the Pindar of Wakefield**: 'Graff': 'A twig, shoot, scion; *gen.* a branch, plant' (*OED*, citing this passage); 'pinder': 'A person in charge of impounding stray animals' (*OED*). Possibly an allusion to the 1599 play *George a Greene, the Pinner of Wakefield* (attributed to Robert Greene). A 'graff' could also be a stylus or pencil. TLP is thus punningly blending the poet Pindar, the office of pinder, the symbol of that office, and the writing instrument of a poet. 'The Jolly Pinder of Wakefield' is a ballad about Robin Hood. The jolly pinder boasts that no one, not even a baron, can trespass at Wakefield. Robin, Will Scarlet and Little John hear him. They fight with swords, and Robin offers to take him into the band. The pinder gives them some food and says that, at Michaelmas, he will take his fee from his current master and join them. The oldest MS was published in 1632, but it is thought to derive from works at least a century older. A fragmentary version appears in Percy, *Bishop Percy's Folio Manuscript*, vol. 1, pp. 32–6.

9 **feelings . . . passions**: In his review of Edgcumbe's *Musical Reminiscences*, TLP contrasts 'the language of passion' in Italian opera and old English songs with the 'false sentiment' of 'modern songs' (Halliford, 9.232–4).

10 *en famille* **with your domestics**: *en famille*: informally; 'with your domestics': cf. the living arrangements of Falconer in *GG*, ch. 4.

11 **hobby**: The *OED*'s first instance of 'hobby' meaning 'a favourite occupation or topic . . . an individual pursuit to which a person is devoted (in the speaker's opinion) out of proportion to its real importance' dates from 1816 (in Scott's *Antiquary*), but TLP is also drawing on the idea of the 'hobby-horse', esp. in *Tristram Shandy*: 'WHEN a man gives himself up to the government of a ruling passion, – or, in other words, when his HOBBY-HORSE grows head-strong, – farewell cool reason and fair discretion!' (Laurence Sterne, the Florida Edition of the Works of Laurence

Sterne, gen. ed. Melvyn New, 9 vols. (Gainesville: University Press of Florida, 1978–2014), vols. 1–3: *The Life and Opinions of Tristram Shandy, Gentleman*, text ed. Melvyn New and Joan New, notes by Melvyn New with Richard A. Davies and W. G. Day (1978–84), vol. 1, p. 106). Sterne's 'hobby', like TLP's 'crotchet' ('A whimsical fancy; a perverse conceit; a peculiar notion on some point (usually considered unimportant) held by an individual in opposition to common opinion', *OED*), is also partly indebted to Pope; Johnson referred to the poet's 'favourite theory of the *Ruling Passion*, by which he means an original direction of desire to some particular object, an innate affection which gives all action a determinate and invariable tendency, and operates upon the whole system of life, either openly, or more secretly by the intervention of some accidental or subordinate propension' (*Lives of the Poets*, ed. Lonsdale, vol. 4, p.44). See *An Essay on Man*: 'So, cast and mingled with his very frame, / The Mind's disease, its ruling Passion came' (epistle 2, section 3, lines 137–8) and the 'Epistle to Bathurst' (1733): 'The ruling Passion, be it what it will, / The ruling Passion conquers Reason still' (*Moral Essays*, epistle 3, lines 155–6; Pope, *Poems*, vol. 3, p. 1). On *An Essay on Man*, see ch 7, n. 16 (p. 251).

12 **herald**: 'one skilled in heraldry; a heraldist'. The *OED*'s first instance of this meaning dates from 1821, in Scott's *Kenilworth*.

13 **love in a cottage**: See also ch. 3, n. 13 (pp. 224–5).

14 **rotten borough**: 'chiefly *Brit. Hist.* a borough whose constituency has dwindled severely or (in certain cases) ceased to exist altogether, but which still retains the power to elect a Member of Parliament; in later use also applied to electoral areas subject to similar circumstances elsewhere' (*OED*). For TLP's use of the phrase, see *Letters*, 1.130 and *Mel*, ch. 22.

CHAPTER 13

1 **Or . . . INNAMORATO**: 'Come, my love, and sit here with me'; Matteo Maria Boiardo (1434–94), *Orlando Innamorato* (1482):

'Or vieni, Amore, e qua meco te assetta' (book 3, canto 9, verse 1, line 5). The poem, an unfinished epic romance in *ottava rima*, is the precursor to Ludovico Ariosto's *Orlando Furioso* (1516, 1532). Episodes of *Orlando Innamorato* in the Ardennes Forest and involving the 'stream of love' ('la rivera dello amore') may have contributed to the setting and atmosphere of this chapter (book 1, canto 3, verses 32–8). TLP's *Sale Catalogue* (74–6) includes M. M. Boiardo, *Orlando Innamorato, rifatto da F. Berni*, 4 vols. (wanting vol. 3) (Milan, 1806); M. M. Boiardo, *Orlando Innamorato, riformato da M. L. Domenichi*, 3 vols. (1824); Bojardo ed Ariosto, *Orlando Innamorato ed Furioso*, with Introductory Essay, Memoirs and Notes by A. Panizzi, 9 vols. (Pickering, 1830–4).

2 **you being picturesque**: In ch. 3 of *HH*, Mr Milestone is described as a 'picturesque landscape gardener'.

3 **the lights and shadows of the present . . . those of the past**: Chainmail is playing on different applications of the Italian term 'chiaroscuro' ('light and shade'). In the 'picturesque' sense, 'chiaroscuro' means 'The treatment or disposition of the light and shade, or brighter and darker masses, in a picture' (*OED*). In the 'poetical' sense, 'chiaroscuro' had recently developed a figurative application: 'Used of poetic or literary treatment, criticism, mental complexion, etc., in various obvious senses, as mingled "clearness and obscurity", "cheerfulness and gloom", "praise and blame," etc.' (*OED*: the earliest citation is from Hazlitt in 1818).

4 **twelfth . . . crusade**: Giraldus de Barri (or Giraldus Cambrensis, or Gerald of Wales, c. 1146–c. 1220/3), archdeacon of Brecon, was refused high office because he was a Welshman. In 1188, he went with Archbishop Baldwin to preach the crusade in Wales (he himself took the cross, but was absolved from his vow in late 1189). He wrote an anecdotal history of the crusade, and of Welsh languages and traditions, *Itinerarium Cambriae* (c. 1191), a work in which Archbishop Baldwin figures prominently. TLP's *Sale Catalogue* (320) includes 'GIRALDUS

CAMBRENSIS, Itinerary of Abp. Baldwin through Wales, A. D. 1188, with historical and topographical illustrations by Sir R. Colt Hoare', 2 vols. (1806).

5 **fascinated with the inn and the scenery**: Chainmail's tour of Wales parallels TLP's. At the beginning of 1810 he travelled to north Wales, where he took lodgings for almost fifteen months at Tan-y-Bwlch, near Maentwrog, Merionethshire, in the Vale of Ffestiniog, which he described as 'a terrestrial paradise' (*Letters*, 1.43). Here, like Susannah Touchandgo, TLP developed a strong attachment to Welsh landscapes, customs and traditions. He pursued a course of study, explored the local scenery, and fell in and out of love. One of the two young women who attracted him was his future wife, Jane Gryffydh (1789–1851), daughter of the parson at Maentwrog. He left north Wales in Apr. 1811 without declaring his feelings, even though he judged her 'the most innocent, the most amiable, the most beautiful girl in existence' (*Letters*, 1.64). He had also fallen in love with another, as yet unidentified 'Caernarvonshire damsel' (*Letters*, 1.55). See TLP's letter to Thomas Hookham (20 Jan. 1810): 'I have taken a lodging here *pro tempore*, while I look about... I should feel perfectly happy in casting anchor here... a picturesque tourist lately made a pause of five months, being unable to tear himself from so fascinating a scene' (*Letters*, 1.43).

6 **tutto... torrenti**: 'all day, determined on fine deeds, / Leaped cliffs, and crossed torrents'; the lines do not appear in *Orlando Furioso*, but see canto 3, stanza 65, for the 'leaped cliffs' and 'crossed torrents' ('e tutto 'l di senza pigliar riposo / saliron balze e traversar torrenti') (*Orlando Furioso, con annotazioni*, 8 vols. (Florence, 1823–4)); TLP owned a copy of this work (see *Sale Catalogue* 36).

7 **One day... torrent**: Aspects of the description resemble TLP's account of his tour of Wales, where 'In the vicinity are many deep glens, – along which copious mountain-streams, of inconceivable clearness, roar over rocky channels, – and numerous waterfalls

of the most romantic character' (*Letters*, 1.43). See also *Letters*, 1.45.

8 **coracle**: A small boat of watertight material stretched over a wicker frame, first fashioned by the ancient Bretons.

9 *recherchée*: 'Recherché' means 'Rare, choice, exotic; far-fetched, obscure' (*OED*).

10 *contadina*: Italian peasant girl. That Susannah should be described in this way may hint at an overlap in TLP's mind between her and another bride-to-be, the maid Susanna in Mozart's *Le Nozze di Figaro* (1786). On TLP's admiration for and knowledge of Mozart, see Halliford, 9.237–40, 244, 294, 321, 430–2. In ch. 15 we are told that Susannah's 'voice had that full soft volume of melody which gives to common speech the fascination of music' (p. 117).

11 **the castle day after day . . . no more**: The phrasing and setting are reminiscent of Gothic fiction; see e.g. Ann Radcliffe, *The Italian*, vol. 1, ch. 1: 'He was lost in revery on this subject, sometimes half resolved to seek her no more, and then shrinking from a conduct, which seemed to strike him with the force of despair . . . He called loudly and repeatedly, conjuring the unknown person to appear, and lingered near the spot for a considerable time; but the vision came no more' (ed. Frederick Garber and E. J. Clery (Oxford: Oxford University Press, 1998), pp. 12–13).

CHAPTER 14

1 **The stars . . . her face**: William Wordsworth, 'Three Years She Grew' (1798), lines 25–30, in *Lyrical Ballads and Other Poems, 1797–1800*, ed. James Butler and Karen Green (Ithaca, NY and London: Cornell University Press, 1992).

2 **four . . . Italy**: Dante, Petrarch, Tasso and Ariosto.

3 *Les Rêveries . . . Solitaire*: Jean-Jacques Rousseau's *Les Rêveries du promeneur solitaire* (*The Reveries of a Solitary Walker*) (Geneva, 1782). As the narrator observes, the book is a fitting one for Susannah's situation. Rousseau wrote it in retirement having

been virtually exiled from France, principally on account of the unorthodox religion professed in *Émile* (1762). The first sentence of *Les Rêveries* is: 'Me voici donc seul sur la terre, n'ayant plus de frere, de prochain, d'ami, de societé que moi-même' (Jean-Jacques Rousseau, *Œuvres complètes*, ed. Bernard Gagnebin and Marcel Raymond et al., 5 vols. (Paris: Gallimard [Pléiade], 1959–95, vol. 1, p. 995); later ('Septiéme Promenade'), he observes: 'Je gravis les rochers, les montagnes, je m'enfonce dans les vallons, dans les bois pour me dérober autant qu'il est possible au souvenir des hommes et aux atteintes des méchans' (p. 1070). On 'a love of truth', see the 'Quatriéme Promenade' of Rousseau's book; on 'children', see 'Neuvième Promenade'; on 'beauties of nature', see 'Cinquiéme Promenade'; on 'simplicity of dress', see 'Troisiéme Promenade' (esp. p. 1014); TLP owned an 1826 edition of Rousseau's complete works (*Sale Catalogue* 540).

4 **sweet poison**: *A Sequel to the Adventures of Baron Munchausen*, 2 vols. (H. D. Symonds and J. Owen, 1792) refers to 'Rousseau, Voltaire, and Belzebub' as 'three horrible spectres: one all meagre, mere skin and bone, and cadaverous, seemed death, that hideous skeleton: it was Voltaire, and in his hand were a lyre and a dagger. On the other side was Rousseau, with a chalice of sweet poison in his hand; and between them was their father Belzebub!' (vol. 2, pp. 240–1). Numerous Munchausen-related publications appeared in the eighteenth and nineteenth centuries.

5 **remained on her memory**: The reference to an image or idea that remains 'on' rather than 'in' the memory suggests that TLP is thinking of the action of something that has impressed itself permanently on the mind, as in a letter to Lord Broughton (10 Dec. 1856): 'He is about to relate things indelibly impressed on his memory' (*Letters*, 2.359).

6 **And . . . solitude**: Wordsworth, 'Lines Left Upon a Seat in a Yew-Tree' (1798), lines 20–1 (with 'his' for 'her'). The poem goes on to note: 'Stranger! henceforth be warned; and know,

that pride, / Howe'er disguised in its own majesty, / Is littleness', lines 46–8 (*Lyrical Ballads, and Other Poems, 1797–1800*).

7 **tippet**: A fur or wool shawl, cape, or cloak.

8 **keep company**: 'To associate with, frequent the society of; *esp.* (*vulgar* and *dial.*) to associate as lovers or as a lover, to "court"' (*OED*).

9 **Harry Ap-Heather**: See ch. 1, n. 40 (p. 202).

10 **One spot . . . favorite haunt**: See TLP's letter to Thomas L'Estrange (11 July 1861): 'The "dingle" in "Crotchet Castle," is a real scene, on the river Velenrhyd, in Merionethshire. There is no chasm on that river which it is possible to leap over; but there is more than one on the river Cynfael, which flows into the same valley. I took the poetical licence of approximating the scenes. That on the Velenrhyd is called Llyn-y-Gygfraen, the Ravens' Pool' (*Letters*, 2.425). For a photograph of the dingle, see 'Landscape and Letters: The Dingle in "Crotchet Castle"', *The Times* (30 Dec. 1932), p. 14.

11 **chasm . . . gleamed**: Compare Coleridge's *Kubla Khan*, where the river runs from the 'chasm', 'Through caverns measureless' (line 4) and 'Down to a sunless sea' (lines 12, 17, 5; 12 and 17 both refer to the 'chasm'), Coleridge, *Works*, vol. 16. Several other aspects of the dingle recall the setting of Coleridge's poem. Susannah has retreated here, having been jilted; Coleridge's 'savage place' is 'as holy and inchanted / As e'er beneath a waning moon was haunted / By woman wailing for her demon-lover!' (lines 14–16). TLP praises Coleridge's poem in 'An Essay on Fashionable Literature' (*NA*, Appendix B). See earlier possible allusions to *Kubla Khan* in chs. 5 (p. 44) and 8 (p. 75).

12 **High above . . . darkness**: The dark cataracts, the oak, the rock and other features of the landscape recall a letter from TLP to Edward Thomas Hookham from Wales (22 Mar. 1810) about 'the *black cataract*, a favorite haunt of mine': 'The effect was truly magnificent. – The water descends from a mountainous glen down a winding rock, and then precipitates itself, in one sheet

of foam, over its black base, into a capacious bason, the sides of which are all but perpendicular, and covered with hanging oak and hazel' (*Letters*, 1.47). See also TLP's description of 'beauteous Meirion' in *The Philosophy of Melancholy* (Halliford, 6.194). The scene is additionally reminiscent of many Gothic topographies; see, for example, Ann Radcliffe's *The Mysteries of Udolpho* (1794): 'The solitary grandeur of the objects that immediately surrounded her, the mountain-region towering above, the deep precipices that fell beneath, the waving blackness of the forests of pine and oak, which skirted their feet, or hung within their recesses, the headlong torrents that, dashing among their cliffs, sometimes appeared like a cloud of mist, at others like a sheet of ice – these were features which received a higher character of sublimity from the reposing beauty of the Italian landscape below, stretching to the wide horizon, where the same melting blue tint seemed to unite earth and sky' (*The Mysteries of Udolpho*, ed. Bonamy Dobrée with Terry Castle (Oxford: Oxford University Press, 1998), vol. 2, ch. 1, pp. 165–6). On TLP's early exposure to Radcliffe's fiction, see his 'Recollections of Childhood: The Abbey House', Halliford, 8.33–4.

13 **perception . . . danger**: See Edmund Burke: 'Whatever is fitted in any sort to excite the ideas of pain, and danger, that is to say, whatever is in any sort terrible, or is conversant about terrible objects, or operates in a manner analogous to terror, is a source of the *sublime*', in *A Philosophical Enquiry into the Origin of our Ideas of the Sublime and Beautiful* (1757), Part 1, 'Section 7: Of the Sublime' (*The Writings and Speeches of Edmund Burke*, gen. ed. Paul Langford, 9 vols. (Oxford: Clarendon Press/New York: Oxford University Press, 1981–), vol. 1: *The Early Writings*, ed. T. O. McLoughlin and James T. Boulton (1997), p. 216).

14 **acclivities**: Upward or ascending slopes.

15 **romantic reveries**: Cf. ch. 8 on 'the state called *reverie*' (p. 75).

16 **lady of the lake**: The Lady of the Lake is the ruler of Avalon in Arthurian Legend. Scott's poem *The Lady of the Lake* appeared

in 1810, drawing on the romance of that legend, but introducing an entirely new plot and setting (in the Trossachs of Scotland). Scott's work in its turn inspired Rossini's opera, *La donna del lago*, which debuted in Naples in 1819 and established a fashion for operas set in Scotland and based on Scott's works, of which Gaetano Donizetti's *Lucia di Lammermoor* (1835) is the best known.

17 **beetle-browed . . . chasm**: See *Hamlet*, act 1, scene 4, lines 70–1: 'the dreadful summit of the cliff / That beetles o'er his base into the sea'.

18 **sleeping beauty**: TLP's reference to the fairy-tale is a reminder that Chainmail hopes to play the role of Prince Charming.

19 **the unknown beauty**: A stock phrase and staple character in chivalric romance and hence in eighteenth-century English fiction: see e.g. Ann Howell, *Anzoletta Zadoski*, 2 vols. (William Lane, 1796), vol. 2, p. 3; Isabella Kelly, *The Ruins of Avondale Priory*, 3 vols. (William Lane, 1796), vol. 1, p. 108.

20 **the nymph of the scene**: The language here is suggestive. To lie 'like the nymph of the scene' makes Susannah appear erotically abandoned (elsewhere in *CC*, however, 'nymph' has happy and innocent connotations: see e.g. 'nymph of the coracle' and 'nymph of the place' (ch. 13)). At one stage TLP planned to write a poem, strongly influenced by Nonnus' *Dionysiaca* (see TLP's footnote to this chapter, and n. 22 [Footnote] below), on the subject of 'Nympholepsy': 'Passion supposedly inspired in men by nymphs; an ecstasy or yearning, esp. that caused by desire for something unattainable. Also: passion or desire aroused in men by young girls' (*OED*). Shelley referred to the work in a letter to TLP of 16 Aug. 1818 (*The Letters of Percy Bysshe Shelley*, ed. Frederick L. Jones, 2 vols. (Oxford: Clarendon Press, 1964), vol. 2, p. 29). Among TLP's manuscripts (British Library, Add MS 36815, ff. 120–2) is a prose abstract of the poem, which narrates how a young man of Bacchus' train, the son of a king, falls in love

with a beautiful nymph. Failing to win her, he runs mad until the nymph breaks her vow of chastity. The bacchanals, deserted by the youth, slay him at Diana's instigation; the nymph melts into a fountain of tears.

21 **plump as a partridge**: The homely phrase is itself comically at odds with 'the beauties of romance'; in 'My Passion is as Mustard Strong', the love-sick speaker complains that, having been 'Plump as a Partridge', he has grown thin and melancholy; his lover, meanwhile (like Susannah) 'insensible of that, / Sound as a top can sleep'. This song appears in many eighteenth-century miscellanies, including *Bacchus and Venus: or, a select collection of near 200 of the most witty and diverting songs and catches in love and gallantry* (1737), p. 47. Book 2 of *The Dunciad* also contains 'a partridge plump, full-fed, and fair' (line 41; Pope, *Works*, vol. 5, p. 298).

22 **features . . . grapes**: TLP's blazon, or inventory of Susannah's features, invokes the Petrarchan tradition. More specifically, the fact that the 'cheeks were two roses, not absolutely damask', and the subsequent hope that her eyes might be like the rising of the sun, may be recalling Shakespeare's Sonnet 130.

[Footnote:] Ἀλήμονα βότρυν ἔθειρας: 'the straying curl of hair', Nonnus, *Dionysiaca*, 1.528. For other references to Nonnus, see chs. 2 (p. 20) and 17 (p. 136). The primary meaning of βότρυς is 'cluster of grapes', but the meaning 'lock of hair' is well-established. The association of βότρυς with the vine has prompted TLP to introduce the direct comparison to grapes. The original context in the *Dionysiaca* is erotic, and chimes with Chainmail's keenness to 'contemplate at his leisure the features and form of his charmer': 'As a lusty youth enamoured is bewitched by delicious thrills by the side of a maiden his age-mate, and gazes now at the silvery round of her charming face, now at a straying curl of her thick hair, now again at a rosy hand, or notes the circle of her blushing breast pressed by the bodice, and watches the bare neck, as he delights to let his eye run over and over her body never satisfied, and never will leave his girl' (tr. W. H. D. Rouse).

23 **fringy portals**: this phrase from TLP is the earliest citation under 'fringy' in the sense of 'Furnished or adorned with a fringe or fringes; covered with fringes' (*OED*).

24 **forehead . . . sky**: From John Milton, 'Lycidas' (1638), line 171 (*The Complete Shorter Poems*, ed. John Carey, rev. 2nd edn (Harlow: Pearson/Longman, 2007). (See also *Sale Catalogue* 647.)

CHAPTER 15

1 **Da ydyw'r . . . delight**: Lines 1–4 of penill no. 39 from *The Cambro-Briton* (Feb. 1820), vol. 1, p. 230. The translation is not the same as the one published in the journal and is presumably TLP's own.

2 **envious**: 'Calculated to excite ill-will, odious; considered obsolete after c. 1640' (*OED*).

3 **eyes . . . forgotten**: Perhaps TLP is remembering 'the radiant eyes of a Caernarvonshire damsel, *not a parson's daughter*' (*Letters*, 1.55).

4 **blubbered till the rocks re-echoed**: Itself perhaps an echo, given the frequency with which rocks echo and re-echo in ancient literature. See e.g. *Odyssey*, book 9, lines 391–6; *Aeneid*, book 3, line 432, book 7, line 563ff., book 8, line 305. These moments are all elemental or manly, especially in comparison with the situation in *CC*: in epic, the re-echoing accompanies great forces of nature or some heroic deed. So perhaps TLP's purpose is epic parody (as with Folliott and the bandits in ch. 8); it is far from heroic that Harry makes the rocks re-echo with crying. On the other hand, the point may be to send up Harry as a pastoral lover. At the start of the First Eclogue, for instance, Virgil has Meliboeus say to his fellow-shepherd Tityrus, 'you, Tityrus, at ease beneath the shade, teach the woods to re-echo "fair Amaryllis" [by singing rustic songs all day on the hillside]' ('tu, Tityre,

lentus in umbra / formosam resonare doces Amaryllida silvas';
lines 4–5). Virgil has in mind Theocritus, *Idyll* 1.1–2. The point
of this is the personification of the countryside in sympathy with
human suffering. So too Propertius (*Elegies*, 1.18.31) declares,
'Let the woods re-echo "Cynthia" for me' ('resonent mihi "Cynthia" silvae'). For more pathetic fallacy of the landscape, respond-
ing and re-echoing with song, cf. Virgil, *Eclogues*, eclogue 5,
lines 62–4, eclogue 6, line 11, eclogue 8, line 22, eclogue 10,
line 8.

5 **They ... murmurs**: The language is biblical, with 'tears' and
'lamentations' recalling the Book of Lamentations (e.g. ch. 2,
v. 18). There is another possible allusion, to *As You Like It*,
act 2, scene 1, lines 40–3: 'and thus the hairy fool, / Much
marked of the melancholy Jaques, / Stood on th'extremest verge
of the swift brook, / Augmenting it with tears'.

6 **original**: Uniquely ridiculous (*OED*).

7 **poiled ... marrow**: Boiled with the bacon, and as good as marrow.

8 **horn**: A drinking vessel formed from, or shaped like, the horn
of an animal (*OED*).

9 **lappets**: 'An appendage or pendant to head-gear of any kind;
esp. one of the streamers attached to a lady's head-dress'
(*OED*).

10 **Shall we ... expatiation**: TLP's narrator indulges in *paralipsis* (a
rhetorical device in which an idea is emphasised by the pretence
that it is too obvious to discuss – or, for some other reason, that it
is hardly worth mentioning). In 'The Four Ages of Poetry', TLP
had complained about similar attempts to document minutiae: in
contrast to the powerful 'outline' and 'simplicity' of 'the Homeric
Muse', he noted 'a verbose and minutely-detailed description of
thoughts, passions, actions, persons, and things, in that loose
rambling style of verse, which any one may write ... at the rate
of two hundred lines in an hour' (*NA*, Appendix C). 'Expatiation':
'opportunity to speak or write at length (rare); literally, to walk

about' (*OED*), and so perhaps an oblique pun when read in relation to 'field'.

11 **steam engines . . . furlong**: 1814 saw the first use of steam in printing (Friedrich Koenig and Andreas Friedrich Bauer sold two of their first models to *The Times*). Robert Cadell bought steam presses and issued reprints of Scott's *Waverley* novels in 1829 at 5 shillings; sales reached 35,000 a month. Colburn and Bentley followed suit a year later and issued reprinted fiction at 6 shillings.

12 **modern literature . . . blacking**: A reference to Robert Warren's boot polish. Warren ran the most prominent and inventive advertising campaigns of the early nineteenth century; Thomas Hood praised him as among 'the best advertisement writers' and commended the 'variety, brilliancy and country circulation' of his puffs ('The Art of Advertising Made Easy', *London Magazine* (Feb. 1825), p. 247). The campaigns were notable for their use of poetry; J. H. Reynolds observed that now '[poetry] was glad to perch wherever she was able . . . she dashed into Warren's blacking manufactory, as a sanctuary, and dipping her wing in an eighteen-penny bottle, took up the cause of boots and shoes' (*Westminster Review*, 2 (July 1824), p. 213). Also in 1824, William Frederick Deacon published, anonymously, *Warreniana; with Notes, Critical and Explanatory, by the Editor of a Quarterly Review*, a book which purported to contain endorsements of Warren's blacking by many leading literary figures of the day. The narrator's feeling that literature is becoming a commodity was shared by many contemporaries; in the *Athenaeum* (July 1830), Reynolds compared the publishers Colburn and Bentley with manufacturers of blacking. History was, however, repeating itself: Swift's 'Description of a City Shower' (1710) was originally published above a long list of advertisements in *The Tatler*, no. 238 (17 Oct. 1710).

13 **Macassar oil**: 'Macassar Oil, an unguent for the hair, grandiloquently advertised in the early part of the nineteenth century,

and represented by the makers (Rowland and Son) to consist of ingredients obtained from Macassar' (*OED*). See Byron's riff on the idea in *Don Juan*: 'In virtues nothing earthly could surpass her, / Save thine "incomparable oil," Macassar!' (canto 1, stanza 17; Byron, *Works*, vol. 5). Alexander Rowland the younger also became an advertising author; titles include *An Historical, Philosophical and Practical Essay on Human Hair* (1816) and *A Treatise on Human Hair* (1828). Like Warren's firm, the Rowlands made extensive use of poetic jingles in their copy.

14 **razor-strops**: 'Strips of leather or textile used for sharpening a razor' (*OED*).

15 **the reading public**: For TLP's sensitivity to this phrase, see his letter to Shelley (30 May 1818; *Letters*, 1.123). He associated it with Coleridge's remarks on the 'Reading Public' in *The Statesman's Manual* (1816) – see *Lay Sermons*, ed. R. J. White (Routledge and Kegan Paul/Princeton: Princeton University Press, 1972), pp. 36–8 and n. TLP had satirized this passage in one of Moley Mystic's speeches in *Mel*, ch. 31, and Mr Flosky twice uses the phrase '*reading public*' in *NA* (chs. 6 and 11). See also a letter to Shelley (4 Dec. 1820), where TLP lets fly: 'the poetical reading public being composed of the mere dregs of the intellectual community, the most sufficing passport to their favor must rest on the mixture of a little easily intelligible fiction & mawkish sentiment with an absolute negation of reason and knowledge' (*Letters*, 1.174). In 'The Four Ages of Poetry', 'the reading public' is 'indifferent to any thing beyond being charmed, moved, excited, affected, and exalted' (*NA*, Appendix C). In his review of Moore's *Epicurean* (1827), TLP refers to 'the most worthless, though, unhappily, not the least influential, portion of the reading public' (Halliford, 9.57).

16 **good . . . bush**: See Rosalind's closing speech in *As You Like It*: 'If it be true that good wine needs no bush, 'tis true that a good play needs no epilogue' (Epilogue, lines 3–5).

17 *ex vi oppositi*: From the opposite view.

[Footnote:] **In this ballad . . . Ballano in giro**: Ferdinando Paër (1771-1839) composed forty-two operas; *Camilla, o Il sotterraneo* was written in 1799. The second stanza translates as: 'One night, someone incautious passed through a street and suddenly heard a deafening scream: it was the ghost of his grandmother, who tweaked him by the nose. Ouf! by day or by night, let's not go through the black forest. (Dance in a circle)'.

CHAPTER 16

1 **THE NEWSPAPER**: A frequent point of reference in *CC*, and a frequent topic of discussion in journals of the period. See, for example, 'Influence of The Newspapers', *Fraser's Magazine*, vol. 4 (Sept. 1831), pp. 127–42.

2 **Ποίας . . . Pind**. *Pyth*. IX: Pindar, *Pythian* 9.33–4. The lines are spoken in Pindar by Apollo. Standing in a cave with the centaur Chiron, Apollo wonders at the fearlessness of Cyrene, a girl who hunts wild beasts and roams over the mountains (akin to 'Miss Susan, as the children called his nymph of the mountains'). Apollo decides in the end to take advantage of the nymph, and a happy marital union follows (according to Pindar's pacific version, at any rate). Cyrene's characteristics and fate are very similar to those of Nonnus' Nicaea (on Nonnus, see also chs. 2 (p. 20), 14 (p. 115), 17 (p. 136)). L'Estrange felt that TLP's translation was incorrect (cf. H. F. B. Brett-Smith, 'The L'Estrange–Peacock Correspondence', *Essays and Studies by Members of the English Association*, vol. 18 (1932), pp. 122–48 (p. 140)). L'Estrange thought the true meaning of Pindar's Greek was 'From what tribe was she [Cyrene] torn away [by bandits] to dwell in the recesses of these shadowy mountains?' He rewrote TLP's couplet, and his own version was duly printed in Cole's edition of *CC* as follows: 'Snatched from what clan has been the maid / to dwell in these cleft mountains' shade?' But L'Estrange's interpretation is by no means certain – indeed, the introduction of 'bandits' is implausible – and TLP's translation cannot be labelled

incorrect. In any case, substituting L'Estrange's translation would give a less close parallel between Pindar and *CC*, since Miss Susan has not been 'snatched away' from her family. Rather, Apollo's question correctly conveyed for TLP the incredulity of the god at finding so remarkable a girl in so unlikely a place.

3 **Giraldus de Barri**: See ch. 13 (p. 107).

4 **dragged … parting**: See Oliver Goldsmith, *The Traveller, or a Prospect of Society* (1764): 'And drags at each remove a lengthening chain' (*Collected Works of Oliver Goldsmith*, ed. Arthur Friedman, 5 vols. (Oxford: Clarendon Press, 1966), vol. 4: *The Vicar of Wakefield, Poems, The Mystery Revealed*, p. 249, line 10 and n.).

5 **nymph of the mountains**: See TLP on his 'Caernarvonshire nymph' (*Letters*, 1.52).

6 **escutcheon**: '*Heraldry*. The shield or shield-shaped surface on which a coat of arms is depicted … fig.; esp. in phrases like *a blot on an escutcheon*: a stain on a person's reputation' (*OED*). Given TLP's comedic take on Chainmail's knight-errantry, see also Miguel de Cervantes Saavedra, *The History of the renowned Don Quixote de la Mancha*, trans. Peter Motteux, 3rd edn, 4 vols. (Sam. Buckley, 1712), part 2, ch. 35.

7 **pluck … mystery**: Hamlet to Guildenstern: 'you would pluck out the heart of my mystery' (*Hamlet*, act 3, scene 2, lines 365–6).

8 **no bottom … a ballad on it**: See Bottom in *A Midsummer Night's Dream*: 'I will get Peter Quince to write a ballad of this dream: it shall be called Bottom's Dream, because it hath no bottom' (act 4, scene 1, lines 214–16).

9 **POOL … FRIAR**: According to an early holograph, this poem was originally meant to have been part of Miss Touchandgo's letter to her father (see ch. 11 (pp. 100–02), Appendix E (pp. 164–6), and Halliford, 1.cxlv). The poem was first published anonymously in the *New Monthly Magazine*, 18 (Jan. 1826), pp. 611–13, as 'Llyn-y-dreiddiad-vrawd; or, The Pool

of the Diving Friar'. See Nicholas A. Joukovsky, 'The First Printing of Peacock's "The Pool of the Diving Friar"', *Notes and Queries*, 219/New Series, 21 (1974), 334–5. On TLP's sense of the serio-comic, mock-heroic inflections of the ballad form, see, e.g., 'Is Wordsworth sleeping in peace on his bed of mud in the profundity of the Bathos, or will he ever again awake to dole out a lyrical ballad?' (*Letters*, 1.27). Later, when in love and bemoaning how long he must wait until he is reunited with the object of his affections, TLP writes that two or three weeks 'is <an> eternity in love, and, in the meantime, I must amuse myself, <as> well as I can, with making "ballads to her eye-brow"', alluding to *As You Like It* (*Letters*, 1.56).

10 **philosopher's stone**: A fabulous stone or substance capable of changing base metals to gold.

11 **Beeves, and the kine**: 'Beeves': oxen; 'kine': cows.

12 **mischief. . . man**: See Henry Fielding, *The History of the Life of the late Mr. Jonathan Wild the Great*, book 1, ch. 1: 'Greatness consists in bringing all Manner of Mischief on Mankind' (The Wesleyan Edition of the Works of Henry Fielding: *Miscellanies*, vol. 3, ed. Bertrand A. Goldgar and Hugh Amory (Oxford: Clarendon Press, 1997), p. 9.

13 **Refected**: To refect is 'To refresh (another, oneself), esp. with food or drink; to restore from weariness or fatigue. Now *rare* (*arch.* and *humorous* in later use)' (*OED*).

14 **made a duck and a drake**: The philosopher's stone skimmed across the surface of the pool (as in the game of ducks and drakes, or drake-stone, in which flat stones are made to bounce on the water and produce circles resembling those created by splashing waterfowl), but with a pun on the squandering of resources, especially money, as in the expression 'to make ducks and drakes of', 'to play (at) ducks and drakes with' (the first known use of the phrase is in John Cooke's *Greenes Tu Quoque, or The Cittie Gallant* (1614): 'This royall Caesar doth regard no cash;

/ Has thrown away as much in ducks and drakes / As would have bought some 50000 capons' (n. p.). See also *OED* 'drakestone'.

15 **dabchick**: A small waterbird noted for its diving.

16 **plummet**: 'A piece of lead or other heavy material attached to a line, used for measuring the depth of water; a sounding lead' (*OED*).

17 **ideal beauty ... flesh and blood**: See Byron, *Beppo* (1818): 'Love in full life and length, not love ideal, / No, nor ideal beauty, that fine name, / But something better still, so very real' (stanza 13, lines 97–9; Byron, *Works*, vol. 4).

18 **Chance ... you**: See Virgil, *Aeneid*, book 9, lines 6–7: 'Turne, quod optanti divum promittere nemo / auderet, volvenda dies en attulit ultro.' ('Turnus, what no god dared to promise to your prayers, see – the circling hour has brought unasked!').

19 **poker ... shield**: This scene has no direct source in *Don Quixote*, but it is indebted to mock-chivalric, mock-epic fight scenes in that work. Harry and Chainmail never come to blows; they are striking combative poses, rather than actually fighting. The scene of domestic combat skewed as comic epic is perhaps reminiscent of battles between women and between Mr and Mrs Partridge in *Tom Jones*, a novel which is itself imitating Quixote as well as Homer (*The History of Tom Jones*, ed. Battestin and Bowers, vol. 1, pp. 177–84).

20 **his outward man**: See *OED* 'man', 3.b.: '*humorous.* The inner (outer, etc.) part of a person's body.' The first citation dates from 1833: 'If he could go on dressing ... but alas! ... He could not expose, even to a poet, the humble arrangements by which his outer man was held together' (*Pearl and Literary Gazette*, 23 Nov. 1833).

21 **petrified**: i.e. hardened, immobilised, paralysed (not necessarily by fear).

22 **Cornelius Agrippa**: Heinrich Cornelius Agrippa von Nettesheim (1486–1535), a German writer whose works on

occultism – esp. *De occulta philosophia* (1533) – earned him a reputation as a sorcerer.

23 **Richard Cœur-de-Lion**: Richard I, King of England from 1189 to 1199.

24 *innamorato*: One who is in love; the lover. Cf. *Orlando innamorato* (and see epigraph to ch. 13).

25 **my own prejudices . . . personal pride**: Cf. Austen, *Pride and Prejudice* (1813). In vol. 1, ch. 5, Elizabeth remarks of Darcy that 'I could easily forgive *his* pride, if he had not mortified *mine*' (p. 21).

26 **daughter . . . to be**: Probably 'The Headsman: A Tale of Doom', *Blackwood's Edinburgh Magazine*, vol. 27 (Feb. 1830), pp. 190–216. The story was set in France and turned upon a legal requirement that an executioner's son-in-law had to take up the office if there were no sons to succeed it. '*Exécuteur des hautes œuvres*': executioner. Blackwood's had a reputation for such tales (William Godwin the Younger's 'The Executioner' appeared in the Feb. and Mar. 1832 issues); see Edgar Allan Poe in 1835 on the style of the journal's fiction: 'the ludicrous heightened into the grotesque: the fearful coloured into the horrible: the witty exaggerated into the burlesque: the singular wrought out of the strange and mystical' (*The Letters of Edgar Allan Poe*, ed. John Ward Ostrom, 2 vols. (New York: Gordian Press, 1966), vol. 1, pp. 57–8).

27 **broken promises**: See the Preface to TLP's *Paper Money Lyrics*: 'a series of paper promises, made with the deliberate purpose, that the promise shall always be a payment, and the payment shall always be a promise', and 'A Mood of My Own Mind': 'The promise is not to be kept, *that* point is very clear; / 'Twas proved so by a Scotch adept who dined with me last year' (Halliford, 7.100, 116).

CHAPTER 17

1 **leman**: 'A person beloved by one of the opposite sex; a lover or sweetheart; †*occas.* a husband or wife' (*OED*).

2 **A cup . . . *Silence***: From Silence's song in *Henry IV, Part II*, act 5, scene 3, lines 46–8. Given that this chapter returns to us food, drink and talk in Chainmail Hall, Silence's song aptly includes the line ''Tis merry in hall when beards wag'. Falstaff's response: 'Well said, Master Silence'.

3 **veridicous**: Veridical, veracious (*OED*). TLP's coinage; the *OED*'s only instances of this word are from TLP, the first from *Mel*, ch. 19: 'Our Thalia is too veridicous to permit this detortion of facts'. Cf. *ME*, ch. 16: 'the present veridicous narrative' (not cited in *OED*).

4 **Christmas-day . . . twelfth century**: The festivities at Chainmail Hall burlesque scenes in Scott's poetry: e.g. *The Lay of the Last Minstrel* (1805), where 'Knight, and page, and household squire, / Loiter'd through the lofty hall, / Or crowded round the ample fire' (*Poetical Works of Sir Walter Scott*, canto 1, stanza 2, p. 3).

5 **flagitious**: 'Of actions, character, principles, etc.: Extremely wicked or criminal: heinous, villainous' (*OED*).

6 **audit feast**: A meal provided on the day on which accounts were settled between landlord and tenants.

7 **old October**: 'A kind of strong ale traditionally brewed in October' (*OED*).

8 **Sir . . . night**: While TLP was writing *CC*, there was widespread agitation for an increase in agricultural wages. Most disturbances took place in Nov. 1830, and the agitation was marked by riots, rick burning and destruction of farm buildings and threshing machines. The events became known as the Swing Riots, or Last Labourers' Revolt. The rioters operated mainly at night, and often left threatening messages. In *Swing Unmasked*, E. G. Wakefield noted that 'A very large proportion of Swing incendiarism has been directed against the property of beneficed clergyman' (quoted in *The Tatler*, 405 (20 Dec. 1831), p. 1).

9 **policeman**: Robert Peel played a major role in setting up the London metropolitan police force in 1829.

10 **education**: Folliott's sense that 'All this comes of education' – and that 'all this' is linked to 'scientific principles' – recalls contemporary debates about education. *Blackwood's Edinburgh Magazine*, vol. 17 (May 1825), pp. 534–51, criticized Brougham's *Practical Observations upon the Education of the People, Addressed to the Working Classes and their Employers* (1825), arguing that if the labourer learned to read, he would study the radical writings 'of such people as Leigh Hunt, Cobbett, and Carlisle, Brougham, Bentham, and Bowring' (p. 540). The review also included gibes at the political economists and at 'scientific' principles (p. 534).

11 **learned friend . . . reading it**: A further allusion to Brougham's many publications for the Mechanics' Institutes. Folliott was not the first clergyman to be disturbed; see, for example, George Wright (Vicar of Askam Bryan), *Mischiefs Exposed: A Letter addressed to Henry Brougham, Esq., M.P., shewing the inutility, absurdity, and impolicy of the scheme developed in his "Practical Observations," for teaching mechanics and labourers the knowledge of chemistry, mathematics, party, and general politics* (1826).

12 **Well, Doctor . . . next week**: Brougham was returned as an MP for Yorkshire in Aug. 1830, but in Nov. the Tory government fell and Lord Grey was charged to form a Whig ministry. Brougham was considered too dangerous to be offered an irremovable post with a seat in the Commons (he coveted the mastership of the rolls), but without him the ministry would be vulnerable. Folliott's reference to a 'week' is accurate: Brougham was offered the attorney-generalship on 16 Nov. 1830, which he angrily refused. He was then offered the Lord Chancellorship, which he at first refused and then accepted on 22 Nov.

13 **Old Philosophy**: See Coleridge, *The Statesman's Manual; Or, the Bible, the Best Guide to Political Skill and Foresight: A Lay Sermon* (1816): 'But alas! the halls of old philosophy have been so long deserted, that we circle them at shy distance as the haunt of Phantoms and Chimaeras. The sacred Grove of Academus is

held in like regard with the unfoodful trees in the shadowy world of Maro that had a dream attached to every leaf. The very terms of ancient wisdom are worn out, or (far worse!) stamped on baser metal: (*e*) and whoever should have the hardihood to reproclaim its solemn Truths must commence with a Glossary' (Coleridge, *Works*, vol. 6, p. 43).

14 **pointed arches . . . twelfth century**: Pointed or ogival arches are among the defining characteristics of Gothic architecture, a style originating in twelfth-century France and persisting into the sixteenth century. Other characteristics include ribbed vaults and flying buttresses.

15 **Nonnus . . . Venus of Cnidos**: Nonnus often describes beautiful nymphs who are subsequently raped by the god Dionysus (for example, Nicaea). 'Zeuxis' was a celebrated painter of the fifth to fourth century BC. Since the context here is erotic, Folliott is probably thinking of the story of how Zeuxis, when unable to find a model beautiful enough to sit for Helen of Troy, produced a composite picture based on the best features of five women. The 'ideal nude' which resulted was much admired in antiquity. 'Antigone' is not famed for beauty. However, she was a woman of impressive moral character (see Sophocles, *Oedipus at Colonus*; *Antigone*), hence a good comparison for Miss Susan's 'virtue and intelligence'; 'plump and symmetrical': on Susannah's plumpness, see ch. 14 (p. 115). On 'Venus of Cnidos', cf. the figures of Venus in ch. 7 (pp. 67–74). Susannah is described as possessing 'one of the most symmetrical of figures' in ch. 13 (p. 109). The combined effect of Folliott's allusions is to emphasise that Miss Susan is the ideal woman: nubile (although she may not know it), physically beautiful and remarkable for her mental faculties.

16 παρθένος . . . **Nonnus sweetly sings**: The Greek cited in the text is not a precise quotation from Nonnus, but it is a perfectly metrical hexameter line. TLP seems to have produced παρθένος οὐρεσίφοιτος ἐρημάδι σύντροφος ὕλῃ by conflating two

lines, namely *Dionysiaca*, 15.169–70: ἔνθά τις ἀγκυλότοξος, *ἐρημάδι σύννομος ὕλῃ, /παρθένος Ἀστακίδεσσιν ὁμότροφος ἤνθεε Νύμφαις*... ('There was one with a crook-bow, a maiden denizen of the lonely wood, comrade hale of fresh among the nymphs...' (tr. W. H. D. Rouse)).

CHAPTER 18 AND CONCLUSION

1 **Vous... RABELAIS, l. 5. c. 7.**: Rabelais, *Le Cinquiesme et dernier livre des faicts et dicts heroïques du bon Pantagruel*, ch. 7 (slightly adapted or misquoted). 'You Men of t'other World say that Ignorance is the Mother of all evil, and so far you are right; yet for all that, you do not take the least Care to get rid of it, but still plod on, and live in it, with it, and by it; for which Cause a plaguy deal of mischief lights on you every Day' (Ozell, vol. 5, pp. 22–3). The words are spoken by Aedituus to the company that has just eaten and drunk huge quantities in 'a Chamber that was well furnish'd, hung with Tapestry, and finely gilt' (p. 22). One implication of the epigraph to this chapter is that *CC*'s roisterers in Chainmail Hall are being asked to take stock of their actions and responsibilities.

2 **cressets**: A 'cresset' is 'A vessel of iron or the like, made to hold grease or oil, or an iron basket to hold pitched rope, wood, or coal, to be burnt for light; usually mounted on the top of a pole or building, or suspended from a roof. Frequent as a historical word' (*OED*).

3 **fire... high festival**: The layout of the room signals both hierarchy and comingling, and is reminiscent of many scenes in Scott; see e.g. vol. 1, ch. 4 of *The Monastery* (1820): 'The idea of the master and mistress of the mansion feeding or living apart from their domestics, was at this period never entertained. The highest end of the board, the most commodious settle by the fire, – these were their only marks of distinction' (Scott, Edinburgh Edition, vol. 9: *The Monastery*, ed. Penny Fielding (2000), p. 50).

4 *rayonnante de joie et d'amour*: Beaming with happiness and love.

5 **your friend** . . . **Vaux**: 'Brougham's vanity impelled him to take the title of Lord Brougham and Vaux, after a barony in fee to which his family claimed descent. This title was a godsend to the wits, who quipped that he should have been dubbed "vaux et praeterea nihil"' (*ODNB*); that is, 'a voice and nothing else'. Brougham was sworn in as Chancellor on 25 Nov. 1830. 'Guy' may allude to Guy Fawkes, whose name conjures up recollections of conspiracy, anarchy and civil discord.

6 **Thank** . . . **delusion**: At this point in the text, in 1837, TLP inserted as a footnote his lines 'THE FATE OF A BROOM: AN ANTIC- IPATION' (see Appendix G, pp. 170–1). As a peer, Brougham had to give up his membership of the House of Commons for a seat in the Lords. Folliott may be implying that Brougham's reformist zeal will therefore be smothered by the strongly anti-reform leanings of the Upper House. But, as his subsequent comments make clear, he may also be sceptical about Brougham's reformist credentials themselves. Similar points had been made for many years by other liberal writers; e.g. Byron, in some draft stanzas of *Don Juan*, where Brougham was described as 'Tory by nurture, Whig by Circumstance, / A Democrat some once or twice a year / Wheneer it suits his purpose' (Byron, *Works*, vol. 5, p. 86).

7 **vested interests**: A pun on 'vested' in the sense of 'Clothed, robed, dressed, spec. in ecclesiastical vestments' and 'Established, secured, or settled in the hands of, or definitely assigned to, a certain possessor' (*OED*).

8 **vaticinate**: 'To foretell, predict, prognosticate, or prophesy' (*OED*).

9 **speech** . . . **duration**: Brougham had a reputation for momentous (and prolix) speeches. Most recently, on 7 Feb. 1828 he delivered a speech lasting six hours (the longest ever in the Commons at that time) on law reform. In 1820, he had given

a speech in the Lords lasting two days in defence of Princess Caroline.

10 **putting salt on the bird's tail**: Proverbially, a bird can be caught if you put salt on its tail. The 'exceeding difficulty' lies in getting close enough to any bird to establish the truth of this claim.

11 **Aristophanes**: TLP admired the Old Comedy, Aristophanes in particular, as 'the most wonderful combination the world has ever seen of splendid imagery, exquisite versification, wit, humour, and moral and political satire' (Review of K. O. Müller and J. W. Donaldson's *A History of the Literature of Ancient Greece*, Halliford, 10.201). Comedy and socio-political critique were, for TLP, intimate allies: 'The Old Comedy thus became a mighty instrument of moral and political censure, and the satiric rod was wielded most effectively by Cratinus, Eupolis, and Aristophanes, whom both Horace and Persius cite as their three great precursors in the poetical denunciation of rascals ... they exercised, during about sixty-four years, a very salutary control over profligates and demagogues' (*Horæ Dramaticæ*, Halliford, 10.76–7). Cf. Shelley's *Oedipus Tyrannus; or, Swellfoot the Tyrant*, a 'political satirical drama on the circumstances of the day', which Aristophanes' *Frogs* helped to inspire, as Mary Shelley pointed out in her note on the work (*The Poetical Works of Percy Bysshe Shelley*, ed. Mary Shelley (Edward Moxon, 1939), p. 191). Shelley's play also features a Green Bag (see below, n. 29) and takes issue with paper money and Malthus's theories.

12 **All the rest ... Nephelococcygia**: TLP refers to Aristophanes' *Birds* ("Ορνιθες in Greek) which contains many onomatopoeic words such as those he quotes. For Τπτιττιμπρό, cf. *Birds*, 314; for ποποποί, ποποποί, 227 for Τιοτιοτιοτιοτιοτιοτίγξ, 738; for Κικκαβαῦ, κικκαβαῦ Τοροτοροτοροτορολιλιλίγξ, 261–2. As is to be expected with such words, the MSS of Aristophanes vary considerably in the forms they give; see the critical apparatus and notes in Nan Dunbar, *Aristophanes: Birds* (Oxford: Clarendon Press, 1995). TLP in his footnote makes the humorous

point that the sounds are 'meaningless', i.e. the Peer's seven-hour speech will be futile. 'Nephelococcygia' is the name given by Aristophanes to the birds' city, which is far removed from the troubles and stresses of the world; 'clouds . . . suggested to Greeks ideas of "unsubstantial", "empty", "deceptive", and cuckoos were thought of as foolish' (Dunbar, *Birds*, p. 5).

13 **day . . . view**: Folliott is punning on 'accounts' and 'reckoning', and again employing 'science' in a pejorative sense.

14 **bill of fare**: Cf. 'The Introduction to the Work, or Bill of Fare to the Feast' (book 1, ch. 1) that prefaces *Tom Jones* (vol. 1, p. 31).

15 **led the van**: To lead the van: 'To occupy the foremost portion of, or the foremost position in, a company or train of people or things moving, or prepared to move, forwards or onwards' (*OED*). The word 'van' has martial and therefore (in this context) mock-epic associations.

16 **tureens**: 'Deep earthenware or plated vessels (usually oval) with a lid' (*OED*).

17 **baron of beef . . . up the rear**: '*Baron of Beef* is when the two sirloins are not cut asunder, but joined together by the end of the backbone' (Johnson's *Dictionary*); there may be a cheeky pun on 'rear'. Cf. also William Kitchiner, *The Cook's Oracle*, 4th edn (1822): 'The Baron of Beef was another favorite and substantial support of Old English Hospitality' (Introduction).

18 **ample indemnity**: Rich compensation for any loss (*OED*).

19 **clamor without**: The immediate reference is to the Captain Swing rioters; as Marilyn Butler points out, 'Christmas at Chain-mail Hall is the actual Christmas that the first readers of the book had just experienced' (Butler, *Peacock*, p. 213). More generally, the rise in extra-parliamentary agitation (or, as it was called, 'pressure from without') was a notable feature of the post-Waterloo years. During the period in which TLP was writing *CC*, the Birmingham Political Union was founded (25 Jan. 1830); over 100 similar groups were formed before 1832 in order to agitate for the reform bill (by early 1831, *The Times* noted that 'The

reform meetings throughout England begin to be almost too numerous for us to notice' (3 Feb. 1831)). The National Association for the Protection of Labour was founded in 1829, and in June 1830 a huge meeting of trade unionists took place. On 'clamor', cf. TLP's comment a few years later to a parliamentary select committee: 'I am more afraid of deference to popular clamour than I am of anything under the sun' (*Report from the Select Committee on Steam Communication with India*), p. 56.

20 **Mummers**: 'Mummers' play': 'A traditional play of a type performed by mummers esp. at the major holidays and popular in England from the 18th cent. These plays were typically performed in private houses by visiting groups of mummers, often masked or wearing other disguises. Different types of play were associated with different festivals (e.g. the "pace egg play" at Easter); 18th-century examples include "Alexander and the King of Egypt" and "George and the Dragon", etc. The term *mummer's play* appears to be the invention of 19th-cent. folklorists' (*OED*).

21 **Stentor**: A herald in Homer's *Iliad*, famous for his loud voice.

22 **Captain Swing**: The fictitious perpetrator of rioting against farmers and farming machinery in 1830. See ch. 17 (p. 133) and n. 8 (p. 303).

23 **Jacquerie**: A bloody uprising by French peasants in 1358; the name derives from 'Jacques Bonhomme', the nickname for a peasant. Given that the Swing Riots originated in East Kent just one month after the French Revolution of 1830, and coincided with a Belgian revolt against Dutch rule, there were also fears that the disturbances might be linked to foreign developments.

24 **disparates together**: Possibly an allusion to Coleridge's renowned formulation about the action of the poetic imagination in ch. 14 of *Biographia Literaria*, where the poet's power 'reveals itself in the balance or reconciliation of opposite or discordant qualities' (Coleridge, *Works*, vol. 7, 2.16).

25 Πολλῶν... μία: Aeschylus, *Prometheus Bound*, 212 (with Shelley's phrasing in TLP's footnote; see also *NA* ch. 11, n. 23). The reference in the original is to Gaia (goddess of earth), but Folliott seems to be using the quotation as no more than a handy tag. TLP apparently had *Prometheus Bound* by 1812 (see *Letters*, 1.93).

26 **poverty in despair**: The 1820s witnessed growing concerns about the plight of the poor. Ricardo's labour theory of value was used to attack the system he celebrated; see esp. Thomas Hodgskin, *Labour Defended against the Claims of Capital* (Knight and Lacey et al., 1825): '[Ricardo's] theory confirms... that the exactions of the capitalist cause the poverty of the labourer' (p. 24).

27 **state seamanship... mutiny on board**: The metaphor reaches back to Plato's 'ship of state' in book 4 of *The Republic*. Given that Hodgskin was himself one of many middle-ranking naval officers who had become expendable since the end of the Napoleonic Wars, the metaphor may again be bringing to mind his work as a radical reformer and 'mutineer' of sorts.

28 **arms**: Calls to (as well as for) arms had become a rhetorical feature of the extra-parliamentary pressure groups. The radical MP Joseph Hume had even intimated a future 'call to arms' in the House of Commons, and another MP, Charles D'Eyncourt, observed that 'Public opinion would soon prevail over the decision of Parliament, and while he trusted that the Government would not precipitate the people into extreme measures, he confidently hoped that the people had too much good sense to precipitate themselves into anything like violence' (*The Times* (4 Nov. 1830), p. 1d.).

29 **green bags**: Formerly used by lawyers for papers.

30 **blunderbuss**: 'A short gun with a large bore, firing many balls or slugs, and capable of doing execution within a limited range without exact aim' (*OED*). Cf. Appendix D (p. 159).

31 **Let me . . . away**: Coleridge had secured a reputation as both
a brilliant and perplexing talker; TLP makes fun of this elsewhere (most memorably in *Mel* and *NA*). Madame de Staël said:
'[Coleridge] is very great in monologue, but he has no idea of
dialogue'; Carlyle noted: 'I have heard Coleridge talk, with eager
musical energy, two stricken hours, his face radiant and moist,
and communicate no meaning whatsoever to any individual of his
hearers'; Samuel Rogers recalled: 'He talked uninterruptedly for
about two hours, during which Wordsworth listened to him with
profound attention, every now and then nodding his head as if
in assent. On quitting the lodging, I said to Wordsworth, "Well,
for my own part, I could not make head or tail of Coleridge's
oration: pray, did you understand it?" "Not one syllable of it",
was Wordsworth's reply' (see Seamus Perry, ed., *Samuel Taylor Coleridge: Interviews and Recollections* (Basingstoke: Palgrave,
2001), pp. 148, 237–8, 225).

32 **when . . . fray**: Falstaff: 'To the latter end of a fray and the beginning of a feast / Fits a dull fighter and a keen guest', *Henry IV
Part I*, act 4, scene 2, lines 79–80.

33 ***Pessimo . . . exemplo***: Petronius, *Satyricon*, 104: 'On the ship,
Encolpius and Giton were shaved and branded to look as if
they were Eumolpus' slaves in order to go undetected, but a sea-
sick man watches them being shaved. When the captain, Lichas,
worries that Tryphaena's dream might mean harm to the ship,
the sea-sick man shouts: "Then who are those fellows who were
being shaved in the dark by moonlight? A mighty bad precedent,
I swear. I am told that no man alive ought to shed a nail or a hair
on board ship . . .".'

34 ***Frere Jean des Entommeures***: See ch. 8 (p. 77) and n. 17 (p. 261).

35 **church militant**: Cf. use of this phrase in *NA*, ch. 1; *MM*, chs.
6, 9, 17; *ME*, ch. 13.

36 ***Pro aris et focis!***: Lit. 'For our altars and hearths!' Normally this
has a wider application, 'For God and our home', but Fol-
liott intends it in its literal sense, as shown by his subsequent

remark about pigs to be sacrificed on altars and fires to roast them.

37 **tilted out on the rabble**: Reminiscent of Don Quixote tilting at windmills, see *The History of the renowned Don Quixote*, vol. 1, part 1, book 1, ch. 8.

38 *hors de combat*: Beyond fighting.

39 **devil**: 'A name for various highly seasoned broiled or fried dishes; also for hot ingredients' (*OED* 'devil', 9), such as 'a turkey's leg and rump, well devilled', mentioned by Folliott below.

40 **wassail-bowl**: 'A large bowl or cup in which wassail (the liquor in which healths were drunk; esp. the spiced ale used in Twelfth-night and Christmas-eve celebrations) was made and from which healths were drunk; a loving-cup; also the liquor contained in the bowl' (*OED*).

41 **arrack punch**: Home-brewed mixed punch.

42 **accinged**: 'To accinge': '*trans.* (*refl.*). To put (oneself) in a state of preparedness; to prepare or apply (oneself)' (*OED*).

43 **excubant**: 'Keeping watch' (*OED*). This is the only instance of the word in the *OED*.

[Footnote:] **Imitated from the Fabliau, De Florance et de Blanche Flor. . . Jugement d'Amour**: Strictly speaking, a metrical romance rather than a fabliau; the English version was adapted from the French into rhymed couplets in the thirteenth century. TLP's is a very free imitation indeed; in all French, German, Scandinavian, Italian and Spanish versions Florance and Blanche Flor are lovers, Florance engaging in many knightly feats.

[Footnote:] **Imitated from the Fabliau, Du Provoire qui mengea des Môres**: Another thirteenth-century French work, 'The priest who ate the mulberries'; more commonly known as 'Le Prêtre qui mangea les mûres'. TLP's imitation stays fairly close to the original tale.

44 **guerdon**: 'A reward, requital, or recompense' (*OED*).

45 **CONCLUSION**: *CC* is the only one of TLP's fictions to end with a separate 'Conclusion' which is not accorded a chapter number; were it not for that Conclusion, *CC* would end (like *NA*) with a drinking scene and a punch-bowl. Given some of the questions it leaves unanswered, TLP may also have had in mind Samuel Johnson's 'conclusion, in which nothing is concluded' at the end of *Rasselas* (1759). See the Yale Edition of the Works of Samuel Johnson, ed. John H. Middendorf et al., 23 vols. (New Haven, CT and London: Yale University Press, 1958–2012), vol. 16: *Rasselas and Other Tales*, ed. Gwin J. Kolb (1990), p. 175.

46 **English mould**: Mould: 'earth... surface soil' (*OED*).

47 **King... Camlan**: According to the *Annales Cambriae*, The Battle of Camlann (Welsh: *Cad Camlan*) in 539 is reputed to have been the one 'in which Arthur and Medruat fell'. In some accounts, though, Arthur was taken to the Isle of Avalon to be healed, and what happened to him after reaching the island is a mystery. Some sources claim that he lies in a cave awaiting the day he is needed by his country. This version of the story appears in the Black Book of Carmarthen of the mid to late ninth century and may well represent much older traditions. The notion of Arthur's future return was widespread by the twelfth century, and was recorded in Breton, Welsh and Cornish folklore.

48 **barbel-pool in the Thames**: 'Barbel': 'A large European freshwater fish (*Barbus vulgaris*) of the Carp tribe, deriving its name from the fleshy filaments which hang from its mouth' (*OED*).

49 **Lady Clarinda... rotten borough**: On the 'fortune', see TLP's own letter of proposal to Jane Gryffydh (20 Nov. 1819): 'your value is beyond fortune, of which I want no more than I have' (*Letters*, 1.169). On the 'gratitude' for what she feels she 'scarcely deserved', see Jane's reply: 'I could not flatter myself that *your* Sentiments warranted such a remembrance

on my part – which knowledge as well as every expression of generosity your very handsome Epistle contains claims my highest Gratitude. I fear you *very* much over-rate my worth' (*Letters*, 1.170). See also Shelley's letter to TLP on learning of the marriage: 'I was very much amused by your laconic account of the affair. It is altogether extremely like the *denouement* of one of your own novels' (*The Letters of Percy Bysshe Shelley*, vol. 2, p. 192).

SELECT BIBLIOGRAPHY

Place of publication, unless otherwise stated, is London.

PRIMARY SOURCES

Anon., *A Sequel to the Adventures of Baron Munchausen*, 2 vols. (H. D. Symonds and J. Owen, 1972)

Aristophanes, *Birds*, ed. Nan Dunbar (Oxford: Clarendon Press, 1995)

Arnold, Matthew, *The Popular Education of France, with Notices of that of Holland and Switzerland* (Longman, Green, etc., 1861)

Austen, Jane, The Cambridge Edition of the Works of Jane Austen, ed. Janet Todd et al., 9 vols. (Cambridge: Cambridge University Press, 2005–8)

Northanger Abbey, ed. Barbara M. Benedict and Deirdre Le Faye (2006); *Pride and Prejudice*, ed. Pat Rogers (2006); *Sense and Sensibility*, ed. Edward Copeland (2006), *Later Manuscripts*, ed. Janet Todd and Linda Bree (2008).

Jane Austen's Letters, ed. Deirdre Le Faye, 3rd edn (Oxford and New York: Oxford University Press, 1995)

Birkbeck, Morris, *Notes on a Journey in America, from the Coast of Virginia to the Territory of Illinois*, 3rd edn (James Ridgway, 1818)

Boswell, James, *Boswell's Life of Johnson, together with Boswell's Journal of a Tour to the Hebrides and Johnson's Diary of a Journey into North Wales*, ed. George Birkbeck Hill, rev. L. F. Powell, 6 vols. (Oxford: Clarendon Press, 1934–50), vol. 4: *The Life (1780–1784)* (1934)

Britton, John, and Edward Wedlake Brayley, *Devonshire and Cornwall Illustrated, from Original Drawings* (H. Fisher, R. Fisher, and P. Jackson, 1832)

Bunyan, John, *Grace Abounding to the Chief of Sinners and The Pilgrim's Progress from this World to that which is to come*, ed. Roger Sharrock (Oxford University Press, 1966)

Burke, Edmund, *The Writings and Speeches of Edmund Burke*, gen. ed. Paul Langford, 9 vols. (Oxford: Clarendon Press/ New York: Oxford University Press, 1981–), vol. 1: *The Early Writings*, ed. T. O. McLoughlin and James T. Boulton (1997); vol. 8: *The French Revolution 1790–1794*, ed. L. G. Mitchell (Oxford: Clarendon Press, 1989)

Burton, Robert, *The Anatomy of Melancholy*, ed. Thomas C. Faulkner et al., 6 vols. (Oxford: Clarendon Press, 1989–2000)

Butler, Samuel, *The Genuine Remains in Verse and Prose of Mr. Samuel Butler*, ed. R. Thyer, 2 vols. (J. and R. Tonson, 1759)

Hudibras, ed. John Wilders (Oxford: Clarendon Press, 1967)

Byron, Lord George Gordon, *Byron's Letters and Journals*, ed. Leslie A. Marchand, 12 vols. (John Murray, 1973–94)

Complete Miscellaneous Prose, ed. Andrew Nicholson (Oxford: Clarendon Press, 1991)

The Complete Poetical Works, ed. Jerome McGann, 7 vols. (Oxford: Clarendon Press, 1980–93)

Carlyle, Thomas, *Sartor Resartus*, ed. Mark Engel and Rodger L. Tarr (Berkeley, Los Angeles, and London: University of California Press, 2000)

Catalogue of the Library of the Late Thos. Love Peacock, Esq. . . . which will be Sold by Auction, by Messrs. Sotheby, Wilkinson & Hodge . . . On Monday, the 11th of June, 1866, and following Day, reprinted in *Sale Catalogues of Libraries of Eminent Persons*, gen. ed. A. N. L. Munby, 12 vols. (Mansell, with Sotheby Parke-Bernet, 1971–5), vol. 1: *Poets and Men of Letters*, ed. A. N. L. Munby (Mansell, with Sotheby Parke-Bernet, 1971), pp. 153–201

Cervantes Saavedra, Miguel de, *The History of the renowned Don Quixote de la Mancha*, trans. Peter Motteux, 3rd edn, 4 vols. (Sam. Buckley, 1712)

Chambers, Ephraim, *Cyclopædia: or, an Universal Dictionary of Arts and Sciences*, 2 vols. (James and John Knapton, John Darby, Daniel Midwinter, et al., 1728)

Chesney, Louisa, and Jane O'Donnell, *The Life of the Late General F. R. Chesney, By his Wife and Daughter*, ed. Stanley Lane-Poole, 2nd edn (London and Sydney: Eden, Remington and Co, 1893)

Coleridge, Samuel Taylor, *Collected Letters of Samuel Taylor Coleridge*, ed. Earl Leslie Griggs, 6 vols. (Oxford: Clarendon Press, 1956–71; repr. 2000)

The Collected Works of Samuel Taylor Coleridge, gen. ed. Kathleen Coburn, 34 vols. (London: Routledge and Kegan Paul; Princeton: Princeton University Press, 1969–2002), vol. 4: *The Friend*, ed. Barbara E. Rooke, 2 vols. (1969); vol. 6: *Lay Sermons*, ed. R. J. White (1972); vol. 7: *Biographia Literaria, or Biographical Sketches of My Literary Life and Opinions*, ed. James Engell and W. Jackson Bate, 2 vols. (1983); vol. 16: *Poetical Works*, ed. J. C. C. Mays, 6 vols. (2001)

Cooke, John, *Greenes Tu Quoque, or The Cittie Gallant* (John Trundle, 1614)

Cooper, James Fenimore, *A Residence in France, with an Excursion up the Rhine, and a Second Visit to Switzerland*, 2 vols. (Richard Bentley, 1836)

Dickens, Charles, *A Christmas Carol and Other Christmas Books*, ed. Robert Douglas-Fairhurst, Oxford World's Classics (Oxford: Oxford University Press, 2006)

The Pickwick Papers, ed. James Kinsley (Oxford: Clarendon Press, 1986)

Disraeli, Benjamin, *Vivian Grey*, 2 vols. (Henry Colburn, 1826–7)

Dryden, John, *The Works of John Dryden*, 20 vols., gen. eds. E. N. Hooker, H. T. Swedenberg, Jr, and Alan Roper (Berkeley and Los Angeles: University of California Press, 1956–2000): vol. 3: *Poems, 1685–1692*, ed. Earl Miner and Vinton A. Dearing (1969)

Duff, E. Grant, *Notes from a Diary, 1851–1871* (John Murray, 1897)

Edgeworth, Maria, *Letters from England, 1813–1844*, ed. Christina
Colvin (Oxford: Clarendon Press, 1971)

Fielding, Henry, The Wesleyan Edition of the Works of Henry
Fielding, 15 vols. in 16, executive ed. W. B. Coley (Oxford:
Clarendon Press, 1967–2011), *The History of Tom Jones, A
Foundling*, ed. Martin C. Battestin and Fredson Bowers,
2 vols. (1974); *Miscellanies*, vol. 3, ed. Bertrand A. Goldgar
and Hugh Amory (1997)

Gay, John, *Dramatic Works*, ed. John Fuller, 2 vols. (Oxford:
Clarendon Press, 1983)

Goldsmith, Oliver, *Collected Works of Oliver Goldsmith*, ed. Arthur
Friedman, 5 vols. (Oxford: Clarendon Press, 1966), vol. 4:
The Vicar of Wakefield, Poems, The Mystery Revealed (Oxford:
Oxford University Press, 1946)

Hazlitt, William, *The Complete Works of William Hazlitt*, ed. P. P.
Howe, 21 vols. (London and Toronto: J. M. Dent and Sons,
1930–4)

Lectures on the English Comic Writers (Taylor and Hessey, 1819)

*Select British Poets, or New Elegant Extracts from Chaucer to the
Present Time* (William C. Hall, 1824)

Hazlitt, William, and Leigh Hunt, *The Round Table: A Collection
of Essays*, 2 vols. (Edinburgh: Archibald Constable and
Co.; London: Longman, Hurst, Rees, Orme and Brown,
1817)

[Hodgskin, Thomas], *Labour Defended against the Claims of
Capital; or, the Unproductiveness of Capital Proved*, 2nd edn
(Knight and Lacey et al., 1825)

Hogarth, William, *The Analysis of Beauty*, ed. Ronald Paulson
(New Haven, CT: Yale University Press, 1997)

Homer, *Homeri Hymni et Epigrammata*, ed. Gottfried Hermann
(Leipzig: Weidmann, 1806)

Hunt, Leigh, *The Poetical Works of Leigh Hunt*, ed. H. S. Milford
(Oxford University Press, 1923)

Johnson, Samuel, *A Dictionary of the English Language: in which the
words are deduced from their originals, and illustrated in their
different significations by examples from the best writers*, 2 vols.

(J. and P. Knapton, T. and T. Longman, C. Hitch,
  L. Hawes, et al., 1755)
*The Lives of the Most Eminent English Poets; with Critical
  Observations on their Works*, ed. Roger Lonsdale, 4 vols.
  (Oxford: Clarendon Press, 2006)
The Yale Edition of the Works of Samuel Johnson, ed. John H.
  Middendorf et al., 23 vols. (New Haven, CT, and London:
  Yale University Press, 1958–2012), vol. 16: *Rasselas and Other
  Tales*, ed. Gwin J. Kolb (1990)
Keats, John, *The Poems of John Keats*, ed. Jack Stillinger
  (Cambridge, MA: Harvard University Press, 1978)
Kitchiner, William, *The Cook's Oracle; containing receipts for plain
  cookery on the most economical plan for private families*,
  4th edn (A. Constable & Co., Hurst, Robinson, & Co.,
  1822)
Knight, Charles, *The Supplement to the Penny Cyclopædia of the
  Society for the Diffusion of Useful Knowledge*, 2 vols. (Charles
  Knight, 1845–6)
*Lexicon Balatronicum: A Dictionary of Buckish Slang, University
  Wit, and Pickpocket Eloquence. Compiled originally by Captain
  Grose. Altered and enlarged... by a member of the Whip Club*
  (C. Chappel, 1811)
McCulloch, J. R., *The Principles of Political Economy: With a Sketch
  of the Rise and Progress of the Science* (Edinburgh: William and
  Charles Tait, 1825)
Menander, *Reliquiae*, vol. 2, ed. Alfred Körte and Andreas
  Thierfelder, rev. edn (Leipzig: Teubner, 1959)
Mill, James, *Elements of Political Economy* (Baldwin, Cradock and
  Joy, 1821)
Political Writings, ed. Terence Ball (Cambridge: Cambridge
  University Press, 1992)
Mill, John Stuart, *Collected Works of John Stuart Mill*, gen.
  ed. John M. Robson, 33 vols. (Toronto and Buffalo:
  University of Toronto Press; Routledge, 1963–91), vol. 26:
  Journals and Debating Speeches, Part I, ed. John M. Robson
  (1988)

Milton, John, *The Complete Shorter Poems*, ed. John Carey, rev. 2nd
    edn, Longman Annotated English Poets (Harlow:
    Pearson/Longman, 2007)
    Paradise Lost, ed. Alastair Fowler, rev. 2nd edn, Longman
    Annotated English Poets (Harlow: Pearson/Longman,
    2007)
Newman, John Henry, *Loss and Gain* (James Burns, 1848)
Peacock, Thomas Love, *Calidore and Miscellanea*, ed. Richard
    Garnett (J. M. Dent, 1891)
    Crotchet Castle, ed. Richard Garnett (J. M. Dent, 1891)
    Crotchet Castle, ed. Henry Morley (Cassell, 1887)
    The Letters of Thomas Love Peacock, ed. Nicholas A. Joukovsky,
    2 vols. (Oxford: Clarendon Press, 2001)
    'Llyn-y-dreiddiad-vrawd; or, The Pool of the Diving Friar', *New
    Monthly Magazine*, 18 (Jan. 1826), 611–13
    Maid Marian and *Crotchet Castle*, introd. George Saintsbury
    (Macmillan, 1955)
    The Misfortunes of Elphin and Crotchet Castle, introd. R. W.
    Chapman (London, Edinburgh, Glasgow: Humphrey
    Milford/Oxford University Press, 1924)
    Nightmare Abbey/Crotchet Castle, ed. Raymond Wright
    (Harmondsworth: Penguin, 1969)
    Nightmare Abbey. The Misfortunes of Elphin. Crotchet Castle, ed.
    Charles B. Dodson (New York: Holt, Rinehart, and
    Winston, 1971)
    The Novels of Thomas Love Peacock, ed. David Garnett
    (Hart-Davis, 1948; 2nd impression corrected in 2 vols., 1963)
    Prose Works of Peacock, ed. Richard Garnett, 10 vols. (J. M. Dent,
    1891)
    'Recollections of Childhood. By the Author of *Headlong Hall*',
    Bentley's Miscellany (1837), 187–90
    *The Works of Thomas Love Peacock, Including his Novels, Poems,
    Fugitive Pieces, Criticisms, etc., with a Preface by the Right Hon.
    Lord Houghton, a Biographical Notice by his Granddaughter,
    Edith Nicholls, and a Portrait*, ed. Henry Cole, 3 vols.
    (Richard Bentley and Son, 1875)

The Works of Thomas Love Peacock (Halliford Edition), ed. H. F. B. Brett-Smith and C. E. Jones, 10 vols. (Constable, 1924–34)

Pegge, Samuel, *Anecdotes of the English Language: Chiefly Regarding the Local Dialect of London and its Environs*, 2nd corr. edn (J. Nichols, Son, and Bentley, 1814)

Percy, Thomas, *Bishop Percy's Folio Manuscript*, ed. John W. Hales and Frederick J. Furnivall, 3 vols. (N. Trübner and Co. 1867–8)

[Petit, Louis], *Discours satyriques et moraux, ou Satyres générales* (Rouen: Richard Lallemant, 1686)

Le nouveau Juvénal satyrique, pour la réformation des moeurs et des abus de notre siècle (Utrecht: A. Schouten, 1716)

Poe, Edgar Allan, *The Letters of Edgar Allan Poe*, ed. John Ward Ostrom, 2 vols. (New York: Gordian Press, 1966)

Pope, Alexander, The Twickenham Edition of the Poems of Alexander Pope, ed. John Butt et al., 11 vols. (London: Methuen; New Haven, CT: Yale University Press, 1939–69), vol. 2: *The Rape of the Lock and Other Poems*, ed. Geoffrey Tillotson, 3rd edn, reset (1962); vol. 3 (2 parts): *Epistles to Several Persons (Moral Essays)*, ed. F. W. Bateson (1951); vol. 4: *Imitations of Horace, with An Epistle to Dr Arbuthnot and The Epilogue to the Satires*, ed. John Butt, 2nd edn (1951); vol. 5: *The Dunciad*, ed. James Sutherland, 3rd edn, revised (1963)

Rabelais, François, *Œuvres complètes*, ed. Mireille Huchon, with François Moreau, Bibliothèque de la Pléiade, new edn (Paris: Gallimard, 1994)

The Works of Francis Rabelais, M.D. . . . Now carefully revis'd, ed. John Ozell [revision of Urquhart-Motteux translation], 5 vols. (J. Brindley and C. Corbett, 1737)

Radcliffe, Ann, *The Italian, or the Confessional of the Black Penitents: A Romance*, ed. Frederick Garber with E. J. Clery, Oxford World's Classics (Oxford: Oxford University Press, 1998)

The Mysteries of Udolpho, ed. Bonamy Dobrée with Terry Castle, Oxford World's Classics (Oxford: Oxford University Press, 1998)

A Sicilian Romance, ed. Alison Milbank (Oxford: Oxford University Press, 1998)

Railroadiana: A New History of England: or, Picturesque, biographical, historical, legendary and antiquarian sketches descriptive of the vicinity of the railroads: first series, London and Birmingham Railway (Simpkin, Marshall and Co., 1838)

Reid, W. Hamilton, *Memoirs of the Public Life of John Horne Tooke, Esq.* (Sherwood, Neely and Jones, 1812)

Report from the Select Committee on Steam Communication with India: together with the Minutes of Evidence, Appendix and Index (House of Commons, 1837)

Report from the Select Committee on Steam Navigation to India; with the Minutes of Evidence, Appendix and Index (House of Commons, 1834)

Ricardo, David, *The Works and Correspondence of David Ricardo*, ed. Piero Sraffa, with the collaboration of M. H. Dobb, 11 vols. (Cambridge: Cambridge University Press for the Royal Economic Society, 1951–73), vol. 8: *Letters 1819 – June 1821* (Cambridge: Cambridge University Press for the Royal Economic Society, 1952); vol. 9: *Letters July 1821–1823* (Cambridge: Cambridge University Press for the Royal Economic Society, 1952)

Ritson, Joseph, *Ancient Engleish Metrical Romanceës*, 3 vols. (G. and W. Nicol, 1802)

Rousseau, Jean-Jacques, *Œuvres complètes*, ed. Bernard Gagnebin and Marcel Raymond et al., Bibliothèque de la Pléiade, 5 vols. (Paris: Gallimard [Pléiade], 1959–1995), vol. 1: *Les confessions/Autres textes autobiographiques*, ed. Bernard Gagnebin, Marcel Raymond and Robert Osmont (1959)

Schlegel, Friedrich, *Kritische Friedrich-Schlegel-Ausgabe*, gen. ed. Ernst Behler (Paderborn: Ferdinand Schöningh, 1958–),

vol. 2: *Charakteristiken und Kritiken I (1796–1801)*, ed. Hans
Eichner (Paderborn: Ferdinand Schöningh, 1967)
Scott, Walter, The Edinburgh Edition of the Waverley Novels, ed.
David Hewitt et al., 30 vols. (Edinburgh: Edinburgh
University Press, 1993–), vol. 3: *The Antiquary*, ed. David
Hewitt (1995); vol. 9: *The Monastery*, ed. Penny Fielding
(2000); vol. 25a: *Introductions and Notes from the Magnum
Opus: Waverley to A Legend of the Wars of Montrose*, ed. J. H.
Alexander, with P. D. Garside and Claire Lamont (2012)
The Letters of Sir Walter Scott, ed. H. J. C. Grierson, assisted by
Davidson Cook, W. M. Parker et al., 12 vols., Centenary
Edition (London and Toronto: Constable, and Macmillan,
1932–7)
The Poetical Works of Sir Walter Scott, ed. J. Logie Robertson
(London, New York, Toronto: Oxford University Press,
1904)
Shaftesbury, Anthony Ashley Cooper, Third Earl of,
Characteristicks of Men, Manners, Opinions, Times, ed. Philip
Ayres, 2 vols. (Oxford: Clarendon Press, 1999)
Shakespeare, William, *The Plays of William Shakespeare; in
twenty-one volumes, with the corrections and illustrations of
various commentators, to which are added notes by Samuel
Johnson and George Steevens, revised and augmented by Isaac
Reed with a Glossarial Index*, 6th edn (J. Nichols and Sons,
etc., 1813)
The Riverside Shakespeare: The Complete Works, ed. G. Blakemore
Evans et al., 2nd edn (Boston: Houghton Mifflin, 1997)
Shelley, Percy Bysshe, *The Letters of Percy Bysshe Shelley*, ed.
Frederick L. Jones, 2 vols. (Oxford: Clarendon Press, 1964)
The Poems of Shelley, vol. 3, ed. Jack Donovan, Cian Duffy,
Kelvin Everest and Michael Rossington (Harlow:
Longman/Pearson, 2011)
Shelley's Poetry and Prose: Authoritative Texts, Criticism, ed.
Donald H. Reiman and Neil Fraistat, Norton Critical
Edition, 2nd edn (New York: W. W. Norton, 2002)

Zastrozzi: A Romance, and, St. Irvyne: or, The Rosicrucian: A Romance, ed. Stephen C. Behrendt, Broadview Literary Texts (Peterborough, ON: Broadview Press, 2002)

Smith, Adam, The Glasgow Edition of the Works and Correspondence of Adam Smith, 6 vols. in 7 (Oxford: Clarendon Press; New York: Oxford University Press, 1976–83), vol. 2: *An Inquiry into the Nature and Causes of the Wealth of Nations*, gen. eds. R. H. Campbell and A. S. Skinner, textual ed. W. B. Todd, 2 vols. (1976)

Sterne, Laurence, The Florida Edition of the Works of Laurence Sterne, gen. ed. Melvyn New, 9 vols. (Gainesville: University Press of Florida, 1978–2014), vols. 1–3: *The Life and Opinions of Tristram Shandy, Gentleman*, text ed. Melvyn New and Joan New, notes by Melvyn New with Richard A. Davies and W. G. Day, 3 vols. (1978–84)

Wakefield, Edward Gibbon, *Swing Unmasked; or, the Causes of Rural Incendiarism* (Effingham Wilson, 1831)

Wilbraham, Richard, *Travels in the Trans-Caucasian Provinces of Russia, and along the southern shore of the lakes of Van and Urumiah, in the autumn and winter of 1837* (John Murray, 1839)

Wordsworth, William, *The Cornell Wordsworth*, gen. ed. Stephen Maxfield Parrish, 22 vols. in 21 (Ithaka, NY and London: Cornell University Press, 1975–2007), *Lyrical Ballads, and Other Poems, 1797–1800*, ed. James Butler and Karen Green (1992)

SECONDARY WORKS

Amis, Kingsley, 'Laugh When You Can', *Spectator*, 194 (1 April 1955), 402–4.

Ashton, Rosemary, *Victorian Bloomsbury* (New Haven, CT: Yale University Press, 2012)

Blake, Kathleen, *The Pleasures of Benthamism: Victorian Literature, Utility, Political Economy* (Oxford: Oxford University Press, 2009)

Brett-Smith, H. F. B., 'The L'Estrange–Peacock Correspondence', *Essays and Studies by Members of the English Association*, vol. 18 (1932), 122–48.

Bromwich, David, ed., *Romantic Critical Essays* (Cambridge: Cambridge University Press, 1987)

Buchanan, Robert, *A Poet's Sketch-Book* (Chatto and Windus, 1883)

Burns, Bryan, *The Novels of Thomas Love Peacock* (Croom Helm, 1985)

Butler, Marilyn, *Peacock Displayed: A Satirist in his Context* (Routledge and Kegan Paul, 1979)

Chapman, R. W., review of the Halliford Edition of *The Works of Thomas Love Peacock*, vols. 2–5 (1924), *Review of English Studies*, 1 (1925), 239–42

Clayton, Jay, *Charles Dickens in Cyberspace: The Afterlife of the Nineteenth Century in Postmodern Culture* (Oxford: Oxford University Press, 2003)

Cronin, Richard, *Paper Pellets: British Literary Culture After Waterloo* (Oxford: Oxford University Press, 2010)

Crook, Nora, and Derek Guiton, *Shelley's Venomed Melody* (Cambridge: Cambridge University Press, 1986)

Dawson, Carl, *His Fine Wit: A Study of Thomas Love Peacock* (Routledge and Kegan Paul, 1970)

Dodson, Charles B. '*Crotchet Castle*, by Thomas Love Peacock: A Critical Edition' (unpublished PhD thesis, University of Nebraska, 1966)

Doren, Carl Van, *The Life of Thomas Love Peacock* (Dent, 1911)

Duffy, Cian, '"One Draught from Snowdon's Ever-Sacred Spring": Shelley's Welsh Sublime', in Damian Walford Davies and Lynda Pratt, eds., *Wales and the Romantic Imagination* (Cardiff: University of Wales Press, 2007), pp. 180–98

Dyer, Gary, *British Satire and the Politics of Style, 1789–1832* (Cambridge: Cambridge University Press, 2006)

Dyson, A. E., *The Crazy Fabric: Essays in Irony* (Macmillan, 1965)

Fain, John Tyree, 'Peacock's Essay on Steam Navigation', *South Atlantic Bulletin*, vol. 35 (1970), 11–15.

Garside, P. D., 'Scott, the Romantic Past and the Nineteenth Century', *Review of English Studies*, New Series, 23 (1972), 147–61

Gill, Stephen, review of Nicholas A. Joukovsky, ed., *The Letters of Thomas Love Peacock* (2001), *Review of English Studies*, New Series, 53 (2002), 449–51

Halliwell, Stephen, *Greek Laughter: A Study of Cultural Psychology from Homer to Early Christianity* (Cambridge: Cambridge University Press, 2008)

Henkle, Roger B., *Comedy and Culture: England 1820–1900* (Princeton, NJ: Princeton University Press, 1980)

Hewitt, Douglas, 'Entertaining Ideas: A Critique of Peacock's *Crotchet Castle*', *Essays in Criticism*, 20 (1970), 200–12

Hilton, Boyd, *A Mad, Bad, and Dangerous People? England 1783–1846* (Oxford: Clarendon Press, 2006)

Hoff, Peter S., 'The Voices of Crotchet Castle', *The Journal of Narrative Technique*, 2 (1972), 186–98

House, Humphry, *The Dickens World*, 2nd edn (Oxford: Oxford University Press, 1942)

Jack, Ian, *English Literature 1815–1832* (Oxford: Clarendon Press, 1963)

James, Elizabeth, 'Sale of the Standard Novels: An Unobserved Episode in the History of the House of Bentley', *The Library*, 5th series 33 (1978), 58–62

Johnson, Reginald Brimley, 'Thomas Love Peacock, Satirist', *Novel Review*, 1.5 (August 1892), 406–15

Joukovsky, Nicholas A., 'The First Printing of Peacock's "The Pool of the Diving Friar"', *Notes and Queries*, 219/New Series, 21, no. 9 (1974), 334–5

'The Revision of Peacock's "Touchandgo" and the Composition of *Crotchet Castle*', *Notes and Queries*, 257/New Series, 59, no. 3 (2012), 386–7

Joukovsky, Nicholas A., and Jim Powell, 'A Peacock in the Attic', *Times Literary Supplement* (22 July 2011), 13–15

Kelly, Gary, *English Fiction of the Romantic Period 1789–1830* (Longman, 1989)

Lichtenwalner, Shawna, *Claiming Cambria: Invoking the Welsh in the Romantic Era* (Newark, DE: University of Delaware Press, 2008)

Madden, Lionel, *Thomas Love Peacock* (Evans, 1967)

Mallock, W. H., *Memoirs of Life and Literature* (Chapman and Hall, 1920)

The New Republic (Leicester: Leicester University Press, 1975)

Mayoux, Jean-Jacques, *Un épicurien anglais: Thomas Love Peacock* (Paris: Nizet and Bastard, 1933)

Monod, Sylvère, 'Meredith on Peacock: An Unpublished Letter', *Modern Language Review*, 77 (1982), 278–81.

Moore, Jane, '"Parallelograms and Circles": Robert Owen and the Satirists', in Damian Walford Davies and Lynda Pratt, eds., *Wales and the Romantic Imagination* (Cardiff: University of Wales Press, 2007), pp. 243–67.

Mulvihill, James, 'Thomas Love Peacock's *Crotchet Castle*: Reconciling the Spirits of the Age', *Nineteenth-Century Fiction*, 38 (1983), 253–70.

Perry, Seamus, ed., *Samuel Taylor Coleridge: Interviews and Recollections* (Basingstoke: Palgrave, 2001)

Praz, Mario, *The Hero in Eclipse in Victorian Fiction* (Oxford: Oxford University Press, 1969)

Priestley, J. B., *Thomas Love Peacock*, reissued with introduction by J. I. M. Stewart (London, Melbourne, Toronto: Macmillan; New York: St Martin's Press, 1966)

St Clair, William, *The Reading Nation in the Romantic Period* (Cambridge: Cambridge University Press, 2004)

Stewart, J. I. M., *Thomas Love Peacock* (Longmans, 1963)

Wilson, Edmund, *Classics and Commercials* (Allen, 1951)

Woolf, Virginia, 'Phases of Fiction', *The Bookman*, 69 (1929); repr. in *Granite and Rainbow: Essays*, ed. Leonard Woolf (Hogarth Press, 1958), pp. 93–145.